Ashok Kumar Banker is regarded as a pioneer among Indian writers. He has been credited with several firsts – including the first Indian crime novels in English, the first Indian television series in English, and now, the first fantasy epic by an Indian author. His work has been singled out for recognition in *The Picador Book of Modern Indian Literature*, received worldwide critical acclaim, and regularly tops bestseller lists in India. He has completed the first two books of his imaginative retelling of the world's longest epic, The Mahabharata, *The Seeds of War* and *As the Blind King Watched*.

Ashok is 41, and lives with his wife and two children in Mumbai, India. To discover more about Ashok and the Ramayana, visit his official website at www.epicindia.com

Please register at www.orbitbooks.co.uk for the free monthly newsletter and to find out about other Orbit authors.

Praise for the Ramayana

'Its epic scale is as globally relevant as Gilgamesh, Cuchullain and Beowulf'
HISTORICAL NOVELS REVIEW

'A milestone. Banker brings a magnificent sense of predestination to his task'
INDIA TODAY

'Banker spins a good yarn, full of colour and atmosphere and authentic touches'
STARBURST

'I'm deeply impressed! . . . Spectacular in scope and vision' ENIGMA

'Sophisticated and absorbing'
DREAMWATCH

'Banker creates a marvellous landscape of princes, demons, mages, and lovers'
Kate Elliott

D1399832

By *Ashok K. Banker*

The Ramayana

Prince of Ayodhya
Siege of Mithila
Demons of Chitrakut
Armies of Hanuman
Bridge of Rama

Look out for

King of Ayodhya

Ashok K. Banker

BRIDGE OF RAMA

BOOK FIVE OF THE RAMAYANA

www.orbitbooks.co.uk

ORBIT

First published in Great Britain in December 2005 by Orbit

Copyright © 2005 by Ashok K. Banker

The moral right of the author has been asserted.

A CIP catalogue record for this book is
available from the British Library.

ISBN 1 84149 330 9

Typeset by Palimpsest Book Production Ltd,
Polmont, Stirlingshire
Printed and bound in Great Britain by
Mackays of Chatham plc, Chatham, Kent

Orbit
An imprint of
Time Warner Book Group UK
Brettenham House
Lancaster Place
London WC2E 7EN

www.orbitbooks.co.uk

Ganesa, lead well this army of words.

For
The Jains:
Smt Prakash Jain.
Vivek, Usha, Prakhar and Moryavansh.
Vaibhav, Pragati and Saumyaa.
The Sahu family.
And the Diwans.

*I think the reason life left me bereft of my own family,
was because I was to be blessed with you, my true family.*

Joy, health and prosperity to you all.

ACKNOWLEDGEMENTS

The author thanks:

Tim Holman, Gabriella Nemeth, Andrew Edwards, and all at Time Warner and Orbit Books, UK.

All those readers in the UK and across the world who have supported this series. Without you, the Ramayana would remain a dusty relic on a musty shelf. Thank you for helping me bring it back to life.

The Epicindians who write to me daily in such numbers, at www.epicindia.com and indianenglish.blogspot.com/ You have made this a living breathing interactive tale, not just a one-sided pravachan. Please keep the comments coming. This is your story too.

And you, dear reader, whoever you are, wherever you are. Thank you for coming this far. Only one more book to go!

Jai Siyaram.
Jai Bajrangbali.
Jai Hind.

PRARAMBH

THE WANDERER

Rama . . .

Deep within a subterranean cavern, in the heart of a great mountain, beneath a vast and nameless forest, the vanar named Hanuman spoke the name clearly, pronouncing it with utmost perfection and reverence, cherishing the soft simplicity of its syllables.

Rama . . .

He spoke it with the dignity it deserved, as the name of a great yodha, warrior of warriors, a champion of humankind. Yet in its inherent softness, it conveyed also the sense of a gentle, affectionate man, a benevolent and just king-in-waiting, a loyal life-sacrificing friend, a selfless brother, a loving husband, and some day, a fine father. So gentle, so soft upon the tongue, so quiet the sound it made upon one's palette. Hanuman repeated it over and over, his protruding vanar mouth nevertheless enunciating it with Sanskrit perfection, the two syllables reverberating down the depths of the mountain, filling every nook and cranny of the sun-deprived caverns with his devotion.

For it was devotion he felt, devotion to a man who had come to mean as much to him as a deity might mean to other beings. His tail curled behind him like an unfinished Om, the vanar warrior-messenger recited the name of the mortal he admired beyond words like a devotional litany.

Ramaramaramaramaramarama . . .

Repeating the two simple syllables over and over, he came to realise with a small shock of delight that when reversed,

Rama became amar. Literally meaning eternal. Immortal. How appropriate, how befitting. How completely right. May Rama truly be amar. He continued his litany, losing himself in the bliss of contemplative meditation, as he had learned from his mentors, Rama and Lakshman. This, he had come to discover, was his own private mantra, the two sacred syllables that opened the doors to his inner vaults. The gates to his aatma. He did not dwell on the how or why of it. Whatever the reason, the simple name Rama functioned as effectively as the infinite Om. He lost himself in his reverie, slipping deeper into the meditative trance. He lost all sense of time and place, aware only of the syllables reverberating in the cavern around him – or in the caverns of his immense heart, he could no longer tell which. His mind, heart and soul were occupied solely with the recitation and the utter absence of thought that was the doorway to true self-awareness.

'Maruti.'

The voice was not his own.

The rhythm of the chant continued unbroken. Yet he could not deny that voice, nor that word. Maruti. It was one of his given names, after Marut, the wind god, his father. Not many people knew that name, nor that he had been called by it once, as a child. No one other than a few vanars, and there were no vanars here in these subterranean caverns. Only the ones he sought. And surely the ones he sought could not know his childhood name, could they?

'Anjaneya.'

His recitation went on, the litany uninterrupted, for he had learned the art of being able to continue one task even while his mind roved across another problem, or another realm. But his meditation was halted: the whole point of meditation was to shut out all the physical world.

This second word was also a given name of his, culled from his mother's appellation, Anjan. This one was more widely known, for it had been his mother who had raised him, almost entirely in the absence of his father.

'Sun-Stealer. Broken Jaw. Whiteleaf.'

They were all his names, given at different times to commemmorate his different antics, most of which he did not remember now. These things had been told to him when he came of age, mainly by his mother, one or two by the other tribe-mothers of his ilk after his mother's passing. It was unthinkable that any one person could know all these names, let alone any person inhabiting these deep subterranean places. Yet he had not imagined the voice. It had spoken the names as clearly as his own recitation of his favourite name.

'Hanuman.'

He opened his eyes now. The cavern remained as dark, as inscrutable as before. But there were presences nearby, approaching him. That last word had been uttered from mere yards away. By a voice filled with great knowledge, ancient wisdom. It was a voice he thought he recognised, not by direct familiarity, for he had never met its owner in person, but by the distinct intonations of its race.

'Beloved servant of Rama, we have waited aeons for you to come and call on us. My people are ready to serve your cause. You need but ask us, in Rama's name, and we shall follow you to the ends of the earth.'

He saw now. The faint fuzzy outlines of shapes in the darkness, shambling towards him, surrounding him on all sides. Their scent was powerful, overwhelming to a vanar accustomed to the open outdoors, not to these closed-in spaces where smell accumulated to potent levels. And before him towered the owner of the voice himself, a good head or two taller than himself, oak-like in width, implacably sturdy and strong. The name of the creature was a legend unto itself, its secret history known only to a few. Yet he had come here in search of it, for his king had willed it, and he in turn had willed it because of the signs, the ancient portents and omens that said it was time, time for the vanars to call upon the ancient race that had sworn fealty to them for a great favour once granted. And so he had found his way here, to these underground caverns, and recited the name of Rama as he waited. And, as promised, they had come.

He ceased his chanting. The purpose was served. The hours – or was it days? He could no longer tell for certain – had passed remarkably quickly owing to the deep meditative trance into which he had fallen, aided by the chanting.

He joined his palms in a namaskaram. 'Greetings on behalf of King Sugreeva of Kiskindha. We call upon you in the name of our ancestors.'

The being before him stood silently, swaying ever so slightly from side to side – he realised finally that it was rocking upon its feet, keeping rhythm to some silent chant of its own, perhaps only the beating of its own heart.

'We call upon you to honour the old bargain,' Hanuman said.

'There is no need,' said the ancient one.

Hanuman blinked, nonplussed.

'You have no need of old bargains or oaths to ask for our help this time,' said the great one. 'We volunteer. It is our dharma to follow you on this mission.'

Dharma. It was a word his new friend and master used rarely, but thought often. The word that summed up the code by which he lived. How could this ancient one know of dharma? He had assumed that it was only—

'—a concept devised by mortals, yes, so it is often mistakenly assumed.'

Hanuman swallowed drily.

The creature did not comment on the fact that it had somehow discerned the content of his thoughts. It simply went on in its gruff, relentless way. 'But it is not Rama's creation, nor his forebears'. It is the way of the world. The law of nature itself. Mortals only choose to interpret it and apply it to their own world. And even that interpretation will change as the aeons go by. In another age, far distant, it will come to mean merely duty, like a given task or chore. And still later, in a dark age filled with garish, soul-blackening light, the age of iron and death, it will mean merely religion. A series of rituals the true origin or purpose of which will have been long forgotten, obscured, and worst of all, perverted. But today, here and now, in this last phase of the Age of Truth, it means what it means to us. A way of life. A way in the world and beyond. And it is the reason we await you and follow you.'

And then the being did something remarkable.

It bowed its mighty head, lowered itself to its knees, and showed respect to Hanuman. Him! A mere vanar, messenger of an adopted prince, not even a general or a commander. A mere angadiya!

'And yet,' it said, its dark eyes gleaming now in the darkness, like rubies drawing the faintest light to themselves, selfish stones greedily drinking the atoms of illumination and returning them tenfold, 'and yet, you shall discover your true worth now. For you are more than the sum of your parts and greater than the whole.'

And it raised its stocky furred arms and uttered an invocation. The air crackled and sparked, the flashes of brief illumination dispelling the darkness to reveal an astonishing sight: the entire cavern, a vast and endless catacombed chamber that Hanuman had thought deserted and desolate, was filled to capacity with the ancient ones, with more of them than he had ever known existed even.

'Rise, Maruti Anjaneya Broken-Jawed Sun-Stealer! Rise, and become all that you are destined to be. In the name of Rama, rise, Hanuman!'

And then the whiteness took him, and every cell in his body exploded, giving up its energy. The entire cavern echoed with first his shriek of alarm. Then with his cry. A single word, called out as exclamation, declaration, incantation . . .

'*Rama!*'

And so it began.

KAAND I

THE QUEEN OF AIR
AND DARKNESS

I

Sita.

The word caught at the edge of her consciousness. Out of her mangled thoughts came a single coherent image, or memory, or vision – she knew not which. She felt the rustle and crackle of dry leaves and gritty earth beneath her cold, damp skin; dampened by sweat or blood or both, she did not know. Her body felt battered and broken, abused and discarded. She dared not move. Someone she knew was speaking her name, softly, anxiously, tenderly . . . someone she loved.

Sita, my sweet.

She opened her eyes slowly. The eyelashes stuck, as if she had been asleep or unconscious a long time.

A dark face loomed large in her field of vision. A man's face. She knew him. His skin was so dark, it appeared almost blueish when caught by the light in a certain way, as it did now. He was leaning over her prone form. She could just make out the silhouettes of overhanging branches above, shirring softly in a slow breeze. Nearby, she heard the gentle lapping of a body of water and wondered if it was the reason she had come to this place. But she could not recall what exactly she had come to do here – drink water, fetch it, bathe? Perhaps she had not come for the water at all? She was not sure. There was very little she was sure of.

It was night in a forest, that much was certain. Distant whip-poorwills hooted, cicadas kept the rhythm of the night, crickets provided a backbeat. The mulchy odour of vegetation, the taste

of sweet dew on her lips, the sound of his voice, the knowledge of her great love for him, and of his love for her, these
things alone were certain to her disoriented mind.

Sita, my beautiful Sita, wake now.

She tried to focus on the man leaning over her, to see his
face clearly. But a full moon backlit his head, casting an aura
so fulminous, it threw his features into darkness. His hair, tied
usually in a tight hermit's bun atop his head, had come loose,
and strands of it splayed out around his face, silver-dyed by the
moonlight. She smelled his familiar odour: coppery, earthy, but
with a pungent tinge of . . . blood? Yes, she sensed rather than
saw that he was bleeding from some small, insignificant wound.
The hilt of a sword gleamed at his waist. He had been fighting
– but whom? And why? She felt a twinge of unease, a sense of
impending danger, of being fenced in by assailants, a desperate
struggle against daunting odds. A memory flashed in her mind's
eye, of a clearing atop a hill where bears and brigands were
locked in a fight to the death, and she and a companion stood
shoulder to shoulder, prepared to meet their makers rather than
yield. Was he that companion?

She peered up at the achingly familiar blue-dark face and
struggled to recall something more than just the fact of her love
for him. What were these circumstances? Where was she? Had
not she been through a great and arduous journey? Had she
been in a battle? Why was her mind so addled, her memories
fogged and inscrutable, her thoughts obscure?

'Rama,' she said slowly, her tongue a parched leaf on the
forest floor of her mouth. She tasted mud, and had some faint
recollection of falling face down in a sandy place. Why could
she not *remember*?

'Yes, my love,' he said, as softly, tenderly, he laid his hand
upon her shoulder, gentle and reassuring. So familiar, so
comforting . . . yet something nagged her mind, gnawed at her
ragged nerves. Something about his eyes? Were they too large,
too luminous, almost . . . catlike? No. It must be a trick of the
light, the dappling play of moonlight cast through the leaves.

Frustrated, she scanned his face as intently as she could manage, given the dim light and her own disorientation. 'What happened?' she asked. 'Where am I?'

He smiled. She sensed the smile rather than saw it, his face being so starkly backlit by the moon. Felt it in the closing of his grip upon her shoulder. 'Time enough to speak of those things later, my love. For now, you must take some refreshment, regain your strength. You have not eaten or drunk anything for too long. Come, drink some of this.'

He held the back of her head, propping her up, and picked up a clay bowl lying beside him. She leaned forward automatically, so familiar was his manner and the circumstances, and allowed him to guide the bowl to her lips. Suddenly, she realised how thirsty she was, how unbearably neglected and deprived. She could not recall when she had last eaten, but the pounding in the back of her skull, near the base of the neck, when he had raised her up suggested that it had been days. She felt a great outrushing of warmth and affection for him, gratitude out of all proportion to the simple gifts of water and kind words.

She was about to take a sip when a sound came from afar. He raised his head sharply. It was a peculiar, disturbing sound, definitely not human or animal. Over the thirteen-odd years of exile, on the run from rakshasas night and day, she had come to recognise that sound as well as any other forest denizen's cry. It was a rakshasa calling out. Whether in pain, anger or some other emotion, she could not tell. But it was a rakshasa.

She gripped his arm tightly. 'Rama.'

'Quiet.'

She blinked. His response had been too curt. Even in the most pressing of emergencies, he had never spoken to her in that tone. They must be in great danger. Yet the glade in which she lay seemed so calm and peaceful. Even the sound of that rakshasa had come from far outside, from somewhere beyond a wall or several walls. As if they were in some palace courtyard and the cry had come from just outside the garden wall.

Were they in a palace garden? Where? Not Mithila, surely. Nor Ayodhya. The flowers were different here. The air smelled different too. But they were in some city. Within the heart of a great city. There was no mistaking that now. Close on the heels of this realisation came the dawning awareness that her mind was clearing at last, she was beginning to think more clearly. Some momentous fact stared her full in the face, yet she could not recognise its blank, unformed features. It taunted her, mocked her. Why could she not remember? What had *happened* to her?

Rama was still listening intently, turning his head this way, then that, as if trying to track an approaching predator. A sound came on the still night air, a kind of choked grunt. Before she could comprehend what might have caused it, he bent and whispered gently, breath warm against her cheek. 'I will return. Wait here.'

Before she could think of anything to say, or ask, he was gone, a shadow among shadows. The night was silent, too silent, she knew. Something was coming through the woods. Naturally, he must go and see. Yet she felt oddly chagrined, as if she expected him to take her along as well, to regard her as an equal, capable of her own defence, not a frail, fragile companion to be protected and sheltered. It was a minuscule thing, yet it nagged at her throbbing consciousness, troubling her. Had he always been so protective of her? Somehow she did not feel it was so.

As she waited, she realised her head was clearing further. The fog that had enveloped her memory and thoughts when she had regained consciousness was dissipating fast. The dizziness that had churned in her belly when she had tried to raise her head to sip from the clay bowl had lessened. The pounding in the back of her skull had receded to a dull throbbing. She sat up slowly and listened carefully, trying to read her environment the way she had done for so long.

She saw on the ground beside her the bowl that he had put aside when he left. She picked it up and raised it to her face, struck by a sudden suspicion that must be confirmed – or denied. A whiff of the bowl's contents, and she knew at once.

A powerful sense of déjà vu overwhelmed her. An image rose in her mind, like the mottled surface of a pool settling slowly to reveal a shadowy reflection: of herself lying like this, and of him bending over her, giving her something to sip from a clay bowl. Something sticky-sweet and redolent of . . . poppy? Yes. It was poppy. That would explain why she was so confused, and unable to think clearly or remember anything. He had been drugging her with juice of the poppy! But why would Rama—

The sound came again, louder and closer than before. It reminded her of a sound she had heard all too often during the past several years, almost like the sound of a rakshasa beginning to grunt in shock, then breaking off abruptly, followed by a heavy thud. But it could not be. The rakshasas of Janasthana were all dead. Weren't they?

The knowledge came to her, still and clear: *I am not in Janasthana.*

Her pulse began to grow steadily faster, rising from the near-comatose state in which the drug had suspended her for hours, days, weeks – she had no way of knowing – into a sharpened awareness that came from years of living under the constant shadow of mortal threat. She grew aware of a new level of sensations, scents, sounds, and suddenly she knew that she was in grave danger. Something came to her then, some vestige of memory. A golden air chariot floating overhead, menacing and cruel in its magnificence, alien, inhuman. And in that chariot . . .

She remembered then. Everything. In all its nightmarish detail. More than she wished to remember. A moan escaped her parted lips. The poppy juice was preferable to this remembering. It was more merciful. She couched her face in her hands, fighting back the tears that threatened to overwhelm her, the memories.

The same sound broke the silence again. Closer this time, unmistakable. She knew it at once as the sound of a living creature being deprived of life in a sudden, violent action. A groan of abrupt agony, then the shambling thud of a body falling to the ground. A vein began pounding in her head, hammering away at the pain of self-awareness. Where was Rama? Why had he not returned yet?

Her attention was drawn to a bank of trees into which the moonlight failed to penetrate. As she watched intently, mesmerised now, a shadow broke away from its dark siblings and stepped out into the clearing. She continued to lie still, rendered immobile by the shock of returned memories and the numbing dreamlike stasis of her condition. The dark shape stopped a yard away, looming over her, massive, overwhelming, blotting out the moon.

As it bent over her, she saw the ten separate yet interlinked faces atop its immensely muscled form, delineated by the back-light of moonglow. Ten unmistakably masculine heads, some bearded, others moustached, a couple clean-jawed, the eyes of all ten glistening whitely, their bared teeth gleaming in the dappled moonlight as the Lord of Lanka stood over her sprawled and prostrate form.

2

Sita fought to clear her mind of the mists that shrouded it, and stared up at her nemesis. After an eternity, one face – she couldn't tell which one in the shadowy light – spoke in a rumbling baritone.

'Awake at last, and about time too.'

She lay utterly motionless, unable or unwilling to accept the extent of her predicament, the enormity of the crisis that had overwhelmed her life. This could not be happening, she could not really be a prisoner of Ravana, her husband's worst enemy, leader of the demon legions sworn to decimate her kind. No. It was not possible. Some part of her, albeit a very small and weakening part, still prayed desperately that this was but a dream, a nightmare brought on by the poppy juice. But then she recalled that it was the poppy juice itself that proved that it was *not* a dream! In fact it was her identification of the drug that had washed away the last vestige of foolish hope. For it meant that those who had her in their clutches had known she would baulk at accepting this rough reality, and had administered it to her to help her weather the very shock she was now experiencing.

Suddenly, she wished she had drunk deeply of that bowl of sourish effluent, deeply enough to sink back into the comforting caress of unconscious bliss in which she had been ensconced. It would have delayed this moment a while longer.

The ten heads examined her, separately and individually, yet with an uncanny coordination. It was like watching a family that was so close-knit, they knew one another's every thought and response, yet retained their distinct individuality. *A tribe of wedded skulls.* A fragment from some Sanskrit drama she had seen or read sprang to her mind unbidden, irreverent in its irrelevance. A secret terror bubbled up within her, threatening to burst its way out of her gullet. She choked it down fiercely. She would not show weakness to *him*. Not here, not now, not ever.

'You will die for this,' said a voice that she barely recognised as her own, so cold and steel-hard was its tone, so utterly devoid of any compassion. 'By this rash act, you have condemned yourself. For committing this transgression, my husband and his brother will wreak upon your lands the most terrible war ever conceived. Not one number of your kind will be spared. You are a fool to have abducted me.'

The ten heads hung over her, some turning this way and that, examining one another as well as her. She could not discern all their individual expressions, but from what she could make out in the dim light, it was evident that they did not all share the same visage, nor the same responses. She distinctly heard one head rattle off a string of words that she recognised as belonging to the distant lands of Hellenia, for she had heard ambassadors from those far-off barbaric kingdoms speaking the same tongue at her father's court in Mithila. Other heads spoke highspeech, lowspeech, commonspeak, and a variety of dialects both local and foreign, at least two of which were utterly alien to her.

For a long moment she feared that he would be enraged by this outburst from the hapless human lying at his feet, drugged and semi-senseless, unarmed and apparently alone.

Instead, he issued a deep and sincere sigh – or one of his heads did, she could not tell which exactly – and spoke in a voice that was shockingly devoid of either anger or pique. 'Your response is understandable, princess. As is your anger and hostility. But I did not come here to have words with you; there will be time enough for us to talk later, when you are rested and nourished.

I came only to ascertain your condition and to see to your needs. Apparently there has been some lapse in your caretaking. I left my cousin in charge of you, but she seems to have been somewhat remiss in her attentions. I apologise for her lack of efficiency and will make up for it by seeing to your arrangements myself. I will ensure that you are provided with nourishment and the opportunity to cleanse yourself and don fresh apparel. Then, when you have rested and recovered sufficiently from your ordeal, we shall meet once more. Perhaps at that time I may persuade you to see the error of your assumptions.'

Of all the approaches she might have expected, this was the one she had no defence against. Politeness, courtesy, concern, even compassion? It was a trick, of course. This was his gambit, to play the noble villain. She had seen enough Sanskrit dramas, heard poems recited in her father's court. She knew all the ways and wiles of warcraft. Did he think to deceive her so easily?

'Play no games with me, rakshasa. I see your subterfuge. Did you really think to get away with it? To kidnap me and bring me to your wretched lair of demons without any consequences? And now you think that by treating me like a house guest, you will gain my forgiveness? You are wrong. This time you have gone too far. Even now, as we speak, my husband will surely be amassing an army. Soon he will arrive here and wreak his vengeance upon you and your people. And this time he will spare none, nor show any mercy. This time his goal will be the total annihilation of your species. He will not let you escape again through the use of your dark Asura art. Your fate is sealed by your own rash actions.'

The rack of heads tilted a little to one side, contemplating her as well as other things. She saw at least two of the rightmost heads look up, as if trying to peer at the shadowy recesses of the dense foliage above. From another direction, she caught the faintest rustle of dried leaves and held her breath, hardly daring to hope. He did not seem to know that Rama was here. Perhaps if she continued to distract him, Rama would have a chance to make his move.

But even as these thoughts flowed through her mind, so did the questions. How could Rama possibly be here? How had he got into Lanka undetected? For surely that was where she was now – in Lanka? It did not seem logical. But she had to continue the charade to the end now. The drama was begun, and must be played out.

'You alone will be responsible for the massacre of your own people,' she added with a vehemence that was easy to project, for she felt every bit as angry as she sounded.

A head on the left shoulder swivelled upwards to examine some inscrutable aspect of the overhanging branches and vines; another turned right to peer sharply at a bush rustling softly in an eddy of night breeze. He seemed to be looking everywhere at once, seeing everything, and yet, she observed distastefully, at least half his heads seemed preoccupied, as if focused on intense mental processes.

The central head yawned briefly, displaying its contempt for her words, then replied laconically: 'And you think I am so naïve that this possibility did not occur to me?' The head immediately to the left of the central one continued the dialogue seamlessly, while the central head frowned and began some kind of subvocal mumbling conversation with the head to its right. 'Do you think that I, leader of the united Asura hordes since the Satya-Yuga, would not be aware of your husband's likely response?' The speaking head yawned and slowly shut its lids, apparently falling asleep. Another head on the opposite end of the rack took up the dialogue. 'You do me little justice, Princess Janaki.'

She was somewhat taken aback at his use of her formal title – Janaki derived from Janak, her father, the King of Vaideha. Then she reminded herself that this man – nay, this *Asura* – had been in her father's palace, had been received and treated as an honoured guest, a suitor for her affections no less; although, on that occasion, he had sported only one head, and the rest of his appearance had matched that very handsomely mortal appendage.

'You are of course right about the consequences of my kidnapping you. I have no doubt that Rama will come here with an army at his back, to do war with me and repossess the object of his affection. I am in fact counting on him to do just that. It is an integral part of my plan. As for his invading my realm and decimating my people, we shall see what transpires as and when he eventually arrives upon these shores. I will not even dignify your comment on my personal survival. You seem to forget that I have a somewhat obdurate resistance to dying, princess. You should know better than that, Maithili.'

Maithili. Literally, Daughter of Mithila. It was a term her father favoured, and the head that intoned the word spoke it with an emphasis that eerily echoed Maharaja Janak's own manner of speaking.

She stared up at Ravana, feeling suddenly foolish and naïve. She had spoken the first, most obvious thoughts that had sprung to her mind, and had expected him to respond in like manner, as a typically villainous demon, the Dark Lord of Lanka – an inappropriate name, for his skin was far whiter than that of the most palace-bound belles of Gandahar. Clearly, her assumptions about his true nature were as shallow as that common misconception about his skin colour. *This is no ordinary more-muscle-than-brain rakshasa, like those brainless brutes you fought in the wilderness of your exile*, she reminded herself sharply. *This is Ravana himself.* If the myths and legends about him were true, the precious few details collected over the millennia by Arya historians even partly accurate, then he was no less a mental giant than the most learned sages of mortalkind. She must not make the mistake of underestimating him. Rama and Lakshman had already done that once, when they believed him destroyed in the wave of brahman unleashed by the brahm-astra at Mithila thirteen years ago. Yet here he stood before her, very much alive. And if he was alive, then . . .

'You survived the brahm-astra,' she said slowly, the implications of her own words chilling her to the bone. 'It did not destroy your Asura army.'

One head snapped around, seeking out something that rustled in the shadowy branches behind Ravana. A small animal of some kind made a squalling noise, then grew quiet. 'Your argument is tiresome in its fallaciousness, princess. Just because I stand here before you, it does not necessarily follow that my army survived the assault at Mithila as well. No. Brahmarishi Vishwamitra's desperate ploy was quite effective. The largest Asura army ever assembled in the history of the world was turned to ashes and dust on the Gangetic fields of your capital city. The terror device he unleashed with such brutal disregard for the rules of war destroyed every last Asura left upon the physical plane. Only a few ragged bands of rakshasas survived that day of destruction. And you and your husband and your band of outlaw companions did away with the last of those survivors during the years of your exile in the southern woods. So, to answer your question, no. The great Asura army that came so close to decimating and subjugating the mortal world that fateful day is no more. Nor can such an army ever be assembled again. Virtually all the Asura races perished for ever in that final holocaust at Mithila. As the good brahmarishi no doubt was aware when he thrust the burden of that great and terrible responsibility upon your adolescent husband's gullible conscience. Your Rama is responsible for the most widespread Asura genocide ever accomplished. You must be quite proud of him.'

'Silence!' she said, her eyes burning with sudden tears. 'How dare you speak of my Rama in that tone! What he did that day at Mithila was a sacred duty. He saved all mortalkind with his actions. The Asura races you speak of were bent upon the destruction of all mortals. You were the aggressors, not us. You invaded our world. You sought our destruction and our subjugation. Had we not stopped you by the grace of the devas, it would be our kind who would be the victims of genocide!'

Several heads turned to examine her with varying degrees of interest. One had yellow eyes that smouldered with murderous rage. Had that head been in charge of the whole rack, it seemed to convey silently, she would be in a far worse predicament than she was right now.

To her astonishment, instead of responding to her angry outburst with like sentiment, Ravana was silent a moment. His heads twisted and turned, each moving as if of its own accord, almost frustrated by its enforced limitation in being an integral part of a larger group. She was reminded of a Nilgiri stag, those enormous blue bucks that grew to near-elephantine size in the lower Himalayan ranges, with their antlers as profuse and extensive as small trees. For a brief interval, the heads muttered and mumbled to one another. When he spoke again, she could not tell which head was responding. He seemed to be having one of those brief moments when all ten heads agreed on something unanimously. She sensed that such moments did not occur often, and perhaps never on matters of any import.

'There are things that you are not given to understand, Sita-devi.' His tone was quiet and reasonable, tinged with empathy and compassion. A thinking man's response, not a berserk demonlord's outburst. That disturbed her even more than the words themselves. He sounded so . . . sane. 'What seems obvious is not always the truth. Often satya lies concealed in the shadows, just out of reach of our keenest gaze. Your outrage is entirely understandable. As is your anger and resentment. Yet there is much you have left to learn, knowledge that will alter your thinking irrevocably, dispel the foolishly naïve notions you have grown accustomed to regarding as absolute truth.'

He paused. 'But this is neither the time nor the place to begin such a mind-cleansing. As I have said, before you insisted on issuing your tirade against me, you are in need of succour and rest. It would not be seemly for me to continue this debate with you in your current state. You are depleted and drained from your long and arduous journey. If I have not yet apologised for the rigours of your abduction and the difficulties of your journey to Lanka, then let me do so now. I only did what I did because it was necessary. Why and wherefore, you will come to understand in due course. Right now, you have need of nourishment and rest. Once you have partaken of these essentials, we shall resume our dialectic. Indeed, I look forward to it.'

So startled was she by the unexpectedness of his response and manner that when he began to walk away, she barely realised that he was leaving. He was almost at the edge of the thicket when she overcame her shock sufficiently enough to regain her power of speech. 'Wait,' she blurted out.

He stopped, a tree unto himself beneath the panoply of dark-enshrouded branches. The heads at each end turned to look upon her. She could not tell what their expressions might be in the dimness of that place.

'I beseech you, return me to my husband and his brother forthwith. Return me at once to Rama and we may yet prevent the catastrophe that is to come. I entreat you. *Send me home.*'

Into his silence fell the soft soughing of leaves buffeted by the wind. It riffled the bushes behind her, wafting the fragrances of night-blossoming flowers, the pervasive odours of a large garden.

'You *are* home, Janaki,' he said softly.

Then melted into the darkness whence he had come.

3

She was still trying to make some sense of Ravana's last words, that change in manner and tone that was far more unnerving than any display of brute force or animal rage, when the bushes beside her rustled softly and Rama emerged from their midst. Sita started and sat up, reaching towards him. 'Rama, where were you? I expected you to appear at any minute, to—'

She broke off when she saw his face. His handsome features were contorted into a mask of ugly rage. He stood with hands clenched into fists, staring in the direction Ravana had gone. 'He dares,' Rama said in a voice that quivered with anger. 'He dares to use sugary-sweet words and tender voices to deceive you? Does he think then to seduce you through such wily strategems? Does he think he can cajole Sita into climbing into his bed just by treating her delicately?'

Before she could think of anything to say to this extraordinary outburst, he turned to her, clutching her shoulders. 'My love,' he said, breath hot and rank on her face. He must have been eating something overripe, she thought, resisting the urge to turn her face away, for never had she known Rama's breath to smell so awful, so . . . rotten. The words spilled sourly from his mouth, all in a rush. 'Do not be seduced by his strategem. He knows that if he treats you roughly and displays his true, bestial nature, then you will shrink away. He wishes to have you succumb to his caresses willingly, not take you by force. That is why he employs this tactic. Do not be fooled by him, my sweet. Do not listen to a word he says.'

'Rama,' she said, struggling to keep from grimacing before
the foulness of his breath, 'let us just leave now. Take me from
this place. Let's escape while he is gone.'

He stared at her dumbly. His hands slipped from her shoulders, falling back by his sides. He turned away, looking up at
the moon through a gap in the branches. Moonlight fell upon
his face like a beam from a lighthouse. She thought his eyes
looked strange, wild, almost animalistic. She put it down to
anger . . . but still a seed of doubt took root within her heart.

'Rama,' she said again, urgently, 'why do you hesitate? We
must make our escape while he is away. It is our only chance.'
She caught his arm. It *felt* like Rama's arm, the rock-hard
muscle beneath the sleek skin. But was that hair she felt? Rama's
skin was almost hairless, smooth and bare. Surely it was only
particles of dirt she was feeling?

He shook his head in a snarling negation. 'It is no use. He
has the place surrounded with his tribesmen. And even if we
were to escape from this level, we cannot escape the tower itself.
It is a sorcerous thing, it responds to his command. Every turn
we take, it will change its shape and form to thwart us.'

She didn't understand what he meant. Level? Tower? What
was he talking about? This was some kind of garden, was it
not? There was the moonlight above, and soil below their feet
. . . surely that meant they were on firm earth. 'But you came
in, Rama. You came here by some means, did you not? Let us
go out the same way then. Take me the way you came into this
place and let us escape quickly. Quickly, my love! I will not
abide here a moment longer!'

But still he would not move, but remained there standing
silently in the moonlight. Until the seed of doubt that had
been planted in her breast took root and grew tendrils of
suspicion. She released his arm, certain now that there was
hair upon it, where Rama had no hair. And that those eyes
that she had mistakenly thought were Rama's deep kohl-black
eyes were in fact slitted and cat-like. Not Rama's. Not human
either.

She backed away, shaken. 'Who are you? Where is Rama?'

He sighed, bowing his head, Rama's head, with its scalp of crow-black hair. 'It always happens to me. If I lose control of my emotions, it triggers the change. I . . . slip back into my own shape.'

He turned to look at her, and a slow, sly smile grew upon his face. 'But I fooled you completely at first, did I not? You had no doubt that I was Rama! If my brother had not interrupted us with his unscheduled visit . . .'

'Brother,' she repeated.

He cocked his head, the moonlight catching his left ear and that side of his face. The ear had changed, she saw, grown long and curved at the tip, unmistakably feline. He was some manner of cat, she realised. A very large cat-like Asura with the ability to change its shape. And his voice was changing too, gaining a more feminine tone. She knew that voice. She had heard it before, on a night as terrible as this one, in a vale by a pool upon the hill of Chitrakut, thirteen long years ago. 'Cousin, actually,' said the Asura. 'Although we are different tribes.'

Something shimmered in Sita's vision. She blinked blearily, thinking herself still nauseous and groggy from the poppy, and struggled to focus on the man whom she had thought was Rama. Then she realised that the fault did not lie with her vision; it was the man himself who was shaking, melting, changing . . .

The name came to her unbidden, a cursed word, responsible for so much pain and grief and bloodshed. Supanakha. Yes, it could be no other.

She watched as Supanakha transformed herself back into her natural form. Her face had changed quite dramatically, to its original feminine rakshasi-yaksi lines. Ugly though they were, yet they remained unarguably female. Her features melted and ran like hot wax, sloughing off the aspect of Rama's handsome mortal masculinity, altering before Sita's harried eyes into the familiar form of the rakshasi who had been the bane of her existence for so long, the rakshasi who had coveted her beloved Rama, who had attempted to kill Sita once and had been savagely repulsed by Rama and brutally mutilated by Lakshman, and who had waged a war against them in order to seek her revenge. She stood transformed before Sita, a sleek, glossy-furred beauty with razor-sharp talons and teeth who radiated sexual heat and vigour like a Banglar tiger in mating season. Sita stared, barely recognising this beautiful animal as the same bedraggled, ear-chewed specimen who had disrupted her and Rama's lives so brutally thirteen years ago, in the idyllic settlement of Chitrakut. Yet below this newly acquired sleek perfection, there was no mistaking the catlike features. After all, this was the creature responsible for those thirteen years of unassuaged warfare in the forests of Janasthana.

Sita spoke the rakshasi's name aloud, hatefully, for she could not feel any other emotion for this creature. 'Supanakha.'

The demoness smiled. Then snarled, like a cat showing her power to a mouse.

Sita allowed herself no room for fear. If she only had a sword at hand . . . 'Why do you disguise yourself as my husband?' she demanded with barely restrained anger. This rakshasi, she sensed, was more dangerous than Ravana himself. The Lord of Asuras had a definite strategem, an intellectually devised scheme to accomplish some masterplan in which she, Sita, was but a pawn, albeit an important one. Already she had understood that he would play by the rules of his own game, and that he meant her no immediate harm. But Supanakha was a different story: the rakshasi had reason enough to wreak violent vengeance upon Rama and all those he loved. And of all those beloved of Rama, there was none she despised more than Sita. Her 'rival', as she had once put it.

She stood before Sita, restored to her true form. The ruined, scar-toughened flesh around her nose and ears marred her sleek new beauty, coarse reminders of Lakshman's rashness. Oh, why had he inflicted such drastic violence upon this Asura? Better that he had engaged her in combat and fought her to the death, than make her suffer this glaring humiliation. The years fighting rakshasas had given Sita greater insight into their minds and workings, and she knew now what she had not known thirteen long years earlier – that the slicing-off of Supanakha's nose and ears was more humiliating to the rakshasi than simply being unable to gain Rama's affections.

'Sita,' growled the rakshasi softly.

Sita resisted the urge to back away further. She must not show fear or weakness before this wily and unpredictable creature, still seething with an ancient grudge. Why had she not shown herself when her cousin Ravana was here moments ago? Why had she disguised herself as Rama? What was her game plan?

'What is it you want of me?' Sita asked the rakshasi in a level voice. 'Have you and your brother rakshasas not spilled enough innocent blood in the jungles of Janasthana?'

Supanakha purred, her tail flicking up over her furry head, then down again. It moved rhythmically from left to right as she regarded Sita, cat eyes gleaming luminously in the moonlight. Her fur was sleeker than when Sita had last seen her, her body well fed and stronger than before. She was a wholly different being from the emaciated, mangy beast that had ranged along with the armies of Khara and Dushana and Trisiras. 'Nothing much,' she replied slowly in that soft, rolling purr. 'Just some of your blood. And the skin and flesh and bone marrow as well.'

And before Sita could act or respond, Supanakha had gathered herself and leapt, all in one smooth, oily motion, across the small clearing. The rakshasi was in the air before Sita quite knew what she was up to – her senses were still dulled by the poppy. In an instant, the demoness would have been upon her, tearing her throat and belly open and feeding upon her hot, steaming innards. Supanakha moved like dark lightning.

But someone else moved even quicker. Sita had barely begun to turn her face away, choking back the involuntary cry that rose to her lips, when a dark shape flew out of the trees and intercepted Supanakha in mid-air. They collided and rolled, crashing down less than a yard from the stunned Sita. She had a glimpse of Supanakha's startled face, eyes glinting demon-aically with rage, then the rakshasi howled with frustration and struck out with her inches-long claws.

The blows were caught by more nimble hands and the rakshasi's limbs twisted back by arms far stronger. Supanakha struggled hopelessly for a moment more, snarling and twisting in the grasp of her cousin-brother, until the Lord of Lanka spoke a single word, like the crack of a whip on a flank. '*Enough!*'

Reluctantly, Supanakha subsided. Ravana held her down, forelimbs akimbo, until he was certain that the fight had gone out of her. She writhed briefly, then looked up into the eyes of one of his heads and saw something there that sobered her at once. She grew still. Ravana used his second – or perhaps it was his third; he had brought all six arms into play – pair of hands to hold her lower limbs down and apart, and at that moment, Supanakha resembled nothing more than an over-grown house cat held down with her limbs splayed. She stared up with dangerous glinting eyes at the Lord of Asuras, down but not wholly subdued.

He released her and stood, turning to face Sita.

'You are unharmed,' he said, stating it as fact.

Sita nodded, not trusting herself to speak just yet.

He folded his lower pairs of arms back into their slits in his back. Sita found herself watching with frank fascination; she had never seen such a thing before. She forced herself to lower her eyes to the ground, but before she did so, she caught at least one of his heads watching her watching him with amused interest.

He looked down at her briefly, as if ensuring that she was unharmed and well. Some of his heads continued to examine her intently, while the rest swivelled on his massive muscled neck and glared at the prone form of his cousin. Supanakha lay with splayed limbs on the ground, her belly bared. Yet even in this hapless posture of defeat, she retained an air of threat. Her eyes smouldered darkly. As Sita watched, they closed almost to slits, and her thick lips parted to reveal a flash of tapering fangs.

Supanakha hissed at her brother. She had thought he had left earlier. That was her mistake. She should have checked to make sure. But she had been so focused on the mortal female, so overwhelmed by the opportunity that had provided itself, that she had forgotten how canny Ravana could be at times.

He stood above her now, staking his dominance. For a long moment, silence prevailed, broken briefly by the distant sound of panicked roaring. Finally, Ravana spoke, this time in a male baritone of exquisite power.

'You were forbidden, cousin,' he said in clipped, brusque tones. 'And yet you have slipped past my clansmen to come here. Four of them have died for their inefficiency – or, should I say, sexual indiscretions, for I scented your musk on each one. They are mindless brutes, barely worthy of claiming any link to the Pulastya line; I expected little more of them than to guard the princess well. But from you, I expected much more. Above all, I did not expect such insubordination. I gave you a direct order, which you violated. Worse still, you have been drugging her. While I waited for her to resume consciousness, believing her to be in shock, you have been keeping her in this senseless, mindless state. If I had not been preoccupied with matters of governance these past days since my return, this would never have happened. But now, seeing as it has happened, I wonder. What am I to do about you? An infraction such as this cannot be allowed to go unpunished.'

Supanakha rolled over, snarling softly. 'What infraction? So I mated with some of your guards? What of that? This entire tower is little more than a breeding area designed to multiply the numbers of your hordes, is it not? There are countless matings occurring here every hour of the day.'

Ravana pointed a finger at her in warning. 'I speak of your

attack upon my guest. And of your drugging her these past days.'

Supanakha licked a spot on her right elbow in a sly feline gesture, keeping her eyes on Ravana. 'That!' she said scornfully. 'That was nothing. If I really wanted to harm her, she would have been dead days ago. I was protecting her.'

'Protecting her.' Ravana's voice dripped with irony.

'Yes,' Supanakha spat. 'By keeping her drugged and taking her husband's form to calm her each time she regained consciousness briefly, I was ensuring that nobody would know the identity of your prisoner. Even mating with your guards was part of the same purpose – to keep them from growing curious and coming to examine her. Why, had I not satisfied some of their mindless lust, perhaps they might have slaked their thirst with your precious princess inst—'

'Impossible,' Ravana rumbled. 'They were fools, surely, but loyal fools. You can't talk your way out of this one, cousin. Those sentries were more faithful to me than you will ever be, ungrateful wench! I know what you intended – you wished to destroy Sita and take her place, *become* her. But in order for the subterfuge to work, you had to get to know Sita better. Learn her every thought and gesture and habit. That was what you were doing these past days and intended to go on doing. Then, when Rama arrived to claim her back, you would be able to successfully play the role of his wife. But then something happened just now that made you lose control, did it not? That has always been your failing, cousin-sister. The best laid plans come to naught because you lack the temperance to restrain your bestial impulses long enough for the plans to come to fruition.'

Supanakha was about to counter his accusation with a few choice abuses of her own devising when something registered belatedly upon her vision. She peered around Ravana's massively muscled right thigh, narrowing her eyes. It was a low-hanging branch, swishing. She snarled softly. 'Ravana.'

'Do not interrupt me. I will not hear any more excuses from you on this matter.'

'Brother!' Supanakha roared, rising up to her haunches. 'See for yourself. She is gone!'

Quick as a whiplash, Ravana's rack of heads turned to look at the spot where Sita had been lying moments earlier – and was not any more.

4

Sita ran through the benighted woods. The forest blurred past her. Branches loomed like chopped limbs, vines trailed and twined like the hairs of a giantess, gnarled roots snaked across her path. Fear and shock had shaken off much of the effect of the drugs, and her body, bruised and sore though it was, was toughened by over a decade of hard living and incessant fighting in the wilderness; it responded well enough for the nonce. But she was depleted and drugged and would not last long; she knew she must put as much distance between herself and her abductor as possible before her resources ran out. What then? A cranny to hide in, perhaps. A place to stow away until she could find a way to get across the ocean to Aryavarta. She had no plan, only the determination to be free. To not have to play the hapless heroine of this nightmare fairy tale.

She had said to Ravana, boldly, that Rama would raise an army to come and rescue her; she did not doubt he would. It was the massacre that would result that she feared. The killing beyond count, the epic violence of war. If she had understood the Lord of Lanka correctly, that was exactly what he desired. Why? She did not care right now. All she cared about was making her escape, perhaps preventing this catastrophe.

Her flight seemed to go on endlessly. As she progressed, she became aware of the peculiar lack of life in this forest. Never mind rakshasas – even the guards that Ravana and Supanakaha had both mentioned in their argument – she could not sense even the smaller wildlife that would be rife in such a place. No sounds disturbed the eerie, deathlike stillness of the woods she ran through: not an owl hoot, not a nightbird's sweet chords, not the chirring of insects. The place sounded as dead as . . . as any man-made habitation. Even the inevitable bruises and cuts she should have suffered by now from clawing branches, tripping roots, thorny brambles and the hundred nameless obstacles of a forest at night were absent. She had been able to run with curious ease through miles of forest at night, virtually unobstructed, her way illuminated by moonlight that was suprisingly bright.

She slowed to a halt, the nape of her neck prickling from the awareness that her nemesis and his crony might be close on her heels. She did not doubt Ravana's ability to outpace her, nor Supanakha's. Yet, even after a long moment of breathless anticipation, listening and sniffing and waiting, there was no sound of pursuit, no sense of threat approaching from behind. And if she didn't know better, she would think that in this strangely still and silent wood, she was all alone.

After several moments, using the benefit of close to fourteen years of forest-sharpened senses, she was ready to believe that she *was* alone. She could not sense so much as a hare munching clover anywhere.

There was something wrong with the moonlight.

It shone too evenly, too perfectly, casting a uniform silvery glow over everything. The angle at which it shone was odd too. She crouched and examined the way it fell upon the top of the leaves of a fenik bush – and the sides and underside of the leaves as well. The instant her eyes took stock of this unnatural phenomenon, she backed away, as if the bush itself was to blame. Spinning around, she saw that everything around her was lit by this strange all-illuminating moonlight. She ran out of the thicket in which she had stopped, into a clearing filled with flowering bushes of a variety she had never encountered before, and looked up.

There was no moon.

Just moonlight. Beautiful, silvery, perfect. All-illuminating.

She ran again, sprinting unobstructed and unharmed through the unnatural forest, beneath the unearthly moonlight, across a landscape occupied by no other living creature except herself. She ran and ran until her lungs could pump no more air, her muscles were tight with fatigue, and the back of her head was throbbing.

There was something ahead. Something that her senses could not discern as anything natural or comprehensible. Yet it was unmistakably there. She slowed as she approached it, unsure of what to expect or how to guard herself against it. The jungle stopped abruptly at one point, giving way to a lush green grassy patch. Looking left and right, she saw that the grassy patch continued in either direction as far as she could see, curving gently backwards like the ends of a bow. Without knowing exactly how she knew it, she understood what that meant: a circle. The entire forest was encircled by this ring of grass. And from the look of it, the ring of grass was a perfect band, as precise in its edging as any band of gold wrought by a Kosala jeweller. Which itself was unnatural. What forest could grow within a perfect circle of kusa grass? This was Asura maya at work for certain, like the moonlight that was not moonlight, and the forest that considerately allowed her to pass unscratched and unscathed, and the utter absence of animal life. She was, after all, she reminded herself, in Ravana's Lanka.

The patch of grass was several dozens of yards broad. From where she stood, she saw that it ended suddenly, like a place where the ground fell off into a cliff or ravine. Except that this edge was immaculate, a perfect rim. And that the grass did not give way even slightly to rocky land or dried gritty patches as would be the case if it were real grass growing upon real earth. It went on in its lush green-trimmed perfection, and stopped.

She went across the grass, feeling its cool softness beneath her bare feet like a benediction. It was hard to believe it was not real. Perhaps . . . perhaps it *was* real, but controlled by Ravana's sorcery? After all, the seer-mages of Aryavarta could control the elements, so why not Ravana? Who knew the extent of his powers?

The grass gave way to a decline. She gasped as she reached the edge. It neither sloped down gently, nor gave away abruptly, as in a cliff-face. It simply ended. Looking down at the rim below her feet, she could see nothing beneath the ridge of grassy land. It was as flat as a plate. She stepped back, her knees wobbly from the long run. Her mind refused to accept the evidence of her eyes. But it was there: a flat, circular plane of forest ringed by a band of grass. What was the word Supanakha had used? Level? Yes, that was what this was, a level of some structure, not a forest upon Prithvi's blessed earth as she had thought at first. Her understanding grew . . . Ravana would not dare to place her upon Prithvi itself, for the earth-mother that had birthed her would embrace and keep her safe, away from his clutches, as she had done in the course of Sita's abduction, by calling the pushpak to her and forcing it to crash in the wilderness. That ploy had almost succeeded. Ravana would never make that mistake again. Hence this lofty prison.

She peered down over the rim for a moment, seeing only misty opaqueness, as if looking at a large plate of glass obscured by a coating of grime. She could hear no sounds of pursuit but expected them at any moment. She considered throwing herself over the edge, to whatever fate awaited at the bottom of that opaque abyss. Even if she crushed all her bones, it would be better than remaining here, a hapless prisoner of Ravana, waiting for the last war between rakshasas and mortalkind. She took a step back, preparatory to flinging herself over. Then she remembered the unborn life within her womb and hesitated.

Something must have sensed her intention, for even as she prepared to hurl herself off the rim of the artfully deceptive forest, the view below altered itself miraculously. Her change of heart occurred at the last instant, as she was poised to leap, but the invisible force must not have realised it, for it continued to alter the view. In moments, the misty obscurity below had cleared, like a glass surface being wiped clean by a magical dusting cloth, and revealed a view so stunning it took her breath away.

A great city lay below. All white and beautifully, artfully structured and shaped. Streets flowed organically through elegantly organised clusters of habitats. She could see tiny figures moving about in those tree-lined avenues and airy esplanades. It was too far to be certain, but she did not doubt that the minuscule figures she glimpsed were rakshasas all. For this was Lanka. There was no doubting that. Except that it was so beautiful! So magnificent. How could this be? A lair of rakshasas, so breathtakingly engineered? So pristine and pure and perfect?

'It is my wife's doing,' he said from behind her, and she knew without turning that the quarry had been found, the hunter had triumphed yet again. 'During the thirteen long years that I lay in suspended animation as a result of the brahm-astra unleashed by your husband in Mithila, my island-kingdom was razed to the ground in the civil conflict that erupted between the many Asura factions that survived the decimation at Mithila. When the fires died down, only the rakshasas remained in substantial enough numbers to repopulate, and my wife Mandodhari, whom you shall meet shortly, took over governance of the land. All this is her doing. As you can see, she has artistic pretensions.'

She observed with an emotion that was calm bordering on hysteria that he did not seem enraged at her escape attempt. If anything, he sounded like he had been standing behind her all this while, watching her, knowing every thought that passed through her addled brain. She wondered if that was truly so; what was the extent of his sorcery?

'It is beautiful,' Sita said, speaking her mind. It seemed pointless to rant and rail – or to scurry and sprint either. It was obvious that she was dealing with forces beyond her comprehension. Best then to attempt to study her captor, hoping by that strategem to glean some morsel of insight that could help formulate a more practical plan of escape. She turned to look at Ravana. Most of his heads seemed morose, inwardly focused, but one head, to the left of the central one, watched her with a bright sharpness in its gaze. She expressed herself honestly and sincerely; there seemed no reason not to do so. 'It seems a renewed land, a land of promise and hope.'

The watching face nodded calmly. 'It is all that. This is the new Lanka.'

'And you will lose it once more,' she said sharply, pressing home her point with intensity born of frustration and fear. If there was no escaping this place physically, then she would not yield mentally at least. 'It will be destroyed yet again when Rama comes. His army—'

'Yes, yes,' he sighed. 'You have said that before. But you still do not understand many things. I apologise again for the unfortunate display of violence. My cousin is not the most reasonable of beings, especially now. As you may recall, there is a history of passion and conflict with your husband and your brother-in-law. She lost her senses earlier. I have reprimanded her. It will not happen again. First, your needs. Then we shall talk. You have much to learn, and unlearn. Much to understand. There is more to this situation than meets the eye. Far from escaping, you would do well to stay and attempt to bridge this rift that has grown so wide already, to apply the methods of peace and ahimsa that your father lives his life by, rather than the easy way of the arrow and the sword.'

She stared at him in utter confusion. 'What do you speak of? I do not understand you!'

'You will, very shortly. Until then, I advise you to make your peace with your current situation. Escape is pointless. Pushpak can anticipate your every move.'

'Pushpak?' The name was a half-mythic mention in the annals of the tales of the devas and their heavenly deeds. She remembered the golden flying vehicle in which he had abducted her and brought her to Lanka.

He gestured at the forest around them. 'This structure. It is an extension of the same celestial chariot. It is a device with great abilities. This entire tower is made of its own . . . manifestation.

While a smaller portion remains as an akasa-rath, a sky-chariot, the selfsame one in which you were brought her.'

She looked around her at the trees, the flowers, the earth, the moonlight . . . questioning, wondering.

He nodded again. 'All this is illusion. Created by Pushpak's fertile and flexible transformative abilities. In view of your brave but regrettably unsuccessful attempt to flee, it will now re-arrange itself to take new shapes and forms. Do not be alarmed. It will cause you no harm, so long as you do not attempt to exit its environs. And now, I must leave you. This time, I will not lurk in the shadows. My cousin has already been removed from the tower and will trouble you no more. Refreshment and fresh garments will arrive shortly. Use the leisure time you have to calm yourself and accept the inevitability of your situation. I am not your enemy.'

And with those final cryptic words, he left her. This time he did not return, and nor did Supanakha. A little while later, Sita felt the ground beneath her feet tremble ever so slightly, and turned to see the view of the city below growing smaller. She puzzled over it for a moment, then with a shock of recognition she grasped that it was not the city that was growing smaller, but she who was rising higher above it. Somehow, through Ravana's Asura maya, this entire level of the 'tower', as Supanakha had called it, was rising up, up, into the sky. She did not understand how such a thing could be possible, nor had she ever encountered any such phenomenon before in her life, but she intuitively grasped that it was not unlike the tree-lifts that the vanars of Kiskindha used, little wooden platforms suspended from rope harnesses. By pulling on one set of ropes, the vanars could raise anyone standing on the tree-lifts up into their palaces above. She looked up, almost expecting to see a harness of rough jute ropes hanging over the entire forest, but of course there was none. Only a blurring of the sky above and a faint flickering in the false moonlight that illuminated this place of deceit.

She watched the city below, her only point of comparison.

And her heart sank as it grew so small as to be virtually invisible. With an outstretched thumb she could cover the city entire; so great was the distance now, that she had no previous experience with which to compare such a height. Yet she felt no different. The air smelled the same, the light had settled once more to the same luminous moonlike incandescence, and the place was as still and calm as before.

Finally, the rising stopped. She knew this because the thumb-sized city below ceased its shrinking. She could glimpse the island around the city now, a lush green land of rolling valleys and sloping hills, studded with diamantine lakes and traversed by slender silvery streams that were not quite rivers. It seemed very beautiful, not at all like the frightful nightmare land Lanka was believed to be in the numerous legends and myths of Sita's people. Or in the nightmares she had suffered before the siege of Mithila. The new Lanka, Ravana had called it. It was new indeed. Pristine and perfect, a jewel in the ocean. She could scarcely believe that this was the dreaded land of Asuras. And Ravana himself? He was not what she had expected or anticipated. What had he said? That she misunderstood him? Words to that effect, yes. What could he possibly mean? Was that yet another subterfuge? Possibly. But what if he was sincere? If the rakshasas had truly changed?

Then she recalled Supanakha and the way she had lunged at her. The hate and malice in those rancorous feline eyes. And the manner in which Ravana himself had abducted her from her little hermitage in the wilderness. No. She would not be deceived so easily. She must guard against Asura maya, such as this magical tower in which she found herself imprisoned. Ravana may have kidnapped her body as easily as carrying away a babe, but she must not allow him to steal away her mind and loyalties, no matter what his methods.

She steeled her heart, preparing herself for the worst.

And reminding herself, like a mantra to ward off the evil influence of this place of deceit and illusion, that Rama would surely come for her soon. She had only to wait and ward off

Ravana's advances, be they ever so civilised and humane, polite and charming. Surely she could do that much, could she not?

And if he used force? How would she defend herself against that mighty monolith of a being?

She had no answer to that. Except . . . she would use whatever means necessary. Somehow, she would defend herself and her honour and survive until Rama came. *By any means necessary*. She did not care to dwell too much upon the implications of that phrase.

Not just for her own sake, but for the sake of the unborn life growing within her. She touched her belly lightly, realising with a shiver that this was yet another thing she must conceal from Ravana – assuming that it was possible to conceal anything from his powerful sorcery. Devi alone knew how he might alter his intentions if he knew that he had not only Rama's wife but his unborn child as well within his power. She was about to embark upon a war of her own. A war of wills.

Maa, mujhe shakti de, she prayed. Mother, give me strength.

The night remained still and silent around her. After a moment, the forest began to alter its appearance, changing to a new form. She waited in the midst of the shape-shifting jungle, waited for whatever destiny her karma had brought her to.

5

'Rama!'

Even above the crashing of the waves, the sly whining of seagulls and the thrumming of the wind in his ears, he could never mistake Lakshman's voice, faint and distorted by wind and distance though it was. He turned his head into the wind and scoured the mist-obscured landscape. He was on the highest point, overlooking the shore, but despite the height advantage, he could barely see anything. He had to strain his crow-perfect sight to see what he sought.

To his right, the rocky pile overlooking the shore undulated into the mist, parts of it alternately swallowed by and revealed by the mist bank. The incessant thunder of the ocean below, rendered completely invisible by the mist, made the rocky bulge upon which he stood seem detached and unanchored to the earth, a floating island in a world besieged by white darkness.

'Rama.'

Lakshman's faint voice resounded and wavered and seemed to come from several directions at once. It was accompanied by the more reliable sound of fast-approaching footfalls crunching distantly upon the gravelly sand. He estimated that Lakshman was still a good quarter-mile away. He waited patiently. His bow and his sword were close enough at hand, should his senses prove to be deceiving him and the source of the voice turn out to be something other than what it seemed. Anything was possible, here on land's end, within crow's flight of Lanka.

Overhead, the mournful shrieks of unseen seagulls mocked the fading echoes of his brother's voice, overlapped by the relentless grinding crashing of the ocean, the eternal clock by which all things measured themselves; Rama had measured his own patience against that remorseless pounding rhythm these past days and found it tested to the limits. And this mist . . . Even standing high and squinting hard, it was several moments before he could glimpse the shadowy silhouette of Lakshman sprinting toward him across the grass-topped rise. The dimly viewed figure of his brother leapt lithely to avoid the slimy barnacle-encrusted black rock that lay like demon droppings everywhere. Rama's heart thudded briefly: Lakshman would not be running and yelling with such vigour unless some new crisis was looming, or unless he had very good news. Either one would be better than this endless waiting in mucky weather upon the cusp of the world.

Through the swirling eddies of mist below, he could make out something . . . *there*. An approaching shadow, moving with a peculiar bearing that was neither wholly vanarlike nor mortal. His brother was loping across the sandy dunes with the speedy but languid gait they had both acquired over the past weeks of hard long-distance running. It was far more effective to maintain a steady if slightly slower pace than to sprint and endanger oneself needlessly. They had learned this from Angad and his vanars; vanars did not sprint in breath-stealing bursts, instead they bounded steadily in a four-pointed loping gait that could be maintained all day – as indeed they had maintained it for most of the days since the company had left Kiskindha. Adjusting their own stance to suit their not-so-flexible mortal spines, the two humans had been able to pace the vanars well enough, earning further admiration from their proto-simian comrades.

As he watched, the tiny figure began to take the shape of a man running. Strips of fog clung to Lakshman as he loped, entwining themselves sinuously around his limbs before dissipating. Denser banks obscured him completely, like a thick veil pulled across then away. This wretched fog. It had rolled in overnight, blocking all sight of the ocean and coast, and by noon today it had grown thick enough in patches to obscure one's fingers if held outstretched. Rama thought of what it might be like to fight a battle in these conditions, then dismissed the thought. He had heard enough of Lakshman's laments about the ill-preparedness of the vanar sena already. They were too indisciplined, too unpredictable, too superstitious, too . . . everything except what a formidable fighting force ought to be, by Lakshman's standards. The mist had been just one more factor to feed his brother's anxiety.

For the vanars feared ocean mist greatly. They even had a term for it, rakshasakaluka. Cloak of rakshasas. They believed it was conjured up by the rakshasas of Lanka to steal across the ocean to the mainland. No amount of persuading by Rama or Lakshman about the fear that rakshasas themselves felt for the ocean could convince them. As long as they could recall, vanars had regarded ocean mist to be an unnatural phenomenon created by Asura maya – the powerful art of demonaic sorcery – and was literally a living thing capable of transforming into demon warriors at any moment. The fact that it came from the ocean, that vast saline desert, certainly fed their superstitious fear.

Cowed by the combined presence of ocean mist and the ocean itself, the entire vanar army of Kiskindha had retired to the nearest thicket, a yojana or two inland, where they crouched miserably on treetops, awaiting the passing of the mist (and, hopefully, the disappearance of that vast expanse of saline water as well!). No amount of persuasion, coercing, and even outright threats from their leader, Angad, could made them come down. Two whole days passed in this way.

After seeing no demons emerging from the mist, and reluctantly accepting that this was not the mythic rakshasakaluka of their legends, the vanars of Kiskindha then began to claim that it was an evil instrument of the Lord of Lanka, sent to confuse them into losing their sense of direction and drowning in the vast water-desert. At that point, early this morning, Lakshman had stormed away from them in disgust, telling Rama that at this rate they might as well raise an army of rabbits to fight Lanka.

Rama took it in his stride. Before leaving Kiskindha, Hanuman had explained to him how unthinkable a concept the ocean itself was to vanarkind. It was one thing for them to be ordered by their king to go forth, cross the ocean and invade Lanka, and quite another to actually be confronted by that vast undulating desert of briny death. To most vanars, the ocean was a mythic thing, something they had heard about in tribe-mothers' tales while they nursed at the breast, or at best a legendary artefact mentioned in the adventures of famous heroic vanars of long ago. To actually see it with their own bulbous vanar eyes was a shock to their system that would take some overcoming.

Rama suspected that now that the vanars were here upon the shore at last, the enormity of the task ahead had struck them immobile, and they needed time to recover their wits and courage. He had let them skulk. They had to wait for Hanuman to join up with them anyway. The vanar was a long time overdue: they had expected to find him here when they arrived three days ago. But perhaps there was news of him at last, or why else would Lakshman be running and yelling at the top of his voice in these weather conditions?

'Rama!'

Lakshman's voice was louder and clearer now, but still the illusion remained that they were in some kind of a canyon or closed-in valley. The two syllables of Rama's name seemed to hang in the air for a moment, then were absorbed by the distant crashing of invisible waves against the monolithic black rock. Lakshman had broached the rise and was running uphill, closing in with strong, swift strides. As his brother came closer, Rama saw sand and tiny shellacked pebbles flying up in spurts behind his feet, puncturing the mist.

For a brief hallucinatory moment, he thought he saw a shadow some yards behind Lakshman, a dark, top-heavy shadow with a head too wide to be human. He frowned, his fist tightening upon his sword hilt, starting to draw the blade out. Just then the mist swirled and cleared briefly, leaving naught but an open space behind Lakshman, and he blinked, putting it down to a trick of the weather. Still, his hand remained upon the hilt of his sword.

If only the sun would shine through just for a few moments. He could almost empathise with the vanars. Being near the one place that every vanar feared from birth – a vast, bottomless body of briny fluid that would swallow you up without a second thought – was bad enough in this fog; not being able to see the sun overhead was pure torture. Rama's skin, burned black as it was through years of over-exposure, had never been fair to begin with, and to him, the feeling of sunlight on his back, warming his skin and searing his senses, was as much a part of normalcy as the air he breathed and the water he drank. Now the absence of sunlight bothered him, though he was disciplined enough not to let it distract him. After all, he was of the Suryavansha line; the dynasty that claimed proud descent from the sun god Surya-deva himself. It was not for nothing that the brahmarishi Vishwamitra had picked high noon as the time for him to make his final assault upon the giant demoness Taraka in the Bhayanak-van. The sun was his totem, his energy-giver and succourer. Not having its warm hand upon his shoulder made him feel bereft, abandoned.

'Rama,' Lakshman said, dropping to his knees on the sandy patch below the rock on which Rama stood. 'He is here. Hanuman has arrived.'

Rama's heart leapt. Finally! He dropped down from the rock, putting himself on the same level as his brother. 'Where is he? Why did you not bring him with you?'

Lakshman was quiet. Not because he had run himself out of breath – it would take many days' running to put Lakshman out of breath – but because he was unable to find words to express himself. Rama waited, knowing his brother well enough to give him the space and time he needed. But he was impatient to see Hanuman, to embrace the vanar, to clap him on his bony back and smell his sour odour again.

'One of Angad's vanars brought the message. He said Hanuman was close on his heels.' Lakshman's tone gave no clue to his emotions, but Rama sensed a faint whiff of disappointment. Lakshman had awaited Hanuman's return as eagerly as Rama.

'And the armies?'

Lakshman shrugged. 'The angadia' – for that was what Angad's vanars called themselves, a term that was synonymous with 'courier' or 'messenger' – 'spoke only of Hanuman. He said nothing about any armies.'

Rama was unperturbed. 'They must be close behind. King Sugreeva said that Hanuman would round up the other vanar tribe-armies and bring them here. I am sure he would not come unless he had gathered them.'

Lakshman raised his head and looked up at Rama. His face had grown intensely thin these past months, too thin, Rama felt. Such thinness gave him a slight aspect of cruelty, as of a man who had endured much at the hands of his enemies and was willing to make his enemies endure much more in return. It was not dominant on his face – his strikingly intense close-set eyes and broad nose still made him as attractive and wholesome as ever – but that touch of cruelty, a warrior's aspect, had not been there a few months earlier. 'Perhaps we have placed too much faith in Hanuman.'

'There is no such thing as too much faith, brother. One either has faith or does not have it.' Rama smiled reassuringly at Lakshman. 'Have no doubt, Hanuman will come with the armies we were promised. We shall have a force sufficient to invade Lanka.'

Lakshman shrugged, rising slowly to his feet. He had a defeated air about him that Rama did not like. 'Perhaps he will at that. And even so, it may not matter.'

'How could it not matter? If he brings a vanar sena large

enough to make a strong assault, we shall have a fighting chance of breaching Ravana's defences.'

Lakshman sighed. 'A vanar sena. An army of talking ape-men. How large could it be? We saw what King Sugreeva called the army of Kiskindha. It was barely equivalent to one regiment of PFs. And untrained, undisciplined and inexperienced to boot. What good would a few thousand more vanars like that be?'

Lakshman turned away from Rama, looking out to sea. There was nothing to be seen in that direction – the mist bank was thickest there. Rama saw his profile, thin and hard, and felt his brother's frustration, saw the bitterness glistening in his angry eyes.

'It would take the king of devas to raise an army fit to invade Lanka anyway. What were we thinking, going to vanars for help?' Lakshman turned suddenly, clutched Rama's sword hand. 'Rama. It's still not too late. Even now we can return home, to Ayodhya. Raise the Kosala army. Why, we could ask the other united Arya nations for aid, they would not refuse us. We could be back here within a month with a real army! With ships! And siege machines! Then we could sail to Lanka and knock on Ravana's doors with the might of Aryavarta at our backs.'

Rama gripped Lakshman's hand tightly. 'Lakshman, I told you, I will not debate with you any more. I cannot take us back to Ayodhya until our term of exile is done. Why do you persist in arguing this point?'

'Because our exile is only a season and a half away from ending, bhai!' Lakshman's voice was plaintive and pleading. 'A few months! What difference can it make?'

Rama released Lakshman's shoulder and turned away. 'Fourteen years, the terms were clear. On my naming day in the month of Chaitra, we shall return home to Ayodhya, not a day before.'

'We shall all be dead by the month of Chaitra!' Lakshman blurted.

Rama turned to look at him. Lakshman's face was flushed,

from running or from emotion, but he stood his ground and did not look away, nor take back his words. Rama reminded himself that Lakshman had endured much, and he weighed his brother's outbursts in the light of that knowledge. His voice was still calm and gentle when he spoke again. 'My brother, why do you lose faith so easily? When faith is the greatest weapon in our pitifully small arsenal?'

'No, Rama,' Lakshman said bitterly. 'It is the *only* weapon. Your faith is our entire arsenal.'

Rama considered that. 'It is a great weapon. Faith can move mountains.'

Lakshman issued a brief sound that might have been a choked laugh. 'And cross oceans?' He gestured behind Rama. 'That ocean in particular? Because I don't know how else we can take a force of cringing talking monkeys across that particular ocean to fight the king of demons in his own stronghold.'

'You must not lose hope, Lakshman,' Rama said, worried now. Lakshman had never been happy about their turning to the vanars for help, but Rama had thought he had come to accept their new-found allies. He was alarmed by this display of bitterness and dejection. 'We will cross the ocean. The vanars have great reserves of strength. It is we who must learn to tap those reserves, to show them what they are capable of achieving. If we lose hope, how can we lead them? They look to us for inspiration and example.'

Lakshman shook his head, sinking to the rock on which Rama had stood earlier. He sat upon it in an attitude of dejection, burying his face in his hands. 'I'm sorry, Rama. You can continue stoking a spark in a winter storm. I don't possess such unshakeable faith. All I see is a group of mangy monkeys who skulk in trees at the sight of a little mist and ocean. How we can transform that ragtag bunch into a fighting army capable of invading Lanka is beyond my comprehension.'

'But Hanuman is here now,' Rama said, unwilling to accept Lakshman's dejection. He had talked his brother out of these depressions before; he would do so a hundred more times if need be. 'He will have brought the remaining vanar armies with him. And the additional army that Sugreeva spoke of, which we know nothing about. Now we shall have a substantial enough number to launch an invasion. Our strength in numbers will make up for the lack of war experience our sena possesses.'

Lakshman stared up at Rama with glistening eyes. 'Listen to you. Planning to cross an ocean with an army terrified of water! But nothing can dampen your spirits. You still speak and act with as much vigour as if you were leading the combined forces of all mortalkind!' He struggled back to his feet with a weariness that Rama knew was more spiritual than physical. 'But I fear that even your stout heart will shudder when you see what Hanuman has brought with him. I fear that your hope and your faith have been unfounded, Rama. Our efforts to raise an army to rescue Sita have come to naught. We have no army worth speaking of.'

Before Rama could respond, a voice boomed through the mist.

'No army you say, brother Lakshman? Then what do you call this force that follows me?'

Rama turned to see a great vanar striding towards him. It took him a moment to comprehend what his eyes were seeing. He could not believe at first that this magnificent specimen, massively muscled, bold of step and glittering of eye, could possibly be the meek, reedy, thin vanar who had first approached him so hesitantly in the wilderness of Janasthana. 'Hanuman?' he said, shocked. 'Anjaneya? Maruti Whiteleaf?' They were all the names he knew for his vanar friend. 'Is it truly you?'

Hanuman approached Rama and Lakshman with great loping strides, then dropped to one knee before them, joining his hands together in a perfect namaskaram, something most vanars could not achieve because of the way their hands were shaped. He bore a great gleaming golden mace upon one shoulder, and he held it easily in the crook of his arm as he greeted Rama and Lakshman in a voice of warm reverence.

'Pranaam to you, my lord Rama, my lord Lakshman. I have

returned with your grace to serve you and your cause. Behold, I bring with me the fruition of your hopes and the vindication of your faith in me.'

And as he gestured behind him with a proud flourish, a deep rumbling rose from the ground beneath their feet like an earthquake announcing its approach.

6

A wind sprang up, as if called by Hanuman himself. Rama had sensed its approach for a while now, had been awaiting this very change in the direction of the breeze that had brought the ocean mist to obscure the shore. But even so, its timing was remarkably coincidental. Or perhaps, as some wise sage had once said, maybe even one of Rama's own venerable ancestors, when you take positive action without fear or doubt, then your well-deserved victory is not a coincidence. The wind tugged at the ends of his matted locks, ruffled the coarse cloth of his garment. The mist that had enveloped them so completely until now was shredded into fluttering strands that clung hopelessly to the edges of things before being cast away. In moments, the entire ridge began to clear, the seashore swept by an invisible broom. Above, the cloudy murk that had obscured the skies was dissipating fast, worked on by the same ocean gale. The glimpses of sky through the opening gaps was not the steely azure blue Rama had wished for; rather, it was a wild and stormy sky, the kind of sky one would expect over a storm front. But the sun was coming through, and the fleeting touches of warmth and spears of brilliance penetrating the clouds were reward aplenty.

As the light and wind show rose in intensity, the rumbling sound grew ever louder. Rama had guessed at its origin, but even knowing the likely cause of the disturbance did not diminish its sheer power. The very rocky ridge upon which they stood was trembling beneath their feet. Few things short of an actual earthquake could produce such an effect. It was impressive.

Hanuman regained his feet. He stood before Rama, hands still clasped in the reverential namaskaram. His face shone with a glow of pure vitality. What has he been feeding on? Rama wondered. The nectar of the devas?

'My friend. It is so good to have you back.' Rama went forward without hesitation and embraced Hanuman. The vanar opened his arms and clasped Rama with an intensity that made Rama feel he could as easily have been crushed as hugged. Was this truly the same Hanuman? It hardly seemed possible. 'You are well returned to us, by the grace of the devas.'

'Nay, Rama. With your grace,' Hanuman corrected mildly. 'Your name was the mantra which led me to the successful achievement of my goals. All this that I am about to present to you is the fruition of your own great deeds and adherence to dharma. I am only the courier who bears the glad tidings, not the creator of this glorious karma.'

Rama looked at Hanuman. The vanar's eyes shone with a light of powerful intensity. His words were mesmeric, the deep-throatedness of his speech wholly unlike the hesitant, self-doubting Hanuman of only a few weeks ago. 'And this transformation that has been wrought in your person, my friend? I am so pleased to see you in such excellent form. To what is owed this wonderful change?'

Hanuman inclined his head. 'Again, it is your grace, my lord. You alone have sustained me through the past several weeks of questing and fasting.'

'Fasting?' This came from Lakshman, whose surprise was great enough to overcome even his deep reservations. 'You look like one who has been feasting, not fasting, vanar!'

Hanuman inclined his head respectfully at Lakshman. 'In that case, brother Lakshman, perhaps you may call it the result of my spiritual feasting and physical fasting.'

He turned back to Rama. 'My lord, I will gladly relate to you the adventures that I have experienced since taking your leave at Mount Rishimukha. Now I have something wonderful to present to you. The purpose of my travels was fulfilled. The armies that you sought have been assembled. All of them and more besides. I give unto you, as promised by my lord and liege, King Sugreeva, in exchange for the favours done by you that helped him regain his usurped kingdom, in his own words, the armies that will lead you to victory against the forces of Lanka.'

While they had been speaking, the wind had blown away the last vestiges of ocean mist. The sun had begun shining down through the stormy, cloud-ridden sky, illuminating the landscape with a purple-tinted light that enhanced the desolateness of the place. The cape on which they stood was a rocky shoal tinged with a little sand, a black stone border between the subcontinent and the vast indigo ocean. Behind the ridge of black stone was a lush green valley, sloping down to the edge of the jungle that was brethren to the countless undulating yojanas of similar jungle that traversed the whole sub-continent, all the way up to the slopes of the mighty Himalaya itself. The valley extended a mere thousand yards before it was overrun by the jungle.

From that jungle, as Rama and Lakshman watched, emerged an army. Nay, *armies*. For as he had been instructed, Hanuman had travelled to secure the support of all the separate vanar forces scattered across the land. Rama recognised the familiar brown-black pelts of the vanars of Kiskindha, lured from their treetops by the arrival of their compatriots. They emerged from the edge of the thicket at the rightmost end, whooping and cheering loudly, beating their chests with their paws. Some came somersaulting, turning cartwheels, bounding in that ape-like way that only vanars could achieve, loping, shambling, rolling as younguns were wont to do, for there were many younguns here, and olduns too, which itself told him how extensive the mobilisation must have been, for the tribes to give up every vanar, male and female, young and old, as long as they were capable of fighting. They streamed out from the cover of the jungle and on to the narrow stretch of sloping grassy valley, emerging endlessly, until the valley was filled with vanars standing chest to back and shoulder to shoulder and no more could be accommodated, and still they came, climbing on to one another's shoulders, building little pyramids the way he had seen the Kiskindha vanars do when they wished to reach some high object that could not be attained by climbing, and after a moment he realised that it was he they were crowding to see, the mortal yodha whose war they were going to fight, whose mate they were seeking to retrieve, Prince Rama Chandra of Ayodhya, trusted ally of King Sugreeva of Kiskindha, slayer of Vali the Usurper, bloodfriend of Hanuman.

The valley below was thick with vanars now, so densely packed that not a blade of grass was visible any longer. While they had assembled, for the large part silently, marked only by the natural grunting, snuffling, wheezing-sneezing of vanars, the sun had emerged from its jungle of mist and cloud as well, and shone now upon them all, bathing them in a golden late-morning glow, beaming down in pillars and pathways of light that seemed to reach all the way up to the heavens, like lights beamed down by the devas themselves to illuminate this great gathering. And still they came, from the cover of the trees into the open land which was no longer open but covered from end to end with vanars.

Rama turned to look at Lakshman, who was staring down with round, amazed eyes. A trace of his earlier bitterness still remained on his face, like a crease in a wrung cloth, but in place of his anger and despair was a light of incredulity. He sensed Rama's gaze on him then and looked up, meeting his brother's eyes. Lakshman seemed to choke on whatever he meant to say, then cleared his throat and said: 'How many?'

The question was directed to Hanuman. Both Rama and Lakshman turned their eyes to him. Hanuman stood with his mace on his right shoulder, his left arm crossed across his chest languidly, like a man who had battled a war and won already.

'We do not count as you do, my lords. But you see here before you every single living vanar capable of combat in our collective tribe-nations.'

Rama was not sure he had heard correctly. 'Did you say

every single living vanar, my friend? Surely you do not mean that literally?'

Hanuman looked puzzled. 'What else would I mean?' He gestured at the great mass of life below them. 'Apart from the carrying females, the nursing and the nursed, the sick and invalid, the old and feeble, I have collected every one of my kind and gathered them together.'

Rama exchanged a glance with Lakshman, who seemed as flabbergasted as Rama felt. Lakshman shook his head, unable to speak. Rama had to search his mind to find words to express what he was feeling: it was not easy. 'This is more than an army, my friend. This is . . .' He did not know what name to give such a thing.

Hanuman came to his rescue. 'You speak truly, my lord. Such mobilisation has not been attempted any time before in vanar history. There are legends, of course, but none living today was present at the time of those legendary occasions. Still, we have a term, passed on in our songs and myths. The term is janaya-sena. It is what we call such a gathering.'

Janaya-sena.

A generation army. An entire generation of vanars mobilised into an army.

Rama caught the look on Lakshman's face. His brother looked sobered. They gazed down together at the great mass of vanars huddled together in the valley below. Now he could see them perched even in the trees at the rim of the clearing, hanging from the thinnest branches in an attempt to view the mortal whose cause had brought them together. The trees were bent over with their weight. The foliage rustled and stirred for as far as he could see, as the vanar armies filled even the jungle for miles around. How many were there? How large could a janaya-sena be? These past few weeks, living and travelling with vanars, he had gained some understanding of their ways. They were far more sophisticated than they had seemed at first. Although instinct was prized over rationality in their culture, nevertheless there were vanars who had acquired some knowledge of the sciences, especially of astronomy, for vanars loved to gaze up at the stars from their treetop habitats. And astronomy required counting to high numbers.

He thought that the combined numbers of these vanar armies assembled before him would reach beyond ten lakhs for certain. Perhaps even into multiples of ten lakhs. He doubted that there was a clearing large enough in the forests of Aryavarta where he would be able to line them up and count them all.

'My friend,' he said to Hanuman, 'I do not have words to express my feelings. This is more than I expected. Much, much more. I had no notion that you would return with such large numbers. This is a great army indeed. The greatest I have ever had the pleasure to witness with my own eyes.'

Hanuman bowed his head. 'It exists only to serve you, my lord Rama.'

'I am honoured, Anjaneya. But surely you have exceeded your orders? Will not such a total mobilisation endanger the very continuation of your great tribe-nations? How will life go on with every able vanar gone to war?'

Hanuman tilted his head to one side reflectively. 'How does your life go on, my lord Rama? Without your beloved wife, can you truly live as normal?'

Rama felt his throat harden. He shook his head.

Hanuman shrugged. 'Then how can we, your friends and allies, go on either? The vanar nations cannot rest until Sita-devi is returned to your side. If one goes to war, then one must go fully to war. There are no half-fights and part-battles. One either gives all or one gives nothing.'

Rama was lost for words. He turned to Lakshman to see the effect these words were having on his brother. Lakshman was staring off to the side, in the direction of the shoreline. Rama thought that Lakshman was so overwhelmed, as he himself was, that he could not meet Hanuman's eyes any longer. The vanar's efforts had truly been gargantuan.

'Rama,' Lakshman said softly, 'it is impossible. This is beyond belief.'

Hanuman glanced back in the direction of Lakshman's gaze. He smiled and turned back to Rama. 'My lord, if you recall my king Sugreeva's last words, he spoke of another army that might possibly join us as well. We had scent of only rumours then, but on my journey I met with a happy accident. I am pleased to present to you the rest of your fighting force in this war against Lanka.'

Rama stared at Hanuman incredulously. 'Another army? But you said that these were all the vanars on earth assembled here already . . .'

Hanuman came forward to take Rama's hand. 'The other army does not consist of vanars, my lord. See for yourself.'

He led Rama by the hand, like a child might lead his father to show him a great sandcastle he had constructed, or a tree house. They stopped at the edge of the black-rock ridge overlooking the shoreline. A thin, straggly line of sandy beach stretched raggedly as far as the eye could see, backed by the same rise of black rock upon which they stood. The mist had cleared further and the whole shoreline was now visible.

Along the beach, covering every square yard for miles into the distance – as far as Rama could see – was a vast assemblage of creatures. Dark-furred, thick-pelted, each one a mammoth in its own right, even the smallest one at least thrice as high as a vanar, and twice as high as Rama or Lakshman. Some stood even taller, perhaps thrice as tall as a mortal male, and built like the trunk of a Himalayan fir. Their dark beady eyes glistened in the sunlight as they peered up short-sightedly at Rama.

'Rksas,' Lakshman said, almost to himself, like a man in a dream. Rksas, or, as they were called in the common tongue, balus.

Bears.

An army of bears.

7

Hanuman raised his mace and waved to the army of bears gathered on the shore below. In particular, Rama saw, he directed his gesture at a great black Himalayan bear at the head of the vast army. The great black was accompanied by an equally large brown, and together they responded to Hanuman's wave by raising their arms and issuing a series of chuffing sounds that Rama took to be some form of bear tongue. They were echoed by their army, the combined effect loud enough to drown out the pounding of the surf momentarily. On the other side of the black-rock ridge, the vanar armies hooted enthusiastically too.

Hanuman turned back to Rama. 'That is Jambavan, king of the bears. He desires greatly to meet with you, Rama. He says he owes you a blood-debt and will do anything to repay it.'

A blood-debt? A great army of bears, as well as the largest army of vanars ever assembled in their history? It was too much to take in all at once. Rama understood what Lakshman had meant. It was impossible, beyond belief. And yet . . . it was there before his eyes. As real as the rocky rise upon which he stood.

'This is more than I ever expected,' Rama said slowly. 'I thought King Sugreeva was referring to another force of vanars. But bears . . .'

Hanuman frowned. 'Are you not pleased, Rama? Do you not scent bears well for fighting your war?'

A smile came to Rama's face. 'My friend, I am more pleased than you can imagine. This is truly a great fighting force. The largest army of vanars ever assembled. And a gathering of bears so great that I believe any mortal or Asura army would be struck dumb at the very sight, as Lakshman and I were indeed struck dumb just moments ago.'

He glanced at Lakshman, who nodded and said, 'A single angry bear is enough to take on a dozen armed mortals at times. I cannot imagine what havoc such an immense number of them could wreak.' He added thoughtfully: 'I wonder how they fight when in groups . . .'

Hanuman beamed. 'They will be glad to show you, Lakshman-bhaiya. They are very eager to please Rama and will do anything he orders.'

Rama had a moment to wonder how and when he had gained such mastery over a race of creatures with whom he had barely had any real contact in his lifetime, but before he could think of a way to express this in words without causing offence to Hanuman or the bears, a vanar came up to them. He was a little fellow, really only a youngun, as they called them. A scraggly furred chap, barely half Hanuman's height. As he reached the top of the rise, heading purposefully towards them, he suddenly came into view of the ocean. He screeched and fell back on his rump, scrabbling frantically, then turned his face away from the sight, burying his head in his hands on the ground, while his rump stayed raised high, facing the dreaded expanse. His mouth continued to issue a stream of vanar sounds which Rama construed as invocations to various devas and devis.

Hanuman issued a bark of laughter at his fellow's reaction, then called out, 'Sakra, it will not cause you any harm. It is the ocean. It only lies there, it does not come up and attack you.'

The vanar raised his furry little cone-shaped head fearfully to look at them. Rama saw that he had managed to get sand stuck all over it. 'But it does, Maruti! It comes rushing up and catches hold of your feet and drags you into its maw!'

Hanuman shook his head, grinning apologetically at his mortal companions. 'That's called a wave, Sakra. And waves don't come this far inland. We're quite safe here, as you can see.'

Sakra looked at them doubtfully, as if ascertaining for himself whether they were indeed as safe as they claimed they were, then stole a quick glance at the offending expanse of brine behind him. The sight was more than he was ready to absorb, and it caused him to quiver from head to toe in a perfect imitation of a wind-struck sapling. It took several more words of reassurance from Hanuman before he finally regained his feet and faced them once more.

'You have nothing to fear here, my friend,' Rama called out. 'If you do not wish to look upon the ocean, then take three steps to your right, and walk quickly to us.'

Lakshman muttered something under his breath about how was an army of vanars expected to cross an ocean without being able to even look at it.

The vanar did as Rama said, taking not three but a half-dozen steps to his right with an enthusiasm that almost carried him back down the hillside. Regaining control of himself by use of his tail, he glanced nervously in the direction of the ocean and seemed surprised that it had suddenly vanished. After a moment he grinned, elated, and issued a happy, '*Cheeka!*' before bounding with astonishing speed towards them. He stopped a few yards away, and scratched first his backside and then his head violently, scattering sand and dirt everywhere, then showed his gums to Rama and his companions.

Hanuman grinned. 'Sakra! Sakra, you little rascal! I have missed you sorely, my brother.' He picked up and hugged the little vanar. So vast was the difference in their sizes that the smaller vanar seemed to almost disappear within Hanuman's arms. He licked Hanuman's face happily, then sniffed him in several key places, as Rama had seen vanars do when greeting a stranger or a new arrival.

'You scent so different, Anjaneya,' Sakra said wonderingly. 'Looking at you, I thought it was a shapeshifter disguised as you. But now I see that it is you.'

Hanuman laughed. 'Yes, it is!'

'Yes,' Sakra went on seriously. 'For I can scent your old smell underneath. It is not that you have a new scent, just that your old scent has changed so much. It is as if you have grown years in a single moon! And so healthy and strong!'

Hanuman laughed. 'We will speak of those things later, my brother. For now, pay your respects to King Rama and his brother Prince Lakshman.'

He put Sakra down again. The little vanar looked at Rama and Lakshman, baring his gums and scratching his backside vigorously a time or two, until he found some offending particle of dirt, yanked it out and examined it closely. Then he suddenly remembered his manners and the mortals before him, and abruptly bowed his head nervously several times, low enough to bang his forehead on the rocky ground.

Rama smiled, amused at his nervousness. Many vanars still regarded him as a god, or at the very least an avatar, after his defeat of Vali and his restoration of Sugreeva: it was a misapprehension he had been unable to dislodge thus far. 'You may approach, youngun. I do not bite friends of Hanuman.'

At that, the vanar's round eyes grew large, seeming to fill his entire little face. 'But you *do* bite others who displease you? With giant teeth you can summon up at any time you please?'

Hanuman prodded his brother lightly. 'Sakra, you're as liceheaded as ever! King Rama was making a jest. He does not bite at all.'

'But he does!' Sakra exclaimed. 'We have seen him biting the flesh of dead boars and even a great bull he and his brother downed just the other night.' He imitated a mortal tearing roasted meat off a bone, then leaned closer and whispered to Hanuman, loud enough for both Rama and Lakshman to catch easily, 'They eat rakshasas too, I heard! Boiled and buttered!'

Hanuman laughed. 'And they snack on vanars between meals, then use their finger bones to clean their teeth afterwards.'

'*Cheeka!*' Sakra screeched, leaping backwards a good yard or three. 'They will eat me! They will eat me! That is why they sent for me. They know that I opened the gate to Vrindavan so we could get in and drink the honey-mead. They will catch me and cook me and eat me! Save me, brother. I beg you, save me from them!'

Hanuman looked back at Rama and Lakshman. Both of them were grinning widely, amused at the little vanar's antics. 'You will excuse my half-brother,' Hanuman said. 'He is prone to over-excitement and exaggeration.'

He turned back to Sakra. 'Don't be foolish, Sakra. You are not here because of any mischief you have committed. Although,' he raised his eyebrows meaningfully, 'I have no doubt that you have committed much mischief that would bear looking into. For the present time, it was not Rama and Lakshman who sent for you. It was me.'

'*You?*' Sakra looked simultaneously curious and relieved. 'Because you missed me and regretted not taking me along on your mission?'

Hanuman glanced at Rama as if to apologise again for his brother's childishness. 'No, Sakra,' he said impatiently. 'I sent for you because I have work for you to do.'

Sakra stared at him goggle-eyed. 'Work? For *me?*'

'Yes, important work. Now, listen carefully. I wish you to tell Generals Susena and Satabali below to take up positions to convey Rama's words. He will speak to our people shortly. Go, quickly!'

Sakra hesitated, looked nervously – but with a shrewd reappraisal – at Rama and Lakshman, saluted his brother smartly, then bounded down the hillside toward the generals Hanuman had spoken of.

Hanuman returned to Rama. 'I apologise for my brother. He is . . .' He searched for words, then shrugged helplessly. 'He is Sakra,' he said at last. 'We used to call him Cheeka as young-uns because he always behaved more like a monkey than a vanar.'

Lakshman flashed a rare grin, nodded as if recalling his own lost childhood, and asked, 'And what did he call you back then?'

Hanuman looked at Lakshman, then at Rama. He grinned

shyly. 'Any of my childhood names. Maruti. Anjaneya. Whiteleaf. Broken Jaw.' He paused. 'And sometimes Shard-shrak.'

Lakshman frowned. 'Shard-shrak?'

Hanuman sighed. 'One who has too thick a skull and not enough sense in it.'

'Oh.' Lakshman nodded, understanding. 'I know that one. Bone-brain.'

'Yes,' Hanuman said, straight-faced. 'And I would much appreciate it if you forgot I ever told you that, brother Lakshman.'

Lakshman shrugged, trying to keep a straight face too, and having some trouble doing so. 'Of course, brother Hanuman!'

Rama chuckled. 'If you two have finished with your little banter, I would like to speak with the leaders of all the armies, Hanuman. Both the vanars and the bears.'

'Certainly, my lord Rama. That is what I have entrusted Sakra with doing. They will set up a chain of speakers who will convey your words to even the farthermost soldiers, a full yojana away.'

A full yojana? That was a good nine miles! How many vanars and bears were there anyway? Rama made a mental note to ask Lakshman to make some kind of a rough count, if only to satisfy his curiosity. Aloud he said, 'But should we not speak to the generals alone first?'

Hanuman joined his hands together. 'Respectfully, my lord, the soldiers would be greatly pleased if you addressed them all together first. Among us vanars, and similarly among the bear races, we do not follow the mortal system of captains and other hierarchies quite so rigidly. Organising an army and giving orders when going into battle is one thing, but when not fighting, each vanar is virtually equivalent to all others. By addressing the troops at large first-hand, you will gain their respect.'

Rama nodded, understanding. 'It is most fitting,' he agreed. 'Very well, we shall do as you suggest.'

Sakra came bounding back to Hanuman. He whispered a few quick words into his half-brother's ear. Hanuman nodded and said something in response and Sakra bounded away downhill.

Rama saw several other vanars take up positions along the slope of the hill, each close enough to hear the other's words. Hanuman looked at them, acknowledging their waves and sounds of greeting with gestures of his own. Then he turned back towards Rama.

'We are ready, Rama. You may speak at any time you wish.'

Rama took a deep breath and released it slowly. 'First of all, then, please tell them all that I feel truly graced by the Creator Himself. For only Lord Brahma could have provided the means by which such a great force could be assembled.'

Hanuman translated Rama's words, calling them out loudly in the vanar tongue, the primitive language of half-words, grunts and teeth-showing grimaces that was understood by all the various tribe-nations and gotras of vanars. Sakra, who had positioned himself closest, rose upon his hind paws and began issuing a series of like communications, ending with an ululating cry that carried across the suddenly hushed valley. For several moments, Rama could hear echoes of Hanuman's translation being passed along by the vanars below in undulating waves that carried into the jungle and beyond, as the message was repeated with lightning swiftness until every last vanar had received it. Meanwhile, Hanuman had turned already to face the bears and was translating Rama's words into their tongue, producing a passable imitation of bear-talk. On the bear side of the ridge, Rama heard chuffing sounds and loud, resounding grunts, as the bears passed on his words in like fashion.

A brief pause followed the end of the translation.

Then, as one enormous beast, the entire vanar army bared its collective teeth and issued an ululating cry that seemed to resound across the world. The bears followed them with an enormous roaring that put Rama in mind of a glacial waterfall he had once seen in springmelt high in the Gangotri region of the mighty Himalayas, source of the great river Ganga. Birds took to the air for yojanas around, startled by the sheer volume of sound.

Hanuman said, 'They are pleased by your praise. Pray, mouth more words. They would hear the great Rama speak further.

They have heard so much about your courage and prowess in battle. If you will say some wise, noble words of inspiration, they will feel blessed.'

Wise, noble words of inspiration. Rama looked down at the veritable sea of vanars on one side and the army of bears on the other with trepidation. He hardly knew where to search within himself for suitable things to say. His body – not just his mind, heart and soul, but his entire being – ached for his lost wife. Losing a limb in battle might have been less painful. Never a willing speaker, he now sometimes went days without saying a single word. He was tired, drained from the long weeks since Sita's taking, barely able to find respite at night from the hellish visions that tormented him, consumed by guilt and remorse. And when he struggled with cares of the day, worries assaulted him on every side. There was Lakshman's constant griping and nagging about the inefficacy of the vanars as a fighting force, the impossibility of crossing the ocean, their utter lack of knowledge of what size of force or defences Ravana possessed in Lanka, what sorcerous Asura maya he might unleash against the innocent vanars, who had never seen so much as a seer levitating. A thousand thousand worries, and little succour to be found.

But a look at Hanuman's face, so filled with pride at being here on this rocky hilltop beside Rama and Lakshman, at having brought to Rama such a vast gathering of his race, and such a great bear army, and Rama knew he must fulfil the vanar's wish. All those waiting vanars and bears down there, hushing each other now as Hanuman's associates and their generals passed on the word that the mortal king was about to issue a pravachan. King. That itself showed how deep Hanuman's faith and loyalty lay. Rama was hardly a king. A prince in exile, yes. The throne of Ayodhya awaited his return from banishment, no doubt. But to Hanuman and the vanars – and presumably the bears as well – who followed him now, he was already King Rama. Rightful master of the throne of the Kosala nation.

He glanced down this way, then that, still unable to assimilate the sheer magnitude of the force that Hanuman had gathered in so short a time. Truly, some force above in Swarga-loka must support his cause to enable the raising of such a vast army in a few weeks. He wondered if in some age past mighty Brahma himself had indeed charged the other devas with the task of populating Prithvi with such multitudes for just such a day, so that he, Rama, could raise an army to seek out and regain his stolen wife.

An army that was gazing up adoringly, almost reverentially, awaiting his next words as eagerly as shishyas awaited their guru's words of wisdom at a forest kul. Or as keenly as disciples awaited their master's pravachan.

A pravachan? That was something venerable sages issued. Religious proclamations, divinely received knowledge, speeches made by Rama's fabled forebears, those mythic heroes of yore: Manu Lawmaker, regarded by some as seed-sower of the entire mortal race; Surya, the sun god himself, taken human avatar to combat evil in the mortal realm; Harishchandra, the benevolent king who gave away all his worldly possessions rather than deny any who asked for alms; Rama's own great father, Dasaratha. These brave and honourable vanars deserved a leader of that stature. A demigod-like personality. A divinely ordained hero. A deva on earth. Or at the very least, an avatar of Vishnu.

Instead, he stood here, wind-buffeted, sun-baked, a weary, heartbroken, care-burdened creature, groping for words, searching for something to say, anything that sounded inspiring. Not a deva. Not even an avatar. Just a man.

A man bent low by the weight of long exile and recent loss. Bone-tired, battle-weary, soul-sick.

Yet even as the enormous gathering waited patiently in almost reverential silence, something rose within Rama's heart, slowly, like a submerged lotus floating back to the surface of a pond, seeking the warmth of sunlight.

What was it Lakshman had said? *Rama, you could stoke a spark into a fire even in a winter storm.* Words to that effect. Yes, it was true, the one thing that kept him going was faith.

Utter and absolute, unshakeable. For what else did he possess now, if not faith? It was all that drove him on, kept him alive, made him eat to sustain himself, even though every morsel seemed like it had been washed of all flavour and nourishment, as if the very water he drank, be it from the purest glacial spring, tasted foul and tainted by some nameless dead animal's corpse. Faith was his touchstone, his whetstone, his millstone. His curse, his sustenance, his salvation. He could not shed it even if he tried. He would raise an army. He would go to Lanka. He would seek out Sita, dead or alive. It did not matter if he succeeded in his aims or not, if Sita were alive or not – or worse. All that mattered was that he had set his mind to a purpose and he would not rest or turn away until that purpose was fulfilled. That was what drove him. How could he put such a thing into words? How could he describe the love that he felt for Sita? The duty that demanded he seek her out and rescue her, no matter what the cost, or the odds. Not duty, for that was a given thing, a choice made. Dharma. Dharma was the centre of his faith. It was an iron bond welded to the very spurs of his skeleton. Like the hilt of his sword. The string of a bow. Dharma defined him, made him, shaped him. And dharma demanded that he do this and not let anything stand in the way of his doing it. Dharma. And yes, love. Above all, love.

Suddenly the sun was hot on his cheeks, and he found his eyes wet. He looked around and saw the still faces of Lakshman and Hanuman. Turned the other way and saw the vanars on the slope, already calling out communications in the same primitive vanar tongue. Heard the passing on of the communications in waves across the vanar sena below. And through the masses of the bear army as well. Saw the armies respond, not with the ululating exultation and chuffing grunts they had emitted earlier, but with white noise. A silence so deafening, that the world seemed stopped, held still. The breeze moved the leaves in the trees below, the sun shone, seagulls called indignantly at the usurpation of their habitat, and Rama realised that he had not merely been thinking those thoughts, but that he had spoken them aloud, had shared with the vanars his innermost feelings, doubts, despair and hopes.

Then he heard Hanuman's voice speak into the silence. The vanar's voice betrayed his own emotions, and without looking, Rama could tell that Hanuman had tears running down his distended vanar cheeks too. For that much had not changed. Outwardly he had become a giant instead of the puny stripling he had been at Rishimukha, but at heart Hanuman had always been a giant. And that too-large heart cried out in its mighty breast now, answering Rama's clarion call. Hanuman spoke three simple words. Rama did not know if all the various vanar tribe-nations and bear nations even understood the first two of those three words. But Hanuman spoke them anyway, and the vanars and the bears passed them on, and the vanar army and the bear army repeated them to their comrades behind until every last vanar and bear soldier for miles around had heard them.

And then with one voice, both armies replied, with a cry so resounding that the world itself was overwhelmed by the tidal wave of sound. They roared the phrase once, then repeated it, then again, and again, and again. Until Rama saw Hanuman raising his arms and chanting the words aloud, and Lakshman beside him, a grim death's-face grimace on his features, saying them too, albeit softly, and the multitudes below chanting them, chanting them, chanting them.

He had heard the words spoken before, with respect, to those heroes of yore who undertook terrible vows and then suffered great hardship to enact those same vows. It was a phrase that was used for the rarest of rare, those who dared to undertake the most self-penalising of missions and then would not be thwarted from seeing them through to the very end.

Maryada Purshottam.

One Who Fulfils His Oath.

But they were shouting it with his name attached. *He* was the one who had taken this great and terrible oath, placed his feet upon an impossible path, and now must follow it through to the very end.

Maryada Purshottam Rama. *Rama, Fulfiller of Oaths*.

He turned and faced the ocean. That was where his path lay now. He would have to walk on water to cross it. He raised his arms, and the armies behind him raised their arms as well, issuing a roar that was part exultation, part cheer, and part battle cry.

8

It was mid-afternoon when they sat around a fire and took their afternoon meal. Or fast-breaking meal, for it was the first that Rama had eaten since rising that morning. Either way, the food was less important than the company, for after the endless introductions and decision-making about a hundred different matters – where to billet the vanars and the bears, and how to supply such enormous numbers without them straying yojanas away in search of food and water, and how to enforce such decisions in the absence of a strong hierarchical structure – this was the first opportunity that Rama had had to truly sit with the chief leaders of the two armies and get to know them better.

It was an odd gathering that sat in a rough semicircle in the sand around the black rock on which Rama and Lakshman were perched. They were on the rim of the beach, about a mile or so north of the black-rock rise on which Rama had made the speech. The sun was baking the sand only yards away, but they were seated in the cool, leafy shade of a grove of palm trees. When they had found the spot and decided it would be suited to their purpose, the bears had stopped and peered dubiously up into the shade of the close-growing palms, and Lakshman had asked them what they were looking for.

'Bats,' Jambavan had replied. The great black had a way of growling words that was intimidating, especially to the vanars. Rama had noticed how most of the vanars kept their distance from the bears, but all of them kept twice the distance from Jambavan himself. Apparently, Hanuman whispered to him discreetly in response to his query, the vanars believed that the king of bears was wont to swallow vanars up whole on a whim. Like most vanar superstitions, Rama guessed that this one probably had its origin in some mother's warning to babies in order to get them to sleep – 'younguns who play at night get eaten whole by the king of bears' – but he had no doubt that it suited Jambavan to let the rumour live and thrive. The fact that Jambavan was an oak of a creature, towering a good yard higher than Rama himself, and almost twice as high as most vanars, added to the aura. But it was also a species thing: the bears seemed willing to tolerate vanars, but clearly considered themselves far superior in the natural order of things. As Lakshman noted quietly in Rama's ear, that was yet another factor that would have to be taken into account when deploying this vast, unwieldy amalgam of an army.

'Bats?' Lakshman had replied incredulously, peering up at the tops of the tall swaying palms. 'What would bats be doing here?' He looked up and down the blinding-bright sunlit beach – the last of the sea mist had dissipated long since. 'They live in caves deep in mountains, don't they? Not in sunny places like this.'

Jambavan looked down his snout at Lakshman as if pondering the relative intelligence of their species. Then, with a visible effort at patience: 'There are no caves for yojanas around here, brer-Lakshman. Yet there are flying insects by the millions, nay, hundreds and thousands of millions. And where there are flying insects there are always bats.' He jerked his snout upwards. 'Those trees are full of ripe sweetheads and stickyfruit. Even a human can scent them, I expect.'

Lakshman blinked, then Rama saw his face clear as he managed to mentally translate Jambavan's words into human-intelligible terms – coconuts and dates. 'Ah,' he said. 'And coconuts and dates are sweet, so they attract fruit flies and other flying insects, and so the bats come to eat the flying insects. But that would be at night, not in bright daylight, wouldn't it?'

'Yes, but by day, the wretched things sleep in the palms. A place such as this is a bat's paradise.' He looked back at the direction of the beach and the mile-distant black-rock ridge whence they had come, and sighed. 'But it is shady, I warrant, and it will be suitable for our purposes. Therefore, we may seat ourselves here for the present. As long as we move to alternative locations before sundown, for that is when the wretched fur-wetters awaken. I would bet my left claws there are more bats up there in those trees than there are grains of sand on that beach.'

Lakshman looked as if he doubted there could be more bats anywhere than sand on any beach, but thankfully he kept his argument to himself. Rama had already had to play mediator to a number of small but needless arguments about points of protocol and custom. If he understood anything about such matters, those little differences would blossom into full-blown debates before the war was done. But for now, he only wished to learn a little more about his new-found comrades and allies. Especially the bears. He knew how he had won the loyalty of the vanars, but he still did not understand why an entire race of creatures unfamiliar to him would suddenly rise up in support of his cause.

They found a clearing between the allegedly bat-infested palms that was wide enough to accommodate the whole company – there were some twenty in all, by Rama's quick count – and some of Hanuman's vanars cleared away the fallen fronds and branches and rotten coconuts. After they were seated, they were brought fruit and freshly broken coconuts to eat. The bears had carried urns of honey with them, and Jambavan's associates, Kambunara and Tiruvalli, dipped their immense paws into the urns and doled out generous dollops of the thick, viscous stuff to each one, repeating proudly how this was the finest honey on all the planets of the world, for they had scoured the entire universe to find the special bees that produced it.

Nobody dared ask how bears travelled from planet to planet, nor how it was that bees lived on those other worlds, but the honey was truly delicious. It put Rama in mind of the honey and fish that he, Sita and Lakshman had been fed by Guha, Lord of the Nisadas, in the forest on the banks of the Ganga, soon after the start of their exile. He remembered feeding Sita honeyed fish and she feeding him, beneath the overarching, all-embracing foliage of that gigantic banyan, the legendary walking tree, Nyagrodha. The taste of that sweetwater fish, so soft that its flesh melted like snowflakes in his mouth, and the warmth of Sita's presence by his side all came to him as clearly as if it were here and now, and she were by his side, waiting patiently for him to finish his mouthful so she could feed him another.

He turned to look in that direction, almost expecting her to be there. But there was only Lakshman, who glanced up at him from his sparsely eaten honeyed fruit and seemed to sense at once that he was seeking out Sita. Lakshman put his leaf-plate aside and sat hunched, staring out through a gap between palm trunks at the sunlit ocean, his eyes inscrutable. Rama tried to bury the heaviness in his chest with another mouthful or two, then put his own unfinished meal aside as well.

'Friends,' he said softly, his voice carrying easily to them all in the quiet shade of the grove. Outside on the beach, several of Hanuman's vanars and Jambavan's bears kept the large numbers of their curious compatriots away from the grove. Rama had requested this, explaining carefully that it was not because he did not wish the rest to know what they spoke of here, but because they must themselves reach some consensus before involving the rest in their plans, lest confusion reign. Both races had agreed without much fuss, understanding instinctively that these were circumstances that called for special behaviour, and yielding easily and instantly to Rama's wishes. 'I have already thanked you all collectively for joining this campaign. Yet allow me to do so once more. It is a great, invaluable service you are rendering unto me, and I do not know how I will ever repay you.'

Jambavan stirred noisily, spitting out the seeds of some fruit – a custard apple, one of Rama's own favourites, and because

of which Sita, who had always thought she hated them, had
agreed to try again and come to enjoy even more than he did,
so much so that he had taken to teasing her by calling them
sitaphal, literally Sita's fruit. The bear king spat the seeds into
his own paw, in a manner that Rama could tell was exceedingly polite for animals who were otherwise wont to spew seeds
out at random as they ate, not caring where or upon whom
they might fall, and growled, 'It is you who do us a service,
Rama. We have waited many thousands of years to return the
great favour you rendered unto us.'

Rama was taken aback. 'I do not understand you, my friend.
Did you say many thousands of years? I am barely thirty years
of age myself.'

'Nonsense, Rama,' Jambavan said gruffly in a tone that
brooked no argument. 'You have existed for countless millennia
and will exist for many millennia to come yet. You were here
upon earth in many different forms, and this form you now
choose to garb yourself with is only the newest one of all. But
we see beyond the physical and discern the personage within,
for we are oathbound to you.'

Rama looked around at the company, nonplussed. He did
not know what to make of Jambavan's mystifying words.
Lakshman was staring at the bear king like a man poleaxed.
Angad and all the vanars were eating quietly, neither disturbed
nor confused by the bear king's extraordinary outburst. Rama
looked at Susena, Satabali, Nila, Vikata in turn and saw nothing
in their faces to help him. He then looked at the other vanars,
many of whom had arrived with Hanuman and had been introduced to Rama only hours earlier – Gaja, Gavaksa, Sarabha,
Gandhamadana, Mainda and Dvivida – but they were all eating
as if nothing unusual had occurred. He looked to the bears,
Tiruvalli, Kambunara, Shamasthan, Parithran, Jagadasthi and
Gyana, but they were watching him so intently that he could
not bear their gaze and looked around again. His eyes fell
on Hanuman then, and there he found something. A trace of
reassurance. Of solemn dignity. Clearly, Hanuman understood

what Jambavan had spoken of and had been expecting him to say such things.

'Hanuman,' Rama asked, 'what does Jambavan mean?'

Hanuman set his leaf-plate aside. Like the two mortals, he had hardly touched his food. All the others were still relishing their victuals. 'Rama,' he said gently, 'you must understand, the bears are a wise and ancient race, and they do not regard the world as you mortals do. Their concepts and precepts are very different from your own.'

'We follow the old ways,' Jambavan said. 'The true ways. You ought to understand, Rama. You are a soldier of dharma. That is the essence of our beliefs. Dharma.'

'That is most heartening, my friend,' Rama said. 'And I am warmed to the core to hear you speak of dharma. But when you speak of my being on this earth for thousands of years and of blood-oaths you owe me that I have no recollection or knowledge of, then I am bewildered. What do you mean?'

'We mean what we say, Rama,' the bear king said around a mouthful of custard apple, the large black seeds spilling freely out of the corner of his mouth. 'Although we do not always say what we mean, for we find that the world has changed greatly, and as this age comes to a close, the same words mean different things to different beings. It was not always so. There was once a time when we were all one, and we all lived in the forest, and there were no divisions between us, even though we were of different colours, races, species, furred and non-furred, limbed and limbless, bodied and bodiless. There was no conflict between the devas and the Asuras in those days, and the race we call mortals now did not exist as a separate thing. For that matter, this realm itself was of no real consequence, merely a way-station between planes, a place where gandharvas came to make love, and apsaras frolicked, and rakshaks came to hunt and play – for they were not called rakshasas then as they are now, and were not considered evil.' He spat out the last of the seeds, looked at the scoured-out greenish peel of the fruit and shook his head. 'For that matter, this word evil. In those days, there was no such demarcation, *good* and *evil*.' He emphasised each word with accents of bitter irony. 'It was all one. Sometimes someone wronged another. That did not make one evil, nor the other good.'

Rama's head was spinning. He saw Hanuman looking at him and tried to convey a plea through a look; he could not think of a way to convey his confusion without offending the bear lord.

Hanuman nodded almost imperceptibly, reading his plea, and spoke up. 'My lord Jambavan. Perhaps it would be helpful to let King Rama know the circumstances of your earlier meeting' – he made a show of clearing his throat carefully, a conspicuously un-vanar-like gesture – 'in this lifetime.'

From somewhere along the beachfront came a curious thudding sound, followed by a loud vanar cheer.

Jambavan frowned at the rind of the custard apple, as if only just noticing it. 'Oh. Yes. Of course. There are wars to be fought yet. Time enough for such talk at the end of days.' He popped the rind in his mouth and apparently swallowed it without chewing, for his jaws did not work for several moments. Finally, he started as if from a reverie, shook his snout vigorously, spewing a seed or two upon his companions' heads – they continued eating unperturbed – and said, 'It was before the unleashing of the brahm-astra at Mithila. You came to the aid of the Princess Sita and her bodyguard Nakhudi, although they were disguised then and you did not recognise their true identities. You and they fought side by side against some brutish oafs.'

'Bearface!' Lakshman exclaimed. 'He and his outlaws were killing bears; they had cornered a mother and her cubs, and Sita and Nakhudi were fending them off. When we came on the scene, they gave up the fight in a hurry.'

'You?' Rama said incredulously to the enormous black-furred bear seated before him. 'You were one of those cubs?'

Jambavan shrugged, then gestured at the black bear beside him, whom he had introduced earlier as his brother Kambunara.

'We both were. Along with our sister Sharik, who was eager to join your war but was heavy with child again – her fifteenth, actually. But other than that, she is alive and well too. Our mother, whom you also saved that day, gave up her present form some few dozen moons past. But her spirit accompanies us. Even now, as we speak, she sits there on the branch of that tree and watches over us intently.' Jambavan squinted upwards as if listening to an inner voice. 'She finds you quite handsome still for a human. Although she feels you have grown too thin and straggly. Eat more honey. Honey mends all wounds.'

Rama resisted the temptation to glance at the branch of the tree behind his left shoulder. He also wondered how, if bears could die like any mortal creature, they presumed to know things that had occurred thousands upon thousands of years ago. But he had no desire to get Jambavan launched upon another of his baffling meandering monologues, and said instead, 'And that is why you came to help us today in our effort? Because we saved you that day as cubs?'

Jambavan lowered his head and squinted at Rama, the way an old lady might peer to correct her shortsightedness. Rama recalled that bears were indeed believed to be shortsighted. The thudding sound came again, closer this time. 'If you wish to believe so, you may. These are minor matters.'

Rama decided to leave it at that. 'Then I am doubly honoured by your support. First, for the purely selfish joy of having saved your and your family's lives those long years ago, and twice, for your nobly offering those same lives to my cause.'

Jambavan snorted. 'You are most welcome, Rama. But make no mistake of it. We have no intention of doing any sacrificing. We have come here to fight alongside you and help you win! The sacrificing will all be on the Lankan side! Ho ho ho ho!'

He slapped his great thighs, coughing violently with bearish laughter. The rest of the bear entourage all joined him, gruffly chuffing their merriment. After a moment, the vanars laughed too, showing their wide white teeth, and Rama and Lakshman allowed themselves the luxury of grinning along. Somewhere nearby, the sound of thudding came again, this time in a rapid sequence, like a pile of rocks falling through a roof during an avalanche. Rama glanced back over his shoulder and finally discovered the source: the vanars had climbed the palm trees in the grove beside theirs, and were throwing coconuts down to crack them open. Other vanars followed their example, and in moments every tree along the beachfront was filled with vanars climbing and plucking and tossing coconuts. Those on the ground below offered enthusiastic encouragement, dancing to avoid the falling rain of coconuts, snatching the broken ones and fighting to drink the sweet nourishing milk and malai within. Not to be outdone, the bears were standing in groups beneath the date palms and were shaking them vigorously enough to dislodge large clumps of dates, grunting as some clutches fell on to their well-insulated heads.

Kambunara gained his feet, roaring, 'Fools! Rotten fish-smellers! Stop that! You will wake the—'

Before he could finish, a new sound arose, a susurrating hissing, like a thousand serpents awakened in a nest. All the bear leaders pricked their ears up, their button-black eyes glinting with an unnameable emotion, and Rama saw Jambavan sigh deeply, then raise his paws to cover his head as he bent over.

'Brace yourselves,' Rama heard him say, with exaggerated calmness.

Pandemonium erupted as a cloud of black-winged chittering things burst free from the eaves of the trees in which they had been hanging in inverted sleep. The bears had been right after all. There were bats in the groves. Lots and lots of bats.

9

They were on the beach, baking in the sunlight after being evicted by the foul-smelling exodus of bats – the 'bat-sena', as Jambavan ironically referred to it – when Sakra came bounding up the beach with a whoop of excitement, sending showers of sand flying over a clutch of bears sitting morosely around. Hanuman calmed him down sufficiently to understand that some vanars foraging for food a few miles south had brought word that they had discovered Mount Mahendra. The news brought grins to the snouts of all the vanar generals. The Kiskindha vanars who had accompanied Rama and Lakshman here had been aiming for that very spot but had been disoriented by the sea mist. Angad was exceedingly pleased that they had found the legendary mount.

From all accounts, it appeared to be the closest point on the coast to the strait that separated the continent from the island of Lanka. The scouts claimed that there were two mountains on the promontory and that from the top of the taller mountain you could just manage to glimpse Lanka. Rama decided that they ought to go and see for themselves right away, and of course, everyone wished to follow their inspiring new leader, so it turned into a veritable march. The distance was easily enough crossed, and it was still afternoon when they climbed the first 'mountain', which turned out to be little more than a large mound, barely worthy of being called a hill. The legendary Mount Mahendra itself was no more than two hundred yards tall and seemed unlikely to be the peak mentioned in so many ancient legends and tales, but Rama had no wish to question the identity of what was clearly a talismanic place to both the vanars and the bears – and, come to think of it, to his own kind as well.

He glanced back from the promontory of the mountain – for he was resigned to referring to it thus to avoid needless controversy – and saw a remarkable sight.

The mountain was unevenly raised, the north side closer to sea level than the south. The south side gave way on to a raised cliff-like runway that extended for at least a mile before losing itself in a thickly wooded spur where the coastline curved sharply inwards again. So looking south, you could certainly term this a mountain, and a quite majestic one at that, with its white-flowering cactuses and snow firs, a most unusual flora for a coastal locale. Looking north, as Rama was right now, it was much less steep, of course, but that only added to its sense of grandeur, the deceptive ordinariness on one side and the sweeping picturesque swoop on the other. The west side gave way sharply to a precipitous fall. Glancing down cautiously, for the foam-flecked waves were a good four hundred yards below, he saw that the drop was almost sheer, the face made up of the same black rock that was seen so plentifully along the coastline here, and covered with lichenous moss, freshly green from the recent rains. The ocean lay spread out below like a great blue quilt, patched with darker and lighter sections which he thought at first were caused by clouds. Then he observed the absence of clouds in the sky and puzzled over the phenomenon for a moment before dismissing it to a remote section of his mind. He often did that when he encountered a problem or puzzling thing that could not be resolved at once: tucked it away into some basement chamber where the idle part of his mind ticked away relentlessly, until suddenly hours, days or even years hence, he would find an answer to the question and fit both parts together to complete the picture.

Stepping away from the edge, he glanced back the way they had just come and was heart-stopped by yet another breath-taking sight. He could see his armies more clearly now than he had been able to from the black-rock ridge, and they made an incredible sight. A dense forest of black, brown and mottled mixtures of furry bears shambling towards Mahendra, alongside hundreds of ragged lines of scampering vanars. The lines extended so far, it seemed that the army must go on for ever, along the length of the coastline and across the stubbly chin of Jambudwipa's face, which was a term Rama had learned from the bears. Their geography described the sub-continent as a giant face surrounded by ocean on three sides. By their reckoning, they were now on the lower left side of the chin. They used the ancient name for the land, Jambudwipa: literally, land of the jambun tree, for as Rama was fast discovering, bears tended to name virtually everything with reference to food.

His attention focused on the vanar armies below, winding their way along the narrow beachfront and through the rim of palm groves and denser forests that lined the coast, and he found he could make out the various tribe-nations easily from this vantage point.

At first the vanars had seemed all much alike. But as the day had passed and he had come into closer contact with many individual vanars, including their appointed captains and generals, he had come to see them as quite distinct breeds. There were the Kiskindha vanars with whom he was already so familiar, and he had come to think of them as typical of their race, their fur a motley variation of browns, the males usually darker-furred than the females, the younguns more thickly furred, the olduns whiting at the tops of their heads and along their spines. Their tails were all a more or less similar yard or so in length. But then there were the Mandara vanars, whose occupation was silver-mining, and who proudly displayed jewellery fashioned from their product. Their most striking feature was their immense earrings, often dangling pendulously down to their shoulders. They had silver piercings on their belly buttons, and elsewhere on their light-coloured bodies as well, but the earrings were mesmeric in the elaborateness of their design and symbolism. These vanars were covered with creamish, wheatish shades of fur, and their tails were thin and long, as much as a yard and a foot. They stood a good foot or more taller than their Kiskindha comrades, and looked noticeably more delicate, bearing themselves with a noble dignity that, coupled with their silver ornamentation and slender forms, was quite beautiful to behold.

In stark contrast to the Mandaras were the Mandehas, who claimed to come from a place where they hung upside down (like bats, as Jambavan remarked inevitably) from mountain crevices and abjured exposure to the sun. If exposed unwittingly – or on account of some important work, as in the present circumstance – they believed that they would be burned by the heat of the sun and fall into the ocean to die, and would be resurrected the next dawn to repeat the same cycle all over again. This mythology notwithstanding, they were possessed of fur that was strikingly jet black, nary a spot of brown or any other shade on even a single one, and were taller even than the Mandara vanars, but with much shorter tails, barely a foot and a half long, which they wore curled up close to their bodies, giving them a near-human gait. At first glance they seemed utterly hairless. Then Rama saw that they had as much fur as their brothers, but that it was softer, thinner, sparser, more downy, and clung close to their bodies, giving them that peculiar hairless appearance. They stood in a gloomy, fatalistic manner that was striking beside the cheerful childishness of the Kiskindha vanars or even the proud vanity of the Mandaras. And their numbers were substantially more than any other vanar tribe-nation, so much more that Rama thought they might compose a good third of the entire vanar corps. They had a tendency to cluster close together, and to stand in the shade, staying very still, so that with their dark colouring they blended in masterfully with the landscape, virtually becoming part of it. They followed an ancient female whose pelt had no doubt once been as jet black as their own but had been whitened by time's inevitable repainting. General Vinat was the grandson of this venerable leader.

Next came a breed of vanars that was shockingly distinct.

At first, Rama thought that these were the elders of all the other tribes, collected into one large contingent, the way that Kosala marshalled all its veterans into a single regiment which was named the Purana Wafadars. He thought this because these vanars were all grey-backed, or whitefur as they were known in vanar parlance. When he looked at them more intently, however, he saw that their pelts were not so much grey or white as a dense silvery texture that actually glimmered in the emerging sunlight. And they were young, as young and virile as any of their coloured-fur vanar compatriots lined up beside them. They moved with a jaunty confidence that naturally attracted attention, several turning cartwheels, some springing off the linked palms of their comrades to somersault madly in the air, issuing ululations, others yodelling and rolling across the grass like little balls of vanar fur. For they were smaller than the other vanars, and broader too. The other distinctive feature of this group was the splash of colour each one of them sported on their forelocks. Dying their heads with vegetable inks, they evidently used colour groupings to mark their troops into marching groups, for the pink-tips were all in more or less one cluster, the yellows in another, the indigos in a third, and so on. They seemed somewhat fewer in number than any of their fellow-nations, but more than made up for it by attracting more attention than all the rest combined. These were the Jatarupas.

Rama could have spent several hours more observing the differences between the various vanars, and he had yet to come to differentiate between the different breeds of bears, but the company on the promontory was already engaged in an intense discussion of the various means to be used to cross to Lanka.

'Ships,' Lakshman was saying. 'We must build ships to take our armies across the ocean. There is no other way.'

Jambavan raised his snout as if to sniff the sky itself. Atop the mountain, clothed in golden afternoon sunlight, the bear king was a formidable sight, his fur bristling, its tips gleaming. His black eyes glinted against the sunlight, his ears twitched. 'No,' he said finally. 'It cannot be done by ship.'

Lakshman folded his arms across his chest and stared coldly. 'How else does one cross an ocean?' He jerked his head down at the breathtaking view below the cliff. 'By swimming across?'

Jambavan wiggled his ears, the rest of him staying absolutely still. Amusing as it appeared, Rama had a feeling that the bear king's intention was not to entertain. He decided he must master bear language as well as the various vanar dialects. How was he to communicate effectively and quickly with the troops upon the field of battle if he did not even know what their gestures and actions meant? Unlike mortals, who considered the concealing of true feelings and their responses to be a sign of maturity, vanars and bears naturally expressed themselves freely through such gestures.

Kambunara spoke for his brother. 'If you wish, we will swim the ocean. Bears hunt for their food in waters far colder than these sun-baked salt springs.'

Lakshman rolled his eyes despairingly. 'The question is not how warm or cold the water is. Unlike the springs you may be accustomed to wading through to catch your fish, this mass of water is vast, vaster than anything you can imagine. There are great sea creatures living within these waters that are as large as this mountain itself.'

'This we know.' Kambunara sniffed. 'The children of Varuna are kith and kin to us bears. Our ancestors lived and mated together until our forebears chose to come upon the land to populate it in accordance with Lord Brahma's wishes, while Varuna and his offspring chose to remain in the salt springs.'

'I doubt that will stop them from swallowing you whole if you attempt to swim across that ocean.'

Kambunara gazed placidly at the endless horizon-spanning expanse of bright blue water. 'We did not say we wish to do it; we only said we shall do so if Lord Rama insists upon it.' He added tartly, 'And we wished you to know that bears can swim.'

'Yes, but can they float? That's the question.'

Rama broke in hurriedly before Lakshman's natural tendency to sarcasm got him into something more than a mere argument about the swimming talents of bears. 'Jambavan, why are you opposed to the notion of building ships?'

Jambavan stopped twitching his ears and regarded Rama patiently. 'Because, Rama, who will build these ships? Will you go to your countrymen to ask them to construct them?'

Rama shook his head slowly. 'Nay, my friend. That I cannot do. I am sworn not to turn back my steps until the completion of my exile.'

'Then who *will* build them? Us bears? The vanars? You and your brilliant brother here? I do not think we could raise very seaworthy ships between us, and if you propose to teach us, it would take a very long time to build sufficient numbers to convey such a large force, would it not? And even supposing we were to achieve this miracle somehow, no bear will set foot upon one of those water-defying monstrosities.'

Rama frowned. 'All your reasons are indisputable, Lord Jambavan. I have no argument with any of them but for the last. Why would bears not sail upon ships?'

Jambavan snorted as if the thing were self-evident. His entire entourage snorted in collusion. 'My mortal friend, it is true what we hear tell of your kind, that you have grown so removed from your roots that you are willing to violate even our mother Prithvi-devi herself to further your own interests. We have seen some of these ships of yours being built, for we bears dwell close by your human settlements oftentimes, as you seem to multiply and spread like plagues through the world. You murder living things in order to build ships, do you not?'

'Living things?' Rama was perplexed. Then he understood. 'You mean trees?'

'Do they not breathe and grow and flower and fruit and multiply like other living beings? Do we not agree that they possess spirits and souls just as we ambulatory creatures do? And do you not hack them down with enormous bladed things then chop their bodies into sections and then mangle and denude those sections until you finally have pieces suitable for your purposes? How many trees do you kill to build one ship?'

'I . . . I am not sure,' Rama admitted, completely at a loss.

'You will kill none for this crossing. Let us be agreed upon that.'

Lakshman sighed, clearly irritated by the argument. 'In any case, there's no possible way we can obtain enough ships, or even build rafts to carry us all across.'

'Yes,' Rama said, relieved at being given an easy escape route. He was afraid that Jambavan's tirade would soon extend itself to mortal dwellings, for most Arya houses were constructed of living wood. 'In any case, we must find some other means of crossing.' He turned to the towering vanar beside him who had stood silently all this while. 'Hanuman, do you have any ideas?'

Hanuman was silent another moment. Everyone waited for his answer. Even the bears fell silent and waited respectfully. Rama desired greatly to know all the things that had befallen his vanar friend since taking his leave of him at Rishimukha. Not only had Hanuman changed so drastically in appearance and mental make-up, he had also earned the respect of all the vanars and bears. That kind of respect was not won easily. Nor did a mere messenger rise to the stature of more-than-a-general in so short a time by normal means. There must be a remarkable story behind Hanuman's transformation. He resolved to learn the tale when he could.

Finally Hanuman shook his snout sadly. 'I am sorry, Rama. But it cannot be done.'

Rama's heart fell. 'Cannot? But it must be done! The only way to Sita is across that ocean.'

'Yes, Rama, but as you have just agreed, ships are impossible to build. Swimming is out of the question. With due respect to my bear friends, Lord Varuna's domain is no salt spring to be waded across. Why, we do not even know how far it is to Lanka. All we do know from our flying friends like the late, great Jatayu, who is much mourned, and his cousin Sampati, whom we encountered in our travels—'

'One moment,' Rama interrupted. 'You met a cousin of Jatayu?'

'Yes, Rama. We did. His name is Sampati, and he gave us much useful information. It is thanks to his generosity of knowledge that we were able to detect the closest point to Lanka and find this spot, Mount Mahendra. For Ravana's Asura maya would have led us astray to a point where it would have been impossible to cross the ocean.'

'But you just said that it is impossible to cross the ocean from here as well,' Lakshman said, frowning.

Hanuman shook his head slowly. 'I said that it cannot be done by the means that have been described thus far. Namely, by ship or by swimming. I did not say we cannot cross the ocean at all. As Rama reminded us all, our lady Sita lies there, across this very ocean. We must cross it to free her from that demonlord's clutches.'

'Then how do you propose we do it?' Lakshman asked, in a manner that was more challenge than query.

Hanuman took no offence at Lakshman's tone or manner, perhaps because, like Rama, he understood the strain under which Lakshman laboured. 'This place we see below,' he pointed at a little jutting finger of land that stretched out from the bay, made of the same black rock as the cliff on which they stood, 'marks the closest point to Lanka. From that place to the shores of Lanka is a distance of many yojanas. Our winged friend Sampati does not measure distance the way we land creatures do, so it could be as little as three yojanas, or as many as three hundred!'

'Three hundred?' Lakshman laughed shortly. 'It might as well be three million! For that matter, even three yojanas would make it close to thirty miles of open sea to cross. You haven't told us a way to get across. You have only defined how impossible it really is.'

'Pray, brother Lakshman, allow me to finish,' Hanuman said calmly.

Rama shot Lakshman a glance. Lakshman caught the look and held his breath. Rama noted that everyone else was listening closely to every syllable Hanuman uttered.

'As we already agree, it is impossible to cross that ocean. But while it cannot be crossed, it can indeed be broached. By a bridge.'

'A bridge?' This time it was Rama who spoke involuntarily. He could not help himself. The idea was so incredible. 'A bridge extending many yojanas over ocean?'

'Just so,' Hanuman said.

Rama waited for him to go on. But the vanar seemed to feel he had said all that needed to be said. Rama ventured doubtfully, 'Hanuman, even if our bear friends did not object to our cutting down the trees that would be needed to make such a bridge, and even if we could find a way to engineer such a great construction, there is no bridge, no matter how great or how cleverly engineered, that could stand over an open expanse of so many yojanas! Even the great Mithila bridge is no more than a hundred yards in span and it is considered a marvel of architectural—'

He stopped. Hanuman was looking at him oddly. He glanced around and saw that the others were also frowning and shaking their heads at his words. 'Did I say something wrong?'

'Rama,' Hanuman said gently, 'we are not speaking of a wooden bridge. We do not have any knowledge of such things, so it would be pointless even attempting it. Nay, my lord. We are speaking of building a bridge of simple rock.' He pointed down at the ground on which he stood, at a bald patch where the coal-black bedrock was exposed through the grass and weeds, gleaming dully in the harsh afternoon sunlight. 'This hardy black rock will serve our purpose well. Sampati said that the strait here is the shallowest for yojanas around. At places, it is only a few dozen yards deep. All we need do is break and carry black rocks and boulders and throw them in the sea until they rise higher than the water. Then we shall have our bridge to Lanka. Rama's bridge.'

Mandodhari awakened in her bower to find the day turned to night. Or perhaps it had been night when she slept and she had slumbered the day away to awaken the next night. Perhaps it was really day now but appeared to be night. She could not tell the difference. The light in the tower was controlled by Pushpak, and Pushpak had the power to make it seem night when it was day, and vice versa.

Yet at this moment, looking out from the floor-to-ceiling wall of glass at the sun newly risen above the northern ranges of Lanka in the distance, its slanting rays gleaming down upon the peaks and rooftops of the city below, it was impossible to tell whether she was seeing the true image of the world without or merely an illusion portrayed by the celestial vaahan. She had ceased trying to tell the difference. It was easier to accept the evidence of her senses and live by that evidence than to question even the most fundamental realities of day and night, cold and hot, summer and winter, for within this enclosed, self-sufficient universe Pushpak controlled everything, even weather, climate and the substance of things, like a god supreme in its own plane of existence.

Except, of course, that Pushpak was no god, merely a god's device, a celestial plaything. And Ravana was its master.

She sat on the edge of her flower-soft bed. The bed itself was shaped like an enormous lotus, and felt as soft and smelled as fragrant to the senses. To complete the illusion, the entire bed floated upon a pool of crystal-pure water in which real lotuses drifted, their pink flowers unfurling and blossoming at the first caress of sunlight – surely Pushpak could not trick lotuses into mistaking its artificial emissions for real sunlight? But that was assuming the lotuses themselves were real. She rose slowly to her feet, sighing softly. After only a few steps, she looked back at the bed she had just vacated. Its yards-wide, yards-long expanse lay empty, as it usually did when she arose. She never knew when her husband left her side or how long he had been gone. But his nightly disappearances was a small thing in the face of thirteen years of not having him in her bed at all. It was the only reason she did not question where he went or what he did and with whom, although she had a fairly good idea. He had never been a monogamous husband, for it was not the rakshasa way, and since he was not only lord of the race but its propagator as well, it was not only necessary but honourable for him to spread his seed freely. That had never troubled her. It was the suspicion of his other preoccupations that did. And it was to confirm or deny those very suspicions that she had finally let him coax her into coming to live with him here, in this towering white palace – or was it a palatial white tower? – leaving behind her the more traditional rock-hewn apartments in the caverns beneath Mount Nikumbhila where she had spent the past thirteen years.

She stepped off the bed on to the white-carpeted floor.

The bower was large, its ceilings vaulting, a dozen or more yards high, and circular. The walls surrounding it were all of the same glasslike substance, polished to near-perfect transparency, and as she left the little platform on which the lotus bed rested, her feet sank into the deep, soft pile of pristine white that covered every inch of the floor. The carpeting was made from snow-tiger pelt, but she could not imagine where one might begin to seek out so many snow tigers bearing such perfect unblemished coats. It would take a thousand such immaculate specimens to carpet this bower alone. And snow tigers were not found in Lanka, only on the distant slopes of the Himalayan ranges, across the ocean and a thousand miles north.

Until she came here to live in the white tower, she had only heard tell of snow-tiger pelts, never seen one with her own eyes before. And even now, she reminded herself, she might not have seen one yet.

But the illusion was perfect. Stepping barefoot across the white floor, freshly risen from a deep, long sleep, she felt as if she were cloud-walking on the insubstantial matter of the heavens themselves. This was what it was supposed to feel like to walk the roads of Swarga-loka, where the paving of the paths was celestial grass, and the grass itself was burnished gold. Mandodhari walked a complete circle, circumnavigating her bower, until she had returned to the north-east-facing side. She stood there a moment, basking in the sunlight, then began to prepare for her morning ritual.

She had barely begun her first surya-namaskara, the elaborate yogic posture by which one greeted the newly risen day, literally a sun-greeting, when a voice broke her concentration.

'Mistress . . .'

A shudder racked Mandodhari. She faltered, caught herself in time, and gently unwound her limbs from the asana. The first time a disembodied voice had come drifting through her chambers thus, she had been startled out of her wits, spilling an entire bowl filled with pomegranate juice across herself, staining her trademark white garments beyond salvage. For all her years of being married to one of the greatest users of Asura maya, she had never been able to develop a liking for sorcery, let alone embrace it the way so many rakshasas did these days. But unlike the mysterious shakti of Pushpak, at least she understood Asura maya, and was familiar with its conventions, rituals and illusions. Through the use of sacred Sanskrit slokas, two-line rhymed verses of power-coded syllables in unique combinations, Asura maya invoked the powers of various deities to achieve some specific purpose. So, for instance, a sloka praising and invoking Lord Vayu, governing deity of wind, could, if rendered correctly by the right user, persuade him to calm a storm, or raise one, depending on one's requirement. The greater the task to be accomplished, the more powerful the sloka required, the more dedicated the recitation, and the mightier the incantator. So, for instance, for her own husband to attain a boon from Lord Shiva himself, the Destroyer, it had taken a thousand years of painful penance to obtain the required sloka, and that sloka could only be uttered over Ravana by Shiva himself. The sloka in that case had conferred the gift of indestructibility upon Ravana. There were laws governing the use and misuse of such power-wielding, and despite the difference in names, Arya shakti and Asura maya were by and large the same thing.

But this was something altogether different.

The white tower had no doors or windows. Instead, Pushpak sensed where one desired to go and opened routes to facilitate one's progress. This was unsettling enough to someone who was accustomed to living in cavernous chambers carved out of solid bedrock, but even more disturbing was the manner in which Pushpak could detect when someone was seeking you out and convey that person's voice directly to you, regardless of the distance involved. So, for instance, the voice Mandodhari was hearing she recognised as belonging to one of her sakshis, the class of inherited servitors euphemistically referred to as 'friends'.

'Mistress, a dream. I must have words with you at once. Pray, milady, let me in.' It was Trijata, one of Mandodhari's oldest sakshis and a rakshasi with rare clairvoyant abilities.

Another voice added in wary confusion, 'Where the devil is the doorway? It was right here the last time I came, only yesterday.' This was Vikata, a particularly ill-tempered sakshi whom Mandodhari tolerated only because of her efficacy in keeping the male rakshasas of the royal household in check. She could hear other voices speaking as well: Champadari, Praghasa and Vikuti. Together, the five of them comprised her inner circle of sakshis, since rakshasas tended to group in packs of six, the same as the number of digits they had on each limb.

The voices were so clear and close, they might have been only yards away. But though she was scouring the entire chamber, she could see no sign of them.

A voice spoke inside her mind. It was Pushpak. It used no words to communicate, yet she was able to understand its message clearly enough. It was asking her if she wished to permit entry to the five sakshis. But in place of their names, it projected images of their faces into her mind.

She shuddered, uncomfortable at this invasion of her privacy by a *thing*, a machine that possessed no heart, lungs or vital organs, only pure divine shakti.

'Yes,' she forced herself to say. 'Allow them to enter.'

She remembered belatedly that with Pushpak she did not even have to speak the wish aloud, simply will it. It was something else she was not able to accustom herself to.

A portal opened in the far wall of the bower. Framed in the oval opening, five startled rakshasas stood a moment, then caught sight of their mistress within and surged forward. Predictably, fair-skinned Vikata strode ahead of the group, her thickly muscled arms swinging ponderously, her massive thighs quivering with each step. Her face was a garish painting, decorated with every unguent and cosmetic known to rakshasas. One might imagine she would be thought ugly, monstrous, ogre-like, and generally fearsome to males. Instead, she was considered the epitome of desirability, the most pursued of all the palace sakshis. In contrast, Mandodhari herself, wheatish almost to the point of being called dark, slender, and curved not unlike a mortal woman, was considered unattractive and 'mannish'.

'It's nothing, mistress. Trijata's had another of her wretched dreams,' Vikata said in her rasping voice, glancing suspiciously around the bower. 'What the devil? Mistress, this place looks different every time I come here. Have you changed something?'

Mandodhari didn't bother explaining – for the umpteenth time – about Pushpak's constant self-initiated alterations. Instead, she raised her arms to receive the elderly albino rakshasi who was walking with the aid of two other sakshis, visibly weakened and shaken by her sleep-vision. 'Trijata, my dear one, was it so bad then? Come, come to me.'

The elderly rakshasi embraced her mistress with a fierce

strength that belied her decrepit appearance. 'Forgive me if I disturbed your slumber, milady. But I had to see you at once.' She glanced around the chamber fearfully, not to note the change in design or decor as Vikata had done, but to make sure that the master of the house was not present. Trijata harboured a perpetual fear of Ravana, for he had a long-standing loathing of all clairvoyants and had even outlawed future-reading in Lanka. The ban went so far as to prohibit even speculative trading, the harmless hoarding that merchants indulged in to benefit from expected price rises. The only reason Trijata was permitted to survive, and to live beneath Ravana's own roof, was thanks to Mandodhari's patronage. She had no doubt that the day she turned her back on the frail old sakshi, Ravana would have her fed to the wolves. Literally, for the wolfhead clan regarded living rakshasi flesh as a rare delicacy, and families with excessive numbers of children, or wives, or husbands were often known to sell off a couple or three in exchange for a fat bag of goldegles, the Lankan currency. In her more brutal moments, Vikata often reminded Trijata that she had been valued at a mere thirteen goldegles and was depreciating with every passing day.

Mandodhari led the shaking rakshasi to the eastern wall, where Pushpak had anticipated her need by producing a variety of seating arrangements, all as soft, comfortable and luxuriant as the rest of the apartment. Mandodhari deliberately ignored them all and sat down on the soft floor itself, seating Trijata before her.

'There, there,' she said. 'Calm down, little mother.'

Among rakshasas, sakshis played a multitude of roles: starting as daiimaas at the princess's birth, then acting as playmates, companions, chaperones, aunts to her children, and even surrogate mothers when required. A rakshasa was given free choice of all his wife's sakshis – just as she was given free choice of all his brothers, as well as his friends. It was yet another mark of Trijata's uniqueness that she had never been touched by the prolific Ravana, otherwise so generous with his seed. Vikata, of course, was a favourite. Of all her sakshis, Trijata was the only one who had been in place even before Mandodhari's birth, a daiimaa – wetnurse, nanny and governess – to her, and later, when her mother died prematurely in a battle against the mortals, all but a mother.

'It was a very bad one, was it?'

'That it was, milady,' Trijata said between gasps, for Mandodhari's touch and kind words had provoked a fresh outburst of the tears that the ageing sakshi always had a plentiful supply of. 'But it was not so much the fearsomeness of the dream-vision that affrighted me. It was the fact that it concerned you.'

Mandodhari's throat clenched. 'Me?' she managed to say aloud. 'You have seen visions concerning me before, little mother. What could be so fearsome about this one?'

'It was a dream of the ending, milady. The ending of Lanka.'

'Ah, I see.' Mandodhari's heart eased a little. She thought she knew what Trijata's dream was about. 'It has been a long time since you last saw that dream. But it is past now, my dear one. Thirteen years have elapsed since Lanka's ending. This is the new Lanka now. A better, brighter Lanka.'

'Nay, milady,' the old rakshasi said. 'You mistake my words. I do not speak of the old burning, the destruction that happened thirteen years ago. That was naught compared to this new ending that is soon to befall us.'

'A new ending?' Mandodhari looked at each of the other sakshis. None of them had said very much since entering, except to whisper soothing words and sounds to their companion. Only Vikata stood with her back to them all, staring angrily at the lotus bed, as if it was somehow to blame for this whole mess. To Vikata, everything was a mess and would remain that way for ever.

Trijata's voice was little more than a whisper, growing softer with each sentence, as if the old rakshasi was running out of breath. 'Aye, milady, a new ending. This new ending will be the last one. An end of days. When it comes upon us, the Lanka of the rakshasa races will be gone for ever.' She paused to gasp for breath, as if remembering that she required air to sustain herself. 'And it will be brought about by the new wife your husband has taken for himself.'

'New wife?' Mandodhari stared at the old sakshi. 'What are you talking about? What new wife?'

Vikata made a sound of exasperation, then hawked and spat into the lotus pool. Mandodhari hardly noticed. Her full attention was riveted to Trijata. The sakshi's last words had chilled her to the bone. Even the touch of the morning sun falling upon her skin felt suddenly ashen and icy.

Trijata turned her eyes away, as if unable to meet Mandodhari's. 'The mortal woman he keeps in the top of the tower,' she said. Her gaze was directed upwards. 'The mortal woman—' she repeated. Then her eyes rolled back in her head and she went into a trance. Mandodhari had seen this happen before and braced herself. Trijata's hands shot out, fastening on to Mandodhari's wrist and forearm in a vice-like grip. Despite her weakened condition and her age, the withered hands were very strong, strong enough to cause pain to Mandodhari. But the old sakshi meant her mistress no harm; the grasping was simply a means to communicate her vision. Usually when this happened the sakshi's voice spoke directly into Mandodhari's head. But this time it was different. Instead of hearing a voice speaking words, Mandodhari began seeing the vision itself. It began with flashes of shocking lucidity, electrifying in their sharpness and immediacy. It was as if *she* were the one having the vision. Not a dream, for that suggested a bleary, dimly glimpsed suggestion of some inscrutable picture. No, this was like seeing the future unfold before her very eyes, experiencing it with all her senses. She could hear things, sounds, voices . . . smell the odours . . . It was real enough to touch, if she could only reach out and catch it . . .

She was standing on the peak of Mount Nikumbhila, before the ancient mandir, the Shiva temple that she had visited so religiously all the days of her life since coming here to Lanka. She had her back to the temple entrance, but within its dark stone interior the bells were ringing madly, furiously, continually, as if the end of the world had come. As if the Destroyer had assumed his final avatar of Nataraj the Dancer and was dancing the final dance at the end of time, the tandav. She could hear the bells on his ankles chiming as his feet stamped the stone floor, hear the dumroo drums clattering and the larger dhol drums pounding, pounding like the swollen heart within her breast, sending blood fleeing through her veins. She could feel the grass beneath her naked feet, wet and splintery, the blades cutting her bare soles like a bed of knives, feel the earth writhing underfoot, as if worms and insects were abandoning their nests within the soil in a hopeless attempt to flee the coming destruction of the universe. The scent of marigold flowers hung thick and cloying in the still morning air.

The time of day was before dawn, early enough that the sun had not yet appeared on the eastern horizon though its arrival was imminent. The island of Lanka lay sprawled before her like a great green rug, rolling and undulating over its many hills and valleys, forests and dales, brooks and lakes, all wreathed in a fine porous mist, like steam rising from a dish of boiled rice. Behind her, the drums pounded, the bells rang incessantly like a maddened bull in heat, and the Destroyer's feet thumped and slapped the stone floor in that final dance at the end of time.

A light rose in the sky and she thought it must be daybreak. Something was obstructing her vision and she tried to brush it away, then was surprised to find that it was a ghunghat hanging over her brow, a bride's veil. She happened to glance down and was surprised to find that she was bedecked in full bridal garb. She felt the weight of heavy jewellery upon her limbs, jewellery that had not been there a moment ago, the same traditionally ornamented gold jewellery that she had worn on her marriage day to Ravana those many years past. A chill ran through her body. If this was Trijata's dream, then how could she be wearing Mandodhari's wedding jewellery and trousseau? But the vision commanded her full attention and rational thought fled her like a bird in a gale. After that she gave herself over to the dream and thought no more.

Clouds boiled and rolled in the sky before her, above the Nikumbhila valley, and within the seething firmament was something that emitted a blazing white light. A light so fierce, she had to shield her eyes. Just as she did so, the clouds parted, and a great chariot stood revealed, riding across the sky itself. Not like Pushpak, for the celestial vehicle was a sky-chariot in name more than form, but a normal wheeled chariot drawn by horses.

It was carved entirely of ivory, pristine white and intricately patterned, but still unmistakably a war chariot, a vehicle designed to carry a monarch into battle. The face of the sun god, Surya-deva, was carved into each side of the chariot, and the chattri, the overhanging cupola above the chariot-well, was shaped like a sun whose rays descended to the four corners of the earth. The chariot was driven by a mortal male, a man neither very young nor old, his face displaying great strength of character and purpose, and a hint of cruelty. Standing beside him, holding a great bow in one hand and bearing a sword in a scabbard at his waist, was a man with skin so dark it was almost blue in tint. This man's face was wondrous to behold, like that of a great enlightened seer or of Lord Vishnu the Preserver portrayed in Lankan religious artworks with his customary nidra-yoga gaze, neither asleep nor awake. His skin caught the sun's rays in a manner that gave the illusion of light issuing from his very being. She could almost see motes of light floating from the pores of his blue skin.

There was a slight resemblance between the two men, and she knew at once, as one knows in dreams, that they were the brothers Rama Chandra and Lakshman, sons of the late King Dasaratha, princes of Ayodhya. The chariot rode on, turning in the sky like any road chariot might turn at a bend in the road, and continued in the direction of Lanka. A conch-shell trumpet sounded from somewhere nearby, issuing an alarum that was taken up and repeated by other unseen conches near and far, and she saw the blue-skinned Rama take up the bow and fix an arrow to it, aiming directly at the white tower that rose above the city. From somewhere far below, the sound of an unseen army rose, roaring an unfamiliar battle cry. It was not a mortal army, she knew that from the sound itself, but neither could she tell what manner of soldiers it comprised. All she knew was that it was vast in number and was pressed to a righteous cause.

Abruptly then, as happens in dreams, the vista before her changed. Suddenly she was gazing upon a white mountain rising above the ocean. Atop the mountain's peak was a mortal woman dressed all in white, in the fashion that Mandodhari herself favoured, flowing silks in undulating layers. The mortal woman was very beautiful, but very sad. Then a mortal male appeared from nowhere, stepping out of thin air on to the mountain. First his foot appeared, then his entire leg, then the rest of him became visible. It was the same mortal who had been riding the ivory chariot, leading the army against Lanka. Rama. He came to the woman and they embraced with great passion, and dazzling white light blazed out at their union, blinding her.

When she could see again, Rama, Lakshman and Sita were standing before an enormous four-tusked white elephant that stood in the empty sky. They were all clad in brilliant white now. Rama helped Sita mount the elephant, then climbed on beside her. Lakshman took his place behind his brother and sister-in-law. The elephant carried them up through the heavens. Sita rose up in her seat and stroked first the sun and then the moon reverentially, the way one might stroke a stone idol while bathing it with milk kheer and curds. The elephant took them to Lanka, where somehow it transformed into the ivory chariot that had appeared before, but Mandodhari saw now that it had the sun carved on one side and the moon on the other, and it was drawn not by white horses but by eight white bulls.

Then, without a break, she saw Ravana. He had been riding in Pushpak and she saw him at the moment that he fell from the celestial vehicle. He tumbled to the ground, and she saw that he was dressed all in black and was unconscious. A woman began dragging him away. Before she could see who the woman was, the scene changed and she saw Ravana again, this time bearing a garland of red flowers and riding a ramshackle chariot drawn by asses. The chariot's wheels were mired in mud and it was struggling to make its way southwards. She saw a dark-skinned woman clad in red ochre, smeared in mud and dirt as if she had just wrestled with Ravana and won, dragging the Lord of Lanka by a cord strung around his thick neck. Then, in quck succession, she saw Ravana riding a boar, her eldest son Indrajit riding a crocodile, and her brother-in-law Kumbhakarna on a camel, all heading south. Of her younger son, Akshay Kumar, there was no sign.

She saw Lanka, resplendent and beautiful as it had become under her regency, filled with its rakshasa inhabitants enjoying a great celebration. There was music everywhere, and flowers; everyone wore garlands and drank the oils of intoxication and danced gaily. All the rakshasas of Lanka were drunk on oil. They danced and danced and laughed drunkenly, hysterically, and suddenly Lanka was all ablaze, the proud, beautiful structures turning to ash instantly. To escape, Kumbhakarna and the other rakshasa leaders of Ravana's court ran howling and jumped wildly – falling into a giant pit of dung. The rakshasas screamed and tore their breasts and pulled their hair out in bloody clumps, while the entire island crumpled and sank into the ocean and was swallowed up.

And then she was back on the pelt-carpeted floor of her sleeping bower, her hand clutched tight by Trijata, the smell of her own nausea filling her nostrils. She tore her hand away and lurched back, almost falling over. The sakshis caught her and held her upright, soothing her. Behind her, by the bed, she heard Vikata hawk and spit again into the lotus pool. 'Dreams and omens, portents and plagues. Bah!'

She found Ravana in his sabha hall. It was the first time she had had a reason to enter the place since his resurrection. The contrast between the new hall and the old court in which he had once presided over the kingdom's governance was immense: from what was indisputably a place designed for rakshasas and other Asuras, it had been transformed into a chamber that would not have seemed out of place in any Arya palace. She felt as if she had left Lanka and stepped into Ayodhya all of a sudden, or Mithila or Gandahar, or any of the seven great Arya nations. She recovered from the shock and walked on without letting her surprise show.

Pushpak deliberately let her in at the far end, forcing her to walk the entire length of the hall under the watchful gaze of the bustling sabha. The clan chiefs were present, all two hundred of them, reposing on the kind of decorative high-backed seats previously seen only in mortal palaces. The enormous chamber, some two hundred yards long and fifty wide, and lined with numerous carved pillars in the Arya fashion, was filled to capacity, and all eyes were on her as she walked the long carpetway to the far end, where Ravana sat on the large white-and-gold throne, his five closest generals seated in a semicircle around him: Bhasakarna, Virupaksa, Duradura, Yupaksa, and Praghasa. Four additional seats on either side of his own were reserved for herself, their two sons, and his older brother

Vibhisena. Kumbhakarna, the eldest of the three Pulastya brothers, of whom Ravana was the youngest, was too large to be accommodated in this hall, let alone on any seat. And in any case, he was in one of his endless sleep cycles. Two of the four seats were empty. One was Mandodhari's, of course. The other belonged to Akshay Kumar, who was conspicuous by his absence. Vibhisena, in his seat, seemed to have been speaking just as she entered. His voice died away as he turned to see what had caused the commotion. Ravana himself was reclining languidly on his great throne, his rack of heads as always watching everything and everyone at once. She distinctly saw a head turn to watch her enter through the portal and follow her progress intently as she approached.

Pillars. There were so many pillars, she felt like a chariot riding along a tree-lined forest marg. It seemed unlikely that Pushpak required them to provide stability, which meant that they had been deliberately included for some other purpose. From the efficient way in which they separated the clans and obscured a direct view of the throne, it was obvious that the intent was to create distance and command respect for the lord of the kingdom. She fumed silently as she walked the long carpet up to the throne, feeling the lascivious eyes of the rakhsasas undressing her, ravishing her.

Much had changed in Ravana's court in the new Lanka. No more unbridled displays of lust or anger or violence. No weapons were permitted here. Nor were outbursts tolerated. With Pushpak at his command, Ravana could dispatch any dissident with only a mental command, a hole in the floor swallowing up the offender and whisking him down a slide chute that deposited him on his rearside in the avenue outside the tower. Or, if he so desired, he could simply cause offenders to disappear into the bowels of the celestial device. But rakshasas could still lust, even if they were not permitted to pursue the object of that lust. And the mate of the highest-ranking rakshasa was always the most lusted-after rakshasi. The more so in Mandodhari's case because she was monogamous to a fault, something unheard of in their race.

She could not begin to count the number of lascivious faces in this sabha belonging to rakshasa chiefs who had tried in vain to seduce, overpower or sexually assault her during the 'lost years', as they were now referred to, the period of Ravana's incapacitation.

Her son Indrajit rose to greet her as she finally approached the upper hall, but the generals made a show of remaining seated. Turncoats. Only months earlier, with Ravana still imprisoned in his bed of redstone, they had kowtowed to her as if she were the queen of air and darkness. Now they treated her as if she were just one of Ravana's many concubines, although when pressed they would perfunctorily mumble the usual formalities, as they did now, before turning their faces back to their king, making it clear where their loyalties now lay. Offended by their manner, she brushed away her son's greeting with a clipped response of her own, and went straight up to Ravana's throne. He was reclining easily on the royal seat, clad in a simple white ang-vastra and dhoti, and sporting the gold armlets and other decorative ornaments of an Arya king. With his fair buttermilk complexion, he might actually have passed for Arya, were it not for the ten heads and six arms. She found it laughable, this masquerading at being the very thing he claimed to despise: mortal.

She launched without preamble. 'My lord, I hear you have brought a hostage to Lanka. A very important and dangerous hostage.'

A head or two smiled balefully at her. The rest continued gazing at his various ministers, as if emphasising that he was not perturbed by her unannounced entrance, nor by her challenging manner. 'What of it?' he asked indifferently.

'Do your people know what you have done? Have you informed them of this newest indiscretion on your part?'

A head yawned. Another squinted sharply at her and babbled a string of incomprehensibles in an alien tongue. 'My people do not expect me to inform them of everything I do, or they would grow weary of hearing of my every fart and belch.'

Titters of laughter drifted down the long rows of seats and were slowly suppressed. Too slowly.

'I think they would want to know of this particular error of judgement.'

One head smiled pleasantly down. 'And what gives *you* the right to question my judgement?'

'The same right that every citizen of this kingdom possesses. The right to demand that the Lord of Lanka takes no action that endangers the safety of the land.'

The muttered comments and whispers died away suddenly. A silence grew in the chamber, buzzing in her ears like a swarm of sleepy flies newly roused from a carcass.

'And what action have I taken that endangers Lanka?' asked the central head, watching her impassively. 'Pray tell me, my lady.' His tone had a mocking indulgence to it, as if he were challenging one of his concubines to demand her choice of amulet at a jewellery merchant's display.

She ignored his tone and addressed his query. 'Why have you abducted the wife of the mortal prince Rama and brought her here to our land?'

Instead of the outburst and commotion she had expected, nay, desired, a silence fell across the crowded sabha hall. As moments clicked by and Ravana took his time responding, the silence thickened, like treacly molasses flowing languorously into a jar.

'Where have you heard this treasonous rumour?' Ravana asked quietly. 'Tell me plainly, that I may have the person originating it tried with due process and punished for the offence. It is against our code to accuse a king falsely, and punishable to spread a rumour accusing him as such. The penalty for this offence will be death.'

Mandodhari was taken aback by his calm demeanour. She had expected fireworks at her bold interruption of the sabha, at the very least a reprimand of her negligence of protocol; some anger at her accusation would have been nice too. But instead he seemed so cool and collected. So . . . *human*. She suppressed her self-doubt and pushed on.

'In that case, my lord, you will have to slaughter half your populace. What you call a rumour is news, repeated by every person in the marketplace of Lanka.'

'A marketplace is a breeding ground for rumours and gossip. It little behoves you, my lady, to waste your time on such trifles.'

'Then you deny this rumour has any basis in fact? There is no truth in it at all? You did not abduct Rama's wife and bring her here to our land?'

Ravana turned one of his heads to face his brother. Vibhisena, clad in his usual brahmin's garb, anointed with the caste-marks and tikka from his morning ceremonies, looked even more subdued and morose than usual. He did not raise his eyes to meet Ravana's glance. 'Perhaps my brother should answer that question. He raised the issue in this sabha not many moments ago. He seemed to be labouring under the same delusions that you are afflicted by, Lady Mandodhari.'

Mandodhari resisted the temptation to frown. This was not going as she had anticipated. 'I would prefer to hear it from you, my lord. Once more I ask you, is there or is there not a mortal woman held captive in the topmost level of this tower?'

Ravana's heads watched her with calm amusement. 'There is a mortal woman on the topmost level, most certainly. But she is not a captive. Nor was she abducted by myself or by anybody. She is here of her own free will.'

Mandodhari baulked, her hand flying involuntarily to her chest. She lowered it with difficulty, struggling to maintain her composure in the face of this astonishing response.

'I find that difficult to believe, my lord,' she said.

He waited a moment before asking, 'Are you presuming to call me a liar?'

She chose her next words carefully, aware that her every syllable was being noted by Lanka's most powerful leaders. Her dignity was at stake here. She turned her upper body slightly, allowing the rest of the sabha to see her face at least partially, and herself to view their reactions. This was very quickly becoming dangerous.

'My lord, I have travelled to the topmost level of this tower. I was denied entrance, but from the guards posted on duty outside that level, I learned that there is indeed a person incarcerated there. And she is none other than Sita, the wife of Rama Chandra of Ayodhya, whom you kidnapped and tore away by force from her husband, for reasons unknown. I have come here to ask you for your purpose in undertaking such an act, and that is what I am presently doing.'

The entire court watched her now, their pale, white-ringed rakshasa eyes glinting in the torchlight. Why did he require torchlight? Pushpak could provide illumination without revealing a specific source. Then she understood: to complete the illusion. It was an Arya court in all but reality. A perfect masquerade.

'And have you received a satisfactory response?' Ravana asked.

She hesitated. 'My lord . . .'

'Go on, speak your mind, Mandodhari. Now that you have the full sabha's attention, you may as well satisfy yourself entirely.'

She tried not to yield to the feeling that the ground was yawning beneath her feet, preparing to swallow her up. Literally. 'My lord, a rakshasi suffered a vision last night. Terrible omens, portents, ill symbols, signifying awful things.'

'Such as?'

'The destruction of Lanka, the disgrace of the royal family, the defeat of our armies.' She dared a glance at the generals – they seemed interested but unalarmed. 'The end of the rakshasa races.'

'Your basic everyday doomsday prophecy then,' Ravana said laconically. 'Available from any cornerstore clairvoyant for a dram or two of som-daru.'

There were sniggers throughout the hall in response to that one. She waited for them to die down. 'The source of the catastrophe was the abduction of this mortal woman. The vision showed her husband and brother coming to Lanka with a great army with the intent of rescuing her, and bringing about the downfall of our kind. Naturally I was concerned and alarmed. If, as the vision portrayed, you have indeed kidnapped the wife of this mortal, then there is reason to be worried indeed. This same mortal once wiped out the greatest Asura army ever assembled, by uttering a single mantra, and condemned you to thirteen years of immobility. He made extinct virtually every other Asura race except for our own rakshasas. Imagine then what havoc he could wreak were he to bring his army here and launch an assault upon our kingdom.'

She glanced at Ravana's face, then at the sabha hall. She saw the most unexpected reaction.

Ravana was smiling. He was actually beaming at her, the entire rack of heads amused and apparently delighted by her little speech.

He laughed. The laughter was picked up by one, then another, then the rest of his heads.

His generals laughed. It spread to the clan chiefs, and soon the entire hall was echoing and reverberating with the laughter of two hundred large rakshasas, kumbha-rakshasas included. She glanced around, face burning, and saw that even the sentries and servants, all lower caste, were sniggering. Even Indrajit joined in, if a little less enthusiastically, and meeting her eyes once to show that he was only participating in the general mood, not specifically trying to insult her.

Only Vibhisena did not laugh. He stared glumly at the polished marble floor, his ang-vastra trailing down from his right arm, unravelled. After a moment, she saw him sigh softly, then raise his eyes to look at her sympathetically. He shook his head once, as if commiserating with her in her embarrassment.

The laughter continued filling the sabha hall, turning her queenly dignity into a farce for all of Lanka to enjoy.

12

Mandodhari stormed out of the sabha hall in a fit of cold rage. The laughter of the chieftains echoed in her head, even though once the portal squeezed shut behind her, not a whisper could be heard. The continuing assault was upon her ego, not her ears. She exited into one of the endlessly winding corridors that Pushpak opened up for those who were undecided about their next destination, and strode along it, going nowhere, for what seemed like hours without successfully venting or calming her pent-up rage. Finally she slowed to a halt, and began to think of what she might do next. The options that flashed before her did not please her.

'Sister.'

She turned and saw Vibhisena emerge from a portal in the wall. She had probably walked a mile or two since leaving the sabha hall, yet Vibhisena had appeared mere yards from her. She almost hated the power Pushpak wielded over them all now, its magic a prison as much as a boon. One could never have privacy if Pushpak decided not to grant it. And Pushpak did only what its master willed it to do.

Still, she was not entirely displeased to see her brother-in-law. 'Vibhishan,' she said, pronouncing his name the old way.

His face was as long-drawn as always, his manner hangdog and abject. 'It was most unseemly, the manner in which they treated you in the sabha, my lady.'

She shrugged, refusing to reveal the depth of her outrage and humiliation. 'They are rakshasas after all. Even if they do play dress-up and sit about like mortals.'

'No doubt, but I was still shocked at the way my brother dismissed you out of hand. He ought not to treat his queen in such a manner before such a congregation. It will diminish their respect for you.'

She exhaled. 'There is now a new queen in Lanka. Or have you not noticed? In any case, Vibhishan, I am inured to it. This has happened before.' And it had: Ravana had had his share of dalliances and she had seen a long line of queens-of-the-moment come and go, had survived them all with equanimity and dignity. Although, she noted mentally, none of those had been mortal women. She had no idea how things might be different this time around.

He looked at her with those sad, tired blue eyes, the caste marks on his forehead luminous in Pushpak's unnatural fluorescence. 'This is not one of those occasions. I fear that this time he has gone too far.'

She almost smiled at Vibhisena's naivety, accustomed though she was to it. 'When has Ravana *not* gone too far? Excess is his trademark. It is the way he acts, Vibhishan. You above all others ought to know that by now. It is why he bears his given name. Ravana: He Who Makes The Universe Scream.' And makes the kingdom roll with laughter when he outwits his wife, she added silently.

But for once the normally docile and acquiescent Vibhisena was adamant. 'No, my lady, do not be fooled. This was not his usual trick. His deception in the sabha hall was but a glimpse of the new wiles he has acquired. Since his resurrection, my brother is not the same. No longer does he charge like a bull through a pottery store. He has learned subtlety, charm, and the art of using rhetoric and diplomacy to achieve his ends. Thirteen years ago, Ravana would have done as he pleased and cared not an ounce what you or I or anyone else thought. Today's Ravana plots his actions carefully, maps out his every course, then strikes like a lunging cobra. See how cleverly he has defanged us, his only two potential opponents in the sabha hall. Moments before you came, I raised much the same questions as you had, albeit in a more diplomatic and couched manner. I received more or less the same treatment.' His eyes flickered away awkwardly.

She read between the lines and understood that he was embarrassed about the difference in their approaches. She could guess how his own confrontation had gone: he would have questioned Ravana with the mildest of phrases, politely enquiring and all but pleading to know, while she had stormed in like a queen – which she was – and loudly demanded answers. Ravana had dealt with each of them with differing levels of severity, as their respective approaches merited. But she was more interested in what Vibhisena had just said. If he had been questioning Ravana about the same things . . . 'Then you knew about the mortal woman too?'

He stared at her momentarily before blinking. 'Of course, sister Mandodhari, every soul in Lanka knows.'

Every soul in Lanka . . . Again she cursed this wretched Pushpak. Her suspicions had been right after all. Ravana had cajoled her into coming here to live with him not so that it would be easier for them to share their conjugal bed – as if they did that any more – but so that he could keep her virtually imprisoned by this infernal magical structure. She had been played for a fool. From the moment she stormed into that sabha hall, he had been prepared for her, had expected her even, and had certainly desired her to make that faux pas, the better to bring her down a notch or two. She had long suspected that he would never forgive her for lording it over Lanka while he was incapacitated, ruling the island-kingdom as she pleased, erasing virtually every trace of the old Lanka, *his* Lanka. So this was his way of putting her in her place.

But now that Vibhisena had put it to her so analytically, she saw he was right. She had been taken unawares because she had never expected Ravana to act so subtly, so cleverly. The old Ravana would simply have ranted and railed and slashed a neck or two at random to vent his frustration. Instead, he had not only anticipated her confrontation, he had prepared for it, had planned and manoeuvred her into that state of humiliation. This was wholly unlike the Ravana she had known all her life, something new. 'You are right. He has changed his methods. And we have both been played for fools.'

Vibhisena nodded glumly. 'Perhaps more than we know.'

She frowned. 'What do you mean?'

He glanced around nervously. 'We are still in his tower, my queen. As you know . . .'

Pushpak watches over everyone for him, and no doubt reports to him if anyone says or does anything amiss, she thought bitterly. One of the many advantages of having ten heads and the ability to switch instantly from one line of thought to another was that Ravana could keep track of dozens of different threads all at once.

She nodded, approving his caution. 'Come. My head is dizzy from all this debating and discussion. I need to clear it. Let us take in some fresh air.'

Vibhisena cleared his throat. 'Perhaps we could perambulate the apsara gardens, my queen? It would be an invigorating change.'

'Excellent.' She smiled, and willed a portal to open, permitting her exit from the tower.

She had expected resistance from Pushpak, perhaps even an outright refusal. Instead, she was shocked to find a portal opening almost at once, and through it open sky and distant mountain ranges visible. Was it this easy then? She cursed herself for a fool again. Ravana had never said she was a prisoner here. It was she who had been seduced by the comforts and luxuries of this self-contained world. Perhaps the air itself had contained some kind of drug, softening her resolve and numbing her normally suspicious nature.

They stepped out on to a path that led directly to the apsara gardens, even though the gardens were a good yojana outside the main city limits. Looking back, she saw the portal wink shut, and beyond it, amidst the cityscape of whitewashed rooftops and gleaming gold-encircled spires, the white-and-gold spear that was the tower of Ravana rose above the city. She looked around. They were standing on the avenue that led to the arching gateway of the gardens. Ahead was a plaque she had commissioned herself, commemorating her parents, to whom she had dedicated this botanical preserve. Within this protected space were the rarest plants, most of which had been all but extinguished in the destruction of Lanka thirteen years ago. She herself had painstakingly restored their lines and overseen their sustenance. Few rakshasas ever came here. Apart from the rare exceptions like Vibhisena and herself, most of her kind preferred the sweaty noise and bustle of big cities. Even now, there was only a crippled broken-sur munching desultorily at some shrubbery, probably one of the many semi-tame creatures that wandered in from the surrounding wilds. The creature raised its head briefly to eye Vibhisena and Mandodhari warily, seemed to find them unalarming, then continued its listless munching.

Pushpak had gone so far as to deposit them directly at their destination. She wondered if the celestial device would pick them up again when they wished to go back . . . *if* they wished to go back. She thought it might. A suspicion entered her mind and she looked around sharply, trying to discern whether the sunlight she felt on her pale skin, the flower-redolent wind that blew her tresses, the insects buzzing in the air were all real and not more of Pushpak's chicanery. Finally, satisfied that they were indeed out of the tower's realm of control – or at least out of its physical boundaries – she told Vibhisena to walk. Once they were through the arched entranceway and on one of the labyrinthine paths, she turned to him.

'What did you mean? What else has my husband been plotting?'

He hesitated as if deciding where to start. 'Sister, I cannot know everything that occupies Ravana's myriad minds. I can only tell you what I have observed for myself and deduced rationally.'

She nodded, eager for him to go on. 'Very well, tell me everything you know.'

He began by describing a visit he had made to the tower some weeks ago. The many levels he had seen, the mass orgies in progress, the unspeakable sights. She did not question him on any of those matters; fornication was the opiate of the rakshasa race, and despite Vibhisena's brahminical disapproval of such behaviour, she was not overly troubled by it. From all that she had heard of mortal myths and legends, they indulged in their share of fornication too. As did their venerated devas. Did that make them any less divine? She would not narrow her thinking and focus on things that caused no real harm to her or to her people.

But when he spoke of his encounter with Supanakha, masquerading as Ravana, and of her comment that Ravana himself was away on urgent business, she frowned and shot off questions like darts. Where had Ravana gone? Why was Supanakha permitted to occupy his private quarters? Had Ravana allowed her to morph into his form or had she cheekily done as she pleased?

Vibhisena shook his head. 'I do not know, sister. But pray, hear me out to the end.'

She listened as he explained how, after that encounter, he began lurking and listening at corners, paying attention to the smallest scrap of news. He heard tell of a new level on the topmost floor of the tower, and visited that level – at the time it was not barred to anyone, since there was nobody there yet. He described the place to Mandodhari.

'It sounds like any forest glade,' she said.

'Exactly, my lady. And why would Ravana wish to have a forest glade within the tower? To house a prisoner whom he wished to deceive as well as conceal, I thought.' He had tried visiting the place more recently, after he'd heard about the prisoner ensconced there, but by then it had been barred to all. Only Ravana himself could enter . . . and, until recently, one other person.

'Who?' she asked, curious as well as a little jealous. Who did Ravana trust enough to share his secret with?

Vibhisena looked at her closely. 'Would you meet this person? She is the source of my most accurate information about Ravana and his great plan. She has much valuable information to share with us, information that may be crucial in helping us prevent yet another war. That is why I suggested the apsara gardens. I was to meet her here after the sabha in any case.'

She thought she could already guess at the identity of the person of whom Vibhisena spoke. Since his resurrection, Ravana had shown little or no interest in matters sexual or persons female. His present abduction of the mortal woman notwithstanding, he seemed to have lost much of his former virility. Even the few nights he had shared her bed had been desultory and wholly unlike his former bull-like self, his appetites diminished, almost vanished. But one female had always been close by his side, and despite the humiliation Mandodhari had suffered in the sabha hall, she had not failed to notice the absence of . . .

'Supanakha,' she said, turning her head. 'Why don't you join us? For once you can pay for your eavesdropping by sharing a bit of your own gossip too.'

She looked at the decrepit broken-sur on the path behind them. She had been certain that it had not been there the instant they had come through the portal, that it had appeared a few minutes later. And she was well aware of Supanakha's talent for self-transformation.

With a grunt and a belch, spitting out a mouthful of half-chewed leaves and curdled cud, the broken-sur began to morph, some of its bones shrinking, others elongating, changing shape and curvature. Skin crackled as it stretched and changed colour, softening and turning glossy and shiny.

In moments, the sleek, catlike form of Supanakha stood on the pathway beside them, incandescent yellow eyes squinting at Mandodhari in the bright sunlight.

13

Supanakha flashed her fangs at the Queen of Lanka. Mandodhari looked down at her imperiously from her tall frame, her thin, disapproving mouth curled in a small moue of dislike. There had never been any love lost between them, and at times Supanakha had fantasised about pleasuring with her cousin's snobbish wife, replacing that superior sniffle with moans of wild, undignified abandonment; and then, when the haughty rakshasi was at her most vulnerable, rendered as naked and wanton as the cheapest flesh-whore in Lanka, tearing into her vitals and eating her alive. Mating with and eating one's enemies while they were in the throes of ecstasy was a long-honoured tradition in many rakshasa tribes, but it was usually reserved for enemies captured after loss in battle. Now, looking at that proud face with its still-unlined cheeks and barely visible traces of maturity, that aquiline profile and pale creamish skin, Supanakha wished fervently that some day she had cause to do battle with this woman, if only to earn the right to enjoy the spoils of that battle afterwards.

She flicked her tail hard and snarled softly at both the rakshasi and her spineless, mortal-loving, deva-worshipping brother-in-law. Pathetic allies these, but she had little choice. Since Ravana had exiled her from the tower, she had been forced to wander the city, passing her time with indiscriminate matings and prolific quantities of the som-daru her mates brought her. She had managed to kick up a row or two, killing and maiming a number of stout fellows, and that had passed a few hours satisfactorily.

But she was hugely resentful and frustrated at having been shut out by Ravana. How could he? After all she had done for him? She snarled again, making no secret of her hatred for this rakshasi who trotted about on her hind legs like she was superior to her sisters, and her scorn for the pious, celibate, self-righteous fool, but curbing her sudden longing to take out her fury on them. She had made use of lesser allies than these before. They might prove useful yet, if Ravana persisted in keeping her out. And if he relented, as he had done so often before, then their little treasonous chicanery would no doubt be of great interest to him. Either way, she stood to gain.

'I don't trust her.' She addressed her words to Vibhisena, disdainfully ignoring Ravana's wife. 'She will go running to him and tell him of our talks.'

Vibhisena looked pained at the accusation. 'Don't be silly, cousin. Mandodhari is the most honourable rakshasi alive. Besides, even if she,' he paused, and added pointedly, 'or anyone else were to tell Ravana what we discuss here, he would have no reason to be upset. We only want what is best for Lanka.'

'And what if what is best for Lanka is not what is best for Ravana? What then? Don't you think your tête-à-tête with his wife and cousin might fall under the heading of treason?'

Mandodhari spoke up, the tightness of her tone indicating that she had taken affront at Supanakha's allegation. Good, it was nice to get through that iron façade. 'Preposterous. I am Ravana's wife. I care as much about him as I do about Lanka.' She shot a reproving glance at Vibhisena. 'It is futile to separate the two. Ravana is Lanka and Lanka Ravana. What is best for one is best for both.'

Vibhisena opened his mouth to answer, then shut it. Mandodhari gave them both a moment to speak, then went on tartly, addressing Supanakha. 'In any case, what is your grievance with my husband? The last I knew, you two were closer than a tick and a kumbha-rakshasa's rump.'

Supanakha flicked her tail, severing a rare, fragile orchid from its stalk with the sharp-pointed tip. She changed the tail back into its normal furry form before curling it behind her own rump. 'We had a disagreement over the mortal woman.'

Vibhisena spoke up hurriedly, as if eager to dispel any hostility between his sister-in-law and his cousin. His eagerness to avoid violence was one of the things she despised about him. How could a rakshasa shy away from violence, the most basic fact of existence? It was like denying one's very desire to survive!

'Supanakha attacked the mortal woman and tried to kill her. Ravana was enraged at her and exiled her from the tower.'

'He might as well have exiled me from Lanka itself,' she snarled. 'Everything that matters happens in there now. It's a city unto itself.'

Mandodhari looked intrigued. 'So you tried to kill Sita?' She nodded thoughtfully. 'I can see why you would desire her killed. Her husband was the source of much unhappiness in your life.' She was silent a moment, as if recalling Supanakha's long history of conflict with the exiled princes of Ayodhya. Then she asked, with expertly feigned casualness, 'How is the mortal woman? To look at, I mean? Is she as ugly as most of them?'

Supanakha sniggered throatily. 'You mean, does she look like you, or is she even halfway attractive? Why? Isn't my cousin parting your thighs often enough to satisfy you, my lady?'

Mandodhari stared down at her coldly. Over her shoulder, she addressed Vibhisena. 'You know, brother dear, I wonder if this creature will be of any help to us at all. It seems she has little more than petty gossip and lewd remarks to offer.'

Vibhisena tugged on his pigtails in dismay, licking his lips nervously. 'Supanakha, cousin. Please, just tell Mandodhari what you told me earlier. About Ravana's master plan and how Sita fits into the whole scheme.'

Supanakha shrugged. She was tiring of this discussion anyway. She would rather be fornicating with a few virile rakshasas or quaffing a gallon or two of bloodwine in one of Lanka's cave-inns. 'Ravana didn't kidnap Rama's wife only to satisfy his own lust. There's a much bigger plan behind it all. It was at my suggestion that he brought her here in the first place.'

'At your suggestion?' Mandodhari looked openly sceptical.

Supanakha bared her teeth. 'I don't really care if you believe me or not. But it was I who provided the key to Ravana's resurrection, if you remember. And part of my price for rejuvenating my dearest cousin was that I would be avenged on Rama.'

Mandodhari's eyes glinted. 'What *was* that key? I have never been able to understand that. We tried for thirteen years using every spell, herb and ritual known to Asura maya. How was it that you, a mixed-breed, were able to do it in moments? Were you somehow ordained by greater forces? If so, then why? Why you, of all persons?'

'What do I look like?' Supanakha shot back. 'A streetside astrologer? I don't have all the answers. All I know is that when Rama and his companions killed the last of my tribe-brothers in the wilds of Janasthana, I felt compelled to take something belonging to him and return to Lanka. And I did. Then, when I was within reach of Ravana's mindvoice, he bade me come to him and give me that thing of Rama I had brought back. And it turned out to be the very thing he needed to break the spell he was under. But don't ask me the how or why of it. I don't bother myself with such things the way you fools do. It's enough to eat, mate and kill. The rest I leave to you wretched politicians!'

Mandodhari seemed unperturbed by the outburst. 'You underestimate yourself, shapechanger. You are quite the politician yourself, or you wouldn't be here at all!'

Supanakha turned around to show the Queen of Lanka her rump, raising her tail to make sure Mandodhari had a good look at her nether end. The hastily covered face and pinched nostrils were very satisfying to behold. 'Shall I go on, or would you like to continue speaking to my other, better half?'

Vibhisena waved hastily at her, as if showing a peace flag. 'Cousin! Enough bickering. Go on with your narrative.'

Mandodhari regained her composure faster than Supanakha

had expected. 'What was the thing belonging to Rama that you brought back from Janasthana, which magically revived my husband?'

'A trace of Rama's blood,' Supanakha purred. 'I swallowed it and placed it in my second stomach, the one I use to store food for later use, the way a camel stores water in its hump in anticipation of the summer.'

'We know about winter bellies, Supanakha,' Mandodhari said, her expression one of distraction. She was digesting Supanakha's revelation. 'His blood, you say? That is fascinating. Why would Rama's blood be the key to resurrecting Ravana?'

Vibhisena spoke up hesitantly. 'It implies a deep connection between them. Something we have not understood fully thus far.' In his usual ponderous way, he added, 'Whatever the significance, I have no doubt that it was ordained thus by the devas themselves, for nothing happens without their knowledge and assent. For some good reason, they have linked the life of my brother to that of Rama Chandra of Ayodhya, and that must mean their fates are intertwined as well.'

'There is no such thing as fate, Vibhishan,' Mandodhari said impatiently. 'Only karma. As we act, so shall we reap. You of all people should know that.'

'What you say is true, and yet . . .' Vibhisena shook his head. 'The more I study the history of my people, the more I wonder. The three tenets of dharma, karma and artha seem to have little bearing on the rakshasa races. I often wonder if even my long prayers and devotion will ever bear fruit and bring about the salvation of our kind.'

'Perhaps you expect too much too soon,' Mandodhari said, still distracted by her inner chain of thoughts. 'Have faith.'

'It is all I have,' Vibhisena replied.

Supanakha growled, spitting to remind them of her presence. 'If you want to talk this rotten-flesh talk, then I'm leaving.'

'Go on then, Supanakha,' Mandodhari said. 'Tell us what your plan was, to avenge yourself on Rama. And why did Ravana agree to go along with it? Because I know my husband well enough to know that he would never undertake any step that did not profit him directly. What did *he* stand to gain by kidnapping Rama's wife?'

Supanakha rolled her shoulders, thinking. 'I don't know, or particularly care,' she admitted. 'I demanded of him when he was still in that redstone block inside that cave in the earth that he would help avenge myself on Rama and his brother, and in exchange for that I would give him the thing he said he needed to come alive again. And he agreed. I gave it no more thought.'

'That's obvious. So your plan was simply for him to go to the place where Rama was living in exile and kidnap his wife. Then what?'

'Then we were to wait.'

'Wait for what?'

'For Rama and Lakshman to come to Lanka.'

'To rescue his wife, you mean. And then what?'

'And then we would kill them.' Supanakha smacked her chops, relishing the very thought. 'I would finally have my vengeance on them both for humiliating and scarring me and for killing fourteen thousand of my tribe-brothers.'

Mandodhari was looking at her with an odd expression.

Supanakha sniffed at her suspiciously. 'What?'

'Did you really think that Rama and his brother would come to Lanka alone? Knowing that this was the lair of the rakshasa race on the mortal realm?'

Supanakha squinted. 'What else? He is in exile, he has only a few ragtag outlaws in his camp.'

'Didn't those same ragtag outlaws, led by Rama and his brother, make short work of your fourteen thousand tribe-brothers?'

Supanakha snarled, not liking Mandodhari's insinuation or the reminder of all her dead cousins. 'It took them thirteen years. And they lost a lot of their number as well, in that last battle at Janasthana. Besides, this time, they would have to come to our ground, so we would have the advantage.' She grinned. 'And there are many times more than fourteen thousand rakshasas in Lanka now, led by Ravana himself.'

Mandodhari shrugged. 'That's assuming that Rama doesn't raise an army.'

Supanakha sneered. 'An army?'

'Yes. He is the crown prince of Ayodhya, after all. A king in waiting. He could have access to a huge mortal force in no time at all, could he not? One morning we may wake up and find a fleet of a thousand ships at our shores, and then who would have the advantage?'

Supanakha smiled, enjoying her power over this woman. 'He will not go back to Ayodhya until his term of exile is ended. That is why it was so important to abduct Sita and force Rama's hand now, before he went back to Aryavarta.'

Mandodhari raised her eyebrows. 'Very impressive. So, assuming that he cannot raise a mortal army, he and his ragtag band of outlaws, a few dozen at best, will come to Lanka, be destroyed out of hand by Ravana and our immensely superior forces. And then what?'

'Then I do what I will with both of them.'

'While my husband does as he will with Rama's wife, no doubt,' Mandodhari said drily. 'Yes, I see the bones of your plan. It is interesting and simple-minded enough to be workable. Although I would have expected something much more dramatic from my husband after all these millennia and so many great campaigns of warfare.'

'And I would not wish to disappoint you.'

The words came from around them, and from nowhere. Then, like a ghost form materialising out of sheer mist, the ten-headed silhouette of Ravana appeared, and assumed solid physical form. Wind dervishes sprang up around him, uprooting plants and flowers, raising a small dust hurricane. He strode forward slowly, looking at each of them in turn. Supanakha slunk backwards, preparing to turn and flee, even though she knew that she could not escape Ravana's sorcery. She was caught! She knew she should never have agreed to talk with these wretched ones.

'Cousin,' she gasped. 'Master. She was the one who insisted I tell her everything. I—'

To her surprise, Ravana displayed beaming smiles across his rack of heads. 'Do not fear, cousin. I am not angry with you. With any of you. Your curiosity is understandable. And I am here to invite you back to my chambers that I may explain the situation to you in greater detail. Despite what Supanakha thinks, she has told you nothing.'

Mandodhari eyed her husband sharply. 'Nothing?'

For a moment Supanakha thought Ravana would deny everything, would make her the villain of the whole piece. It would be in keeping with his new approach, using lies and wiles rather than brute force and violence.

But he surprised her completely.

'Nothing important,' Ravana said. 'You still do not know the real story. That is why I have come to fetch you.' He looked over Mandodhari's shoulder at the partly hidden Vibhisena. 'Both of you.' He glanced back at Supanakha. 'You are welcome to join us as well, cousin. I have long since forgiven you for your trespass in the lady Sita's quarters.'

'You have?' she asked suspiciously, hearing the uncertain croak in her voice.

Mandodhari said sharply, 'After the way you humiliated me in the sabha hall, I have no wish to speak to you anywhere, my lord.'

'That is why I came to you, instead of sending my minions to summon you. My dear, before you condemn me for your humiliation, remember that it was you who stormed in and attacked me before my entire assembly. Surely you could not expect me to treat you humbly and respectfully under those circumstances? I would have been the laughing stock of the kingdom. You got what you deserved.'

Mandodhari looked at him, as if considering his words seriously. 'It's true I did storm in, but—'

'If you had chosen to speak to me privately, in your usual quiet and dignified manner, I would have gladly explained all to you. As I am willing to do now.'

Mandodhari exchanged a glance with her brother-in-law. Even Vibhisena seemed taken in by Ravana's charm. Supanakha marvelled at her cousin's ability to turn two potential betrayers back into allies. She found herself intrigued too.

'Very well, then,' Mandodhari said quietly. 'I will give you a few moments' hearing to explain yourself.'

'And in those few moments, my love, you will learn more than you could learn in a thousand hours of skulking around behind my back and gossiping in gardens!' Ravana's central head smiled balefully at Vibhisena. 'Come, my brother dearest, let us repair to the comfort of my chambers and I will tell you the real reason why I brought the lady Sita here to our island-kingdom, and why Supanakha's simplistic scheme for avenging herself upon Rama fits in so well with my own plans for restoring Lanka to her former glory.'

And with a gesture and a mantra, uttered too softly to be heard by even Supanakha's cat-sharp ears, he transported them away.

Sita heard the sound of approaching voices and looked around frantically for a place to hide. Then she realised how futile it would be. No matter where she fled in this forest of illusions, she would still be Ravana's captive. She looked around the little enclave where she had been sitting. A waterfall tumbled over rocks nearby, spilling its waters into a small pool. Early this morning, shortly after Ravana's departure, his rakshasi minions had arrived and led her to this spot, indicating that she could bathe and cleanse herself here, then change into the fresh garments they had brought. She had spoken not a word to them, and they had left quickly, no doubt instructed by their master not to offend or assault her in any manner. But even hours after their departure, she still sat here, having barely moved. The garments lay untouched on a rock beneath a tree, as did the fruit and meat they had brought. She had no intention of eating any of Ravana's food, or of enjoying his hospitality. She had not touched so much as a drop of water, but had only sat hugging her knees tightly, the sound of falling water soothing her after the horrors of the past days.

She stood now, sensing the approach of visitors. There were many voices speaking at once, strange, harsh rakshasa voices using that guttural language of theirs. She knew they were most likely the same rakshasi guards, sent to replenish her food and drink and check on her, but a shiver of unease passed through her, like a fine needle inserted into her right side and pulled out through her left. She put a hand to her belly, feeling vulnerable and defenceless, and hating the sensation. For a moment she felt like a doe must feel at the approach of a pack of lions, paralysed with fear and fascination and self-disgust at her own frozen state. Then, with a soft prayer to the Devi, she willed herself to have confidence. Rama would come. This would end. All she had to do was retain her dignity and her composure and show no weakness to these Lankan swine. She was a princess of Mithila, a future queen of Ayodhya, a mother-in-waiting of princes and princesses of Arya. She need fear nothing and no one.

She stood, straightening her back, lifting her chin, folding her arms across her chest and assuming a deliberate attitude of callous indifference. It had been most effective when the rakshasas visited earlier, and they had left in obvious awe at the human female who stood as straight and silent as a queen even in this state of captivity. They had probably expected her to behave as mortals did when subjugated; as a girl, she had heard tales at her father's court of northern white-skinned folk who went down on their knees before their captors and put grass between their teeth to show their allegiance. She would put no grass between her teeth.

The visitors broke through the shrubbery at the other end of the little glade, on the far side of the pool. They came into the dappled shade and looked around, seeking her out. The pattern of light and shadow through the leafy trees overhead and the reflections of sunlight from the falling water camouflaged her effectively, and it took them a moment to see and recognise her. When they did, they nudged each other and pointed with their stubby six-fingered rakshasa claws, whispering to one another. At least one of them opened her mouth wide, baring a mouthful of shattered yellow fangs in a universal gesture of threat.

Sita resisted the urge to react.

She had seen rakshasas before, as ugly and menacing and large as these. But of course, on all those previous occasions, she had been fed and rested and armed, and secure in the knowledge that there were others supporting her. And those encounters had been on land that was only wild and unexplored, not tainted by foul Asura sorcery.

Never before had she been utterly defenceless, unarmed and isolated, captive in a strange land, weak from hunger and thirst, faint from the residual effect of the poppy drugs administered by the shapeshifter. Even so . . . She held her ground and her stance, meeting the rakshasas' eyes, ready to defend herself against them by any means should they attempt to assault her. Ready to fight to the death if need be. Although a small voice within her, a timid and humble voice, prayed that she would not need to sacrifice herself. Not because she loved life too dearly to lay hers down with dignity, but because she cherished the unborn life growing within her womb, wished to give that delicate one at least the chance to properly enter the world it had been conceived in.

There were a half-dozen of them. The largest seemed the most belligerent, showing Sita her broken fangs again before turning to the others and barking a series of commands. Then she made her way around the side of the water, issuing what seemed to be curses when her own clumsy gait caused one of her feet to splash in the pool. Sita recalled what she knew of rakshasas and their loathing of fresh water, and toyed with the idea of using the vine hanging above her to propel herself forward, kicking the approaching rakshasi and knocking her into the waterfall pool. Then, with a mental flicker of regret, she suppressed the urge. All that would achieve was to enrage the rakshasas and perhaps cause them to take their wrath out upon her. It would be a poor bargain just to dunk one in a little harmless water, however much the creatures feared the innocuous substance.

The rakshasi stopped a few yards from Sita and barked a harsh command. Sita had no idea what the creature was saying, and even if she had understood every word, she would not have cared. She met the creature's fierce red-eyed glare with a cold, quiet stare, refusing to yield in the battle of wills. But she had not expected what came next.

Instead of yelling in frustration or repeating her insistence that Sita eat the food, or wear the clothes, or whatever other instruction she assumed the creature had been given to fulfil, the rakshasi lurched forward with shocking speed, and before Sita could react or move had landed a resounding smack on her left cheek. The blow was hard enough to knock Sita off her feet, and she found herself on the ground, her hip throbbing where she had landed on her side, her mouth filled with dust and dry leaf fragments. She spat them out and turned her head quickly to place her enemy, fearing that the rakshasi would land upon her, using her immense weight advantage to crush her – and the delicate life growing within her belly.

But the beast was still standing, leering down at Sita with those cracked yellow fangs, hands on her own ample hips. She said something in her guttural tongue, eliciting peals of raucous laughter from all the other rakshasas but one, and hawked and spat into the pool, mere inches from Sita's outstretched feet. Sita pulled her feet up closer, trying to adjust her position to brace herself in the event of another assault. But the rakshasi seemed contented with the one blow and stood laughing and spitting and saying incomprehensible offensive-sounding things.

One of the other rakshasas came forward at a half-run, blabbering something equally incomprehensible. This one was short and squat and evidently much older than the others. Her long white hair streamed out around her thick, flat-topped head like a garment, its leathery strands as thick as hide-strings. She screamed in a hysterical tone at the larger rakshasi, who leered in her face and said something which made the older one shrink away hastily. The larger rakshasi laughed and called out something to the others, who roared with a fresh burst of laughter.

The older rakshasi came towards Sita cautiously, bending over and peering as if her vision were partially impaired. As she came closer, Sita saw that her eyes were covered with milky-white patches and guessed that she suffered from some rakshasa variation of old-age blindness. Sita pulled her legs up and dragged herself away until her head and back struck the trunk of a weeping willow that hung over the pool, its fronds dripping into the water. She reached back, grabbing the sinuous trunk, and pulled herself up, glaring a warning at the approaching rakshasi. She would not allow herself to be taken by surprise a second time. She glanced around quickly for a tree branch she could snap off, a stone, anything to be used as a weapon in her defence. The old rakshasi paused, as if sensing her hostility, and said something in a placatory tone. Behind her, the larger rakshasi echoed her words, mocking her tone, and was rewarded with more sniggers from her audience. The old rakshasi ignored them all and repeated herself, speaking very slowly and gently, as if by doing so Sita would be able to understand her better.

Sita wished she *could* understand, if only to know when one of them intended harm to her so she could prepare herself. No sooner had she thought this than the quality of light in the glade altered fractionally, like the blinking of an eye, and suddenly she was shocked to find that she could understand every syllable as clearly as Arya commonspeak or Sanskrit highspeech.

'Forgive us, my lady,' the old rakshasi was saying. 'Vikata does not know what she does and to whom. I beg your pardon for the way she treated you.'

Sita swallowed, struggling to comprehend whether she was imagining things or whether she had suddenly gained perfect knowledge of the language of rakshasas. She remained silent, watching the old rakshasi carefully, ready to leap aside if the demoness made any sudden hostile move. She could go into the water, where the rakshasas would be loath to follow her. It would buy her a few precious moments at least. There was little else she could do. Running was out of the question. She was backed up against the waterfall on one side and this weeping willow behind her, and the large, bullying rakshasi was blocking the only other avenue of escape. In any case, where would she run?

'My name is Trijata,' the old one said, folding her hands together in a namaskaram, 'and I am greatly honoured to make your acquaintance, wife of Rama. I pray, do not curse us for our foolish actions. We are all victims of the same celestial plan.'

'Daughter of a whore,' roared the large rakshasi, 'speak for yourself! We are princesses of Lanka all. We have no need to debase ourselves before puny mortals. They are food on our table, no more. A few choice morsels to fill our bellies, a little entertainment for our beds perhaps, maybe even slaves to work our farms and clean our sewers. We do not need to fold our hands or bend our heads before them! Get away from her, you old hag!'

The one who had called herself Trijata turned her milky eyes up to her associate. 'Curb your tongue, Vikata. Do you not recall my vision of last night? If we do not have care for how we treat this lady, she will bring about the end of all rakshasa-kind! I have seen it in my dream, and my dreams are never wrong.'

The yellow-fanged rakshasi hawked throatily and spat at the older one, the disgusting effusion almost striking the crouched rakshasi's thigh. 'I spit on your dreams and visions. Debase yourself before the mortal if you will; I would rather cut off my own head than bend it before her.'

'There will be no bending of heads, nor cutting off.'

The voice came from the far side of the pool, behind the other rakshasas, who had been watching the exchange between their two companions with unmitigated glee. At the sound of the new rakshasi's voice, they stopped laughing at once and turned to bow their heads, greeting the arrival with a show of respect. From this, and from the manner in which the large rakshasi scowled, Sita deduced that the new visitor was a rakshasi of high rank.

She was tall and slender, but full-bodied, her curves well delineated in the flowing silken white robes she wore. At a glance, she could almost have passed for a human female. Except for the two white horns growing from the top of her head, curved backwards in an almost feminine way, less threatening than ornamental. Her skin was pale, nearly as white as the colouring of the emissaries from foreign lands that oftentimes had visited Sita's father's court at Mithila, people from strange distant lands where they ate cheese and wheatcakes and drank red grape-wine and spoke of philosophy all day long. But her skin was much thicker than that of any of those foreigners, so thick that it appeared almost milky, like the hide of some albino beast. Her features were unmistakably rakshasi, but were much finer and more delicately shaped than the coarse bluntness of the others. She bore herself in a manner that was imperious and haughty, like a queen secure in her power.

'So this is the she-devil who seduced my husband,' she said now, staring at Sita from across the pool of water with a barely suppressed resentment seething in her pale sky-blue eyes.

Sita started. Not at the hatred in the look cast by the rakshasi, but at her words. *Seduced my husband?* Who was this creature? What did she mean?

The white-clad rakshasi walked slowly around the pool, the others moving aside to make way for her. Even the large rakshasi stepped back, albeit with another scowl, and the older one moved away to allow her mistress to approach Sita.

Sita stared defiantly into the pale eyes.

'See how she stares at me,' said the rakshasi. 'As if she would drive her claws into my breast and pull out my heart.'

If I did possess claws, I wouldn't be averse to putting them to such use, you demoness. But within her own breast, her heart pounded relentlessly, the unease she had felt earlier grown now into a full-blown terror. In a way, she sensed, this person was more dangerous than Ravana himself. Her hatred of Sita glowed in her eyes, reflected in the murderous stares of the other rakshasas – all except the old white-haired one who crouched now beside her mistress.

'Do you know who I am, mortal wench?' asked the rakshasi disdainfully. 'I am she whose husband you desire to possess. The queen you seek to replace. But you will never succeed in your foul scheme. I have just come from my husband's chambers, where he informed me of all your machinations and manipulations. Surely only a human could act so dishonourably. You have been exposed and your fiendish plot laid bare.'

15

Sita stared at the pale, haughty rakshasi in astonishment. What was she talking about? The only sense Sita could glean from the rakshasi's words was that she was probably Ravana's wife. Who else could she be referring to? But what did she mean by all those other accusations? Still, Sita kept her silence.

The rakshasi went on disdainfully, her hatred evident in her words. 'I admit that at first I too was deceived by your apparent plight. An innocent mortal woman, abducted from her husband's house and brought here by force against her will? What honourable rakshasi would not have sympathy for such a one? When Trijata told me of her nightmarish vision of the downfall of Lanka and the rakshasa race, I thought it must be due to his transgression against you. But my eyes are opened now. He has told me the full story. Never have I heard of such a devilish plot, hatched by a woman against her own husband!'

Sita's head was throbbing. For a brief moment, she wished that she could be blessed with ignorance of the rakshasa tongue once more – and at once her wish was granted, the rakshasi's next words turning into incomprehensible gibberish. But then she knew that she must listen, for it was better to possess knowledge than to live in animal ignorance. So she willed the Asura sorcery that had enabled her to understand their tongue to grant her understanding once more, and listened with sick horror as the rakshasi's monologue continued.

'The seer-mage Vishwamitra had long since prophesied the destruction of the Asura races, and had promised that he himself would play a significant part in their decimation. So when he interrupted his own long tapasya in the Southwoods, my husband Ravana knew that the time had come at last. From compatriots of the Asura cause within Ayodhya he learned of Vishwamitra's recruitment of the young prince Rama Chandra and his brother. Later, Vishwamitra used magic to imbue the two brothers with superhuman powers, and fielded them against the unsuspecting yaksi Tataka in the Bhayanak-van. They massacred the innocent Tataka and every last one of her blameless children, then laid waste to the entire forest, which was all Asura land since ages past. This was no less than an act of declaration of war against the Asura races, who had lain quiet since winning the last war, some two decades past.

'Ravana marshalled a great army of Asura races, and marched towards the mortal kingdoms, believing offence to be the best defence. But he was honourable enough to attempt one last time to bridge the divide. He attended the swayamvara of the daughter of King Janaka of the Vaideha kingdom in the capital city of Mithila, knowing that King Janaka was renowned for his pacifism and unswerving adherence to dharma. By winning the hand of Janaka's daughter, namely yourself, Ravana hoped to forge an alliance between the mortal and Asura races, and put an end once and for all to the endless warfare. His plan was a good one. He triumphed in the challenge posed at the swayamvara, and by rights you should have been given to him in matrimony. But there your deceptions began. Instead of doing the honourable thing, and accepting him as your rightful husband, you allowed Rama to intervene by force, and through the use of Vishwamitra's vile sorcery, Rama equalled Ravana in the challenge. This was patently unfair and immoral, violating all social laws as well as the premise of the swayamvara ritual. When Ravana saw that justice would not be done at that venue, he understood that he had lost more than a richly deserved bride; this was the mortals' way of spurning the Asura offer of peace and brotherhood. Ravana returned to his waiting armies and led them on a charge towards Mithila. But again Vishwamitra's magic enabled Rama to unleash the terrible brahm-astra, the forbidden weapon of the Creator Himself. And genocide was committed.'

Sita stared at the wife of Ravana with rapt horror. All she could do was listen, and learn, with indescribable dread, how events that she had thought she knew so well could be perceived in such dramatically different fashion by these people. Not people, rakshasas, she reminded herself fiercely. But still, that did not change the pain it caused her to hear of herself, her father, her husband, even the venerated brahmarishi Vishwamitra, spoken of in such terms.

'As a result of his war crime and a-dharma, Rama was punished by the devas and spurned by his people, even his own family disowning him, and banished to the wilds for a long forest exile, deprived of the crown of Ayodhya he coveted so desperately. The devas did this in order to allow the rakshasa race, which had been wronged so heinously, to recover and replenish itself. Even then, Rama's evil war against our people continued. First he insulted the modesty of our cousin Supanakha, then his brother mutilated her and left her in a condition that among our kind is considered worse than crippling. When she appealed to her tribe-brothers for protection, Rama raised a force of like-minded rakshasa-haters, and waged unceasing battle upon them. He slaughtered fourteen thousand more of our people, wiping out the last of them at the brutal battle of Janasthana, only a season or two ago. And even then, this was not sufficient to slake his bloodlust.

'Rama knew that in a few seasons, his exile would end and he would return home to Ayodhya, where at the very least he would face further humiliation from his people and bitter infighting within his own family over the rightful successor to the throne. At worst, he would not be permitted back into Ayodhya at all, or into any Arya nation. For as you well know, daughter of Janaki, your husband had not only insulted his dying father and refused to abide by his last wishes, but had also defied the moral code of dharma by unleashing the brahm-astra which exterminated the Asura armies – and to make amends now, Rama felt the need to bring home some kind of trophy that would make him indispensable to his people, compelling them to grant him, however reluctantly, the throne of Ayodhya. So his gaze fell upon Lanka. Assuming it already depleted of its great Asura hordes, and the rakshasas cowed and submissive after their historic defeat at Mithila, Rama thought it would make an easy target for conquest. By conquering Lanka, he would be able to return home and claim that he had single-handedly rid the mortal realm of all Asura threat. But to achieve this goal, he needed an army, and since no mortal army would follow his command – even the outlaw bands had fled from him the minute the battle of Janasthana ended – he fell back on desperate measures.'

Sita could barely breathe, so sickly fascinating was the rakshasi queen's story. Yet she was compelled to listen. To hear this litany of shame and horror being heaped upon her honourable, noble, self-sacrificing Rama. He who was all but a deva in human form was being demonised. It broke her heart to hear such things said of him, but she wished to hear this out in order to take the full measure of this monstrous mountain of lies.

The rakshasi went on, her loathing of the events she was relating unequivocal. Whatever her husband had told her – and it was Ravana who had fed her this pack of lies, Sita reminded herself – he had done a very thorough job. Every angle was secured, every nail hammered in tightly. The rakshasi clearly believed what she said, and considered her husband the honourable one for being pitted against such a foe. Sita clenched her fists into balls, her fingernails digging into her own palms deep enough to draw blood, and forced herself to listen. It was one of the hardest things she had ever done.

'Everyone knows that the vanars are great in number and inclined to war. Even though their battle skills are laughable, they more than make up for their lack of knowledge by their sheer numbers alone. And Kiskindha is the greatest vanar city of all. Rama heard of the civil conflict in Kiskindha from some wandering exiled vanar and saw an opportunity waiting to be exploited. By murdering the rightful king, Vali, and staining the throne of Kiskindha, he gained an uneasy alliance with King Sugreeva the Usurper. He convinced the vanars that in aiding him in his conquest of Lanka, they would gain rich booty as well, besides rising considerably in the scheme of things. Vanars would forever be regarded with awe and respect after ridding the world of the last rakshasas. The scheme he proposed was to march south with the vanar forces, bridge the ocean and invade Lanka.

'And that is what he is now doing, even as we speak, preparing to build a bridge across the narrowest strait. Once that bridge is ready, he will lead his unsuspecting vanars across the sea to Lanka, expecting to find a rich kingdom languishing for want of a leader. He surely knows of the celestial device Pushpak and its fabulous powers, as well as other great wealth my husband possesses, which he received in past times from his brother Kuber, the lord of worldly wealth appointed by the devas. He intends to wipe out the surviving rakshasa clans, and take command of Lanka for himself. No doubt he means to place some surrogate upon the throne, while he returns to Ayodhya and uses his new-found glory to inveigle his way back on to the sunwood throne. It is a fine plan he has schemed up, and were it not for my husband being rejuvenated and in full possession of his powers, it is a plan that would have succeeded. Rama would have committed genocide once more, wiping out the last of the Asura races, and wresting a rich kingdom for his own.'

She paused, her proud mouth parting in the semblance of a sneer. 'No doubt he hoped to enjoy the other spoils of such a conquest. I hear that ever since his ravishment and subsequent betrayal of Supanakha, he has developed a taste for rakshasi bodies that—'

Sita's hand shot out and slammed into the jaw of the rakshasi queen. The blow was so fast and filled with such fury, for it came instinctively and without any predetermination, that it rocked the rakshasi, nearly twice Sita's size, upon her heels, then caused her to lose her balance. She would have fallen but for the ashoka tree beside her, which she caught hold of just in time. The other rakshasas, standing and sitting around, listening with rapt attention to their mistress's tale, were shocked at the sudden assault. In the brief moment that they were incapacitated by the sheer suddenness of the blow, Sita could have leapt upon the rakshasi queen and torn her throat out – with her own teeth if need be. But instead, she only stood over the fallen rakshasi and spoke to her in measured words that came out like arrowheads from a wound, so painful was the act of defending what ought not to have needed defending in the first place.

'Rama is no less than a deva,' she said. 'It is your husband who is the demon! He has warped the truth and fed it to you as a sheaf of lies, and you are foolish enough to have believed him. Rama and I were at the end of our exile and on our way home in a few moons. Your husband came and abducted me by using force and trickery. If Rama does come here with an army now, he is justified in doing so. But he has no designs on your damnable kingdom, nor on you or your other ugly-mouthed rakshasas. Rama is a warrior of dharma. It is the only thing that drives him. How could you ever hope to understand that, you creature of hell!'

She would have gone on, but by then the first of the rakshasas had reached her and pulled her away from their queen. She was slammed back against the weeping willow, a rakshasi hand pressing her throat until she choked, and the foul breath of the one whom they called Vikata washed over her. 'Let me kill her, mistress. I shall kill her and then we shall all eat her, piece by piece. Or, if you prefer, we can tear chunks out of her body and eat her while she still lives. They taste much better when the blood still flows through the flesh.'

'No!' screeched the old one named Trijata. 'If you harm her then the gods will rain destruction upon us all!'

'Kill her! Kill her! Kill her and eat her!' cried the other rakshasas in an irregular chorus.

'Silence,' said their mistress, regaining her feet shakily. The side of her face was discoloured from the blow. Sita's fist ached as well, but she hardly cared. She would rather be beaten and tortured than listen to any more lies defaming Rama. Even now, she struggled defiantly against the large rakshasi's iron grasp. The queen looked at her with a strange equanimity, as if Sita's outburst had only confirmed her worst beliefs about mortals. 'There will be no killing and no eating. She is a valuable source of information to my husband. And a hostage of war. That is the only reason he agreed to her request to bring her here to Lanka, and keeps her fed and cared for. When the time comes, she may provide him with important information about Rama's war tactics. And when her information runs out, then she may be usable as a hostage. Not that a warlord as evil as Rama would care what happens to one of his many trifles. No doubt he has found a dozen to replace her already. But still, until then, she will not be harmed physically.'

Vikata turned her head back to Sita, her fangs dripping saliva on to Sita's shoulders. 'Hear that, puny mortal? If not for my mistress, you would be meat in my belly now. But some day your time will come, and then Vikata will be here to take her pound of flesh – and liver. I relish mortal livers. But for now . . . go! Live!'

She shoved Sita backwards, hard enough to make her fall and strike her head against some unseen object. For a moment the world turned black.

When she was able to see again, the rakshasi queen was standing over her, the other rakshasas close enough to defend her if Sita attempted another assault.

'Would that Ravana had never set eyes on your husband Rama. Would that their paths had never crossed. Would that Ravana had not agreed to your demand for asylum and brought you here. But all that is done. It is written in the books of karma now. And so we must play the game that is dealt to us. I shall honour my husband's wish. You shall be kept alive and unharmed. He has given me the responsibility of your care, and these companions of mine, my own sakshis, will be entrusted with the task of guarding you night and day.' She started to raise her hand to her injured jaw, then stopped, too proud to show her pain before her enemy. 'But know this. The devas watch us every minute. And though they do not judge us, yet we are judged by our own selves, for each word we say and deed we commit adds to the weight of our karma, for better or worse. And your evil husband Rama will not succeed in his plans. If we need your help for that, so be it. We will do what we must, and we shall prevail, as we have for so many millennia.'

She turned and walked away, calling out instructions to her minions. 'Stay with her. Watch her closely. But do not lay hands on her or harm her in any fashion. I shall not tolerate any who disobey. Vikata?'

'I hear you well,' said the hulking rakshasi, hawking and spitting angrily into the waterfall pond.

Sita sat up. 'Wait!' she called. 'Listen to me. You have been wrongly informed. My husband is not what you say he is. Rama is the most honourable man alive. You must believe me.'

The rakshasi queen paused and turned her head. 'What is the mortal woman blabbering about?'

One of the others, an enormously fat, big-bellied rakshasi, shrugged. 'Who knows, mistress. She yelled some gibberish earlier too, when she attacked you. No doubt she is cursing us all in her own tongue. These mortals cannot speak without using the vilest blasphemies and oaths. I hear that the first words a mortal babe utters are insults against her own mother and father! They have no shame or morality.'

'No!' Sita cried, and there were tears running down her cheeks now. 'Why do you not understand me? I can follow every word you say. Use your magic to translate my words as well. You must hear what I say. Rama is innocent! He is blameless of the crimes you accuse him of. *He* is the one wronged and maltreated. It is your husband Ravana who is the perpetrator of this whole plot. Please, in the name of the Goddess our Mother, heed my words!'

One of the other rakshasas cocked her head to one side. 'It sounds so ugly, their talk, does it not?'

'Like crows squabbling over scraps,' said the fifth and last one.

The rakshasi queen gazed at Sita a moment longer. 'I will pray that you find peace here,' she said quietly. 'That you repent the error of your ways and ask forgiveness. When and if you are ready to do prayaschitt for your sins, I will be there to help you. We are honourable followers of dharma. That is why we will triumph in the end over your evil husband.'

And with those words, she turned and was gone.

'Wait!' Sita cried again. 'Hear me!'

But nobody understood her. Her words remained incomprehensible to them, the blasphemous blabbering of a heathen pagan mortal. It was the supreme irony, and Sita knew now that this was Ravana's doing as well, the perfect way to promote his jaundiced version of things and suppress all other versions, including the truth, which only he and Sita knew. He had used his sorcery, or the sorcery of this place, to translate their words for Sita's benefit, but not the other way around. For all Sita knew, even the rakshasi queen had spoken her long tirade only to unburden her own heavy mind, not caring if Sita truly followed every word or not.

Their mistress gone, the other rakshasas looked at each other and suddenly broke out in a clamour. They converged on Sita, who drew herself up, striking and bruising her shoulder against the tree, not the willow this time, but the ashoka tree, the one which the queen had caught hold of. There was a whole grove of them here, neat, perfect rows of ashokas. At one time Sita had loved to see groves of the trees. Loved the way they bent over in the strongest wind, but never broke. She leaned against one now, and stared with throbbing head and watering eyes as the clutch of demonesses surrounded her, laughing and gesturing.

'We cannot touch her,' the one named Vikata reminded them all, flashing her yellow fangs. 'But our mistress laid no bar against our calling her names. Let us tell her what we think of females like her. Mortal women who assault our queen and attempt to seduce our king. Let us show her how language itself can be an instrument of torture.'

Vikata leered at them all, then turned to Sita, grinning even wider, showing her rotting, pus-suppurated gums. 'She can scream as loud as she likes. She has no champions here.'

KAAND 2

PRAYERS TO BROKEN STONES

I

_____

Rama heard the scream across the ocean and looked up. Squinting against the dazzling late-morning sunlight, he saw the silhouette of a bird far in the distance, floating above the ocean, its wings parted to catch the high air currents. The sound came again, a distant, mournful scree, and this time he recognised it for the bird's cry. But for an instant, just a brief heart-stopping moment, it had sounded like . . .

He shook his head and turned away. Hanuman was watching him intently. 'What is it, Rama?'

Rama exhaled slowly. 'Nothing, my friend. Only the ears playing tricks on the mind.'

Hanuman looked at him as if he wished to ask a question. The vanar was about to speak when a cry alerted them both. They turned and looked up.

They were standing on the far end of the crescent-shaped beach overlooked by Mount Mahendra, upon a cluster of large black-rock boulders that framed this end of the sandy strip. The ocean lay to their right, receded several dozen yards as the tide was out. Across the strip, the sand rose in undulating dunes to the foot of the mountain, then ran up at a sharp concave angle to the jutting lip of the mountain's flat top. The summit was crowded with hundreds upon hundreds of vanars and bears, all intent upon their work. Rama could see Lakshman shouting orders to the vanars, gesturing animatedly. Jambavan's distinctive head was visible too, looming above the vanars and even above his fellow bears. The bear king's ears were twitching furiously, which meant he was agitated. Both Lakshman and Jambavan were superseded by Nala, a Kiskindha vanar known for his prowess at building and architecture, who was officially the master-builder in charge of constructing the bridge to Lanka.

The lines of vanars and bears extended to the right, disappearing briefly where the cliff-face of the mountain twisted, then appearing again, running down the side of the range, and further back out of sight. Rama and Hanuman had only just come from there, and he strained to see how the work was going. It was hard to tell: all he could see right now were vanars and bears milling about in what seemed to be outright chaos. But he knew that there was purpose in that chaotic milling, and that each individual was performing a pre-designated task. After much trial and error they had come to this division of labour, and it was only today that Nala had politely but firmly suggested to Rama and Hanuman that they take charge of the beach detail.

Rama looked to the left, seeking out the vanars and bears under his and Hanuman's command. They were lined up along the dunes, extending back over the edge, the majority of them following the order to keep the beach itself clear. But it had been a long, searing-hot morning, with little to do but wait, and several dozen had trickled down to the beach, some to gain a better view of the work atop Mahendra, others, vanars mostly, to get a closer glimpse of the feared salt desert. Some of these, emboldened by having stayed successfully unharmed for so many hours, had plonked themselves down on the sand and were reclining in attitudes of bold indifference, demonstrating their courage to their less confident fellows up on the dunes. Rama saw one vanar sitting on the sand only a few feet from the foamy lip of the receding tide, dipping his tail into the froth then raising it high, eliciting hoos and haas from the watching vanars on the dunes. It was Sakra, of course. Hanuman's half-brother seemed to find new and innovative ways of causing mischief each day. The little vanar was so clumsy that Nala had begged Hanuman to take him off the mountain and put him anywhere, just to keep him out of his way. Hanuman had found some make-work task for the fellow to do – ferrying fresh waterskins to slake the thirst of the bridge-builders as they worked. Right now, Sakra's skins of water lay beside him as he played the dip-the-tail game to show off his lack of fear of the sea desert. No doubt he hoped to impress the females on the dunes by this antic.

Rama shook his head in exasperation. 'Tell that idiot to get out of there now.'

Hanuman glanced impassively at the tail-dipper. Even his infinite patience had been tested to its limits by Sakra's antics. 'Ignore him, Rama. He'll move quickly enough in a moment. Vanars learn better by example and experience than by following orders.' He didn't need to add that Sakra revelled in drawing attention to himself. The more loudly he was berated, the more mischief he got up to.

Another cry from the top of the mountain alerted them. They gazed up, shielding their eyes against the sun, and saw the crowd on the clifftop parting to leave a space clear. Lakshman and Jambavan had vanished. The roaring and shouting along the dunes died down, leaving only the ceaseless pounding and shirring of the sea. Gulls flew overhead, calling. Rama heard a crab scuttling between the boulders on which he stood, and then splashing into the water below. The vanars and bears on the beach looked up, aware that the moment they had been waiting for all morning had arrived. Most of the curious line-breakers retreated up the dunes, behind the boundary that had been marked out by Hanuman earlier. Still the foolhardly vanar sat by the tideline, dipping his tail and holding it up. For a moment, the universe held still, waiting.

Then a large black shape appeared on the top of the moun-tain. It moved very slowly, in tiny increments of distance, as it had moved all morning. It was a gigantic boulder, twice as large as the one on which Rama and Hanuman stood. It was easily the height of a palm tree, and as wide. Black as pitch, and misshapen from millennia of erosion, it was nonetheless rounded enough to be rolled up the mountainside by a few thousand vanars and bears all pushing at once. Even though Rama could not see it, he knew of the mighty struggle going on up there. What strain those creatures must be labouring under, to push that great rock all the way up the mountain. He and Hanuman had been there to help pick out a suitable boulder to start the enterprise, had given a hand themselves in dislodging the giant from its ancient perch. Hard as it had been to overcome inertia and get that monster moving, it had been tortuous to push it up the side of the mountain. Hundreds of vanars had been delegated the task of clearing the path, picking out stones and pebbles, filling in and tamping holes that could cause one of those pushing to lurch or stumble. A hundred bears were the backbone of the effort, doing the actual pushing of the boulder. Hundreds more fanned out in a giant formation, each pushing the back of the one above, in order to spread the weight and pressure. The vanars took the awkward smaller places in between the bears, taking the pressure where the larger creatures could not fit, stabilising the overall load. Slowly, painfully, working all morning, they had managed to move the boulder to the top of the mountain. At that point, Rama and Hanuman had set off for the beach, to prepare for their side of the work. When they left, Nala had been hopping from one foot to the other, screaming orders nonstop.

Even this method was the result of much trial and error. Pushing giant rocks up mountains did not come naturally to either bears or vanars – or to any species, for that matter. Lakshman had taken Rama aside and suggested that by placing sheared tree trunks beneath the boulder, they could roll it along more effectively. Rama had disagreed, not only because of the bears' staunch refusal to 'murder' trees, but because he felt the boulder was much to heavy and because the added height would make it near impossible for the bears and vanars to place their hands upon it to push. Now he wondered if he had been too hasty in dismissing Lakshman's suggestion. They might have used ropes, he realised, long ropes to pull the boulder uphill.

Anything to make it easier. Several vanars and bears had already died or been maimed in the initial efforts, crushed when the boulder rolled too quickly down little slopes or when it fell back upon those pushing. Rama's heart had wept for those brave souls who sacrificed themselves, and swelled with pride at the hordes who had stepped up to take their place.

Nala, of course, had been inconsolable, feeling personally responsible for each death. As Rama had comforted the master-builder, he had wished there was some better way, some method that reduced the risk to life and limb. But in the same instant, he knew that there was no way to eliminate loss completely, that there would always be a price to be paid, that there were no ropes to be had, and even if there were, that they could break, the logs splinter. He must trust in the stout hearts and wills of his followers and believe that those hearts were stronger than the thickest ropes could ever be, their wills hardier than even the densest logs.

The boulder came into view in stages, first only its rounded top appearing above the mountain's flat top, then a larger wedge, then, after several anxious moments of waiting, a semicircular portion. Over the next half-hour or so, it came entirely into view, dwarfing the tiny silhouettes of the animals around it, making Rama wonder how they could possibly have manipulated such a great bulk. And yet there it was at last, a boulder the size of a large house, standing on the rim of the cliff, proof that strong wills could move mountains – or boulders at least.

A figure appeared to one side of the boulder, and from the way the sun caught the figure's brown fur, Rama recognised Kambunara. The bear raised both arms into the air and waved them slowly from side to side. Hanuman waved back in response, then turned to Rama.

'They are ready, Rama. Shall we proceed?'

Rama scanned the shore. The tide was almost fully out now and thrice the usual span of beach was visible, the wet sand glistening in the sun. The ocean seemed enormous and placid, sunlight catching rising waves and twinkling at him, a giant wink of amusement at the thought of these puny creatures attempting to bridge its vast expanse. The day was clear and the sky almost empty of clouds. The world seemed to be watching curiously, to see if Rama could achieve the next step in this enormous undertaking. He experienced a moment of great trepidation, a self-questioning instant wherein he wondered if it was truly worth all this, so many labouring so hard, struggling against such great odds, before they could even begin a war. And if the struggle to reach Lanka was so enormous, imagine what the war would be like. He felt his resolve falter a brief instant, and heard his own voice speak doubtfully within the echoing space of his mind: Is it really worth it? Why are we making such a huge effort? Look at the way these people have toiled all morning, just to raise one boulder, a single rock. Do I really expect to build an entire bridge this way? To span an ocean? Miles upon miles of undulating sea? How many boulders? How many broken backs and crushed bones and lives sacrificed? And then what? Another war. Yet another terrible, doomed, life-extinguishing, horror-wreaking war. How do I justify it all?

A bird cry broke through his thoughts. Without turning to look, he knew it was the same bird that had called earlier. A sea hawk perhaps, or a falcon, perhaps even a vulture. He did not know. But its cry, so mournful and soulful and filled with sadness and longing, cut through to his heart. And it brought the image of Sita flooding back into his mind: Sita sitting by his side in their little hut and talking to him about returning to Ayodhya; Sita dreaming of home and peace and children; Sita before her abduction; Sita, who had done nothing to merit such a fate, who depended now on him and him alone to come and free her. It sounded as if the bird spoke for her, with her voice, tugging at his conscience, calling to him. *Come, save me. Save me, Rama.*

Was it worth the price? So many lives, so much effort, to save only one person? He did not know. All he knew was that he could not fail her, he must go on, and he would not cease trying.

More than this, he did not know.

'Yes,' he said at last. 'Proceed.'

Hanuman did not comment on the long wait for his response, or say anything else. He only raised his arms again and waved in a pre-arranged gesture, and was answered by the tiny silhouette of Kambunara. The bear turned away and shouted something to those pushing the boulder. There was a scurrying around, as positions were altered to prepare for the final step of the boulder's journey. Then one last signal from the bear, and the time for going back was past.

The boulder rolled forward in lurching, drunken increments, slowing, then stopping as it reached the very lip of the cliff-face. It teetered on the rim, as those behind it made one final superhuman effort, then gave itself to gravity. Rama could hear the voice of Lakshman now, shouting the final orders, his words indecipherable at this distance, but the urgency unmistakable. Then even Lakshman's voice was stilled, and silence fell upon the bears and vanars once more, as the matter went out of their control and was given over to nature.

The rock hung on the edge of the clifftop, like a marble hesitating before rolling into a little hole in a child's game. For a moment it seemed as if it would stay suspended there for ever, stuck to the cliff. Then it relinquished its hold on the earth and fell.

It plummeted for perhaps a hundred and fifty yards without encountering any obstacle. Then it brushed against an over-hanging rock, which shattered to smithereens, sending debris flying dozens of yards in every direction. Rama saw one fragment rise in an arc that took it thirty yards or more out into the sea, where it landed with a splash like a whale's spout. The sound of the impact, so slight and seemingly negligible, was like a stroke of thunder in the silent morning, crashing against the face of the cliff and echoing back.

The rock continued its downward descent as if the overhang had never existed. It reached the point where the cliff-face curved outwards again, the slope more gentle. Here it landed with a second impact that dwarfed the first, an explosion of sound that boomed like a bolt from Indra's fist, and Rama felt the rock on which he stood shiver. The vanars on the dunes screamed and screeched and retreated further back, only their eagerness to see more keeping them from bolting outright. Sakra, still bravely sitting by the tideline, leapt up into the air as if launched by a bent sapling, and scampered up the beach to join his fellows, quivering with fear. All thought of impressing the females had fled from his mind.

The boulder rolled down the slope at the bottom of the mountain, gathering great momentum. It bounced and leapt into the air, flying a good twenty or more yards out, then thudded with yet another ground-shaking impact on the exposed sand of the tide-abandoned beach. Here, its powerful forward motion was absorbed almost entirely by the soft, yielding sand, and after a half-roll it came to an abrupt halt some few yards from the lip of foam. Had the ground been hard and rocky here, instead of soft and wet and sandy, the boulder would easily have rolled right up to the place where Rama and Hanuman stood, crushing them as easily as a bladder-ball crushed two blades of grass.

But the sand had taken possession of the boulder now.

It lay there, silent and still, its energies expended, its travelling done. In its wake, debris and fragments continued to roll down the cliffside a moment or two longer. The ocean sighed and soughed rhythmically. Gulls cried out angrily, furious at this violation of the natural order.

Then, as one, the armies cheered. Their collective throats roared out their satisfaction and pleasure at this task accomplished. They had beaten the rock. These puny beings had raised that great weight up the side of the towering mountain and flung it down to the beach below. They had moved it as they had intended to move it.

Hanuman and Rama leapt down from their perch and ran across the beach. The bears and vanars on the dunes, after a moment's hesitation, let out a chorus of whooping cries, then ran down too. Rama felt the wet sand yield beneath his feet, his soles leaving deep prints that would be filled with brine. He felt the wind on his sun-burned face, the salt chafing at his chapped lips. He heard Hanuman's steady, deep nasal breathing beside him, felt the pounding of his heart echoed in the impact each footfall made as it landed on the sand, and saw the vanars and bears upon the mountaintop raise their arms and roar with delight as they looked down upon the fruits of their labour.

Hanuman reached the boulder a fraction before Rama did. Barely touching the jagged side of the rock, the vanar launched himself up, up, seeming to leap almost in a single bound to its top. Rama had to pause and climb, seeking out footholds and handholds and working his way upward with effort. Hanuman's hand reached down to haul him up the last yard or two, and then he was standing beside his vanar ally, a dozen yards above the beach.

He raised his arms and let out a cry of triumph.

It was echoed by a million throats.

2

Work progressed slowly.

With each passing day, more lives were lost. Mainly vanars, for the smaller, less muscled creatures were crushed easily beneath the huge boulders. Bears were not spared either. Seven bears were killed when a boulder rolled back after one of them put his foot into a rabbit hole and lost his balance. Almost twice that number fell and were smashed on the sea-washed crags below the cliff when the ground at the edge gave way as they were manoeuvring a boulder over.

And that was the least of their problems. On the beach below, it was proving very hard to move the boulders those last few precious yards. The original plan had been to roll the boulders down to the beach, then move them to the edge of the promontory, extending this natural jetty farther and farther out into the ocean. But they had not reckoned on the unfamiliar terrain of wet sand. The soft, yielding surface became a sucking pit beneath the weight of the huge boulders. And for several valuable hours each day, when the tide was in, it was virtually uncrossable. This was despite the vanars overcoming their natural fear of the ocean – dry or wet, low tide or high, the sand simply would not support the great weight.

After a series of brave but futile attempts, Rama and Hanuman decided that each boulder must be carried over the promontory. The rocky crag itself would then act as firm ground over which to move. It took most of a full day to move the first boulder to the end of the promontory. The moss and lichen growing on the wet rocks could be cleaned away, but what was to be done about the never-ending bombardment of seagull guano that fell all day long, splattering the tops of the rocks and making them dangerously slippery? Or the waves that washed continually over them and caused the rock-carriers to lose their footing? And there were gaps between the rocks on the promontory, into which legs slipped and whole vanar torsos were swallowed.

A total of seventeen vanar and bear lives were lost that first day on the beach. Rama was nursing a gash on his right shoulder, caused when the boulder he, along with a hundred others, was helping carry slipped a fraction of an inch. Had it slipped more than an inch, it would have shattered his collar-bone to powder. He ignored the running blood and stayed under the rock, determined that nobody would do anything that he would not do himself.

Within a week, the overall death count – on the mountain-side as well as the beach below – went easily into the hundreds. Every night the pyres burned at the top of the beach, a sobering reminder that for those unfortunates, the war was already over. But each day before dawn, they were all ready and at work once more, even those nursing broken limbs and cracked skulls and other minor or major injuries. By the end of the week, there were too many such partially injured to count easily.

By the tenth day, Rama began to feel his heart sinking, like a boulder into the soft sand. It was evident now that the bridge would take a great deal longer than anticipated. In these ten days, they had amassed enough rocks to extend the promontory about fifty yards into the sea. Fifty precious yards, wrested from the ocean by copious blood-sacrifice and great toil.

He was standing on the farthermost edge of that extension, at the tip of Rama's Bridge, as they all called it now. Two or three yards below his feet, the ocean swelled and sank, an occasional wave washing high enough to spray him lightly. The sun was angled in the western sky, somewhere between noon and sundown. On the top of the mountain, a new boulder was being brought up. Meanwhile, Hanuman and the others were moving not one but three separate boulders across the promontory. Rama had been under one of those three black monsters since daybreak, toiling without a rest, until Hanuman had ordered him replaced and scolded him roundly for not taking any nourishment since waking. The vanar seemed to grow in strength and confidence with each passing day. His strength was amazing. There was a heart-stopping moment when a bear had slipped between two rocks, his spine snapped in two, and two vanars had leapt in to take his place, for they were all now inured to the constant toll demanded by their work. Even as the vanars replaced their fallen bear comrade, another vanar at the other end of the boulder had lost his footing, and the whole gang was unbalanced. In another moment they would have lost their hold and the boulder would have come crashing down on them all, killing scores.

Hanuman had leapt beneath the boulder, on the side where it was faltering, and grasped it with both hands, squeezing into an impossibly narrow space between two bears. Even then, his normal strength would hardly have been sufficient to restore the lost equilibrium. Rama had been under another boulder himself, close enough to the edge to see what was happening, but unable to break away or help. He had watched, horrified. But then an astonishing thing had happened. Hanuman had grown. Rama saw it with his own eyes, or he might not have believed it. The vanar flexed his muscles, expanding them and taking in a great lungful of air. Any strong person might do the same, but Hanuman's expanding body had not stopped at the limit of his muscles' span. In moments, the other astonished vanars and bears around him found the boulder lifted above their heads, out of the reach of their own arms. And Hanuman had continued growing, until he was twice as tall as any bear, with the entire weight of the boulder resting on his bent arms alone.

'Clear the way,' he had shouted, his voice muffled, yet clear enough beneath the boulder.

His neighbours had moved aside like wheatstalks parting

before a horse, staring with incredulous eyes, gibbering and grunting and pointing. Hanuman had taken a step to one side, staggering beneath the unspeakable weight, and Rama had thought for one soul-chilling moment that his friend would fall into the ocean and be crushed beneath the stone. But then Hanuman had exerted one last enormous effort, and to Rama's surprise the boulder had risen up, lifted by the vanar's own two arms and nothing else, and Hanuman had flung it bodily beyond the edge of the promontory, into the sea. It had fallen with a great splash, drenching everyone for dozens of yards around with brine. Nobody cared. After a shocked moment, they were all cheering, as they had done that first day, and then they crowded around Hanuman, clapping him on the back, hugging him and licking him and nuzzling him.

Hanuman was back to normal size again.

'I can't explain it,' he said that sundown as they sat to eat their evening meal. Rama was still wet from the acamana and the wind was cool on his hair. 'I only knew that I needed more strength than I had, more strength than I could possibly have, and the next moment I had that strength. I don't know how I grew larger. It was as if I was someone else and I was doing it all, and I was aware of it but still not wholly myself.'

He looked around apologetically at the many curious faces watching him. 'That's all I can think of to say. I don't know anything else about it.'

Jambavan grunted. 'Better to have infinite strength yet not be aware of it than to be a puny man who considers himself a giant.'

Lakshman frowned at the bear king. 'What exactly does that mean? How can anyone not know their own strength? How could any vanar possibly double in size and then reduce to normal size again? And how could anyone lift a boulder that size just like that?'

The bear king's eyes glinted in the dusky light. There was no fire. Bears and vanars did not sit around one and Rama had accustomed himself to eating uncooked food. 'Do you know the answers to all the questions in creation, brother Lakshman? What does it matter, the how and the why? This happened. That is all we need to know.'

'But will it happen again tomorrow?' Lakshman demanded. 'Can Hanuman do this at will? If yes, then he can virtually build the bridge on his own! And if he can do it, why not the other vanars? Or the bears? Why not yourself, King Jambavan? With that kind of strength, we could finish this task in days!'

As against months or seasons, Rama added mentally but did not say. 'I am sure we all wish for the same,' he said aloud. 'Even if only Hanuman can summon up such reserves of strength and ability, it would help us in our task a great deal.'

'Ah,' Nala said, releasing the word like a great pent-up sigh. In his eyes, Rama could see visions of Hanuman rolling rocks as easily as bales of straw, and his great bridge being constructed in mere days.

Hanuman looked at Rama. 'My lord, whatever strength I possess is given by you.'

'Well spoken,' Jambavan rasped.

Lakshman looked at each of them in turn. 'Well spoken? What? That Hanuman's strength is derived from Rama? By that argument, Rama should be able to lift a boulder in each hand and toss them over the mountain straight into the ocean!'

Jambavan snorted. 'You take things too literally at times, brother. What Hanuman meant was that his love for and faith in Rama is the source of his strength.'

'Very well,' Lakshman conceded reasonably. 'But that still does not answer the question: Can he or can he not summon up that strength at will?'

'When the time comes, he will summon up far greater powers. What you saw today was only a small demonstration. Once he is ready, he will be able not only to toss boulders over mountains as you suggested, but to pick up whole mountains if he desires.'

Lakshman was silenced. Rama stared at the bear king, unable to tell whether the ancient rksa was being literal now or mystical.

Soon after, the topic changed – everyone had various ideas about how they might carry the rocks more effectively to the promontory. None of the ideas proved workable. The sandy beach made it impossible to take the stones any other way. After debating fruitlessly for a while, they resigned themselves to the existing method and moved on to discussing other matters.

That was yesterday. Today, thus far at least, Hanuman had not displayed any sign of repeating his extraordinary feat, and not for want of trying. Rama had twice seen the vanar put his shoulder to a rock and try to heave it up, and each time the rock had won the contest. After that, Hanuman had decided not to try again, and even the entreaties and encouragements offered by his fellow rock-lifters could not persuade him to make a third attempt.

In the afternoon, the weather began to change. It began with a wind, nothing more. Restless, milling about, causing sand dervishes that irritated all, blowing salt spray into their eyes but doing little harm. Nobody paid it much heed. But then the sea began to rise more than usual, each wave arching higher and falling farther inland. Never had they seen the tide rise so fast or so high. Soon all the fallen boulders were waterlogged and the vanars and bears attempting to carry them were immersed at various levels. It was not so bad for the bears, since the water came up to their haunches at worst, but most of the vanars were floundering, some in neck-high water. And still the ocean kept rising, the wind kept growing stronger, and the temperature dropped steadily, despite the sun's presence.

Then sulky dark clouds began rolling in across the sea, lightning flickering inside their enormous bellies like devas warring listlessly, deep sub-aural grumblings and grindings warning of things to come.

The beach and mountainside were buzzing with ill omens and portents seen and unsuitable dreams experienced the night before. Some had seen flocks of inauspicious birds flying in the wrong direction, others had felt twitching in the eyes and right-hand limbs, and so on. Rama had never been particularly superstitious, and could not have identified an ill omen if it flew over him with banners unfurled and embroidered with warnings writ large, but he knew enough about such things to understand that they indicated some larger disturbance in the natural order. The gurus had taught them how nature always issued warnings to living creatures in the event of any calamity. This was why rats knew to desert a burning house or a sinking seacraft, and why birds lost their sense of direction and flew in inauspicious ways before the approach of a storm.

None of his people was inclined to work. Several of the Kiskindha vanars were already squatting high on the dunes, arranging themselves in mandalas and chanting verses to ward off the ill will of Lord Varuna. The Mandaras were miserable and wet but still struggled to toil on beside their bear brothers to lift the three newly rolled-down boulders, though there was more chance of the poor fellows drowning than actually moving the rocks. There had been much mixing of the tribes these past days, with everyone focusing on the given task rather than on clan or tribal organisation. But the change of weather frightened them all and they were fast falling back into their traditional lines. Rama saw his workers gathering instinctively in clan-clusters, disturbed by the stormy weather and the rising ocean. He did not rebuke or order anyone: it was brave enough of them to stay their ground in the face of such things. Only weeks earlier, few of them had ever seen the ocean in their lives before, let alone dreamed they would come so close to the dreaded thing.

He waited to see how things played out. Surely the storm would pass quickly, surely it was no more than a passing disturbance; the monsoons were over, were they not? But he had heard tell that in these southern climes there was often a second monsoon, one that came during the winter months and which brought fierce typhoons and cyclones. He did not think such a storm might be coming; it could not, must not. He put it out of his mind and continued his work: carrying smaller stones from the beach and using them to plug the gaps and holes in the bridge. As he toiled, a wave rose up over him from behind

– he heard the shouted warning from one of the vanars accompanying him just before it struck – and broke upon his back. The force of the current was almost enough to sweep him off his feet and into the ocean. He gritted his teeth, shutting his eyes against the stinging onslaught, and resisted the watery claws tugging insistently at his feet.

The bears seemed unperturbed by the coming storm. As Rama waited for the line of vanars to hand up another stone, on the far side of the beach a boulder was being hoisted slowly and painfully by the bears. There were no vanars in the group because of the incoming tide. But Hanuman was in the midst of them, at the most dangerous point beneath the stone, heaving manfully. Rama watched as an incoming wave crashed into them, splashing over the boulder itself, and the whole group disappeared from view beneath the wall of water. When it cleared, the bears sputtering and spitting water but unable to shake their soaked fur, he saw that the impact had dangerously unbalanced the whole group. Several tense moments passed as Hanuman shouted orders to bears on his right and left, fore and aft. The bears and vanars on the beach watched tensely as well, and for a few heartbeats it seemed that the group was certain to lose the unequal battle. Rama prayed that another wave did not come crashing into them just then.

Somehow, though, partly through Hanuman's clever commands to adjust their balance and largely through the sheer will of the bears, they managed to regain command of the rock and resume their slow forward motion again. Another wave did come then, and almost buried them again, but they were able to withstand it and carry on. Water foamed and seethed continually around their waists, giving the bears a straggly, wretched appearance that made Rama feel sorry for them. Several of them had bare patches on their fur through which livid wounds and scrapes showed, evidence of the price they paid for their achievements. This bridge, he thought with tightly clenched fists, is being built with the bones and blood of these people, not just with stones and rocks.

'So what do you think caused it?'

Rama had no need to turn to look at Lakshman. He had seen his brother coming down the mountain and over the dunes, pausing briefly to watch the desperate struggle of the bears before making his way over the bridge. He had no need to ask Lakshman what he meant either; he knew the question referred to Hanuman's show of strength.

Rama shrugged, as much to attempt to alleviate the tight muscular tension in his body as to respond to Lakshman's query. 'Nothing so far,' he said. 'He hasn't done it today.'

'I know *that*,' Lakshman said with a trace of impatience. 'It's been the only thing everyone's been talking about since morning. Has he, hasn't he, not yet, not today, not ever again.'

'I wouldn't go that far. I don't think what he did yesterday was a fluke. It was his own doing. I saw it. It reminded me of . . .' He shook his head. 'I'm sure he will be able to do it again.'

'What were you about to say?' He felt Lakshman's eyes on him, watching him knowingly. 'You were going to say it reminded you of the time Brahmarishi Vishwamitra gave us the maha-mantras Bala and Atibala, weren't you? The kind of super-human strength we gained at that time. Maha-shakti. You think Hanuman has been given a similar mantra by someone? A certain wise and inscrutable old bear, perhaps?'

Rama was about to answer when suddenly a cry came to them above the keening wind and the crashing ocean, the chanting of the vanars on the beach and the grunts and gruff shouts of the bears at work. He looked up and saw the silhouettes of bears and vanars on the mountain, crying out and flailing their hands. Jambavan was there too, standing to one side of a huge boulder, certainly the largest they had mined since that monstrous one on the first day. The bear king and his generals were straining at the boulder, struggling. Not to tip it over as they usually did, but to stop it.

Lakshman cursed. 'It must have rolled. The ground is eroded there.'

He sprinted back down the length of the bridge, all fifty or so yards of it, leaping nimbly over the wave-washed, guano-slippery rocks, even though it would be quite impossible for him to run all the way back up the mountain in time. Rama let him go, knowing that Lakshman had come down only because the work on the mountain had been suspended until the boulder being moved below had been carried out of the way. That boulder up there had been much farther back on the clifftop, almost out of sight, when Rama had last glanced up. It must have been set into motion by the ground at the edge giving way. He could see the rim of the cliff-face crumbling a little, debris falling like crumbs from a hungry mouth. The constant rolling of immense boulders over the edge had inevitably taken its toll; the ground at the edge of the cliff had been steadily eroded. At the meeting of leaders the night before, Lakshman had warned that something like this might happen, but Jambavan had only grunted and said that until they built another mountain or removed this one from their way, they would have to make do.

Rama looked down and saw a frightening sight. Hanuman and the bears were directly below the boulder, only a few dozen yards from the bottom of the cliff. If Jambavan's team could not halt that great boulder from rolling over the edge, Hanuman and the bears would not be able to put down their rock and move away in time. One way or another, they would all be crushed to death.

3

The great rock teetered on the rim of the cliff. Without taking his eyes off it, Rama was aware of a single figure running madly up the mountain. He knew it was Lakshman. He would not reach the top in time. It did not matter. Nothing Lakshman or anyone else did could stop what was happening. The rock was too close to the edge and the edge was crumbling too fast. As it was, the bears, supervised by a madly dancing Nala, were desperately attempting to push it back, risking their lives in the process, for they were the only thing that stood between that rock and the fall. Still they strained and sweated valiantly, knowing that the lives of their brothers and sisters below were at stake. At one point, Nala himself put his hands on the back of one of the bears, as if by adding his few ounces of strength he could tip the balance in their favour. There was no place for more helping hands to fit.

On the beach below, Hanuman and his fellow rock-carriers were still labouring beneath their crushing burden. They were a good ten yards from safety, Rama estimated, and even that was uncertain, for who knew exactly how far a rock might roll after falling from such a height?

He turned and sprinted over the bridge, almost dashing into the stunned vanars busy staring at the unfolding calamity. He shouted to them to move, and when he was still a long way from the tideline, leapt off the rocks and into the water. He landed with a resounding splash, and fought his way chest-deep through the swell. An incoming wave almost lifted him off his feet. Glancing up as he half swam, half ran, he saw that the cliff edge was crumbling further, fist-sized stones falling away steadily now. A bear at the very edge lost his footing and fell to his death below, not a word of protest leaving his mouth in that final descent. Jambavan's deep-throated roar urged the others to fight, fight on, as if it was a battle they were fighting, not a rock.

Rama reached the place where the bears and Hanuman were waging a battle of their own. He splashed his way around towards the beachward side of the group straining beneath the weight of the boulder, trying to see the vanar. But Hanuman was surrounded by the press of dark wet fur and the light in the sky had dimmed to twilight duskiness. Rama went close enough to shout above the raging sea and called out his friend's name.

'Hanuman, listen to me. Do not attempt to reply, I know you cannot speak. Only listen to my words.'

He spat out seawater swallowed inadvertently during his frantic run, and took a deep breath.

'My friend, I know you have great power in your veins. I do not claim to understand what infinite source gives you that power. But you said yesterday that whatever strength you possess was given by me. Very well. In that case, I now give you all my strength, all the power I have possessed before, and all I will possess in ages to come. Take it. Take my strength and save yourself and save these brave allies of ours. Act now, Hanuman Maruti Anjaneya. Act now and save the day.'

And he uttered the most powerful mantra he knew, the Maha-mantra Gayatri, whispered into the ears of newborn infants that their souls, that portion of brahman granted to each living being, could awaken and channel the power of the infinite shakti that created and maintained the universe, unlocking the eternal energy of all creation, the invisible force that mani-fested itself as devas, Asuras, mortals and other animals, depending on the need of the hour. He chanted it over and over, with a fervent devotion he had not felt for too long, since that day in the Bhayanak-van when Brahmarishi Vishwamitra had chanted it, starting his cycle of litanies, and channelling the infinite force into both Rama and Lakshman, to feed them in their solitary battle against the warped offspring of the giant demoness Tataka. He was no brahmarishi, or even a brahmin, nor was he that same Rama who had fought half a thousand demonaic creatures in the dark forest that day. He had no maha-shakti infusing his body, empowering him to achieve great super-human feats, nor did he know any of the sacred smriti mantras that brahmins and brahmin warriors used at such times. But he was not seeking power for himself. He was seeking to pass on his own stored energies to Hanuman. It did not matter that he now possessed no more strength than any other exceptional mortal warrior – no more, perhaps, than Lakshman, for instance. What mattered was that Hanuman regarded him as a godlike being, possessed of infinite strength. The vanar's faith was absolute, as solid as the rock beneath which he laboured now. And it was that faith that Rama sought to appeal to, to awaken, to unleash. It was the only thing he could think of to do. For Hanuman did possess the strength required to accomplish this seemingly impossible task he was demanding of him; he had seen him lift and toss that boulder yesterday. The power was there in his veins; it needed only to be unlocked. And if Rama's intuition was right, then he, and he alone, could provide the living key.

A rumbling began above them, pulling his gaze upwards. A chorus of bear howls and shouts broke out atop the mountain. Rama looked up and saw the edge give way completely, crumbling and breaking into fragmented slabs of earth and stone. Bears fell, a dozen, perhaps twice that number, to certain death. But they were not the ones who cried out. The ones crying out were those on the mountain, who were able to move aside and save themselves in time, as the boulder's weight overcame them at last. Rama saw Lakshman reach the summit and grab hold of Jambavan, shouting something incoherent. The bear king shook himself free of Lakshman's grasp and raised his snout to the sky, issuing a cry that carried as far as a conch-shell trumpet on a battlefield. It was a wordless cry, for there were no words to describe what the bear king must feel at such a moment; a final appeal to his parents, the devas. Nala too howled out a last despairing wail, clutching his tail in grief. Around them, bears and vanars scattered away from the disintegrating cliff-edge, screaming with dismay and grief at the calamity that was upon them all, and their inability to prevent it from happening. Lakshman let loose a cry of such anguish that it pierced Rama's heart like an arrow.

The massive rock hung suspended on the lip of the cliff, as debris and doomed bears fell beneath its curve. Then, with a grinding, gnashing sound like a giant pair of iron jaws coming together, it began its great descent.

On the beach below, thousands of vanars and bears cried out. If it would save their fellow bears and Hanuman, Rama knew, they would gladly have rushed forward to put their own fragile bodies in the path of the tumbling rock. But such a sacrifice would be of no avail; it would only add to the death count. He gestured sharply to them to move back out of harm's way, shouting a wordless command. Then he turned and focused his energy one final time upon Hanuman. He put every ounce of will into this plea, knowing that this was their last hope.

'We all have need of your power of faith. Unleash your strength now, son of Anjaneya and Vayu, and save us all! I, Rama, command it!'

Time seemed to crawl like an ant carrying a leaf ten times its size up a treetrunk. Rama heard the rumbling as the boulder left the clifftop and started its descent, striking glancing blows to the cliff-face as it came. Each nick and nudge carried sufficient force to dislodge whole chunks of rock from the cliff, and these followed in the wake of the boulder itself. It would be a small avalanche that fell, not just a stone. He was glad the beach itself was cleared. If his desperate attempt failed, then all of them here on this stretch of sandy, wave-lapped shore would surely be killed in moments, but at least no more lives would be lost.

Lakshman's voice howled in despair from the clifftop, barely audible above the rumbling, gnashing chaos of the mounting avalanche. Rama could make out only one word: 'Rama!'

There was no time to call back an answer, to tell Lakshman to continue the war and retrieve Sita at any cost, not to waste time grieving for him when he was gone. Even this thought barely occurred to his mind, then was gone. He continued to focus his energy upon the vanar beneath the rock. *Awaken. Awaken! AWAKEN!*

A great wail rose from the beach as his followers realised that he, their leader, was in harm's way. There was nothing to be done. Without turning his head, he could see that the rock was almost at the bottom of the cliff: it filled his peripheral vision. Time still continued to move at ant's pace, enlarging each heartbeat to what seemed like whole moments.

He saw the bears before him stirring, their snouts opening to issue forth grunts and growls of an unidentifiable emotion. Brave as they were, it was too much to expect that they would not fear death. His heart swelled with pride that so many had put their lives at risk for his cause. So many brave and great warriors had joined him in this final war. And after he was gone, he knew that his body would be carried in state, a thousand thousand shoulders offering themselves gladly to bear that last burden. As many pairs of eyes would weep copious tears when they heard of his demise back in Ayodhya. To have lived well, loved greatly, fought and won every battle he engaged in, to have remained faithful to the laws of dharma to the very end, and to be remembered by so many after his passing: what more could a man ask for?

I would ask for Sita, his heart cried. *For her freedom from that villain's tyrannous captivity. For justice.*

'Rama.'

He blinked and started to look around. Yet he knew at once that the voice came not from any around him, but from within his mind. The speaking served to dispel the trance he had fallen under, and the world returned to normal time. At that very moment, the rock landed at the foot of the cliff, falling upon the backs of its brother stones.

The impact was shattering. The ground trembled, as if shaken by a giant hand. An explosion of rock and shards and debris issued out, sending deadly missiles flying in every direction, each one a potential life-taker, as the great rock itself, lightly chipped and barely scathed by its fall, struck the hard-rock crags and rebounded into the air, flying directly at the bears carrying the other rock, and at Rama himself. It loomed like a dark sun falling out of the sky on to his world, the final irony in this unequal battle that was his life – the rock meant for his own bridge would be the one to kill him. Like the black fist of Yama-raj, the lord of death, it fell towards him.

'*Rama*,' said the voice again, booming in the caverns of his consciousness, denying that fate, rebelling against life itself, against the falling fist of Yama.

And with a great unified groan, the bears shrugged off their immense burden.

Or that was how it seemed at first. As if they flailed their fur-clad limbs and the boulder rose up into the air.

But then they all raised their snouts and peered upwards with eyes widened by shock and awe.

For the boulder had not been thrown up, it had been lifted. Not by the bears, but by another. It flew up, up, above their startled snouts. Now it stood ten yards above, and was still rising. Fifteen yards. Twenty. Thirty. Forty. Fifty. It rose so quickly that a blink of an eye could not encompass the velocity of that action. The other rock, flying towards Rama, seemed suspended in mid-air, frozen in time, so rapidly did this rock rise in contrast.

But it was not the rock alone that rose.

It was the one bearing it.

Hanuman.

Rama's eyes widened in wonder and delight as he saw the vanar, grown to ten or fifteen times his normal size, and still growing. With each yard he grew, the rock he carried seemed to shrink in comparison. And with what speed! In a sliver of a fraction of a heartbeat, he was a third the size of Mahendra itself, and the enormous boulder, ten yards wide at the least, seemed now a mere ball that he carried in one hand, gently balanced upon his palm.

'*Rama.*'

Reverentially, adoringly, devotionally. It was a chant, he realised now, a chant that seemed to be recited slowly because of the speed at which everything else was taking place. It was Hanuman's voice that chanted his name, but in a manner that could be heard only by him.

The other rock still hung in the air, for all this – Hanuman's supernatural growth in stature and raising of the great boulder upon his palm – had taken place in the brief instant that it had taken the other falling rock to traverse those thirty or forty yards of distance from the edge of the cliff to the place where Rama stood. It now loomed directly over Rama, casting a darker shadow on this gloomy day, and the bears fell in that shadow of the fist of Yama as well.

The giant Hanuman turned. He twisted at the waist, the first rock in the palm of his left hand. His other hand flashed out, as lightning flashes in a dark sky above an ocean, as a humming-bird's wing flutters. Quicker than thought, he snatched the falling rock out of the air, grasping it easily, as a child catches a bladder-ball flung by a playmate.

The shadow over Rama and the bears disappeared. At the far end of the beach, the rest of the debris tumbled and crashed and made a great deal of noise and raised a vast amount of dust and sand. Some fragments rolled this way and that, within yards or even feet of their position. But none of it actually came close enough to harm them. Slowly, as things of nature even-tually do, the debris of the fall settled, and the beach grew still.

The ocean seemed to lie still. The air was still. The sky, preg-nant with laden clouds, was still.

Every one of the thousands upon thousands of souls watching on the beach, on the mountain, on the cliffs was still.

All still.

Like the heart in Rama's breast.

Only Hanuman moved. Gigantic, forty yards tall or more, he turned and moved across the beach, stepped carefully past the bears, as a father steps by his sleeping infant children. Only a heartbeat or two ago, they had been a head or two taller than he. Now he towered above them all, and their snouts turned skywards to gaze upon him in admiration and awe.

Hanuman took a giant step across the beach, his enormous feet sinking into the sand to the depth of a man's height. Then another step, as if assessing the stability of his new-found height and bulk. Then he strode on confidently.

He stepped out into the sea, the water barely covering his hairy feet at first, then rising to his ankles. When he reached the end of the bridge, he stopped. Leaning down, he placed one rock, then the other, at the end of the bridge, adding a good twenty yards more to its length. He did this with careful ease, the way a child might do while building a pyramid of stone marbles.

Then he turned and gazed back, searching for something.

'*Rama.*'

His eyes, big as dark lotus pools now, sought for and found Rama. The bears on the beach turned and looked at their mortal leader.

Hanuman came striding up the beach. In a few quick steps, he was back where he had begun. He fell to his knees, gouging great depressions in the sand, and joined his hands together. Then he bowed his head.

'At your service, my lord,' he said.

4

The sun hung like a golden ball in an expanse of azure blue, like a jewel set in velvet. Not a whisper of cloud was visible anywhere; nothing marred the picturesque perfection of the scene. Flocks of beautiful birds flew in impeccable formation, wheeling and curving as if following pre-ordained paths; even soldiers could rarely be trained to march in such perfect order.

Yet Vibhisena knew that such perfection was itself unnatural.

Following the flight of a flock of herons, he scanned the lush, beautiful rolling landscape that lay to the north and east of Lanka. So clear was the day, so crystalline pure the air, he almost thought he could make out the distant peak of Mount Nikumbhila. He even thought he could spy the familiar shape of the Shiva temple atop the mountain. But that was hardly possible: the peak was many yojanas distant. Then again, who knew what one might see from a tower of this height? The mainland even, mayhap? That stretch of beach before Mount Mahendra where the mortal prince Rama was said to have camped with his army of vanars? Surely that was too distant. And yet he felt as if he had but to concentrate sufficiently, and even that impossible view would be granted to him. That was the power of Pushpak's magic: to render almost anything possible.

'She is in here, brother, not out there.'

The voice was sibilant and susurrant. A serpent hissing at a male it hated intensely but with whom it was willing to mate in order to satiate its seething urge. That was ever Supanakha's way, to invest her every word with sexual malice.

He ignored the tone and responded to the words. 'He has altered Pushpak's height, do you see? The tower is now at least thrice as high as before. To what end has he done it, I wonder?'

She laughed mockingly. 'Why wonder? It's no secret. The matings have yielded good fruit. More bodies need more space. It's a simple enough calculation.'

He turned to look at her. She crouched on the side of a treetrunk, her eyes serpentine, forked tongue flickering in and out of her slightly parted lips. The glistening scaly skin merged unnaturally with her true furry coat to produce an odd, unsettling hybrid. Yet even the chaste, devoutly celibate brahmin within him could not deny the obvious lure of her sexuality, avid and avaricious, burning like a pantheress in heat. 'You speak of the couplings on the lower levels. What do they have to do with this? How many offspring could they be producing? Surely not enough to require such a threefold expansion?'

She snarled impatiently. 'You know nothing, Vibhisena. I don't know why he tolerates you sometimes. You're such a pious fool. The matings are his greatest work, don't you see that? They are the means by which he has ensured that he will win the war, when the mortal arrives with his army.'

Vibhisena stared at her. 'What help can all these little infants be to Ravana in the war? It's only a few months since he began this programme of multiplication. At the normal speed of rakshasa gestation, at best he could have engineered the production of a few hundred—'

'The normal speed of rakshasa gestation doesn't apply. Remember Tataka.'

'His experiments with genetic manipulation in the Bhayanak-van? The creation of hideous hybrid creatures? But he has no more Asura species to work with now. Only rakshasas.'

'It isn't the variety he's interested in. It's the number. He's been doing something to decrease gestation periods, to produce more babies faster, and to . . .' She paused, a wary look coming into her eyes. 'If you don't already know all this, then perhaps he intended it that way.'

Vibhisena shrugged, trying to look uninterested. 'He said something once, took me on a tour of his great experiment, the communes. Even tried to persuade me to join in. I wasn't interested.'

She chuckled throatily, reassured. 'You self-righteous oaf. What are you saving it for anyway? A mortal?'

Vibhisena bristled and tried to hide it. 'How much faster can he make rakshasa babies grow up? It takes a normal rakshasa infant a full year to reach adulthood. How much could Ravana reduce that period? By a month perhaps? Two months?'

She smiled, licking something off the tips of her talons. 'What if I told you that by feeding them a special diet, he can make them grow in weeks.'

'Weeks?' Vibhisena repeated, unable to process the information, let alone accept it. 'Weeks? That's impossible!'

'Not for Ravana. Aided by Pushpak's power. Besides, brother, the results speak for themselves. When was the last time you visited the Nikumbhila caves?'

He frowned. 'There is nothing there. Since Ravana's return, the Pulastyas have moved back into the city. They occupy the finest houses and live like royalty. Many reside here within the tower itself. The caves are abandoned.'

'Is that what you think?' she asked slyly. 'Then perhaps some day you should pay a visit.' She turned smartly, showing him her rear, tail flicking provocatively. 'Then again, you don't need to go to Nikumbhila. The caves extend all the way to beneath this tower now. All you need do is go down to the sub-levels. Way down.'

'Wait,' he said. 'Where are you going?'

She turned back, her eyes gleaming. 'I am forbidden to visit the mortal. Ravana's orders. In any case, I have no wish to see that hussy again. There are better things to do.'

And with a last flick of her tail, she was gone, leaving only a series of rake-marks on the trunk where she had clung.

Better things to do. All for Ravana, no doubt. The discussion the three of them had had that day had all come to naught.

Ravana had won them back with his eloquence and mind manipulation. Even Mandodhari had been convinced of her husband's innocence and had believed the entire jaundiced version of events. As for Supanakha, her motives were always suspect. Even when she had pretended to be willing to act against her cousin, Vibhisena had known that it would take only a few words for her to go slinking back to Ravana. She was like the loyal cat, snarling and hissing when she wanted to be left alone, but always around at mealtimes.

He made his way cautiously through the forest, the immaculately rendered *artificial* forest, towards the place where Supanakha had said the mortal woman lived. He noticed how careful everyone was to refer to her as a visitor or a guest, never a prisoner. But he intended to see for himself just how comfortable this guest was in her new home.

He was still a good distance away when he heard the voices. Harsh, railing, nerve-grating, sanity-stealing rakshasi voices. Badgering, ranting, abusing, threatening, castigating, insulting . . .

His heart pounded as he slowed his pace, stealing through a kamatya grove as quietly as he was able. As he came closer, the voices grew louder, unbearably so, until he was transfixed by the sheer outpouring of hatred and venom that was being heaped upon the poor mortal. His ears burned at some of the names she was being called, at the vehemence with which the colourful epithets and revolting descriptions were vomited out.

Finally he could take it no more. He stepped out from behind the trunk of an ashoka tree, into an entire grove of such trees.

At first, none of them was even aware of his presence. They stood around her, four hulking beasts, spewing out their noxious streams of abuse. And not content with mere words, they poked and shoved and kicked dirt at her, slammed their fists into the treetrunk above her head, beside her ear, spewing spittle and slime over her tender skin. For her part, the poor wretch sat crouched in a foetal posture, her knees drawn tightly into her chest, hands clasped around her head, bent over into a human ball.

His hand curled into a first.

For the first time in his life, Vibhisena longed for a sword, an axe, a mace, anything to stop this torrent of psychological torture, to punish these despicable creatures for ganging up on a solitary, unarmed, unprotesting woman thus. Never before had he been so tempted to violent response.

With a great effort, he reined in the savage impulse and muttered a mantra of peace beneath his breath: *Om Shanti. Shanti Om.*

The moment passed, slowly and reluctantly.

He stepped forward.

'ENOUGH!' he said, startling even himself by the loudness of his command. It sounded like another person altogether, so unfamiliar was he with the sound of his own voice raised in anger. 'Stop this at once,' he said in only a slightly lesser tone.

His hands trembled with barely concealed rage.

As one, the rakshasas turned slowly, unafraid and uncowed. He recognised them at once: Mandodhari's sakshis. He had never paid them much heed until today. Now, he marked their faces closely, carefully, as if memorising the faces of enemies for future reference upon the battlefield. They looked at him unafraid. He realised that shouting had been a mistake: Ravana was the only one they truly feared. And Ravana would never have shouted. He would have killed them all without saying a word if he so desired. Only a dog that did not wish to bite barked instead. They looked at him indifferently, as they might look at a passer-by on a street.

One of them whispered something to the biggest rakshasi of the group – Vibhisena couldn't recall her name – and she chortled. 'So, feeble one. Are you come to have your way with your brother's new keep?'

The other one, the one who had whispered just now, said slyly, 'I hear you can only find arousal with mortals. Is it true, my lord?'

They all laughed uproariously at that.

'Silence,' he said. Then wished he hadn't. Telling them to be silent was as effective as asking a pack of stray dogs to stop barking. 'Leave this place at once. I wish to have words with Princess Sita.'

'Words?' The rakshasi leered knowingly. 'It will take more than words to accomplish what you have in mind, master!'

He glared angrily at them all. They threw a few more suggestive looks and lewd gestures his way, then, to his great relief, shambled off into the woods. He heard them laughing raucously as they went. He waited for their voices to grow distant, until he was certain they were not waiting and watching in secret. Then he crouched down before the ashoka tree against which she was still leaning.

'My lady.'

The curled figure at the base of the tree did not stir.

'Princess Sita Janaki, wife of Rama Chandra, daughter-in-law of Rani Kausalya, First Princess of Ayodhya.'

Still there was no response. Her face remained buried in the cloister of her knees, her hands still covering her ears. There was dirt and bits of dried leaves in her hair, and he could see welts and bruises and nicks where they had scratched and poked and nudged her.

'Devi,' he pleaded. 'I mean you no harm. I come as a friend.'

Still she did not move or respond in any way. An awful thought occurred to him. He leaned closer, to try and see if her body moved with the intake and outgiving of breath. To see if she yet lived. For all he knew . . .

''Tis no use.'

He jerked back, startled. Then realised that the voice had come from somewhere to his right. He peered through the gloom, for it was shadier in this part of the forest level than elsewhere. He could hear the sound of water falling somewhere not far away, and in the silence, the sound of rakshasi voices and water splashing.

She was standing by a sala tree, her white tresses wild and

unmanageable, her eyes drooping and sad. She looked as if she had survived a hurricane.

'I know you,' he said. 'You are . . .'

She did not help him out. Instead she said, 'They have been torturing her continually for the past day and night. I fear for her sanity.'

He glanced back at the huddled woman, alarmed. Then realised who it was who had just imparted this information, and looked back at the rakshasi. 'You people—' he began.

'Not I, master. I tried to stop them. But they would not heed me. My mistress gave them licence to do with her as they pleased as long as they did not harm her bodily.'

Mandodhari? How could she have ordered such treatment, let alone condoned it? He would have words with her at once. But first . . .

'And why do you feel so kindly towards her?' he asked, his anger at the others harshening his tone. 'Did you have your fill of verbal battering and then retire for a brief respite? To regain your strength for another round of mind-numbing brutality?'

She was not insulted by his allegations. Her sad face told him another story. 'I saw this in a vision. The master taking her by force. Her husband and husband's brother leading a great army here. The destruction of our land and our kind. The end of Lanka.'

He recalled her name suddenly. 'Trijata. I remember now, you're the one who claims to be able to see the future.'

'And the past. And the present. I see what I am shown. Mostly, I do not know what it means.' She looked away suddenly, her voice turning sharp, her eyes flashing angrily. 'I did not wish for these visions! I do not want them! Why do you plague me thus, O Goddess?'

He saw an opportunity. A possible ally. 'Trijata, we are all given roles to play. Not of our choosing. We must make the best of what we are given.'

She looked at him with a dead ghostly light in her pupils, as if they reflected scenes from other worlds, other lifetimes.

He resisted the urge to move closer, to look into those pupils and see the tiny reflections that lay within. He had a sense that if he did that, he might never be the same again.

'And what is my role, master? To see nightmares of damnation and destruction? And be powerless to prevent it?' She shook her head, her hair flying hither and thither like a curtain of ragged coarsecloth. 'Better dead than thus.'

'You can help her,' he said gently. 'Save her from the torture of your fellows. Protect her.'

She laughed. It was an ugly sound, teeth-grating. 'Me? Vikata can pick me up and break me upon her thigh with one hand. I am old and weary from too many visions. My brain is curdled from all the terrors I have foreseen. I can do nothing except wait and watch.'

'You must do something,' he said. 'Has she been fed at all? Has she been allowed to take water or nourishment? Bathe? Sleep awhile? She must be allowed to sustain herself, or she will not survive long.'

She shrugged. 'What will be will be. If we can do nothing to prevent it, what good does it do to act at all?'

'Because it is our dharma,' he said angrily. 'Only through the karma we perform, the actions we execute in this lifetime, can we hope to break free of the endless cycle of rebirth. Do you wish to be forever chained to your role? To continue seeing visions of terrible ends and be powerless forever to stop them? You may not prevent what is inevitable, but you can change some part of it at least. And by each action you perform, you redeem yourself. Do it for your own eternal soul, if not for this blameless woman.'

She stared at him silently, her eyes glittering in the dappled shadows of the shaded grove.

The sound of splashing came clearly on the wind, the laughter of rakshasas. 'Trijata,' he said earnestly, 'your fellow sakshis are occupied for the nonce. Use this time to fetch her some food and drink. Try to persuade her to take some nourishment. And keep them away from her for as long as you can. Do this and

you will earn yourself a lifetime's worth of blessing.' He started
to turn away.

'And where do you go, master?' she asked.

He replied grimly: 'To seek out your mistress and put a stop
to this despicable behaviour.'

5

Vibhisena was waiting on the steps of the temple when Mandodhari emerged. A chariot stood nearby, the horses foaming at the mouth. From the paleness of his face and the angry red spots on his high cheekbones, she knew her brother-in-law was angry. It was rare to see Vibhisena in the throes of any strong emotion. And anger was the rarest of the rare.

Yet he was silent and patient as she offered him the pooja thali to take the sacred blessings from the flickering diya flame, applied a red tikka to his forehead, and offered him prasad, the sanctified fruits of the ceremony. Performing these simple ritualistic actions seemed to alleviate some of his anger. When he spoke, only an uncharacteristic tightness in his tone betrayed that he was not his usual serene self.

'Sister, I always took you for a woman of dharma.'

She raised her eyebrows. 'Is that the precept of dharma as followed by us rakshasas, or the mortal interpretation of it?'

He frowned. 'What do you mean? Dharma is dharma. There are no two versions of it.'

'But of course there are. It is written in the sacred texts. Dharma shall be interpreted differently by different peoples, and by the same people at different points in time. In the first age alone shall dharma be universally understood in the same manner by one and all and practised diligently by everyone in the three worlds. In each subsequent one of the four yugas, the great ages into which time is divided, the practice of dharma will progressively diminish as people descend into baser thought and action. And this, as you well know, is nearly the close of the second age.'

'What has that to do with mortals and us? How can the mortal interpretation of dharma be different from our own? What is right is right, wrong is wrong. Nothing can alter that basic truth.'

'Yet truth itself is always debatable. Do you know – of course you know, how could I forget that you are more learned even than I, but still, excuse me as I remind you of these trivial details – do you know that the very word we use for truth, artha, in fact means wealth? Because the ancients believed that truth was wealth, knowledge the greatest possession of all. Yet with every passing age we grow more impoverished, for while we accumulate the physical trappings of superficial wealth, we lose the ultimate source of wealth itself, truth. And that great storehouse is looted by us without respect or regard for its real value. So think carefully, brother-of-my-husband. This truth you speak of. How did you come by it? Did you perceive the events in question yourself, or were you told what happened by another party? What vested interest might that party have? Even if you saw the events unfold with your own senses, from what perspective did you witness them? Everything changes everything, dear brother-in-law. You must know that.'

He gestured impatiently. 'I am not here to debate the laws of causality and metaphysics. I am here to ask you to do a simple thing. Your rakshasas are terrorising the mortal prisoner. You must ask them to stop at once. They will drive her insane if they continue. I beg you, go there at once and command them to cease their verbal torture.'

'How do you know that it is they who are terrorising her and not she terrorising them?' she asked calmly.

He stared at her. 'What do you mean, sister? She is unarmed and defenceless, a mortal woman alone and imprisoned against her will. A gang of fierce rakshasas surround her, badgering and abusing and taunting her at all times. I have seen and heard them doing this with my own eyes and ears. There is no debate about the facts in the matter. No matter how you interpret it, this is a crime against dharma. No prisoner deserves to be treated thus, let alone a woman we claim is our guest!'

She took a few steps, gazing out at the view, pristine and splendid. The evening sunlight was gentle on her upturned face. 'And if a soldier on a battlefield picks up a spear and flings it at a foe, is he going against dharma?'

He shook his head, unable to see her point. 'What does that have to do with the condition of Princess Sita?'

'Everything, Vibhisena,' she said, turning back sharply. She was offended by his use of the mortal female's name. 'This is war. The mortals are at war with us. Do not mistake it for anything less. That woman betrayed her own spouse and seduced mine. She sought to become Queen of Lanka and replace me. She thinks she is shrewd enough to win no matter what happens. If Ravana prevails, as I pray daily he will, then she will no doubt seek to inveigle herself into his bed and upon his throne, to secure her future. Alternatively, if her husband, the conniving mortal that he is, wins the coming war, then she will no doubt turn back to him, batting those big doe eyes, and say she did all this for *him*, to aid him in his campaign. And he would probably believe her – why, for all we know, he is the one who thought up this whole deception! Either way, she is the enemy. And why should we show the enemy any sympathy when they will show us none? Do you think when her husband comes here with an army he will not try to terrorise us? To massacre our people? To commit genocide as he has done before?'

Vibhisena shook his head despairingly. 'You have been deceived by my brother's manipulations again. Do you not see? Everything he told us in his quarters was a lie. He has fabricated a whole tapestry of events designed to show himself as a hero and Rama as a villain. I did not wish to say anything before him because he would only deny it all. So I held my peace. But I have been to see Princess Sita, and what I saw was proof enough of his lies. He has used your rakshasas to break her down by constant terrorising and intimidation. The poor woman is under great duress, even risk of physical harm. You must intervene and tell your sakshis to stop at once. They will listen to you.'

She looked out at the view again before saying calmly, 'It was not Ravana who ordered them to remain with Sita. It was I.'

He reared back in astonishment, his hand flying to his open mouth in a typically effeminate gesture that she had always disliked. 'My lady! What were you thinking? Surely you were misled by Ravana, or manipulated? He—'

'He had nothing to do with it,' she said coldly, seeking to warn him by the steel of her tone. 'I went to see her of my own free will and I put my sakshis upon her. I wish to get the truth from her own ugly lips. Is not that what you seek as well? The truth? What else is the goal of dharma after all? To support the truth. Believe me, my sakshis will get the truth out of her, given time.'

'But that is torture! You cannot—' He stopped. 'My lady, you have been severely misled. Ravana has twisted all the known facts to suit his own grotesque misinterpretation. He has recreated a version of events that only shows himself in the best light and Rama in the worst.'

She waited a beat before asking: 'And do you not think Rama has been doing the same?'

He blinked. 'Doing what?'

'Narrating events to show *himself* in the best light and *Ravana* in the worst?'

He faltered. 'Quite possibly. But that is the truth. Rama—'

'Stop right there, Vibhisena. What do you mean? Rama's version is the truth and my husband's version is lies and deception? On what basis do you reach that conclusion?'

'On the f-f-facts before us,' he stammered. 'Rama is a man of dharma. That is well known.'

'Not to rakshasas it is not. My husband is a man of dharma. Has not Ravana received great boons from the devas for his long penance and devotion?'

'Yes, but—'

'And has not Rama been evicted by his own family because he threatened his brother's rightful ascension to the throne?'

Vibhisena shook his head vigorously, but said, 'Yes, but—'

'And Rama did indeed commit genocide at Mithila when he unleashed the forbidden weapon, did he not?'

'My lady—'

'And what of our cousin Supanakha's disfigurement? You accept that surely – you saw her state yourself when she arrived here months ago. Before she was restored. You cannot deny that? Nor can you deny the destruction of fourteen thousand rakshasas, the last of their clans, whose only crime was their defence of their sister-rakshasi Supanakha and their claiming of retribution for her mutilation, a crime punishable by death under our laws.'

He sighed wearily. 'Of course I do not deny these things. But they are all misinterpreted by Ravana. He has altered the point of view to make it conveniently in his favour. So by his reckoning, he is the one who is following dharma. But in truth, Rama's way—'

She laughed, the sound thin and empty beneath the open sky. He stared at her in mute bafflement. 'So there you go at last. Admitting it yourself, finally. You concede that dharma is interpreted differently by Rama and Ravana, depending upon the perspective from which they individually perceive events. And because all those in conflict must of necessity have conflicting viewpoints, therefore they will interpret dharma by their own standards.' She gestured widely, as if indicating the far-distant future. 'Who knows, millennia from now, when the record of these events is retold by future scribes, there may be two versions of the story: Rama's version, and Ravana's version.'

He looked nonplussed. 'This whole debate notwithstanding, my lady, you must know that Ravana has committed a great wrong. The lady Sita is a prisoner in the tower, not a visitor as he has led us all to believe. She is a prisoner against her will.'

She shrugged. 'Indeed.'

He looked surprised, almost hopeful. 'Then you agree that—'

'I agree that she is a prisoner of war. And she must be treated as such. Besides, no bodily harm has been caused to her yet, has it? We are well within our dharma to demand from her that she confess the truth. War criminals and spies can be questioned, even roughly. That is not a violation of the rules of war.'

'Not harmed?' he asked. 'Yes, you may be right in the most superficial of senses. She has had no bones broken or blood shed, it is true, not yet, that is,' he conceded angrily, 'but at the rate your sakshis are bullying her—'

Wearily, for she was tiring of this argument now, of Vibhisena's whining stubborness, she demanded, 'What would you have me do, Vibhisena? Treat her like a queen, put her in my own apartments, in my husband's bed? And turn against my husband, accuse him as a villain who, according to your interpretation, has engineered this entire grand scheme?'

'I ask only that you treat her humanely. Even if she is a prisoner of war, she has shown no physical threat to us. Therefore, by the rules of war, she cannot be threatened physically either.' He stopped, realising what he had just said, and what she had said a moment earlier. 'All right. Even if she is not being physically threatened, surely there is such a thing as excessive roughness in questioning. I saw what she was undergoing. It was nothing less than abuse. You cannot abuse a prisoner who has shown us no violent threat at all.'

'But I should abuse my husband? Is that what you are saying? I should distrust Ravana's motives and challenge his every word? Call him a liar and a ravisher of other men's wives, a kidnapper and a warmonger? Is that what you call adhering to my dharma?'

He paused, startled by her sudden vehemence. 'You must do what is right. You must follow your own conscience. You are an honourable woman, a pious and highly moral-minded rakshasi. But—'

'But not a human,' she said sadly.

He baulked. 'That is not what I was about to say.'

'It is what you meant to say. I am all those wonderful exalted things, but I can never be the ideal of perfection you aspire to, because I am not mortal. And she is. That hussy who sits in the tower and plays her little pretend game of oh-look-at-me-how-miserable-I-am for gullible innocents like you, Vibhisena. That is what lies within your heart, does it not, dear brother-in-law?'

She looked away grimly, her profile hard and uncompromising even in the soft light of sundown. 'I thought I understood how you felt. When Trijata came to me with her visions of hell and destruction, my first thought was to blame my husband. Why? Because everyone regards Ravana as being responsible for everything. It is his own fault, actually. It is the persona he has built for himself. The truth is, he is only doing what any king would do, seeking the best for his people and his land. That often means taking harsh, even apparently cruel steps. It is something that disturbed me much as a young bride. But there are things which must be done when you are king of a great land, with so many enemies pressing down at all times. And Ravana is a great follower of dharma. Unlike your beloved mortal Prince Rama, who was banished from his own kingdom, by his own father no less! Ravana's fight is against any enemies of our kind, and there are many of those. For every one Ravana there are a thousand Ramas seeking to bring him down by any means, fair or foul. It has made him a strong and hard ruler, but a great one too.'

Vibhisena began to answer, but just then a messenger arrived. Mandodhari heard what he had to say, then turned back to her brother-in-law, a look of bright anger gleaming in her eyes. 'It would seem you picked the wrong victim to champion, Vibhisena. Your allegedly docile little princess has gone and done something even you cannot condone, under the rules of war or the rules of dharma. She has attacked and killed one of my sakshis.'

Vibhisena stared, dumbfounded. 'But . . . but that cannot be. How could . . . It is impossible, my lady. She was defenceless, unarmed. And barely fit to stand or walk. How could she possibly . . .'

Mandodhari looked at him with a tight-lipped expression. 'The how and why of it hardly matter now. She has done it. I will go to Ravana and tell him she must be penalised for this transgression. By taking another's life, she has forfeited her own.'

She strode to the chariot waiting to take her back to the city. Vibhisena followed her, wringing his hands. 'I cannot believe it. How could she have killed one of your fierce rakshasas when there were five of them together against her alone?'

'Apparently it was the foolish rakshasi's own fault,' Mandodhari said with a mixture of anger and sadness. 'She told the others to go and refresh themselves while she watched over the mortal. When they were alone together, she stupidly fetched food and drink and attempted to nourish the prisoner, who exploited the opportunity and attacked and killed the poor rakshasi before the others returned. I am told she slaughtered her in a most heartless manner.'

Vibhisena stared up at his sister-in-law as she climbed aboard the chariot. 'Who was she? The rakshasi who was killed?'

Mandodhari tossed her head at him disdainfully. 'My favourite sakshi, the old and faithful Trijata.'

Vibhisena gripped the golden rim of the vehicle. It was warm and pulsating under his fingers, like touching a living being. He pulled his hand away at once. 'My sister, I tell you, it must be your own sakshis who killed her and are pretending that the prisoner did it. It was I who requested Trijata to feed and succour Sita while the others were away.'

Mandodhari looked down at him. 'Then you share a part in her death too, Vibhisena. How does that sit with your sense of dharma?'

He reared back as if struck with a whip. 'My lady—'

But she did not wait to hear the rest of his response. She commanded Pushpak to take her away, and was gone in the wink of an eyelid, carried up and away by the celestial vehicle, flying at the wind's pace back to Lanka.

6

Hanuman's great size diminished soon afterwards. Any hopes they might have had of the vanar retaining his vastness and putting it to use in their bridge-building effort were dashed. He remained as he was through Rama's effusive showering of blessings and praise and gratitude, and through the deafening rounds of cheering and congratulations that were bestowed by all the workers on the beach and the mountainside. With Rama's permission, Nala called a brief respite from the work to retrieve the bodies of those who had fallen trying to stop the rock on the cliff. Hanuman strode across the beach and picked up the broken, bleeding corpses in his hands, carrying them tenderly to the pyres that had been laid out on the dunes. He deposited them gently upon their final resting places, then knelt down in the sand, bowed his great head, and with palms closed, joined them all in the prayers. When Rama opened his eyes at the end of the prayers, Hanuman had shrunk to his normal size again. Everyone else gazed with awe at the change, but Rama saw the abject disappointment on Nala's face, and the chagrin that flared in Lakshman's eyes.

'I do not know how to make it happen again, Rama,' Hanuman said later, when the leaders sat in an unscheduled council called by Rama himself. The bears had overcome their dislike of bats long enough to agree to meet in the palm tree grove. The weather had changed again unexpectedly, the sky clearing so suddenly, it seemed impossible that only hours earlier a storm had appeared inevitable. The afternoon sun was so hot and searing now, the wind so still and energy-sapping, that the relatively cooler shade of the grove was as welcome as a benediction from stern gods. Rama relished the coconut water that had been handed out by Nala's vanars to each of them, and found himself scooping out and eating each morsel of the soft malai inside. The bears too were eating energetically, their eyes brighter than they had looked for days. The whole occurrence had infused them all with a great swell of hope. Now, if only that hope could translate into something more concrete.

'How can you not know?' Lakshman asked plaintively. 'You have done it twice now. Surely you have some control over it?'

'If he had, then he would gladly use it to aid us, brother Lakshman,' Angad said patiently. 'But we vanars think that this is a gift given to him by the devas only to prevent the vanars coming to harm. On both occasions, the lives of vanars were threatened. We have a belief in our species that when the species is threatened, the devas empower one of us to save the rest. I fear that was all Hanuman's power really was: a temporary gift by the devas to prevent calamities. Once the danger was past, the power was removed.'

Jambavan made an odd sound, halfway between a snorting and a chuffing. Rama glanced sharply at the bear king. 'My friend, you disagree with Angad's assessment?'

Jambavan raised his head from the coconut he was feeding from. Coconut water and malai dripped down the end of his snout. He swatted it off carelessly with the back of one furry paw. 'Smells like rotten fish to a bear.'

Angad frowned. 'Are you insulting our legends, sire?'

'I am respecting them, sire!' the bear king said with unexpected vehemence. 'You, on the other hand, are clearly unaware of your own legends. Do you know the tale of El-ahrairah? Or the many adventures of Shardik? Or any of a thousand other great adventures and exploits?'

Angad struggled to restrain his temper. The young prince had learned a great deal since Rama had first encountered him at Kiskindha, much of it, he claimed, from Rama himself. He glanced at Rama now, then said in a strangled voice, 'Are those names of vanars? If they are, then I have never heard them spoken before.'

Jambavan crunched into the side of the coconut, chewed noisily for a moment, then abruptly discarded the rest of the shell, narrowly missing a couple of bears' heads as it went flying over. His ears twitched furiously for a moment, then he swallowed, grunted, and said, 'Hanuman, then. Have you heard that name before? Or Maruti? What of Anjaneya? Have you heard *those* vanar names in your legends, or were you sleeping too soundly when Granny Vanar was telling her bedtime tales?'

Angad looked offended. 'My lord rksa, are you seeking to insult me deliberately?'

Jambavan waved a thick paw. 'Oh, don't fuss. Don't fuss. It's all fish and bone anyhow.'

He snorted, choked, spat out something – it appeared to be a cone-shaped piece of coconut shell, or perhaps an oyster shell – and grunted with relief. 'Much better, much better on the bellywork. Now, come to the edge of the pond if you want to drink deeply. You should be ashamed of yourself, not knowing your own ur-history, son.' He waved deprecatingly to shoo off an apoplectic answer from Angad. 'Oh, don't get your fishbones in your honey, boy. I was busy helping *participate* in most of those legends back when you were hardly even a speck in your ancestor's seed.'

Rama glanced over at Angad and caught his eye. He lowered his lashes, conveying a message to the young vanar. Angad got the message and subsided.

'Harr,' Jambavan belched. 'The mortal has more wisdom than ten of us combined. That's why *his* legend will survive long after our names are forgotten or mistaken for the labels of items of curiosity on a dusty museum shelf someplace. Anyhow. Anyhow.' He slapped his enormous rotund belly, the fur prickling as he rubbed it hard. 'It's time you knew the worth of your own man.' He gestured to Hanuman. 'Come here, son. Come sit by your old ancestor.' He grinned, adding gruffly: 'So old,

I hardly remember how I begat the vanar and mortal races, let alone this one solitary vanar!'

Lakshman rolled his eyes at Rama as if to ask what they were doing listening to all this ballyhoo when there were more important things to discuss and far more important work to be accomplished. Rama nodded once, firmly, and Lakshman sighed and shook his head sadly. But despite the puzzlement on everyone else's faces, Rama had a feeling that the old bear was about to surprise and shock them all.

Hanuman came and crouched on the ground beside Jambavan. The bear laid a hand on the vanar's shoulder, slapping him hard on the back. 'I blame you not at all for forgetting. The forgetting itself was a curse laid down upon you all. For sometimes, when greatness arises in too proud a form, it needs gentling. The most common flaw among giants is a lack of humility. And so when Hanuman here was very young, his father decreed that nobody should know his true ability, least of all Hanuman himself. And a decree from a deva is a writ of law.'

Angad shook his head in frank confusion. 'I don't understand, bear lord. I grew up with Hanuman in the wilds of Kiskindha, we played together on the slopes of Mount Rishimukha and roamed the red-mist ranges together. He was no giant then. As for his father, he was a fine vanar, but no deva, as you say. Kesari was a great designer of gardens and his work graces the royal grounds of Kiskindha even today, but he was—'

'Harr. Kesari was his father, in the sense that he raised this boy and was a father to him. But Hanuman was not begat by Kesari.'

'He was not?' Angad looked around, uncertain whether this was a jest. The other vanars returned his look with equally baffled expressions of their own. But none appeared very upset or scandalised. Such things were not too uncommon, among vanars as well as mortals.

'No, young Prince Angad,' Jambavan said. 'He was not begat by a vanar at all! He was begat by a deva. This young fellow here, this fine specimen of greatness-in-the-making, is the son of Marut, the lord of wind, also known as Vayu-deva.'

There was stunned silence all around. Even the vanars beyond the grove, conveying the essence of the discussion to the rest of the armies – Rama had not forbidden listening to the council's talk today; perhaps because he had sensed that all should hear whatever was said on this occasion – fell silent. Only the ocean, and wind shirring in the fronds of the palms overhead, continued their eternal dialogue. Hanuman, crouched on his haunches beside Jambavan, looked up at the bear king with an innocent openness that reminded Rama of any young Ayodhyan scholar at a forest gurukul. Undemanding, unquestioning, completely open to anything the guru had to say. For to the truly enlightened seeker of knowledge, there were no real surprises or new things to be learned, only knowledge that one did not know one possessed.

'Punjikasthala was the best of apsaras, the celestial danseuses that graced the court of Indra, lord of the devas. But owing to a curse, she was compelled to be reborn as the daughter of Kunjara, the then king of vanars. Her given name in this rebirth was Anjana. And it was with that name and in that form that she married the vanar Kesari, the king's master of gardens. Now, you may wonder why she did so, being a daughter of the most powerful vanar and able to obtain a prince as her husband if she pleased, or a dozen princes even. For as with mortals, vanar women choose their mates. And Anjana, after all, was an apsara reborn. Even in her vanar form she was the portrait of feminine perfection, graced with exquisitely formed limbs and features that would rouse Indra himself. But despite all this, she still craved to return to her apsara form, for it is ever the lot of living creatures to believe that they were happier yesterday past and miserable today, even though that assumption is proved wrong when they move forward a day and see that they are still unhappy today but felt happier yesterday.

'And so, night and day, Anjana prayed to be returned to her former place in the court of the king of devas. Which, of course, could not be done, because the curse required that she live out this entire lifetime in the form of a vanar. To ease her aching soul, Indra, her former master, found a loophole in the curse.'

Jambavan paused. 'Do you notice that in such tales, someone or other is always cursed by a holy sage, and the person cursed always prays to one deva or other, and the deva always seems to find some way to subvert or otherwise obfuscate the curse?' The bear shook his head, spittle spraying to either side. 'Brrr.' He went on. 'Anyhow, Lord Indra heard his courtesan's pleas and granted her wish, but only for one night. Anjana was given the power to transform back into her apsara form for one moonless night, provided that she did not show herself in that form to any living being. So she proceeded to the top of a mountain.'

Jambavan looked down at the upraised eyes of the silently listening Hanuman, even though the vanar had not spoken a word. 'Yes, my lad, you would not be amiss to think that mountain to be Rishimukha. For it was there that your mother had suffered the curse, and it was there that she repaired to muse on her fate. And it was as a beautiful apsara, beyond the ability of any male to resist, that she wandered the lonely slopes of Rishimukha all that night. Being pitch dark on account of the lack of a moon, she was seen by none, and her night would have passed safely, and in the morning she would have returned to her vanar form and gone back to her husband's embrace and resumed her life in Kiskindha. But then you would not have been born and we would not be sitting here today, would we? Nay. Something did happen that night, and again, it was an event that seems to occur in most such tales of devas and devis.

'One person did lay eyes on Anjana in her form as Punjikasthala that night. For though it was dark and moonless, and not a creature stirred on the slopes of Rishimukha, yet the wind still blew. And in every breath of wind that wafts across the world is part of the essence of the wind lord, Vayu. Or Marut, as you prefer.

'The instant he gazed upon her perfect form, Vayu was smitten.

Her slender waist, her well-shaped thighs, her tapering form, her exquisite face . . . He danced around her, seeing her beauty in all its heavenly perfection even on that pitch-dark mountain, and he could not resist the overpowering desire he felt for her. Taking his corporeal form, Vayu stepped on to the mountain and, without preliminaries, embraced the beautiful apsara. In the darkness, absorbed in her self-pity and misery, she cried out, affrighted.

'"Who dares to lay hands upon a chaste woman? Do you not know that I am already married? How dare you seek to break my vow of fidelity to my husband?" So saying, she struggled furiously to break his embrace, for she was a strong-willed woman willing to fight to defend her honour.

'The wind god gave her sight to gaze upon his form in the darkness. "Do not fear me, beautiful one," he said gently but with passionate intent. "I am the lord of wind, Vayu. I do not seek to ravish you without your acquiscence, but your beauty has overwhelmed my senses. I must possess you tonight, or I will wander for ever upon this mountain and be unable to leave its gentle flower-strewn slopes, languishing out of unfulfilled desire. I urge you, give yourself to my embrace and I shall show you pleasure such as you have never known before nor shall know hereafter."

'Now, many women, mortal or vanar, would have yielded to such an urging. For to accept a deva's coital embrace was to be divinely blessed. But Anjana was a woman of great pride and honour and could not bear the thought of enjoying such pleasure at the cost of her husband Kesari's reputation.

'"I cannot," she pleaded. "For I am wedded to a good and honest vanar. It would not be meet for me to cuckold him thusly. Were I not his wife, and only an apsara, as indeed I was until not long ago, then I would gladly accept your passion, my lord. But I cannot commit a dishonourable act." And she related the story of her curse and exile to the wind god in brief, apologetic words.

'In her reply itself Vayu saw the means to his salvation. "Dear lady, do you not see the truth of your own reasoning? At present you are not in the form of a vanar. You are as you were, an apsara of Indra's court. By your divine master's own command, you are Punjikasthala the apsara, not Anjana, wife of Kesari, for the duration of this night. It is in the form of Punjikasthala that I desire you. And Punjikasthala is not married, nor has she taken a vow of fidelity to any one male. As Punjikasthala, you will be blameless in submitting to my embrace. Before morning arrives and you are transformed back into your vanar form, I will leave you. This I promise."

'In addition, the lord of wind promised that he would beget upon her that night a son who would be a champion among vanars and a legend whose exploits would be related for millennia after his passing. He would be brave and strong beyond measure, and endowed with great wisdom. The wind god continued heaping promises upon promises, in order to persuade the beautiful damsel to acquiesce. And finally his arguments won her over, and Punjikasthala submitted to his desires. When she awoke the next morning, she was alone upon the mountain once more, and was once again the vanar Anjana. She had no memory of her encounter the night before, for that would have been disturbing to the married vanar Anjana, and so Vayu-deva had erased all memory of their encounter. Months later, when she gave birth to a handsome and healthy young vanar son, she assumed it was Kesari's son. The truth was known only by Vayu himself, and he told it to Indra at his court, where he was overheard by the wandering brahmin Narada-muni. And Narada, of course, told everyone who was willing to listen, and a good number who did not care to listen too. And that was how the son of Anjana and Vayu was born in the house of Kesari the vanar.'

_____

7

'When he was but a boy, Hanuman revealed that he was no ordinary vanar. But fate decreed that none were there to see his greatness revealed, albeit briefly. It was because of his father's occupation that he and his mother were often alone in some unsettled part of the wilderness, while Kesari studied flora and sought new methods of intertwining species and designing bigger and more beautiful gardens. Later they would come to live in Kiskindha city proper, where he would meet companions like Prince Angad and where his half-brother Sakra and other siblings would be born. But in those first weeks after his birth, Hanuman mostly played alone.

'One day he saw the sun rising over the forest. He was no more than a babe still and it was the first time he had seen the celestial orb with his own eyes. He took it for a fruit hanging over the trees, and tried to leap to grab it. He leapt once and reached the top of the tallest tree, but could not catch it. He leapt again, leagues above the forest, and still could not put his hands upon the sun. So, with a great intake of breath, he jumped higher still, all the way to the sun itself. The rays of that great ball of fire were powerful and searing, but still he did not falter.

'Lord Indra in Swarga-loka saw what his godson was doing, for ever since Vayu had told him how he begat Hanuman upon Punjikasthala, Indra had felt himself personally responsible for the young vanar – after all, it was he who had sidestepped the curse by transforming her back for that one fateful night, even though he had known the possible consequences, so in a sense he was directly responsible for Vayu's flaring of passion, and Indra himself knew a great deal about the consequences of unbridled passion – and he saw that in another instant Hanuman would reach the sun and wrest that great orb out of the sky, thereby disrupting the whole of Prithvi. There was barely time to act, let alone to think. So Indra took the fastest recourse – he hurled his thunderbolt at Hanuman moments before he could reach the sun. Hanuman was thrown back, his body striking a glancing blow to the moon, which sustained a deep crater still visible on a full-moon night, and then fell upon a mountain of our world, whereupon his jaw broke on impact. This, by the way, was how he came to be known as Hanumat or Hanuman, literally, He Of The Broken Jaw, for until that day he had been known after his mother's name, Anjaneya, from Anjan, as is the vanar custom. On breaking his jaw, at once Hanuman began bawling. For even though he was possessed of divine powers, he was still a babe and knew only one way to express himself.'

Rama looked at Hanuman, and so guileless and honest was the vanar's protruding face that he could well imagine the little babe that this grown hulk had once been. When he looked back at Jambavan, he found the bear gazing at him with a dark twinkle in his grape-black eyes, as if he knew exactly what Rama had just thought, and indeed what he was thinking at any moment.

'Naturally, his true father Vayu, who was everywhere and saw everything that happened, was furious. Greatly offended by Indra's action against his son, he did the worst thing possible. He ceased blowing in the three worlds. At once, all creatures high and low, devas and Asuras and mortals and other creatures, began suffering greatly. The devas were confused and knew that they must appease Vayu at once or all life would cease to exist. So Lord Brahma picked up little Hanuman, rocked him on his knee, and conferred upon him a blessing, softly whispered. This was the boon of invulnerability. From that moment onward, Hanuman could never be harmed by any weapon in battle, be it mortal or celestial, no matter who wielded it. It was Brahma's way of saying to Vayu that in future even Lord Indra, master of heaven's affairs, could not punish his son as he had done that one time. Indra, who was feeling very guilty, for he had after all employed a terrible weapon against one who was no more than an innocent babe, was pleased and relieved. To show that he had not meant little Hanuman any harm, he granted him a boon as well.'

'What boon was that, lord bear?'

It was Hanuman himself who had asked the question.

Jambavan grunted and patted the vanar's head affectionately, tousling his hair as he would any bear cub. 'It was the power to choose the manner and time of your own death, my lad. Considered by many to be the greatest boon of all. For as we know, even the boons of invulnerability and invincibility can prove wearisome after a long life. Sooner or later, all things must end. It is the way of the world. So, to be able to choose when that time comes and in what way, ah, that is the finest gift anyone can be given.'

The bear king sighed and slapped his own thigh again. Several startled bees, suckling contentedly on the honey drops splattered here and there on the bear lord's fur, were startled and flew off, buzzing in protest. 'But of course, there was a caveat to all these gifts. It was decided that henceforth Hanuman's mind would be sealed from all knowledge or awareness of his own divinity and of the great powers he wielded. When the proper time came, it would be revealed again, but for the nonce it was best that he neither knew nor wielded his power. For he was after all a vanar, and for him to be exposed as such a powerful being would mean casting aspersions on his father-hood. And Anjan did not wish her husband to ever doubt his son's parentage during his lifetime. Even now, were the good vanar Kesari still alive on this earth, I would not be telling you this tale, my friends.'

Jambavan looked at the back of his right paw, noticing a

food stain of some kind that had been there for some days. He licked it curiously, then lapped it clean, as he added, 'And that is the legend of Hanuman's parentage and true nature, revealed to you all at last.'

Rama glanced around. Everyone looked stunned. He could see that several had questions, probably too many to be answered, and too controversial to be dealt with quickly and easily, even if the surly bear king deigned to answer one or two. Most stunned of all was Angad, who sat with his gaze riveted on Hanuman's upturned face – still looking at Jambavan – as if he could not believe that his childhood playmate was the same being of whom Jambavan had just spoken.

After a pregnant pause, during which Rama could hear the separate sounds of the surf soughing on the beach below and the ocean crashing upon the cliffside and crags, a great commotion broke out. Everyone began speaking at once, some excited, others shocked, and scores of vanars and bears began crowding the grove, seeking to spy the son of Vayu-deva with newly opened eyes that now saw him for the great being he truly was. It was a cacophony so deafening, the bats in the trees above began screeing their sub-vocal calls and flying about madly.

Rama stood and asked for silence. Few heard him at first. That itself showed the level of excitement.

He shouted. The other vanar and bear leaders heard him and conveyed his desire. A wave of 'Be silent!' and 'Rama speaks!' rippled outward from the grove, travelling miles away, and finally quiet descended raggedly once more. Rama waited a moment or two. He could hear the distant shouts of 'Quiet, quiet!' still echoing and being repeated, the whirring of the bats overhead, and the hammering of his own heart in his chest.

Finally, he raised his hand to indicate he had something important to say.

'All things come at their proper time and place. Thus has it been designed by the creator Sri, the One God of whom even the devas and devis are but many disparate reflections. There is a reason and purpose for Jambavan to be telling us this tale today, not yesterday or tomorrow. And there is a reason why Hanuman's full potential was not revealed to us any other day. As we all know, time is short and the task ahead immense. I know you would all dearly desire to debate and discuss this matter further, but I request you to put it aside. We know our friend's greatness now, and that is all that matters. All our doubts and queries can be answered over time – indeed, I have no doubt that the things we are meant to know we will come to know in due course anyway. But for the nonce, we must give our friend pause to reflect upon the things he himself has learned here about his own self. Now is not the time to press him with a thousand queries. Give him some space, my friends, give him a little room to explore the implications of his own rediscovered history.'

Jambavan rose. 'Rama speaks wisely, as ever. Heed him well. I have told the tale of Hanuman's true identity not to entertain and regale us all, but to help the vanar himself unlock the power embedded in his being. Yet all the power in the world is of no use if he who bears it is not able to comprehend its purpose and put it to good use.

'Let Hanuman sit and meditate on what he has learned about himself. When he is ready, let him come and join us again. We owe him this much at least.'

And the bear king looked at Rama and said gently, 'Rama, if you wish it, let us return to work now. The sun is still high above and there are many fruitful hours of labour to be enjoyed. Order the vanar sena and the rksa sena back to work on the bridge. Hard labour is the best antidote for too much thought and speculation.'

Rama nodded. 'I concur, Jambavan, my friend.'

He gave orders accordingly, and without a murmur of protest all began to move back towards the beach, their vast numbers reminding him of an ocean.

Nala came to him as he walked out of the sweet shade of the grove into the sunlight again. He seemed inordinately excited.

'Rama, I must have words with you.'

Rama thought at first that the vanar wished to discuss the story told in the grove, and what it implied for them all. 'Speak, Nala.'

Nala began to babble, his words stumbling over themselves, stopping and starting, breaking off in mid-sentence, gesturing furiously. He described calculations he had made, estimates of the distance, the likely depth of the ocean, the kind of rocks, the size and variety. He talked about an experiment he had conducted in a little inlet with a troop of vanars over the past days, and the results of that experiment.

Lakshman and Angad came up while they were talking and heard part of Nala's explanations. Rama glanced at them to see if they understood the vanar any better than he did. Neither seemed to know what he was talking about. Out of politeness, and sensing that it mattered greatly to Nala, Rama let him finish.

'So you see, Rama,' the vanar concluded breathlessly, 'this method will be far safer than the method we have been using till now, and moreover, it makes better use of our vast forces. Instead of large numbers waiting for each giant boulder to be manoeuvred into position or carried hither and thither, everyone can work simultaneously. The work will proceed much faster, and with greater efficiency.'

He would have gone on in this mode, but Rama interrupted him.

'Nala,' he said patiently, 'Lakshman and Angad did not hear your full explanation. Can you repeat the gist of your argument for their benefit? But only the main gist, please. Time is short.'

Nala turned to the others and started again with his calculations. This time he even took up a stick he carried with him for such things, and began drawing pictures and numbers in the dirt, showing them some elaborate Vedic system of calculation he had devised involving the multiplication of the number of rocks by the length and breadth and depth of the proposed sea-bridge and—

'Nala, Nala,' Rama said hastily. 'Not the whole explanation. I mean to say, just tell us your conclusion. In one sentence!'

Nala stopped and scratched his head, looking bewildered, as if the idea of reducing his complex calculations into a single sentence was harder than building the entire bridge to Lanka. But finally, after several false attempts, Rama managed to get the gist out of him.

'So,' Rama said slowly, making sure he had understood correctly, 'the idea is simply to switch from large rocks to small rocks. Right?'

'Yes!' Nala said, almost weeping with relief that he was finally being understood. Lakshman and Angad, with their customary impatience, had asked him several pointed questions that had confused and then maddened him. Rama wondered if all creatures endowed with extraordinary mental gifts were similarly challenged when it came to expressing the fruits of those talents.

'Yes, Rama,' Nala went on. 'Imagine every vanar holding a small stone, passed on by means of a great chain from hand to hand, and finally thrown into the ocean. Each stone individually is too small to make much of a difference, but millions of them, thrown continually, all day long, will make up a volume as great as several hundred giant boulders.'

'And there will be no risk involved, for these stones will not be in danger of crushing us,' Rama said, seeing the full import of Nala's new idea. 'And because everyone will be picking up and passing on the stones at once, the majority will not be sitting idle for hours and waiting as they do now.'

'That is what I have said already! Exactly!'

Rama looked at his two companions. They raised their eyebrows sceptically. 'What do you think?'

Lakshman shrugged. 'I am not sure. Would even a million small stones fill up as much depth as a single large boulder?'

'Might such small stones not be washed away by the tide?' Angad asked.

'And what would keep them piled up on top of each other?'

Lakshman added doubtfully. 'At least the big boulders, once thrown, stay firmly in place. Even an ocean squall cannot move them. But little rocks . . . ?'

Agitated, Nala began to repeat his explanations about experiments conducted in inlets and the calculations that showed how the sheer number of hands and the volume of the rocks—

Rama stopped him. 'No need to explain yourself again, Nala. I have made my decision. We shall build it as you propose.'

'We shall?' A stunned smile spread slowly across the vanar's protruding mouth.

'Yes, Nala. You are the bridge-builder. I have seen your work and am greatly impressed by it. We shall follow your plan. Let us put it into effect at once.'

'Now, Rama?' Nala hardly seemed able to contain his emotions.

Rama looked up at the sun. It was already moving low in the west. 'Until we start, we will not know how effective it is. The best way to find out is by implementing it and then judging the results for ourselves. Angad, Lakshman, see to it that all the leaders are given the appropriate instructions. Nala, you supervise the chains as you described to me. You will be the overseer of the operation henceforth. All of us will be guided by you and you alone. There must be no dissension on this matter. Is that clear?'

Lakshman's eyes flashed, but he nodded in a surly way.

Rama was alone for barely a moment before he felt the presence of someone close by.

It was Sakra. The little vanar hovered hesitantly.

'Yes, Cheeka,' Rama said, then corrected himself. 'Sakra, my friend. What troubles you?'

'Hanuman,' said the little one, his mischievously twinkling eyes sombre for once. 'He has gone into the forest. Nobody knows where. The bears say he has gone into the caves. To meditate. Jambavan went with him . . . to aid him in his self-discovery, they say.' He sniffed disapprovingly. 'Smells like rotten fish to a vanar, I say.'

Rama bent down and picked up the little vanar. Sakra was startled at first, issuing a brief 'Cheeka!' then grew still, realising that he was enjoying a rare privilege by being embraced by the great Rama himself.

'That is good, Sakra,' Rama said. 'Great revelations were made to Hanuman today. He needs time to reflect upon it all.'

Sakra looked unconvinced. He glanced this way then that, as if wishing Hanuman were here with them.

'What troubles you still, Sakra?'

'I am afraid, Rama,' he said meekly, a different person from the fellow who played pranks and created commotions in the vanar ranks all day long. 'I fear we will lose Hanuman for ever now.'

'Why do you fear that, Sakra?'

'Because now he knows that he is so powerful, why should he stay with us any longer? He will leave us and go live with his father the wind god and we will never see him again.'

'If that is his choice, then he is entitled to it. He may go anywhere his heart pleases. We must bid him farewell and wish him well in whatever he chooses to do.' Rama paused, looking out at the great azure ocean. 'But I do not think that is the way he will turn. I think your brother – for he is your brother still, have no doubt about that – will do the right thing. He is a great servant of dharma. He will do what dharma dictates.'

Sakra looked up at Rama silently, his large eyes soulful and open in a way that only those of the innocent-minded could be. Suddenly he craned his head upwards and licked Rama's face.

'What was that for?' Rama asked, smiling.

'For showing my brother the way to his own true self.'

'But I did not do that, Sakra. It was Jambavan who told him the story of his origins. I did not even know the tale of Hanuman's parentage.'

'But it was you who gave him his true strength. The strength to unlock his powers and become himself. You are the one who truly empowered him. He told me how, even at your first meeting, you spoke to him with love and kindness, and addressed him as a man. A man! No one had ever treated him so well before. He would speak of you often after he came back, during the months he was watching you and your battles. But after that first meeting, he said that you were not only the greatest yodha he had ever seen, but a god upon earth.'

Rama was embarrassed, even though Sakra's innocence made the praise guileless and easy. 'He was wrong, Sakra. I am just a man. It is Hanuman who is the son of a god living among us upon earth, although I did not know this at the time I first met him.'

Sakra raised his gaze to Rama's face. 'Yet you treated him with great respect. The olduns say that the devas love us all equally. *You* love all of us, vanars and bears and mortals, equally. You treated Hanuman as a man even back when he was no more than a humble vanar messenger. So you must be a deva too, Rama. I think one day some wise storyteller will tell your story too, that the whole world may know your great-ness.'

Rama did not know what to say to that. He was silent for a long time.

Finally he said, 'Come, it is time to go back to work now, my friend. Let us help make Nala's vision a reality.'

He put Sakra down and held his hand. The vanar's head barely reached up to his hip.

'Yes, Rama,' Sakra said solemnly. 'Let us go and build the bridge to Lanka. We will do it together, you and I.'

They went across the beach together, hand in hand.

8

He woke in the early watches of the morning, those hours called bhor suvah considered most auspicious for meditation, prayer and penance. He sat up slowly, unwilling to disturb his companions, and sat breathing shallowly. He had dreamed of his father, standing on the beach, calling his name. He looked around, trying to rub the weariness and grit from his vision.

The beach was covered for as far as the eye could see with what seemed like irregularly shaped stones that he knew were the sleeping forms of bears and vanars. It was not quiet. The combined sound of all the bears snoring and the vanars calling out occasionally in their sleep, still uneasy from their proximity to the ocean, made for an unmusical cacophony of sounds. But as far as he could see, there was no standing form. Certainly nothing that looked like a stocky human male.

The sand felt gritty and faintly damp under his body: a combination of dew and spray, settling slowly every night, usually drying by morning. The land was dark and shadowy; the faint telltale glow over the north-western horizon confirmed that there had been a moon but it had only just set. There were no watch-fires kept burning in this camp, for the crackling flames and wind-blown sparks were more terrifying to both races than any intruders. Sentries were posted, at Rama's orders, but they were on the high points, watching the sea. He craned his head, trying to make out their silhouettes atop the mountain, but it was futile in this light. From up there they had a view of the entire ocean upon which even the smallest skiff would be noticeable.

There had been a couple of false warnings that had turned out to be sea monsters; those immense grey-black elephantine beasts that rolled and churned in the foaming waters, issuing spouts of spray from holes in their heads. Their appearance had caused much consternation but ultimately they had seemed benign. The bears spoke fearfully of the great serpents and other vile beasts that lived in the deep reaches beneath the ocean, but nothing anyone had ever heard of corresponded with those spume-blowing sea elephants. Rama thought they were like their land counterparts: dangerous only if threatened or maddened, otherwise content to live peacefully and spend their days incessantly feeding those immense bodies.

He could not fall asleep again. The dream, or vision, or whatever it had been, had been too vivid and unsettling. Instead he rose and carefully picked a way through the mass of huddled bodies. Going up the beach would be impossible; there were bodies clustered for at least a yojana. It would be morning before he reached a clear area, and if he disturbed even one of the sleeping forms, chaos would ensue. This way there were only a few hundred to get past, and then he was just above the high-tide line, walking down to the ocean buffeted by a brisk sea breeze that carried more than a promise of chill. The vanars claimed that autumn was mild in these coastal parts, but winter would be freezing, the absence of snow more than compensated for by the deathly chill winds that blew nonstop. Already he could feel the first warning in this sea breeze. They must cross before winter set in fully, or Devi alone knew how they would endure.

The gravelly wet sand of the lower beach crunched under his bare feet – the tide was out – and he felt the faint scurrying of sand crabs underfoot, though he could not see them. The surf ran up and fell back a few yards to his left as he made towards the promontory. He leapt the last yard, landing nimbly on the smooth slab placed to improve access. The stone was surprisingly warm and dry to the touch, and he stood there a moment, looking out at the darkened ocean, trying to make out the long finger of the bridge. Yesterday, work had gone exceedingly well. Despite much confusion ensuing mainly from the coordination of tasks and some hilarious errors in direction – some of the lines had ended up carrying stones down to the beach and most of the way back in a circuitous semi-circular fashion before they realised their mistake – the new plan was working brilliantly well. Even though he strained he could not quite see the end of the bridge, but his mind's eye retained the last view he had had of it in fading daylight, as Nala brought him and the others the wonderful news that they had extended it by over fifty yards that day.

'Fifty yards!' Lakshman had repeated. And even his normally surly face had cracked into a wide grin. It was almost as much as they had achieved since they had begun, and all in half a day. There was no question that Nala's change of approach had been a stroke of sheer brilliance. Everyone had stopped work filled with new hope, looking forward to the next day's labour.

'Give me five days, my lord,' Nala had said confidently, 'and your bridge will be ready.'

Rama made his way slowly along the unfinished line of stone, treading carefully for fear of crabs. The bears delighted in breaking the shells off the scuttling things and slurping out the pale, fishlike meat while the claws still scrabbled helplessly. They claimed that the flesh was sweetest when fresh. Rama had declined politely. He had no desire to eat anything that still moved. If that was fresh, he was quite content with stale food, relatively speaking.

When he reached the end of the large boulder portion and stepped on to the small stone part of the bridge, he was surprised once more by how firm and solid it felt. Nala had been proved right about this as well. Far from being crumbly and liable to dissipate in the pounding ocean, the use of smaller stones in place of large boulders had actually proved more stable to walk upon. The surface here was as flat as a road. Rama could almost envision riding a chariot over it, whereas with the large boulders, the path sloped and rose and fell so abruptly, even the sure-footed vanars sometimes slipped, and the bears were constantly in danger of cracking their skulls open like the crabs they loved so much.

Someone was standing at the end of the bridge.

Rama stopped still. He felt at his waist, reaching instinctively for his sword. It was back upon the beach, at the spot where he had lain. So was his bow and quiver. He was unarmed and defenceless. When one moved with a force of over a million strong bodies, one seldom felt the need to remain armed at all times.

But now there was someone on the bridge, at the farthermost end, where no vanar or bear would dare venture at night. It was hard enough to make them come out here by day, where the ocean pressed in on three sides, and only a few sturdy ones had overcome their fear of the open sea and elected to work this part of the chain. They were mainly bears at that. As for mortals, there was only one other apart from himself, and Lakshman was lying fast asleep a yard from his own sleeping spot.

Whoever or whatever was out there, it was neither vanar, bear, nor mortal.

Yet somehow he did not feel alarmed or afraid.

He felt as if he had been expecting to meet someone out here. As if this was the reason why he had awakened – or been awakened – and had come upon the bridge.

He walked the last twenty yards slowly but without fear. The ocean was very loud and encompassing here. It filled one's senses completely: the wind so powerful it felt as if with one impatient gust it could throw you over into the brine. The waves rolled by on their way to the beach with relentless strength, unstoppable by even a giant vanar. The sound itself was eternal and omnipresent, godlike in that it had been here for millennia before the first living beings crawled upon this world, and would be here for millennia after the death of the last one. It filled him completely, wiping out all thought, all fear, all anticipation.

He walked to the end of the bridge.

As he approached, the figure standing there turned slowly. He saw the shadowy profile of a familiar face. And a voice that brought back a torrent of memories said warmly, 'My son.'

They came in the dead of night. Or perhaps it was mid-afternoon outside, or morning, or evening, but in here it was always night, always the dead of night, and the very sameness of it was unnerving, depressing, a literal night without end. The rakshasas had been unusually vicious since the death of their companion. Their ranting and railing had turned obscene and ugly beyond belief. Her arms and back and legs were scored with countless scratches and gouges and slashes. Staying curled up and silently motionless had become a fine art of which she was a master now. Blood had dried on a hundred little nicks and cuts, none deep enough to leave a scar or cause much harm, but all expertly designed to inflict pain. Pain, that was her lot now. Endless pain. And monsters taunting and tormenting her night and . . . night and . . .

She laughed miserably. She could not even say night and day any more, nor think it. For there was no day for her. Only an endless night among rakshasas.

A while back, they had left her suddenly, departing without a word, as if recalled by some mental command that could not be disobeyed. She had heard nothing, felt nothing, but she knew that in this strange, unnatural place, orders were often conveyed wordlessly, objects appeared at the slightest thought. She herself had seen it done, when the rakshasas willed food into appearing, or wine, or jewels to ornament their grotesque bodies. It was all provided in the blink of an eye. What had Ravana called it? Pushpak? The tower? She no longer remembered clearly. Whatever it was, it was bewitched, the stuff of Asura maya. That was how they made it appear to be night always.

She waited for the visitors to come. She could hear them making their way through the forest, their heels crunching on the dried leaves underfoot. Apparently, the illusion being maintained was that it was late autumn in this place. That would correspond with the outside, real world, although she had no idea whether Lanka's climate was like that of the rest of the mortal realm. Was Lanka even a part of the mortal realm? From what she knew, which was very little, it was indeed a real place, a sizeable island-kingdom that had existed and flourished before Ravana took it over, but his sorcery had altered it somehow, making it a suitable place for the Asura races who followed him. And most of all, for the rakshasas.

She regretted not having been more responsive to the rakshasa male. The one who had visited her the day before. Or was it the night before? Anyway, the one who had visited some time back, the one with the strange caste marks on his forehead, black thread around his chest, and white garments, just like any mortal brahmin. Were there brahmins among rakshasas? She had heard there were. After all, even the Asura races had been created by the One God, the same supreme being who had created the holy trimurti and the rest of the devas, mortals and the three worlds. She had heard her father speak of rakshasas who were devout and pious, celibate and honourable. Rakshasas who adhered scrupulously to dharma. It had seemed like a contradiction in terms to her then, but she wondered now whether perhaps it was conceivable. Anything seemed possible now. Even Ravana had appeared so suave and gentle and noble . . . but that was almost certainly a ploy. Look at how she had been maltreated after that. Unless it was the work of his wife, that shrew who had said all those nauseating lies about Rama. She did not know any more: the incessant hammering away of the rakshasas had taken its toll. She hardly knew if she was sane or insane. But she wished now that she had allowed herself to trust the rakshasa brahmin, to speak a word or two. He had seemed to genuinely care for her welfare, had sounded outraged at how she had been treated. And yet she had formed the impression that he was Ravana's . . . brother? Surely that was impossible.

The bushes parted and they emerged into the clearing where she sat. The two of them.

'Sita-devi, we meet again,' Ravana said. 'I believe you have already met my wife Mandodhari? She is the one I entrusted with your charge. I am sorry to say, it appears that you have abused her excellent hospitality and repaid her by committing a grievous crime. I have come to ascertain if this is true.'

The queen of rakshasas stepped forward, her eyes flashing in the eerie glaucous light. 'There is nothing to ascertain. She killed one of my sakshis. And she must be punished for it. The penalty I demand is her life.'

'My son,' the dark figure said. 'My eyes have thirsted so long for a sight of you.'

'Father?' Rama said doubtfully. 'Is it really you?'

The figure held out his hands, the sky behind him just slightly lighter than his dark silhouette, enough to let Rama see his outline, that familiar hulking, bearlike figure that his father had become in his last years. He was not sure of it, but he thought he could see a beard as well, a great bushy beard, something he had seen only in the lifesize royal portraits in Suryavansha Hall. He recalled reading or being told that his father had been in the habit of growing his beard only when he went to war. Since the last Asura war had ended seven years before Rama's birth, he had grown up seeing his father always clean-shaven, groomed every morning by one of the royal barbers who had been practising their hereditary trade for as long as the Suryavansha dynasty had been in power, which was some eight centuries. The portraits that had recorded that imperial facial growth had all depicted his father in younger, fitter days, hard-muscled body plated with armour, bearing gleaming weapons of war, always aboard his chariot, which had been his trademark, for a king's prowess with his chariot was a family tradition in their line, and it was in expectation of his excellence in that art that he had been named Dasaratha at birth: He Who Rides Ten Chariots At Once.

Rama brushed aside these useless musings and focused on the outstretched arms of the figure standing before him.

'Come to me, my son. Let me feel your heart against mine.'

Rama went forward unhesitatingly. With all his being he desired to embrace his father too. He had never been able to accept the fact that Maharaja Dasaratha had died only hours after Rama had gone into exile, had never stopped wishing he had put off his departure by one night. Perhaps then Dasaratha would have put off his own departure too . . .

At the very last moment, something flared in his mind, a bright and fluorescent flame of doubt. He paused abruptly. 'But, Father, you are no longer of this world. How is it possible then that you stand here as flesh and blood, able to embrace me heart to heart?'

Dasaratha sighed. He lowered his hands slowly, reluctantly, but with a decline of his leonine head that suggested he had known Rama would not accept his embrace. That some things were just not meant to be. 'You speak wisely, Rama. The dead are dead. They cannot walk this world again. For their bodies are ash, and their souls, the eternal spark of brahman that burns within every living creature, must move on to their next birth. The only exceptions are those rare souls who have achieved moksh, freedom from the endless cycle of birth, death and rebirth. And I have not yet reached that exalted state of infinite freedom.'

He sighed again. 'The truth is, Rama, I have not come to share a warm moment of reunion with you. Much as I would desire to enjoy that stolen treasure, yet it is not for my own selfish satisfaction that I was sent back here to speak with you. You are not wrong in deciding not to embrace me. I am but a thing of shadow and essence, no more substantial than the curling smoke rising from a funeral pyre. I am garbed in this form and given the power of speech only long enough to communicate the urgent missive I have been given to pass on to you. So listen carefully, my beloved son. For once my message is delivered, I will vanish, and you will never see me again.'

Rama started forward, regretting his moment of indecision, desiring to embrace this dark, shadowy form, to see for himself if he was substantial or not. How could he have been so foolish as to deny himself the heaven-sent opportunity to enjoy one last fatherly embrace?

But the ghost was speaking again. 'Heed me well, my son. I will say this but once, then I am gone. You must go to her with utmost speed and haste. She is in dire distress.'

Rama knew at once that he was speaking of Sita. 'We are building this bridge as fast as we can,' he blurted. 'In another five days—'

He saw the silhouette shake his head sharply. 'In five days, she will be lost to you for ever. Not killed, but something far worse. You must go to her now. This very day, even as we speak, she faces the greatest crisis of her life, and without your urgent assistance she will not survive it. There is little point in waging a war to win her back if you lose her even before the war is begun. This is the missive I was sent to convey to you.'

The figure looked up. Already, Rama saw, he was growing insubstantial, starting to fade. Wisps of his silhouette were being pulled away from his form, like a cloud of smoke being blown apart by wind.

'It is time now. I must go. But in going, I will say one more thing. Ravana. Ask yourself *why* he has ten heads. And what that has to do with you. *That* is the key. Answer that question, Rama, and you will know the secret of defeating the Lord of Lanka . . .'

The last words were lost to the wind, the form itself whipped away like a feather taken by a gust. Where the shape and form of his father had stood a moment ago, now there was nothing but empty air and a hard-built surface of stone.

Rama rushed forward. But his hands closed on empty air. The end of the bridge lay below his feet, sloping sharply down into the ocean. A wave crashed softly against the bottom, spray splashing his feet. The tide was rising, and so was the wind.

'Father!' he cried out wildly. 'Father!'

But there was nothing there. Only the wind, wailing around him, echoing his anguish.

9

'Rama.'

He heard Lakshman's voice calling him for the fourth or fifth time, but did not turn. He was sitting in the same position he had been in since the early hours of the morning, on the edge of the end of the bridge, staring out to sea. The tide had come in since then and the waves breaking around him had drenched him completely, several times over. The eastern sky was vermilion-tinted, with a hint of a blush of peach, and the silhouettes of great flocks of birds, as substantial as large clouds, wheeled and circled slowly high above the distant mountain ranges. The air was less cold now but a nip still remained.

'Rama.' Lakshman's feet appeared in his peripheral vision, to his right. His brother dropped to the ground, seating himself on the rocks beside Rama. 'What is it? What's wrong?'

Rama could not bring himself to even look at Lakshman. Far behind in the distance, he could hear the usual sounds on the beach, the various noises of a million-odd bears and vanars milling about in semi-organised chaos, taking their places, shouting the inane things to one another that fellow soldiers did when performing mindless tasks, but also excited, enthusiastic, eager, something most ordinary soldiers rarely were when engaged in such brainless labour. He felt a pang of conscience again. Was he truly leading this force? To what purpose? What end would this war serve? Was it necessary at all?

His brother was silent, waiting with a patience he had not shown of late. Lakshman sensed the turmoil within Rama: he knew him well. Perhaps better than Sita knew him even. What was it she always said? *My husband, my love, you're like Brahma-dev. Four faces, and no matter which one I happen to see, they are all the same!*

'If it's Hanuman's state that troubles you,' Lakshman said quietly, 'then I will gladly go and seek him out. Kambunara knows the caves they have gone into. It is a labyrinth that tunnels beneath the ranges in the east; the mouth is but a few miles away.'

When Rama did not say anything in response to that for several more minutes, Lakshman said, 'King Sugreeva has come to join us, Rama. He arrived a few minutes ago. He has brought fresh troops with him from Kiskindha, as the city is now secure and he wishes to take part personally in the war against Lanka. Will you not come and greet him at least?'

Still Rama gave no reply. Lakshman made yet another attempt to draw him out. 'Rama, everyone is waiting for us. Nala saw you sitting here and tried to call out to you, but when you did not answer his calls, he came back and was very anxious. He is concerned that you are upset with him because of the change in method. But look, Rama, his impossible idea works! Look at the progress we made in a few hours yesterday. And with everybody confused and unable to understand the new system. Today, we are all prepared and well briefed, and we will do exceedingly well. You know,' he laughed self-deprecatingly, 'I thought that you were mad to trust in these vanars. And when the bears showed up . . .' He shook his head. 'But now, I don't think I would want any other army behind us. What they lack in discipline and training they more than make up for in vigour and enthusiasm. And their loyalty . . . their loyalty is amazing. So many gave their lives carrying rocks and stones! They died without even seeing a day of combat. Think how bravely they will fight once the war itself begins. We are within reach of our goal, Rama. There is no need to despair. Nala says we will finish the bridge in five days. I believe him. Five days more, maybe less, and we will be there, on the shores of Lanka.' He clenched his fist and shook it at the open sea, shouting at the top of his voice, 'And then we shall show that ten-headed pig how we Ayodhyans wage war!'

Lakshman looked at Rama closely for the first time, lowering his hand and his tone of voice as well. 'Rama, whatever it is that ails you today, talk to me, and I will help you rid yourself of it. I know full well the kind of black despair that steals across the heart in the dark watches of the night. I have battled my own inner demons too, as fierce as any horde of kumbharakshasas. It is a war that I fear we kshatriyas wage all our lives, and one that is never truly won, nor ever finished. But we will fight together in this struggle, as in all else. We have set our feet upon this path, and we will follow it to the ends of the earth. Take my hand, my brother. Take my hand and rise again, and face a new day.'

Rama let Lakshman grip his hand tightly and raise him up, half lifting his weight until he was forced to come to his feet. Lakshman's face was anxious and set in a stubborn, determined, no-surrender-no-retreat expression that was so like the face of the little boy Rama recalled from their gurukul days, the little boy who would stand with him against any number of opponents on the battle-training field, even though he was on the verge of tears and knew they could no longer win the practice bout, the little boy who was closer to his elder brother than to his own twin, Shatrugan.

Rama leaned forward and kissed his brother on the side of his face, and said, 'Father came to see me last night.'

Lakshman froze. His eyes met Rama's. There was wild light in them, reflections of the first rays of the sun rising in the east. 'Truly?'

'It was some kind of shadow image of him, a soul-reflection. He did not stay long. He had been sent to give me a message, and once he had delivered it, he vanished like smoke.'

Lakshman stared at Rama silently, absorbing this extraordinary turn of events. Finally he asked, 'What was the message?'

Rama sucked in a deep breath, inhaling the sharp, tangy salt of the spray mist that enveloped them like a cloud, produced by the constant pounding of the waves against the bridge. 'Sita is in grave distress. Extreme peril of some sort. If we do not reach her in time, she will be lost for ever.'

Lakshman's eyes flickered. His jaw shook a little. Then he said, 'Five days. Maybe even four. Nala says—'

'It will be too late. Father's ghost said today was her day of reckoning.'

'Day of reckoning?'

'Or words to that effect. He did not explain. It was all very brief, very dreamlike. He called me here to the end of the bridge in the dead of night. He said that if we do not reach Sita today and aid her, she will be worse than dead.'

'Worse than dead?'

'What are we to do, Lakshman? Can we build a boat? I wanted to wake you and start chopping down a tree that very minute. But I realised that even if we lash a raft or a skiff together quickly, Sampati the vulture told Jambavan – and even Jatayu had told us often before – that the strait to Lanka cannot be crossed in a small craft.'

'Yes.' Lakshman stared unseeingly at the ocean. 'Yes, that is so. The currents from the southern seas are immense, you can see that even now from the force of the tides. A small craft will not survive the crossing, and even if it holds together, you are more likely to be carried off course, out to the open seas, hundreds of miles away from any land mass. It requires a well-weighted ship and knowledge of the tides and currents. Jatayu often told us that this was the reason why it took Ravana so long to launch his invasion. He had first to construct sufficient ships to carry his huge army across the strait. And that construction took over two decades. We would need a large ship, at least twenty tons weight, to cross.'

'And no matter how fast we work, we cannot complete the bridge today, can we?' Rama heard the hope as well as the hopelessness in his own voice. Yet he was unable to stop himself from asking the question.

Lakshman shook his head sadly. 'Impossible. Even four or five days seems a miracle. Not even Nala can find a way to broach this expanse in one day.'

'Then we are lost.' Rama let his hands hang limply by his sides, lowering his head. 'We are truly lost. What good is this war if we cannot save Sita?'

Lakshman looked at him, his eyes mirroring Rama's pain. He embraced his brother, clapping him tightly on the back, held him a long moment, then released him without saying a word. His eyes were glistening when they parted.

'Rama! Lakshmana!'

The voice was that of a vanar. They turned together.

Sakra stood a few yards away, looking more cheerful than usual. His tail was upright behind him, swaying slowly from side to side, like a cat's.

'He's back, my lords. My brother Hanuman is back!'

She was bound and gagged by the rakshasas before they took her away. Gagged! As if she would scream their city down if her mouth was left open! She supposed it was to keep up the pretence that mortals were foul-mouthed creatures who could not stop shrieking obscenities, part of the whole elaborate picture they had built of her. It was supremely ironic: they had simply taken all their faults and given them to her. They did not even have to fabricate qualities, only wrongly attribute them.

A way opened in mid-air, some kind of sorcerous portal. Through it she could see a long winding passageway, with white walls and golden pillars, but around the rim of the open portal, the forest remained unchanged. She recalled seeing something similar before and racked her brains to remember it. She was weak from hunger and thirst and brain-weary from the days of mental torture and anguish. But it came to her as the first of the rakshasas went through. In Mithila. After the swayam-vara. Her swayamvara. Ravana had gone through a portal in the air much like this one. She almost smiled bitterly. And yet Mandodhari had claimed that Rama was a sorcerer who used illusion and magic to propagate the false impression of his superiority as a warrior. It was obvious how the queen of rakshasas had formed her misimpression of Rama; she had been fed a carefully reconstructed self-image of her own husband!

Unhappy with her slowness, Vikata shoved her through the portal with a vicious kick. Sita fell through and landed on her shoulder hard enough to knock the breath out of her. She had twisted her body to avoid landing on her front, protecting her belly. She grimaced at the pain. But they were prodding her and kicking her and she struggled to her feet as quickly as possible before one of them kicked her in the middle.

They snarled as they pushed her along, their foul breath nauseating her. She struggled to keep her balance as she was half shoved and half pulled through winding white corridors lined with elaborately carved gold-plated pillars. At strategic points, enormous portraits had been hung, depicting what seemed to be famous rakshasa kings. She guessed they were Ravana's ancestors, the famed Pulastya line that she had heard the rakshasas mention in the course of their tormenting. Every few dozen yards there was an elaborately carved doorway guarded by rakshasa sentries in matching garb, heavily armed. Everything seemed vaguely familiar, and at first she put it down to her own disorientation and weakness. It took her a few moments more to realise why.

A gasping chuckle escaped her.

The short, rotund rakshasi was sniffing at her mouth in a trice. 'What's that? What do you find funny about all this?'

Sita knew better than to answer. She just kept her head down and kept moving. But in her mind she was laughing incredulously. *It's all modelled on Suryavansha Palace. Ravana's wonderful new palace or tower or whatever he calls it is modelled on the royal palace of Ayodhya!*

And now that she had made the connection, she began to see more similarities at every turn. The garb of the rakshasa sentries, the emblems on their shoulder-clasps, the symbols carved above doorways, the style of art used in the portraits and their framing, the pattern of the pillars, everything was so acutely reminiscent of Ayodhya that she might well have thought she was in some phantasmagoric nightmare if not for the throbbing in her bones and head and the painful prodding and elbow-nudging that never let her forget where and with whom she was.

Finally, the corridor broadened and rose to vaulting heights, and rich deep-pile carpeting appeared, lined on both sides by armed sentries; these were garbed somewhat differently to the others she had seen, their dhotis the same but their oddly patterned ang-vastras sluiced with purple patches. The rakshasas wearing them even looked different from the others, their features less grotesque and deformed, more bestial and anthropomorphic – more like Ravana himself, in short. She guessed they were Pulastyas, but what did all that purple remind her of? Of course. The PFs, the Purana Wafadars of Ayodhya, the king's personal guard, made up of the oldest, most loyal veterans. That fitted as well with the overall design, she thought bitterly, the flash of humour fled from her as quickly as it had arisen. If you were going to imitate Ayodhya so slavishly in the superficials, then you might as well go all the way. What next? A sabha hall like the great court of Suryavansha Palace? A sunwood throne? A queen . . . She sucked in a sharp breath. A queen like Maharani Kausalya . . . or her daughter-in-law, Princess Sita Janaki? Of course. Was this Ravana's plan then? To turn Lanka into a faux Ayodhya, complete with an Ayodhyan queen transplanted to his bed? If so, surely he was going about it the wrong way.

The rakshasas halted before the great doors. Sita took a moment to glance around, rolling her eyes without turning her head – that would have fetched her another good blow or two – and noted that the architecture of the hallway was quite impossible. The ceiling could not have suddenly grown ten times higher, nor the light so much brighter, despite there being fewer mashaals here than in the corridors. Then she remembered sheepishly: Pushpak. It was all Asura sorcery. That was how Ravana could design his entire palace to look so similar to Ayodhya's house of power. Nothing was what it seemed here, not even the light streaming past her face, or the air she was breathing, redolent of jasmine and lotus bloom and the unmistakable, unconcealable reek of rakshasa sweat and ichor.

The great doors opened and she was ushered into the hall, the sound of her own name, along with some arcane rakshasa pronouncements, echoing from the vaulting ceiling and walls of the enormous chamber, proclaimed loudly by a crier who even sounded exactly like the crier in Suryavansha Hall.

And then the great doors shuddered shut behind her with a terrible finality, and she was in the court of Ravana.

'The charge is murder,' Ravana said imperiously, leaning with one elbow on the armrest of the massive throne – which was, as she had presumed earlier, almost identical to the sunwood throne of Ayodhya. 'You will be permitted to present your defence here and then will be judged guilty or innocent, as the court deems fit.'

She was standing at the foot of the great dais, bound in chains, like some dangerous beast rather than the piteously weak and battered woman she was. She had to raise her head to look up at Ravana's face, or rather, faces. Mandodhari sat to his right, dressed more extravagantly than Sita had seen her till now. Around them sat a semicircle of important-looking rakshasas, including one young specimen who was striking in his sheer ugliness. He oozed masculine virility, and his alien eyes roved freely over the length and breadth and width of her body, gleaming with undisguised lust. He bore a striking resemblance to the queen of rakshasas, and he and another rakshasa beside him were positioned strategically to Ravana's left, which made her think they might be sons or brothers of the ruling pair.

She longed for a sword to put out his eyes.

On the other hand, if lustful gazes offended her so, then she would have had to put out a thousand pairs of rakshasa eyes. For as she had walked the long central carpetway to the foot of the dais, a half a thousand rakshasas lined up on both sides, seated as well as standing, had eyed her, grunting and snorting and sniffing in a manner that left no doubt as to their interest in her unusual mortal anatomy. She had kept her head up high, and walked slowly, but with as much dignity as she could muster. It had been painful, but she was determined to hold up her end to the very last. Like the grove of ashoka trees in which she had spent the last several days, she would break but would not bend.

'I will speak for the victim,' Queen Mandodhari said, rising from her throne with a rustling of delicate fabrics and tinkling of jewels. She stepped down the broad steps of the polished granite dais, taking a place yards from Sita. 'I am ready to present my case. Will the court hear me now?'

'A moment,' Ravana said, raising his hand. His heads scanned the hall, seeking out someone. 'We must have someone to represent the assailant as well. Who will present her case?'

From the stony silence behind her, Sita could tell that nobody was in a hurry to champion her. She was not surprised. Which rakshasa would wish to go up against the King and Queen of Lanka? Especially when they had already made their personal bias clear by referring to her as 'the assailant'.

To her surprise, a voice spoke from close beside her.

'I will.'

A figure moved up past her, stepping before the dais and bowing formally. 'Vibhisena of the Pulastyas, my lord.'

Ravana offered an ingratiating smile on a head or two, while the rest remained preoccupied with inscrutable expressions, but Queen Mandodhari's eyes blazed liquid fire at the rakshasa clad like a brahmin standing beside Sita. Clearly the Queen of Lanka was less than pleased at her brother-in-law's volunteering. She turned her gaze back to Sita and narrowed her eyes sharply, lowering her head, as if to say, It makes no difference, you will not escape me. *If she had her way, I would be a mauled, half-eaten carcass just like that poor old rakshasi they tore apart.*

'Very well,' Ravana said, in a tone that suggested he was almost bored with the proceedings. 'Let the matter proceed quickly. The court has more important issues to debate today.

My queen, you may start by telling us the facts of the matter at hand.'

Sita noted his phrasing with wry bitterness: the *facts* of the matter. Not a point of view or observations, but the facts themselves. Despite all the trappings, this was a very poor imitation of Ayodhya's legendary court of dharma. She ought to feel alarmed, she knew. Terrified even. She was perilously close to being branded a murderer and summarily executed. Instead, she felt almost detached from it all. Above this entire farce of a proceeding.

She barely listened as Mandodhari outlined a predictably biased and distorted version of the events that had led to the rakshasi's death. According to the Queen of Lanka, Trijata's kindness had been rewarded with brutal betrayal. It was the duty of Lanka to see that their guest was treated with due right, but the mortal had been stubborn, fasting deliberately to harm herself, no doubt to give her some cause to lay false blame upon her hosts. And when the elderly sakshi had brought her food and drink, the mortal had leapt upon her and attacked her savagely. Taken by surprise, the rakshasi had made no attempt to defend herself, and had succumbed mercifully quickly. And then, as if to mock the very kindness shown by the poor unfortunate victim, the mortal had fed on the rakshasi's still-warm flesh. She had been discovered pawing at Trijata's steaming innards by the other sakshis, who arrived scant moments too late to save their beloved colleague.

Sita's head grew dizzy for a moment, and she blanked out while still on her feet, losing track of the next several moments. It was all she could do to stay upright. When she regained her senses, the queen was summarising the 'facts' in the case. Mandodhari ended by registering a strong demand that the mortal's vicious behaviour should be repaid with like treatment, and proposed the traditional rakshasa sentence for such a heinous crime. 'She must be given to the companions of the murdered sakshi, and they must eat her flesh and organs while she still lives, and they must continue feeding on her until she is dead and reduced to bone and gristle. It is the only meet fate for such a brutal abuse of hospitality.'

Vibhisena was then invited to step forward and present his side of the matter. Sita had no expectation of his testimony making any difference in this ludicruous staging, but she saw that it mattered to him. He spoke briefly but eloquently, describing how he himself had visited Sita and seen with his own eyes her maltreatment at the hands of the rakshasas who were ostensibly to be her friends in distress. In fact, they were tormenting her and abusing her both mentally and physically. When they left her alone to pursue their own pleasures, he had used the opportunity to entreat the rakshasi Trijata, who seemed the only humane one of them all, to at least allow the mortal to partake of some nourishment. She had done so, and had been taking food and drink to Sita, who was in great need of it. When the other rakshasas saw her doing this, they flew into a rage, and instigated by Vikata, they had attacked their own fellow-rakshasi, and had killed her. Their biting and mauling of her flesh and innards had been typical of their brutal nature. If anyone ought to be punished, it was Vikata and the other rakshasas, not Sita, who was completely blameless and inno- cent of any wrongdoing.

There was much disgruntled murmuring and grunting of disapproval during Vibhisena's speech, reaching a crescendo by the end. This was in stark contrast to the respectful silence that had prevailed during the queen's testimony. After Vibhisena finished and bowed, the disgruntlement turned into outraged cries of 'Traitor!' and 'Mortal-lover!' which, Sita noted, Ravana did little to curb.

The final verdict, when it came, was no surprise.

Ravana spoke with a languid voice, conveying an air of near- boredom at the whole proceeding. A few of his heads were actually asleep, Sita saw, their eyes shut and a mouth or two parted slightly, breathing softly. She had no way to tell if this was feigned or genuine, but it seemed real. She tried to stare at him until he felt the power of her gaze but was unsuccesful.

Ravana barely seemed to be aware of her presence. So much for all his noble dignity earlier. But she remained uncertain: had that been an act, or was this?

'Upon hearing all the facts in the matter, and weighing both sides equally, it is the opinion of the throne that the assailant is guilty as charged. Since we are now a democratic nation, as representatives of the clans and tribes of the new republic of Lanka, I leave the final decision to your able minds. Speak, Lanka. What is your decision? Is the mortal guilty of her crime or no?'

'GUILTY!' came the resounding roar.

Ravana sighed softly, as if it pained him that his hospitality and friendship could have been repaid so brutally. He turned one head to look at Sita. Another head yawned and its eyes flickered briefly before it returned to contented slumber.

'And what is your verdict on the manner of punishment to be granted for this crime?'

'*Death!*' came the exultant response. 'Death by eating alive!'

Ravana gestured imperiously. 'So be it. The sentence will be carried out tonight at midnight, as is usual. It will be held publicly, that all of Lanka may witness how justice is dispensed in our glorious republic. Take the prisoner away and see that she is treated appropriately until it is time. Now let us proceed with other matters of the court.'

As Sita was led away, she saw Mandodhari, seated on her throne, smiling with triumph. Vibhisena sat with his head hanging, miserable. The princes of Lanka – they had been addressed as such in passing – sat watching her with lustful regard, as if debating whether it would be more exciting to ravish her themselves or to see her being eaten alive by rakshasas. Ravana was not even looking at her – she could see none of his heads so much as glancing in her direction. It was as if she had been some unknown harlot dragged in off the streets and brought before him to be tried and sentenced. The rakshasas holding her yanked on the chains hard, almost dislocating her right shoulder, and forced her to turn away. Even as she did so, she caught out of the corner of her eye the sight of Ravana winking at her. Winking! So he had been observing her all along, but concealing his interest.

At that, her simmering impotent anger, long suppressed out of concern for the life growing within her womb, flared into full-blown rage.

She grasped the chains that bound her, wrapping them around her hands and yanking them hard. The rakshasas holding them had become so accustomed to their prisoner's docility, they were ill prepared for this outburst. The ends of the fetters flew out of their grasp. Sita whirled the chains in a sweeping arc, lashing out at each of her tormentors. They struck one on the waist, another across the chest, the third on a hip, the fourth on the front of her thighs. They all shrieked, less with pain than with surprise. Sita swung the fetters in a full circle, building up momentum, forcing them to retreat, limping and sniffling, and making clear that she was willing and able to inflict bodily harm.

The sabha hall exploded with a flurry of roars of outrage, howls of anger, cries of glee. Sentries rushed forward, seeking to bar the prisoner's access to the throne dais and the royal family. Sita saw the smile of triumph in Mandodhari's eyes fade to a dull look of venomous anger. The princes watched with arched eyebrows and greater interest than before: the vixen had shown her claws. At the edge of her vision, she saw the sentries she had noticed earlier, posted one at every pillar, rush forward in concerted efficiency, their purple-black uniforms so much like the PF uniforms of Ayodhya that she almost thought she saw Captain Drishti Kumar leading them. She focused her energies and looked back at the dais.

Ravana was giving her his full attention now. All ten heads were turned towards her, watching intently. A few babbled to one another, but for at least that moment, all his considerable power was directed at her alone.

The sentries rushed forward, weapons lowered and ready to skewer her like a joint of meat for the cookfire. She was, after all, a condemned murderer, awaiting only her fate. Even her whirling circle of chains would not keep them away for more than a moment, and she was weakening already, the days of starvation and thirst taking a heavy toll.

But as they came to the periphery, ready to slip through and pierce her with their evil-looking weapons, the King of Lanka's voice boomed out.

'Do not harm her! She is not to be touched. Step back.'

At once the sentries fell back.

The rakshasas, recovered from the shock of her unexpected turnaround, snarled fiercely, flashing their yellowed fangs and teeth, showing their eagerness to carry out her death sentence here and now. She allowed the chains to slow in their arc, but kept them turning still.

Ravana rose from his throne and stepped across the dais. Mandodhari stood as well, seeking to accompany him and no doubt heap new penalties upon Sita for this new transgression. He spoke a few brief words to her, and she stepped back to her throne, bright spots of colour rising on her cheekbones. Her eyes glared like rubies in a cave wall, reflecting the light of mashaals. *A cobra whose eggs I had squashed would not be more malevolent towards me*, Sita thought.

The court hall had become a rabble of noise and commotion. A single gesture from the Lord of Lanka and dead silence fell upon the entire chamber. Ravana's carpet-muffled footfalls sounded as he strode down the dais steps and across the dozen or so yards to where she stood. She lowered the chains, knowing that if she were fighting this opponent, they would hardly be effective weapons. But she kept them wrapped around her fists, if only to give herself psychological strength. It was all she had.

'So,' Ravana said in a quiet tone. The same tone he had used when he first spoke to her after her regaining consciousness in the tower-forest. 'Do you wish to add a murder attempt to your crimes?'

'I am innocent,' she said. 'I committed no murder. This

so-called justice of yours is a travesty. I was not even permitted to speak in my own defence.'

Ravana's heads examined her with interest.

From somewhere in the depths of the ranks of watching representatives, a voice rang out rudely. 'You had the mortal-lover speak for you! What more did you expect? A full pardon and the king's bed to boot?'

Sita ignored the heckler. Instead, she raised her voice and addressed not just Ravana but the entire assembly. 'I was abducted by deceit, stealth and force. I was brought here against my power, against my will. I have been subjected to inhumane treatment, tormented and taunted, threatened and badgered. I am starved and neglected. And when a rakshasi wiser than all the rest of them combined attempted to give me some little nourishment, she was struck down and brutally killed by her own so-called companions. These four,' she pointed a hand wound about with chains at the four rakshasas, snarling and bloody-eyed, 'murdered the one named Trijata, not me. I did not lay a hand on her or anyone else. I am barely able to survive my imprisonment. And now I am brought before this mockery of an Arya court and made to participate in a charade of Ayodhyan justice.

'But whether or not I survive is no longer the issue. You can kill me tonight as your lord has decreed. You can rip my flesh and tear me apart and eat me like a meal for demons. But know this. Retribution is coming. A great and terrible vengeance is upon you all. Trijata saw it coming, saw the end of your city-kingdom, and the end of your race entire. That end approaches fast. And when the day comes, there will be an accounting for all these wrongful doings, and every one of you will be called upon to pay the butcher's bill. On that day of reckoning, being eaten alive will seem like a mercy in comparison with what you will experience. My husband is a soldier of dharma, a great wielder of the sword of truth and justice. When he comes, and he comes swiftly now on wings of fire, he will dispense true justice. And even the devas will not hear your pleas of mercy on that day. This I promise you, one and all.'

She let the ends of the chains drop from her hands. They fell with a clattering that was very loud in the silent, stunned hall.

'Now do with me as you will. As you act, so shall you be judged.'

He stood on the crest of the dunes, his muscled body gleaming like a freshly oiled wrestler about to step into the akhada for a bout. Never as profusely hirsute as his vanar brethren, his new-found vigour made his skin appear almost hairlessly smooth, golden-hued in tone, and near-mortal. He appeared no larger than when he had left, but the look of calm childlike quietude had settled further into a state of blissful contentment, a beatific aura. This was a far cry from the ragged, bedraggled, reed-thin, fangs-flashing creature that had first accosted Rama in the wilds of Janasthana, and noticeably different even from the Hanuman who had met up with them here at the coast mere days earlier. He is complete now, Rama thought. He has achieved self-realisation.

Jambavan stood beside the vanar, his ears twitching, mouth working busily on something chewy. The others stood around them, a short distance away. Rama had already acknowledged and greeted King Sugreeva on the beach, and the king went forward, stopped, and looked Hanuman up and down keenly.

'To think that I had a deva in my ranks and did not know it all these years.'

He folded his palms and began to bow. Hanuman caught him at once. 'Nay, my lord. You are still my king. It is not meet that you bow before me.'

Sugreeva smiled. 'Even kings bow before devas.' He bent and touched Hanuman's feet before the vanar could protest again. 'I consider myself doubly blessed. First for having been privileged to have known a demi-god for so many years, even if I did not realise he was such. And again for having had that demi-god in my service, even though I hardly deserve such an honour. Hanuman, before all of vanarkind I declare you now a free person. You may do as you please with the rest of your life. You are no longer bound to my service.'

Hanuman folded his own hands together and, bowing, touched Sugreeva's feet. 'My lord, I choose to remain in your service. I shall be ever your loyal servant.'

Sugreeva blinked and tears welled in his grey eyes. 'Then I am blessed yet again. Yet I exhort you once more, you are free. Go do as thou wilt. My son. My son's friend. My friend.' Each of the three appellations was filled with such warmth and love, Rama could feel the sincerity in them. He felt glad he had chosen to ally himself with Sugreeva. His first instinct had been right. This was a good king. A great king even. Then he remembered: it was Hanuman who had come to him and asked him to ally with Sugreeva. So it was really Hanuman who was proved correct.

Almost as if he sensed his thoughts, the vanar turned his large soulful eyes towards Rama. Then he looked back at his king, his hands still folded. 'In that case, I ask only one thing, my lord. While still in your service eternally, as you have allied your strength with Lord Rama, let me serve you by serving Rama. It is what I desire most.'

Sugreeva clasped Hanuman's hands, then kissed them. 'So be it.' He raised his voice, loud enough for all the crowd of watching vanars and bears to hear and pass on to those who were out of earshot. 'From this moment on, Hanuman shall serve Lord Rama of Ayodhya. And in doing so, he serves me. Hanuman, you will take all your orders from Rama henceforth, and do as he says. Serve him as diligently and loyally as you have served me; make his cause your own.'

Hanuman bowed his head, thanking the king. A great sigh rose from the watching armies.

Sugreeva paused, then looked at Hanuman uncertainly.

Something passed across his face. 'When you were a boy, I once scolded you for leading the vanars into the Madhuvan gardens, and for stealing the honey wine there and getting yourself and all the vanars drunk, when you should have been working on an errand for me. At that time, I did not know of your divinity. I thought of you only as a young vanar, as my son's friend, and I may have raised my hand upon you . . .' He paused. 'Forgive me for that transgression, forgive me for any time that I may have treated you wrongly in any way—'

Hanuman made a sound, a vanar sound that Rama understood to mean several different things at different times and in different contexts. In this context, it seemed to mean, *No, no, no.* 'Nay, my lord,' Hanuman said in words. 'It is not you who needs to render an apology. It is I who must apologise to you.'

'You? What for?'

'For possessing the powers given to me and not using them in your service. Had I but been aware of the extent of my abilities, you would not have been compelled to wander the aranya in exile. I could have championed you and won back Kiskindha single-handedly.'

Sugreeva shook his head, his grey eyes twinkling sagely. 'It was not to be that way, young master. It was your destiny to seek out Rama and gain his friendship and trust. He was destined to return me to the throne of Kiskindha. Just as he was the one who was to awaken you to this realisation of your powers.'

Sugreeva turned to Rama. Everyone else turned as well.

Rama shook his head self-deprecatingly. 'I have done nothing to deserve praise here. His powers he gained at birth itself, from his illustrious pater. As for now, Jambavan was the one who made Hanuman's awakening possible. He—'

'Was Vashishta your father, Rama? Or Vishwamitra?'

Rama frowned at Jambavan. What sort of question was this? 'Of course not. My father—'

'Was Maharaja Dasaratha. Exactly. A guru, even one who shows his pupils the way to enlightenment, does not become the father of a child. In the same way, while Vayu engendered Hanuman, and Kesari raised him lovingly as his own son, it required one soul more to complete his fathering. You were that soul, Rama. Without you, Hanuman could not have achieved this self-realisation and actualisation. You are as essential to his blossoming as rain to a rose.'

Rama nodded, knowing better than to argue with the bear king when he was in a voluble mood. 'It is my privilege, then, to have been the one chosen to aid you in this journey of fulfilment.' He addressed the words to Hanuman directly.

Jambavan laughed. 'Still you do not understand your true nature, Rama. But it is of no account. In time, you will come to learn all, and mayhap that day will not be a happy one. Not all knowledge is desirable. Some truths are better left unknown. It does not diminish their value as truth one ounce. Some of us, like Maruti here, need to be awakened to our true nature in order to fulfil our dharma. Others, like you, Rama, must needs remain blissfully unaware precisely that you may fulfil your dharma! So the wheel of time turns and we all turn with it, topsy turvy, upside down, inside and out. And the last one standing when the dumroo-dancer ends his dance at the end of time will not be the strongest or the bravest or even the most aggressive. Simply the loneliest.'

After this ominous speech, none seemed to know what to say. Finally, Hanuman broke the uneasy silence by coming to Rama and kneeling down before him.

'My lord, you have brought me to this pass, that I have learned the full extent of my true powers. Now, even my king has released me, permitting me to serve you on his behalf. I exhort you now, my lord, command me. Tell me your will and it will be done.'

Rama laid his hands on the vanar's rock-hard shoulders. 'Then my first command is that you rise to your feet, and stand by me and Lakshman.' When Hanuman complied, he embraced him warmly, and smiled at him. 'I take great pleasure and pride in your self-discovery, my friend. May you tap bottomless reservoirs of strength and agility, and possess the power to achieve all your goals.'

Hanuman inclined his head soberly. 'If you will it, so shall it be, Lord Rama. You have but to name your desire, and it shall be done. The lord of bears has shown me sights of feats I have performed in ages past, and made me aware of the immense possibilities of my state. If there is anything you desire me to do, only say the word.'

Rama exhaled deeply and turned to look at Lakshman. His brother's face showed that he knew what Rama was thinking.

'Hanuman, my friend, our brother Rama hesitates as always to speak his innermost desires. If left to him, he might well urge you to use your new-found abilities to help work on the bridge proceed faster. And I have no doubt that with your help and Nala's brilliant new method, we shall make great progress at great speed. But what use would be a bridge if it achieves its goal too late?'

'Too late?' Hanuman frowned. 'I do not understand, Lakshman-bhaiya.'

Lakshman explained about Rama's pre-dawn encounter with their father's spirit upon the unfinished bridge. 'So, my friend, if we do not cross to Lanka today, we shall be too late to save our sister Sita, Rama's beloved wife. And if we cannot save Sita, then what use is this bridge, this war, this whole endeavour?'

'You speak truly, Lakshman-bhaiya,' Hanuman said, his eyes flashing with determination. 'We must go to Lanka at once. Sita-devi must be saved at all costs.'

Nala, who was standing within earshot, scratched his head vigorously. 'Mayhap if Lord Hanuman expands himself to giant size again, he could help us complete the bridge within the day.'

Prince Angad frowned. 'Are you certain of that, Nala? Just last night, we talked about this, about how, if you had Hanuman's vast size to aid you, you could build it in a day or two. You did say "or two". Not necessarily one day.'

Nala bobbed his head. 'I cannot be certain. A day. Perhaps two. These are not things that can be known exactly until they are done. Never before to my knowledge has such an endeavour been undertaken. Not even Lord Vishwakarma, architect of the devas—'

Angad cut him off gently. 'Yes, Nala, we understand the limitations. But if it takes two days, not one, or even a day and a half, then what?'

'Then we shall be too late,' King Sugreeva intoned sadly. 'And a victory delayed is a victory denied.'

Many more suggestions and comments flew about, and many more ideas were bandied by all and sundry. The air grew thick with the heat of the debate as everyone sought to use their new-found champion's strength as well as their own ingenuity to come up with a solution to their problem.

Finally, Jambavan, who had been eating some variety of fruit whole, skin and seeds and all, said through an over-full mouth, 'Vanars leap.'

Everyone turned to look at the bear king. Jambavan spat violently, spraying a mouthful of discarded seeds and fruit debris over some vanars foolish enough to have crept up too close to the lord of bears. They scurried away, cheeka-ing indignantly. Sakra was among them, of course, and he stopped after retreating a few yards, still eager to watch and listen to what the lords were saying. Jambavan looked around with a bearish grin. 'Is that not what vanars do when the far branch is too distant to swing to?'

Everyone stared at him incredulously.

'Leap? Leap to where?' Angad asked. 'What far branch do you speak of, Lord Jambavan?'

Jambavan snorted. A few flecks issued from his black nostrils; they might have been fragments of fruit. 'To the branch of the nearest coconut tree, Prince Angad! What do you think I mean?'

'To Lanka?' Lakshman asked. 'You mean we should leap across the ocean to Lanka?' He looked around quickly, aware that he had said something laughable.

The bear king raised his dark eyes to the sky. 'Devas grant us mercy. Not all of us, Lakshman, my lad. I said vanars leap.

Not mortals. Or bears. We rksas would rather get our hind fur wet than do any jumping around, thank you, sir. Leaping is what vanars and monkeys do.' He added brightly, 'And fish. Lovely silvery salmon, fat and juicy and soft-bellied salmon, leaping all the way up to—'

Angad interrupted hastily. 'You cannot mean that, Lord Jambavan. It is quite impossible.'

Jambavan looked at him with a dark frown. 'Would you like to accompany me to the glacial river tops? I will show you such leaping salmon as would make your mouth salivate and your stomach growl with anticipation, big as bears almost, and silver-perfect, fat and—'

Sugreeva came to Angad's rescue. 'He means, to Lanka. It is quite impossible to leap all the way to Lanka, Lord Jambavan. It is a distance of many yojanas, several dozens of miles. No vanar in history could leap that far. It is hardly akin to leaping to a high branch.'

'Oh.' Jambavan's thoughts seemed to linger a moment longer on those lovely leaping salmon. Then he shrugged. 'You're right. Can't be done. Forget about it.'

'Forget about it?' Lakshman repeated. 'But you only just suggested—'

'Yes, yes, boy,' the bear king said testily. 'Are you suggesting that I don't know what I just suggested? Of course I do. I suggested that we all leap to Lanka. Which, I agree, is quite impossible. Even the vanars cannot make that great a leap.'

Everyone looked at one another, nonplussed.

Jambavan turned and scanned their frowning faces.

'So it's settled then.'

Rama looked at him benevolently. 'What is settled, Jambavan? Pray, speak more clearly, my lord bear. Not all of us possess your silvery salmon swiftness of mind.'

Jambavan chortled. 'Well spoken, Lord Rama. That's the way to get a bear to open up. Praise him. Praise him to the skies. Or scratch his back. All bears love a good back-scratching.' He paused, as if seeking the thread of his thoughts, then went on. 'I meant it's obvious then that we cannot all leap across the ocean to Lanka. And leaping is the only way to make the trip in so short a while. So it is settled, then. Only Hanuman will do it.'

Hanuman stared at Jambavan. 'I, my lord?'

'Aye, Maruti. You will have to make the leap to Lanka. You must go there and fetch Sita. It's the only way.'

12

They stood on Mount Mahendra, saying their goodbyes to Hanuman before he left. Rama waited until everyone had spoken their farewells and left the mountain. Jambavan had told them that they must give the vanar sufficient distance to expand himself and warned that the force of his leap would endanger anyone who stood too close. The eagerly watching armies had been ordered to retreat to a distance of two miles from Mahendra, keeping the entire mountain and a half-mile on either side clear. Now, as King Sugreeva, Angad and the others strode quickly down the mountainside, Jambavan was close on their heels, shouting orders to his bears to make sure the area was clear of all gawkers, including that pesky half-brother of Hanuman.

Hanuman's eyes moistened as Rama came before him. Rama moved to embrace him, but the vanar was quicker, bending and touching Rama's feet to take his blessings. Rama did not protest, but touched the vanar's matted hair gently, conferring on him the traditional ashirwaad that all elders passed on to their juniors. Then he raised Hanuman up and embraced him. His voice shook as he gripped the vanar's shoulders tightly.

'My friend, my brother, you are now Sita's champion. She depends on you to survive this day. Go to Lanka and seek her out. Do what you must but rescue her. She is my heart's blood, my life itself. Without her, I am nothing. If anything should happen to her, I will die a living death. I entreat you, save her and bring her home to me. I shall be eternally thankful to you if you accomplish this task.'

Hanuman took Rama's hand and kissed it. 'My lord, you have no need to thank me. What I go to do now is my dharma. It is my duty to serve you. Rescuing Sita-devi is a task I now realise I must have been born to accomplish. This must surely be the whole intent of my existence. I wonder if Lord Brahma knew that some day you would require someone to accomplish this task, and so he ordained that the deva of wind, Vayu, should sire me. It feels like the fulfilment of my entire life's purpose. Even if I should lose my life in the process, I will not fail you. I will return here with Sita-devi or I will not return at all.'

Rama squeezed the vanar's shoulder. 'Nay, return you shall. For whatever transpires in Lanka, you must report to me everything you see and hear. I pray that you will be in time to save her, but if for any reason, things should go amiss, you must still return and tell me every scrap of news you have gathered, good or bad, terrible or wonderful. If the devas have willed that I will lose a wife today, then I would not want to lose a friend and ally as well. Promise me that you will return, with or without Sita.'

Hanuman breathed heavily. 'I will return, my lord. But it will be with your cherished one. Even if I must battle all Lanka to free her from Ravana's clutches. This I promise you, in the name of all that I hold dear.'

Rama looked at him with glistening eyes. 'Go then, my friend. Go with the gods' grace and my blessings. Go now, and return victorious quickly to us. I will count the heartbeats until I see your face again.'

He embraced Hanuman once more, then turned away, walking quickly down the mountain. Lakshman, who had already said his farewell, walked with him. Further downhill, Jambavan was roaring at a clutch of mischievous vanars who had been flushed out of a grove where they had been skulking, trying to get a ringside view of Hanuman's leap. Sakra, predictably, was one of them. The bear king trundled down the steep slope, roaring and windmilling his arms, chasing the shrieking vanars before him.

'Rama,' said Lakshman as they descended the steep slope, 'Nala and Sugreeva and Angad have suggested that we continue with the bridge even as we wait for Hanuman to return. There is no point in sitting around and doing nothing.'

'Well thought,' Rama replied. 'The work will keep our minds occupied.'

'Exactly. And we do not know how long we may have to wait.'

Lakshman did not elaborate on that cryptic statement, but Rama understood. Sita's crisis was today, and they all prayed that it would be averted. But for all they knew, Hanuman might return in two days, or twenty, or never. For that matter, who knew how long it would take to reach Lanka? None of them had any knowledge of such a fantastical thing as leaping across an ocean. At what speed would the vanar travel? When would he reach his destination? And then there were the myriad uncertainties of what he might encounter in Lanka itself. Who knew how heavily fortified the island-kingdom really was? Or how many rakshasas and other Asuras now resided there? As Sugreeva had put it in his sage way, where Ravana was concerned, the only certain thing was that nothing was certain. Lies and subterfuge, deceit and deception, smoke and mirrors. 'Sab maya hain,' the vanar king had said disdainfully. 'All is illusion with the Lord of Lanka.'

'Of course,' Rama said as they continued down the mountain, 'if he does return with Sita safe and sound, then there probably won't be much use for the bridge.'

Lakshman glanced at him sharply. 'What do you mean by that?'

'I mean, what use will it be to have a bridge when we don't need to cross the ocean any more?'

Lakshman stopped abruptly. 'Rama, I don't understand your meaning. What does Hanuman's mission have to do with our crossing to Lanka?'

'Well, if his mission is successful, then it makes the crossing redundant.'

Lakshman frowned, adjusted his rig on his shoulder, and shook his head. 'I still don't understand you. Even if Hanuman should return with Sita, and I pray that he does do so, we will still have to cross to Lanka and fight the war.'

'Why, Lakshman?'

Lakshman stared at him. 'Why? You are asking me why? Because he kidnapped Sita, brother! Because he came to our house and took away your wife, my sister-in-law, and carried her off to his fortress as if she was no more than a spoil of war or a trinket he had filched! That's why. What more reason do you need?'

'Lakshman, that is why we are sending Hanuman to fetch her. If he succeeds, then we will have undone what Ravana did. We will have Sita back home safe and sound, and this nightmare will be over. We have no need to wage war.'

'What do you mean? Of course we need to wage war. We *must* wage war!'

'Why do I need to wage war once Sita is returned safely to me? She was the reason for this whole campaign. As long as she is brought back safe and sound, I have no more quarrel with Lanka.'

Lakshman exploded indignantly. 'And what about the insult suffered by you? By me as well? What about the stain on our honour by having a woman of our house abducted and taken by force to a strange man's hold? Who will avenge that?'

Rama sighed. 'Brother, we are not the only ones wronged in this affair. Do not forget, we killed Tataka and her hybrid offspring, and cleansed the Bhayanak-van of Ravana's influence. We wiped out Ravana's Asura armies at Mithila. We humiliated and defaced his cousin Supanakha at Chitrakut. And we slaughtered all her rakshasa hordes during the years of our exile. Even Vali, whom I killed at Kiskindha, was a secret ally of Ravana. We have done our share of harm to him and his forces. We have inflicted many more wounds upon him than he has upon us. Why, we did not even know that Ravana still lived until he appeared that day and abducted

Sita! This is a war we have won already, many times over.'

'Yes, I thought so too. But with this one demonaic act he has altered the balance in his favour once more. By casting this slur upon our reputation and our family name, he has compelled us to wage war. It is the only honourable thing to do, Rama. We cannot back down now, whether we rescue Sita or not. Safe and sound, or not.'

He did not have to spell out what he meant by that last statement. Rama swallowed, feeling his gorge rise at the thought of what Sita might have undergone while in the Lord of Lanka's clutches – what she might be undergoing even now, as they stood here on the slope of Mahendra, arguing. 'Lakshman, what is it you seek? What do you expect to get by waging this war? If Hanuman gets Sita back, then what more do we want?'

'Justice, Rama! To clear our name. What will the world say, today, tomorrow, or a thousand years hence, if we let a vanar save your wife and then go home meekly and quietly? What will Ravana think? We will be branded cowards, yellowbellies, cravens. They will say we did not have the stomach to fight for her ourselves. We sent a hireling to do it for us, and then went home with our tails between our legs, without avenging our honour.'

Rama shook his head. 'We do not need to prove ourselves. We have killed enough to be remembered for a thousand years, if history chooses to remember. People are fickle. Today we are heroes. Tomorrow we may be branded mass murderers. Indeed, to the Asura races, we are probably branded genocidal killers already! We do not need to slaughter more rakshasas to prove our honour.'

Lakshman slammed his fist into his open palm in frustration. 'Who cares about the Asuras and the rakshasas? We never sought war with them. They were the transgressors. We only defended ourselves and our people.'

'And in this war, whom are we defending?' Rama asked gently, trying to calm Lakshman down.

'Our honour! Our family name.' Lakshman paused a moment, seeking to control his tone. 'Rama, I understand your reluctance to engage in another war with no certain outcome. I am our father's son too. I know what Dasaratha taught us: war is the last resort of desperate and foolish kings. But in this case, we have been wronged as surely as if Ravana had led an invading force into the heart of Ayodhya. By abducting Sita, he has struck at the heart of our entire house. If we do not go to Lanka and make reparation for this violation, people will say that the Ikshwaku Suryavansha dynasty does not defend the honour of their women. That a rakshasa can enter their house and carry off their daughters, or sisters, or mothers, or wives, and the men do nothing to avenge the dishonour. It is our dharma to make reparation for this wrong done to us.'

'And what is the price of that reparation? When will our honour be sufficiently redeemed? When we have killed another fourteen thousand rakshasas? Or fourteen lakh, if there are so many left in Lanka? And even if we succeed in wiping out all of Lanka's rakshasas, how do we know that some other cousin of Ravana, or some son, or brother, will not hear of it and come to seek reparation for the loss of *his* house's honour? At what point does the cycle of revenge end? What if revenge itself is the worst crime of all? For by exacting vengeance, a man perpetuates the cycle of sin. Only by forgiving and forgetting can we end the killing and the endless seeking of retribution. I say let the bridge be built, for bridges are necessary to unite and unify. But once Sita is returned to us, let there be no war. For war serves no man well, and only breeds more war in turn. It is the instrument of death and devastation, and has no relation to life, love or dharma.'

Lakshman stood breathing heavily, staring not at Rama any longer, but at the ground on which they stood, the grassy slope of Mahendra. 'And if Sita is violated?'

This time it was Rama's turn to look at Lakshman sharply. 'Lakshman, remember your place. You speak of your sister-in-law, she who is as honourable as your mother, or mine.'

'Yes, she is. And I did not so much as suggest that she would yield to or accept any advances ventured upon her. I know she would die rather than do so. Die fighting, for she is a warrior-princess of Mithila and I have seen her fight myself. But the word I used was "violated". Even the fiercest fighter cannot battle an entire kingdom of rakshasas alone. I am sure Ravana did not steal her away so he could play a game of chaupat with her on rainy afternoons. He took her to make her his—'

'Lakshman.' This time Rama's tone was not just one of warning; it bore open disapproval.

'Fear not, bhai. I will not speak ill of she who is more honourable than Devi herself. I seek only to remind you of the facts of the matter. Even if Sita is returned to us safe and sound in limb and health, as I sincerely pray she will be, what of the violation of her honour? Will you not seek to avenge that at least? I accept that you do not regard the violation of the honour of our house as sufficient justification for waging another war against the rakshasa race. But what of the violation of your wife? Surely you cannot let that transgression pass unavenged?'

Rama's fist, clenched so tightly that the knuckles had turned white, opened and closed slowly. His jaw worked as if he would bite and rend the words to pulp rather than speak them. He took care not to look at Lakshman directly, keeping his eyes instead on the beach below and before them. But his anger was palpable, and several moments passed during which it seemed he must surely strike at his brother. Yet he did not do anything that was not in his normal sphere of behaviour. Finally, he said in an almost level tone, 'I will consider that question if and when it arises. For the nonce, I do not care to discuss this matter further. We shall continue with the building of the bridge with the same haste as planned. We shall await Hanuman's return. And then we shall confer again, take stock of the situation, and decide what must be done. But know this, Lakshman, I will accept facts if they are proved to me. I will accept my fate and the fate of those I love, however terrible that fate may be. But I will not accept speculation and rumour and assumption before

the fact and before that fate is unveiled. Do not speak again of
your sister-in-law in such light. It does not become you, and I
will not tolerate it. That is all I will say at present on this
matter.'

13

The mountain shook. Birds shrieked and left the rooftops in enormous numbers, filling and darkening the sky with their flocks. Swarms of bats, more numerous than anyone might have imagined, left the palm groves and wheeled about in confused dismay, unable to comprehend this disruption of the natural order. Monkeys, those gibbering distant relatives of the vanars, fled the safety of the trees on the rear side of Mahendra and in the valley behind, and scattered north and east, away from the source of the trembling. Other creatures of the forest, deer and buffalo, elephants and lions, snakes and mongoose, all fled as well, terrified by the shaking of the earth.

The entire region shook, in a fashion similar to but different from an earthquake. An earthquake would have been a shuddering from deep within the earth, a subterranean vibration that travelled to the surface. This shaking was only upon the surface itself, and it was not as constant as an earthquake, nor as reverberatory. Rather it was one enormous, bone-shuddering thud, accompanied by a massive pounding sound that rattled the hearing, then was still for long moments, before the thudding and pounding were repeated, this time louder and more powerful than before, followed by a longer pause than the one before, followed by an even louder and more bone-shaking thud, and then a still longer pause . . . The intervals between thuds grew greater, and the impact and sound of each successive thud grew as well, until it seemed like a mad deva was pounding the earth with his celestial hammer.

Upon the beach, two miles from the peak of Mahendra, Rama and Lakshman and the rest stood and watched. Their eyes were raised to the mountain's peak, but after each successive thud, their sights rose high into the sky, then fell again. Each time they brought their sights down, the subsequent thud shook them so mightly, they lost their focus and had to re-adjust their sights. In the trees to their left, coconuts, date bunches and palm fruits fell in showers with each impact. Beneath their feet, sand crabs were abandoning their homes and racing frantically across the beach, seeking shelter in the arms of mother ocean.

On the peak of Mahendra, Hanuman had grown to some fifty times his normal size. He was jumping up and down on the mountain, expanding himself even as he built up momentum for his great leap. Each time his bare feet thudded into the top of the mountain, the ground shook, and with each successive rise into the air, his body grew in size and weight. He was now perhaps one hundred yards in height and growing visibly. A hundred and twenty, a hundred and fifty, two hundred . . . Now, his rate of expansion multiplied, as he exerted greater force over his powers. In moments, he had grown to at least two hundred yards in height, and still he continued expanding. The peak of the mountain was crumbling under each successive pounding of his enormous hairy feet. The craggy rim of the cliff was giving way, slabs and sections sliding and falling into the ocean, or on to the rocky crags below. Entire trees were crushed beneath his feet, snapping like twigs, and Rama saw a boulder, the last one carried up the mountain before Nala hit upon the new plan, come beneath the heel of Hanuman's left foot. The rock was shattered to bits, while Hanuman hardly seemed to feel the impact. Three hundred yards and growing . . . With the next impact, the fragments of rock were turned to gravel. Four hundred yards . . . The gravel became dust, which became a cloud which obscured the top of Mahendra but only came up to the knees of the giant vanar.

Five hundred yards . . . six hundred . . . seven . . .

Now, to look up at Hanuman's head, Rama had to shield his eyes from the risen sun, which blazed in the eastern sky like a halo behind the vanar's gargantuan visage. It was hard to focus on Hanuman any more, for each time he hit the ground, the vibrations jarred every bone in Rama's body, forcing him to lose his balance, and before he could recover sufficiently to focus again on the jumping vanar, Hanuman had descended and hit the ground again.

Eight hundred . . . nine . . . A thousand yards high. Now Hanuman was almost thrice as tall as Mahendra itself, and the mountain was being pounded beneath his feet. What must he weigh? Rama wondered. If his increase in weight was proportionate to his gain in size, that would mean he now weighed . . . The next impact knocked Rama off his feet again, and when he blinked the dust from his eyes, Hanuman was even larger. The vanar's standing jumps were now taking him so high up into the sky, his head was brushing against the bellies of the clouds. Rama stayed on his knees, crouching to maintain his balance, and saw Hanuman grow so quickly that his expanding head pushed through the enormous bank of cloud, disappearing from sight completely for a moment. His descent took longer too, but the subsequent impact forced Rama to clench his jaw to avoid biting his own tongue. Everyone around him was sitting on the ground, the vanars mostly cross-legged, staring mesmerised. Rama lowered himself to the ground too, putting his hand on Lakshman's shoulder to steady himself. Lakshman sat beside him, staring up at the sky. For a moment, Rama was reminded of a kul full of students looking up at their guru as he unfolded the secrets of the sacred Vedas, the storehouse of all Arya learning.

Hanuman landed on Mount Mahendra with an impact that crushed the very rocky veins of the mountain. Rama saw an enormous jagged crack appear in the cliff-face, like a black lightning bolt. It ran down to the foot of the cliff, followed by a great rending and gnashing sound. The entire mountain groaned and settled several yards lower than before. Another dozen poundings like that, he thought, and the mountain would be reduced to a hill.

That turned out to be an underestimation.

Over the next hour, as the sun rose higher into the sky, and the morning drew on, Hanuman continued to expand and to leap higher with each jump. At the very end, he was easily a mile tall, and his outstretched arms spanned a distance hundreds of yards wide. But it was clear that his weight did not grow proportionately, for if it had, then even by Rama's rough mental calculation, he would have weighed enough to drive the entire shoreline into the ocean. Instead, he seemed to strike the ground with more or less the same impact, the thudding heightened only by the increase in the height to which he jumped. Even so, by the time he was ready to make his final leap, the mountain had been completely flattened and the entire shoreline had been altered, with black rock and debris strewn everywhere as far as the eye could see. Gone was the line of miles of palm groves, gone was the golden sand of the beaches. Rubble and rocks were all that remained. And Mahendra was only discernible by the fact that the ground in that place, all black bedrock, bore a curious indentation like that which might be made by a child leaping up and down on soft, spongy wet earth.

Hanuman's last jump took him so high, nobody could see where he went. He rose up into the air, passed through the now-shredded cloud bank, and rose still higher, higher, until he was out of sight. Several moments passed. Finally, cries broke out as the sharpest eyes spied a faint speck reappearing, descending. This time, even Rama's heart was in his mouth as he braced for the impact. Were Hanuman to land even a little to the right or left of where he had left the ground, several tens of thousands of his vanar fellows and bear allies would be crushed to so much bloody pulp.

But Hanuman landed exactly where he should, upon the shattered bedrock of Mount Mahendra, pressing the rock so far into the ground it became a deep bowl, like the bed of an emptied lake. He landed on the balls of his feet, cracks splintering outwards from the centre of the declivity that had once been a mountain, and sending entire ranges of trees toppling with the impact. He crouched, bending low at the waist, his powerful thigh and calf muscles tensing visibly, like giant cords tugged by numberless hordes, his shoulders tight with the strain, his protruding vanar jaw set with determination, eyes as large as boulders gleaming brightly, mouth open to draw in one enormous breath. A bead of sweat left his chin and fell to the ground. It splashed and became a small pond. His tail swung from side to side pendulously, aiding his balance.

For a moment, he seemed suspended in time, like a living statue carved by some unimaginable god.

And then, with one final mighty burst of strength, he leapt again. Not upwards, as he had done until now, but outwards, forwards, towards the gaping sea. With a roar of effort, he rose into the air, launching himself with an energy that was formidable to behold. It was the same manner in which any vanar might leap, say from one rock to another, or one branch to another, but on a scale that boggled the mind.

Hanuman left the earth and rose up into the air, leaping . . . no, Rama corrected himself, flying. For the distance he covered with that great jump was akin to the flight of a bird. He flew up into the air, rising, rising . . . until he shrank in perception, though not in size, to a fist-sized object, then the size of a fingernail, and finally became just a tiny speck in the vast blue sky. The speck disappeared from sight as well, still rising. Rama watched it as long as he could, then blinked.

The sky was clear, except for the enormous cloud of dust still drifting from the debris that was all that remained of Mount Mahendra.

A resounding cheer rose from the ranks of the armies of vanars and bears, filling the air for miles around. Rama added his own voice to the throng, calling out the new name that the vanars had agreed upon for their fellow, a name they had conferred upon him to mark his new-found stature: Bajrangbali, to indicate the great sacrifice the vanar had made when he swore his oath of celibacy back on the mountain of Kiskindha when he first pledged loyalty to Rama's cause.

'Jai Shri Bajrangbali!'

It took great coaxing and prodding to get the vanars and bears to resume work. If not urged, the armies would have been content to stand about and *cheeka* and roar and beat their hairy chests, and leap up and down, imitating Hanuman's mighty leap all day long, chattering excitedly. Even the bears tried to jump up and down to show they could do it as well as vanars; the result was unconvincing, even ludicrous, for bears jumped no better than vanars fished, but none dared tell the bears *that*.

Hanuman's preparatory jumps had taken far longer than anyone could have guessed. The sun was high in the eastern sky by the time he disappeared from sight. Even so, it was closer to noon than morning by the time the leaders were able to marshal their ranks and Nala got the bridge-builders working. Once started, though, work progressed with tremendous speed. Everybody was filled with passion and pride after viewing the fabulous spectacle of the morning, and vanars and bears alike sang songs in unison, alternating between the lays of one species and those of the other. If it was strange to hear bears singing gruffly of leaping from tree to tree and feasting on the highest fruits, it was even more incongruous to hear vanars yodelling about dipping their snouts into honey hives and lunging after upstream salmon.

Whether knowingly or accidentally, Hanuman had made their work substantially easier. By reducing Mount Mahendra and the surrounding cliffs to one enormous pile of rocky rubble, he had provided a huge cache of raw material for the bridge. The crushed rocks were just the right size, small enough to be lifted by even a vanar and passed from paw to paw, and yet heavy enough to sink decisively into the ocean. By the time their shadows had begun to lean eastward, Angad came to Rama with the news that they were progressing at a rate of some hundred yards every clock-hour. Rama was impressed. He had expected speed and efficiency, but this was remarkable. At this rate they could be in Lanka in three days, at best two. The bridge-builders sang on, unmindful of the miles-long cloud of dust raised by their brother's leap, and afternoon turned to evening and the day drew gently to a close.

Supanakha waited impatiently for the last of Ravana's boot-lickers and sycophants – ministers and generals – to file out of the sabha hall before she climbed down from her perch in the ceiling, creeping down the side of the alabaster wall, not caring if she left pugmarks on the pristine white surface, and leapt to the dais. She landed on all fours, preened with pride at her own dexterity, and sprang up to the throne that Mandodhari had vacated a while earlier. She didn't mind the warm seat but sniffed disapprovingly at the remnants of Mandodhari's scent. Was the woman a rakshasi or a mortal? She smelled disgustingly clean, as if she had bathed within the past week. Why anyone would want to immerse themselves in steaming-hot water at all was beyond Supanakha's understanding. Wasn't licking one's haunches a few times a day good enough then? This bathing fetish was a perversion of the natural way of things. She sneezed out the disgustingly aromatic scent, and felt better.

Ravana was watching a clutch of his personal guards carry something heavy up the stairs of the dais. They set it down with exaggerated caution, then retreated quickly, leaving the sabha hall empty except for Supanakha and her cousin. She peered doubtfully at the thing they had left. It was a large shallow-bottomed vessel made of baked clay. It seemed to be filled with water. How repellent. Surely he didn't intend to wash himself as well? What was Lanka coming to? Bad enough that Ravana had had Pushpak insinuate itself into every structure in the capital city, turning everything into a gaudy imitation of mortal architecture and design. Did he have to go and—

'Cousin, shut your mindbabble before I dunk you in this ganga-jal.'

Supanakha swore aloud, leaping backwards. She perched on

the backrest of the queen's throne. *Ganga-jal?* Water from the sacred river Ganges? 'What do you want with holy water? Are you planning to bathe Rama's wife in it?'

Ravana's voice sounded distracted. 'Quiet, cousin. I need to concentrate.'

She stayed sullenly silent, licking her paws and keeping her distance from the cursed water. She watched with disdain as Ravana stood before it with all his six arms outstretched, uttering some arcane mantra too softly and too quickly for her to catch – as if she would steal his stupid sorcerous Sanskrit slokas! Her disdain turned to horror as he bent, dipped his hands into the water and splashed it liberally into the air. She cringed, even though the water was thrown away from her, then gasped. To her amazement, the water rose up, and froze in mid-air. Intrigued, she began to creep forward slowly, then stopped herself. Suspended in the air or no, that was still holy ganga-jal. Even a drop of it would be enough to burn a hole through her flesh like the harshest acid. She remained where she was, crouched on the backrest of the queen's throne, watching in mute fascination.

Under the urging of more slokas, the water began to move and swirl, taking a definite shape and form. It gained colours and hues as well, creating an approximation of reality that was close enough to identify. An image formed in mid-air, like a sculpture wrought out of molecules of water in defiance of gravity. Supanakha narrowed her eyes, recognising the shape Ravana had crafted.

It looked like a vanar, leaping through the air. A not un-attractive vanar, well formed and well built. The image on the water was, well, watery . . . like a rapidly melting ice sculpture. Not much detail was available. But from her point of view, it seemed as if the vanar was leaping across a body of water – a lake or a pond of some sort, perhaps? Or was that only the surface of the water in the vessel itself? No, those were surely waves flecked with foam, and was that a cloud beside his arm? It couldn't be, for the cloud was smaller than his fist. And the look of determination on his protruding face was quite amusing. He looked like he was on a mission!

All in all, it was a very clever imagining. A vanar as large as a mountain, leaping across the ocean on a mission! How droll.

'I had no idea you were artistically inclined, cousin,' she said, swishing her tail. 'That is quite good, you know. Maybe if you lose the battle with Rama, you could take up painting royal portraits for his family?'

She chuckled at her own wit.

Ravana didn't reply.

Instead, he gestured with his uppermost pair of arms and the suspended water sculpture changed its shape, producing a sound like an oar swishing through a lake. When the image settled again, it depicted the same vanar in a much smaller perspective, far in the distance but still recognisable. The cloud by his arm had fallen a long way behind, hinting at the great speed at which he was travelling. Far ahead of him, many miles distant, lay a land mass surrounded by ocean. His destination.

Even with the restrictive imagery of the water-sculpture, she could recognise the familiar black-rock cliffs and the sloping grass-topped peak of Nikumbhila, with its tiny spire of stone that was the monolithic temple of Shiva. Her jaw dropped open, and she lost her sardonic grin. There was no mistaking the vanar's destination. And if the destination was real, then obviously so was the vanar. The giant flying vanar who looked like he was ready to face and fight an army single-handed. The giant vanar who seemed to be leaping across the ocean as easily as she, Supanakha, might leap across that vessel of ganga-jal – not that she would want to chance *that*. Leaping to Lanka.

Ravana laughed. The rakshasa king reached out and grasped the tiny image of the flying vanar in his fist. It dissolved in his hand, droplets leaking through his fingers. The curtain of water cascaded down in a torrent, splashing back into the vessel.

'Come, then,' Ravana said. 'Come and meet your death, fool.'

KAAND 3

BEAUTY

I

The sky pressed in above his head, seeming close enough to touch. It brought back memories of his childhood prank, the time he had leapt to grasp the sun. This exhilaration, this feeling of total freedom, he remembered it well now. It was marvellous. How could he have forgotten how to do this? Now that he had rediscovered the ability, he felt he could fly for ever, a creature of air and sky, eschewing the land and clumsy bipedal motion altogether. Up here, he was free, alone, supreme.

At this height, the sky above him was white, as pale as a duck's belly, while the sea before him, endless and eternal, was deep cerulean blue, the blue of a robin's egg. Clouds drifted slowly by, leagues below him, tiny puffs over an epic expanse. The occasional flicker of a flock of birds flying slowly in an enormous arc, casting rippling shadows over the water, caught his eye. He looked to his left and to his right, below and then back over his shoulder. Nothing was as high as he was. Except the sun. And, faintly glimpsed beyond the uppermost reaches of the air blanket that covered the world, the myriad stars. Surya-deva shone down hard, scorching his back and head. But he did not mind it, for the air was cool and constant up here, the speed of his flight ensuring an unceasing stream of refreshing wind that ruffled his locks, aerated his pores, kept him alert.

At times, the ocean was so clear, so still, he could see down to the bottom itself, glimpse great underwater terrains, rolling mountains and valleys rife with the flora and fauna of the undersea world. Sea monsters frolicked and danced in the deep, enormous grey-backed things as large as mountains that rolled beneath the surface and spat geysers of foaming water high into the air; many tentacled creatures that issued dark inky bursts as they looked up and saw him pass, as if fearing that he would plunge down and attack them; sleek, swift things with jaws full of jagged fangs, biting and slashing and tearing into their prey – and even each other, cannibals that they were; playful, dancing finned beings that leapt in mischievous arcs above the surface, reminding him of salmon and, in turn, of the bears. What would Jambavan say if he could see all this? The profusion of fish in inconceivable numbers, enormous shoals of them, numbering in the lakhs and crores, darkening the ocean like cloud-reflections. He recalled Rama musing aloud to Lakshman that he could not understand how some parts of the ocean occasionally appeared to be darker than others, then cleared soon after, when there were no clouds in the sky to account for such shadowplay. It was shoals of fish that caused that discoloration and darkening. It was one of many things he tucked away in his mind to share with his friends when he returned.

The world scrolled below him as he flew. He remained fascinated by the sheer variety and lushness of life in the waters below. There was an entire world here. Richer and more profuse than on land. He saw predatory creatures hunt and kill smaller predators, and those smaller ones in turn hunt even smaller ones, but the largest of them all, the gargantuan grey and white and black beasts that rolled ponderously through the water like herds of elephants, seemed to hunt not at all, only gulping down enormous mouthfuls of ocean, then spewing the water back out through the spout-holes on their heads. Some of them paused in their swimming, floating with their blunt heads raised upwards, their dark glinting eyes reflecting the sun, watching him. They sang a song for him, in a language he could not understand. But the sentiment was unmistakable. They were praising and honouring him, acknowledging this great land beast, larger even than they were, who flew above their realm as effortlessly as the winged denizens of the air.

Once, a great bird with a wing span almost as wide as a tall ash tree appeared below him, drifting languorously on the air currents. As his shadow passed over it, blocking out the light of the sun, it issued a piercing screech of outrage that travelled for miles. It was furious and humiliated that any creature could rise above it; these high reaches were its realm. It had believed itself master of the air until now. Hanuman cooed softly to it, reassuring it that he was only passing through. It flapped its great span angrily twice, then blinked up and saw that he was no bird, but a wingless land animal. With a final squawk of dismay, it plunged downwards, spiralling with folded wings, fleeing him as fast as it could. He laughed at its panic and flew on.

Towards noon, he looked back and found that he could not see any trace of the land he had left behind. The last time he had checked, a faint black line had still been discernible, rippling with heat waves. Now only ocean was visible. He looked around, sweeping his vision in a full circle. Ocean everywhere. He shielded his eyes from the sun and peered ahead, seeking to glimpse some sign of his destination. There was none as yet. He sighed and lowered his hand. Looking down, he saw that he was still rising. The arc he had traced as he leapt out over the sea was designed to carry him up as high as he could go, then bring him back in a long, slow curve to the ground – right down to Lanka, if his estimation was correct. If he was still rising, then that meant he had not yet reached the top of his arc. The air was growing thinner, and colder. The clouds very far below, the ocean farther still. The landscape of the undersea world lay spread before him like an enormous map seen from a treetop. The almost unchanging regularity of his surroundings, the wafting stream of wind upon his body, the sunlight baking his back and head, all made him drowsy, dreamy. He fell into a reverie, musing on things that were, might have been, and might be again.

He wondered if once, in aeons past, all this had been land as well, emptied of this saline water, and if creatures of the land had dwelled here too. Then he remembered something, a faint memory of an ancient knowledge. It was the other way around: all had been ocean once, and the waters had receded only in some parts, allowing new life to spring up and exist. This was the original state of the world, waterbound. In the first age, all life had existed only beneath and upon the water. It was told in all the puranas. The age when Vishnu had taken his first flesh-and-blood form as Matsya, the fish avatar . . .

Something caught his eye, interrupting his musing.

At first he thought it was a reflection of sunlight upon the ocean, some silvery thing catching the light and casting it up at an angle that met his eyes.

He blinked when he saw that it was no reflection at all. It was something quite impossible.

A mountain was rising up from the middle of the ocean.

It rose at a tremendous speed, matching the velocity of his flight, as if it sought to attain a certain height before he reached that spot. He recognised it as being similar to one of the innumerable sub-oceanic rises he had glimpsed below, their peaks submerged leagues beneath the surface, and their foothills extending many miles further below into unplumbed depths. But this mountain was shooting up from the ocean, growing visibly, just as he had grown to his present size.

And it was rising to block his way.

Hanuman watched in bemusement as the mountain rose up. Water cascaded down its sloping sides, falling back into the ocean. Sea creatures fell with the water, all shapes and sizes and colours and species. The larger ones were pulled back down by their own weight and splashed noisily into the sea, where they lay stunned awhile, before starting sluggishly to swim again. But the smaller ones fared less well. He saw a large shoal of fish suddenly beached on the side of the mountain, only a few of them falling back into the precious life-giving waters, while the majority flopped and gasped, tiny silver pinpoints winking in the sunlight. One of the enormous toothed predators of the kind he had glimpsed earlier was beached too, and he saw it thrash and twist violently, seeking the water that it needed to sustain itself. Yet even in its death throes, it lunged greedily at the nearby gasping fish, its jaws snapping them up and chomping them to bloody bits. Then the mountain's rapid rise caused the slope to straighten out, and the large predator as well as its gasping prey all fell back into the brine, splashing and resuming at once their eternal dance of survival.

The mountain loomed up, already reaching as high as Hanuman himself.

And still it continued to grow. To expand, as he had expanded his own form. To enlarge itself, spreading now to form a mound-like shape that stretched for yojanas from top to bottom – and that was only to the surface of the ocean – as well as miles from side to side. As it passed above his present height and surpassed him, it slowed its upward motion and began to expand breadthwise at a faster rate. Now it was many miles across. And still it grew.

Still, he wasn't concerned. He did not understand what force could cause such a phenomenon to occur, raising an entire mountain out of the sea depths, but he knew what the purpose of this phenomenon was. It was meant to block his flight. To stop him from reaching his destination.

It would not succeed.

He inhaled deeply, spreading his arms and legs wider than they already were, expanding himself even further. Exerting his will, he increased both his speed and the angle of the arc in which he was presently rising. He saw himself fly to the level of the mountain's peak, then crest it, then rise above it. And he was going faster now. In a handful of moments, he would reach the place where the mountain had appeared and fly over it. He would not be daunted in his mission.

The mountain began to grow again. It sprouted tendrils of earth, still damp and cloggy from their millennia of immersion, clad with weeds and undersea plants and growths. Like a row of spears, the fingers of earth shot up, high above where he was, seeming to stretch to the very stars themselves. Then, like a second rank rushing to fill in the gaps, the spaces between the fingers of rising earth were occupied by the mountain's substance too, making a solid wall once more.

Hanuman roared and flew higher.

The mountain grew again to meet him.

Still he rose higher. And higher.

And still the mountain rose.

He darted to the left.

The mountain expanded itself to that side.

He flew to the right. It blocked that way as well.

He was fast approaching it now. For in increasing his size and the angle of his upward arc, he had increased his speed as well. The changed angle had delayed his reaching the spot where the mountain had appeared by a few moments, but now he was finally approaching it.

He set his jaw firmly, and beat his chest with his fists. Roaring a challenge, he flew directly towards the mountain.

He was less than a mile away, and approaching at great speed, when the top of the mountain changed shape. As quickly as it had elongated itself, it moulded its crest into a shape that was surprisingly familiar. Within a fraction of an instant, it became a giant face. An imperfect, roughly hewn face, such as a potter might press out of a lump of wet clay, unfinished and without fine detail. But enough that he could see it had two eyes, a semblance of a nose, and a mouth. The eyes of the mountain's face opened, and within were two mud-brown eyes without pupils, staring back at him.

Hanuman slowed his flight by exerting his will, reducing his speed to almost nil. He floated in mid-air, face to face with the mountain.

'Who or what are you?' he said.

The mouth of the mountain opened. It stretched from side to side and up and down as if unfamiliar with the use of this feature. A great rumbling emerged from deep within the bowels

of the structure, causing a disturbance in the ocean below sufficient to generate waves several dozen yards high. They ran from
the base of the mountain – or from the belly of the mountain
man, as it were – fleeing in panic just as the sea hawk had fled
at the sight of the giant vanar flying overhead. When the mountain spoke, it did so in rumbling waves of sound, each wave
generating its namesake in the ocean below.

'I am Mainika,' said the mountain. 'I am the gold-navelled
one, placed here by Lord Indra to pose an obstacle to the Asura
hordes that dwell in the underworld. Once, I blocked the way
to that netherland, preventing the demon dead from coming to
the mortal realm. But Ravana through his sorcery rendered me
useless. So I diminished in size and lay huddled at the feet of
the ocean lord Varuna, biding my time until the world ends.'

'Mainika, why do you block my way? I am no Asura, as
you well know.'

'I know this,' the mountain rumbled. 'You are the son of the
lord of wind. Once, in the krita-yuga, a long time before your
kind came upon this world, he was kind to me. In that great
age, all mountains had wings and they flew everywhere with
the speed of the breezes that blow across Prithvi. But then the
sages began to live upon the earth and increased in number,
and they feared that the mountains might fall upon them and
crush them to death. So they entreated the devas to help. Indra
complied, and with the use of his thunderbolt, Vajra, he clipped
the wings of all my brothers and sisters. I did not try to flee,
as I wished to share the fate of my brethren. But even as the
celestial thunderbolt approached me, a great wind rose and
carried me away, throwing me into these salty waters with my
wings still intact.'

'But why were you spared?' Hanuman asked.

'I asked the wind lord, for it was he who had saved me. And
Varuna replied that some day he would have use of me. And
it was for that day that I was spared and sent here. For many
millennia I was used to weigh down the entrance to the netherworld, thwarting Ravana's plans to release the demon races.

That long pressing-down altered my structure and the wings I once possessed became a part of me. That is why I can now rise and grow and expand, but not fly as I once could.'

'You still have not answered my question, Mainika mountain. Why do you block my path?'

'I do not block it, son of Marut. I sensed your approach from a long way, for the use of such powers as you possess can be detected by all the elements of the universe, as it involves a great exertion of the force of brahman, the energy that sustains and unites all things, animate and inanimate. When I knew that you were the son of my saviour, I knew I must rise to meet you. So I have come out of my watery home to greet you and offer you my back to rest upon before continuing your journey.'

Hanuman smiled at last, relaxing his guard. 'You are kind, old one. And it is an offer I would gladly accept. But my mission is urgent and time is short. I must reach Lanka before this day is ended, or a great calamity will befall Sita-devi, the wife of my lord Rama. Please accept my gratitude and move aside to let me pass. I must be on my way.'

Mainika sighed a great sigh, the exhalation setting into being a sea typhoon that churned its way westwards at a furious pace. 'If that is your desire, then I shall move at once. I apologise if I have delayed you in the commission of your task. I sought only to honour and aid you.'

'No apologies are needed, Mainika,' Hanuman said benevolently. 'To show you my appreciation, and thank you for staying loyal to my father for so many ages, I shall touch you and offer you my heartfelt thanks.'

And he flew forward and, bending down, touched the tip of the mountain – the top of its head – with his forefinger.

'And now, my friend, I must be on my way.' And he shot up to the top of the mountain, which began to recede and diminish at once, and flew over it.

'May your father's strength speed you,' cried Mainika, the reverberations of its shout causing another enormous wave.

Hanuman raised his hand to acknowledge the mountain's wish, and without glancing back, flew onwards, picking up speed. After a while, he heard a loud groaning, then a huge implosion of water, and guessed that the mountain had returned to its watery bed.

2

He was within sight of Lanka when the second obstacle arose. He had been scouring the horizon anxiously for a glimpse of the emerald island, and was starting to wonder if he had somehow been travelling in the wrong direction, when he glimpsed the first flash of green in the distance. It was only a speck, like a tiny pinpoint, a fleck upon the glimmering silvery expanse of the sea. But it remained still, and grew slowly as he flew on, and he knew that it was his destination.

He roared with exultation and increased his speed. He had lost a great deal of height in the encounter with Mainika, because although he was able to keep himself aloft by sheer force of will, each time he used his mind to do something else – such as speak to the mountain – he slipped down lower and lower. And when he increased his speed, too, he fell correspondingly lower. He was only a few miles above the ocean now. But it hardly mattered. There was Lanka. He would be on its shores before the sun had travelled a finger's length further west.

He pushed his chest out and raced through the air, the wind buffeting his sunburned body feeling as searing as fire.

Lanka was the size of his fist and growing fast when he saw the serpent.

She rose from the ocean, water dripping from her golden scales. Her head was flattened and protruded in a V-shaped wedge. Tentacular appendages streamed from either side of her head, flowing down in multicoloured strands. Her body behind and beneath her opened in thick undulating coils, lashing the sea and stiffening to hold her aloft. Hanuman had not known what or who Mainika was, for as the mountain had explained, he was from a different age altogether. But he knew the serpent at once. She was a legend among vanars and had been for millennia, one of the reasons why vanars feared the ocean. She was Surasa, mother of all serpents of the sea, and sister of Takshak, the celestial serpent who lay coiled around the neck of Shiva himself.

She rose up to meet Hanuman, her coiled body gleaming like a pillar of gold in the sunlight. He knew better than to try to dodge her in mid-air. He was still unaccustomed to the art of flight, while she was in her element here. And, unlike Mainika, she was no mountain of mud and sludge that he could break through with brute force. If the legends were true, then she possessed enough poison to kill him with a single flash of her fangs.

She bared those fangs now, as he slowed and came to a floating halt. Her hood danced, showing him how swiftly she could move and strike if she pleased. The strands around her neck changed colour constantly, traversing every imaginable shade in a dazzling display. He made sure not to stare at them too long, knowing they would hypnotise him into helpless immobility. Instead, he kept his gaze fixed firmly on her ruby-bright eyes. Even so, he could see her fangs, each a hundred yards high and tapered to a razor point. A drop of milky, viscous venom dribbled slowly down one gleaming bone-white fang as he watched, and when it splashed into the ocean, the water boiled and sizzled and seethed. He saw fish turn belly up for a mile around the spilt drop, dead upon contact with the lethal venom.

'Vanar,' she said, and hissed at him, 'it is forbidden for your kind to pass through this ocean. This is my domain.'

Hanuman folded his arms across his chest and stared at her calmly. 'This ocean, like all others upon the earth, is the domain of Lord Varuna, not yours. But I do not pass through the ocean. I pass above it.'

She hissed at his impudence. 'Even so. You annoy me by flying over my home.'

'Then you must get accustomed to being annoyed. I intend to pass this way at least once more, when I return the way I came.'

She opened her mouth and made a horrible throaty sound that nauseated him. For all his bravado, he was still a vanar by upbringing. And to vanarkind, nothing was more frightful than a snake. He thanked the devas that Sakra did not have to see this. The poor fellow would leap off a mountain and drown himself at the very thought that such a being existed. Surasa herself. Queen of serpentkind! And here he was, speaking to her as if she was naught more than a vexatious impediment in his path.

'You do not scare me,' he said sternly. 'Now return to your seabed and let me pass. I have business in Lanka and it will not wait while I tarry here with you.'

'Businesssss,' she hissed, stretching the word into a sibilant nightmare. 'What business would a vanar have in the land of Asuras?'

'That,' he said curtly, 'is none of *your* businesssss.' He stressed the last syllable deliberately, taunting her. Careful now, he warned himself. There might still be a way to handle this diplomatically.

Her eyes blazed, glittering like hot coals in a fire. 'You dare mock me? Do you know who I am?'

He feigned a yawn, then feigned stifling it. He couldn't resist it. She was so pompous and arrogant, so full of her own importance. 'Probably. But what does it matter? I am not here to pay you a visit and discuss pleasantries. Move aside and let me pass. Go on now, slither home.'

'Fool vanar,' she said. 'You do not know whom you insult. I have been given a boon by the devas. Anything I desire must enter my mouth. I will eat you and spend a century digesting your flesh. No creature can escape my maw.'

Hanuman glanced up. The sun was well past noon, moving on towards late afternoon. He glanced over Surasa's quivering head. Lanka was right there, within easy reach. He had only to get past this wretched sea snake and he would be there.

She grinned. 'Do you still think you will reach Lanka in time to save your beloved Sita-devi? You are more stupid than I thought. The only place you will travel to today is the bottom of my belly. And let me tell you, that is a long, long journey. My coils are so long, even I have no idea where they end. I have not seen my tail for many centuries. It could be in another world for all I know.'

'You speak too much,' he broke in. 'If you wish to eat me, then go ahead and do it now.'

She hissed angrily. 'Insolent vanar. I told you, the devas have gifted me a boon. If I desire you, you will not escape my mouth. Even your father the wind god cannot save you now.'

'Is that what you wish?' he asked. 'That I should enter your mouth?'

She grinned at him. 'That is all.'

He nodded, as if thinking it over. 'And if I do this, if I enter your mouth, then you will let me pass?'

Her grin widened. 'Pass, yes. Pass into my stomach!'

'So you presume,' he said nonchalantly. 'But let us assume for the moment that I only pass through your mouth and not enter your undoubtedly fascinating digestive system, will you then let me go on towards Lanka?'

She laughed, a sibilant serpent laugh. 'It is impossible. But yes, if you could do that, then I would happily let you go anywhere you pleased!'

'So be it,' Hanuman said grimly. 'Now, if you're going to eat me, eat me. Don't bore me to death with your mindless patter.'

Her grin vanished. She emitted a hissing cry, producing a sizzle as loud as a volcano's lava flow meeting the ocean. Then she lunged wordlessly at him.

Hanuman danced out of the way, darting backwards. She hissed in frustration and lunged again. Again he dodged her easily and she missed. She screamed a serpent cry, making fish flop madly and swim away in terror around them both. She lunged yet again, and again he was able to dance out of the way just in time.

Eyes glinting, she paused to look quickly over Hanuman's shoulder. He looked as well, and his heart fell when he saw that the three leaps out of her way had taken him miles back the way he had come.

'How will you avoid my mouth?' she said. Now it was her turn to taunt him. 'Will you have me chase you all the way back to your friend Rama? Will you cower by his feet and beg him to save you from me? Come here, you craven vanar!'

He tried to think quickly. He kept moving as he thought, flying this way, then that. He tried to feint in one direction then fly in another, hoping to get past her. But she was too quick and blocked him each time. He knew that this game was wasting precious time, while she could dance all day – or for the next hundred days if she pleased.

Nor could he simply stand still. That was the mistake almost every vanar made when confronted with a serpent. First they froze, stunned by the sight of those lethal fangs, those hypnotic, fevered eyes, that flattened hood swaying slowly to the rhythm of unheard music, those glistening scaled coils. Then they ran, leaping this way and that. Or worse, turning and fleeing back the way they had come. This last was the worst of all, for the turning-around itself slowed them, and gave the snake ample time to lunge and strike. Even leaping to either side was useless: no vanar could jump as fast as a snake could lunge.

There was only one way a vanar could defeat a snake. And that was to leap towards it, grasping its neck in both hands as tightly as possible and then pounding it senseless or dead on the ground or against a treetrunk. He had known vanars who had done this, had seen it done himself on one occasion, years ago, though he had been high on a branch looking down, and the vanar in question had nevertheless sustained a glancing nick from a single fang when his hold on the snake's throat slipped a little. The vanar had not died, but he might as well have. He took severely ill as a result of that single nick, and was unable to leap or run the rest of his days.

But this was not the forest, nor was this an ordinary snake. It was Surasa. And she was empowered with a boon that made it impossible for any creature she desired to escape her mouth.

So he knew that he must enter her mouth. Unless . . . well, unless her mouth wasn't big enough.

An idea blossomed in his mind. Without wasting more time thinking, he expanded his body, putting all his energy into the act. He had reduced himself after the encounter with Mainika, diminishing back to the mile-tall form in which he had left the mainland. Now, he grew himself in the wink of an eye to fifty times that size, then a hundred times. Ten yojanas tall.

Surasa laughed, and before the sound of her laughter reached his ears, she was twenty yojanas tall.

He doubled his size. Now *he* was twenty yojanas tall.

She doubled hers. She was forty yojanas now.

'Grow, grow, foolish vanar. The more you grow, the more meat I shall get to feed on!'

As she spoke, he became forty, then eighty, then a hundred yojanas tall. She followed suit a blink of an eye later. But each time, he observed, she took a breath before her expansion. Just a tiny intake, barely a sliver of a fraction of a moment, but it was there. An inward puff of breath, and then she expanded, another small puff, another expansion.

He knew what he had to do.

She loomed two hundred yojanas tall, twice as tall as he was.

He shot up like an arrow from Rama's bow, up to where her hood swayed high in the sky. Stars glimmered faintly behind her hood. She gaped down at him, ready for his next move, whatever it might be.

He reached the height of her mouth and shouted, 'Is this the tallest you can become? Have you reached the end of your strength? I thought you were the queen of snakes, Surasa. Even an ordinary grass snake with a boon can do better than this!'

She shrieked, the sound echoing off the moon's surface. And

expanded herself to twice her size again. And again. And yet again. Each time she took a tiny breath; each time she wasted a fraction of a moment.

When she was taller than he would ever have believed possible, he flew straight at her mouth. In a blink of an eye, he reduced himself to a hundredth, then a thousandth, then a millionth of his size.

The size of a vanar's thumb, he flew into her gaping maw, straight into those jaws of certain death. Between those poised fangs, dripping venom. She was so huge, he so tiny, it was like a gnat flying into a cave.

He flew out again.

As he emerged, he expanded himself.

At the same time, she realised his trick and reduced her size. She shrank at the speed of imagination, and in a blink she was a yojana high, as when she had risen out of the ocean to confront him. Too late.

By then, he was a yojana tall as well.

He stopped and turned to face her again. 'So,' he said, 'I have entered your mouth and fulfilled your boon. Now your power over me is gone. Slither back into your watery home and let me pass.'

She cried out in sibilant rage. But he was right. She had agreed to his condition and he had kept his part of the deal. He had flown into her mouth and out again.

For a moment, he thought she would not honour the bargain, that this dance would resume, and that he would have to fight her to the death, which he was not sure he could do without wasting a great deal of time or injuring himself gravely in the process.

But then she scowled, and dipped her hood once. Like a duck dipping for a drink of water.

'It is true,' she said. 'You have done what no being before you has been able to do. You have entered my mouth and lived to tell the tale.' Her ruby eyes flashed dangerously at him. 'Clever vanar.'

He shrugged, trying to appear unaffected. 'All the cleverness I possess would not fill a thimble that fits my lord Rama's little finger.'

She inclined her hood. 'I would like to meet your lord Rama then. If his servant is so powerful and shrewd, how great a warrior might he be?'

'And perhaps you shall meet him,' Hanuman said. 'But now, I must be on my way.'

'Goodbye, then, clever vanar. I do not know if you will accomplish your goal. For Ravana has many, many allies like me waiting to defend his kingdom. But I think I will watch with great interest how you fare in the fight. And perhaps it would please me to see you succeed. After all, if you vanquished me but stay unvanquished yourself, then that would mean I was bested by the very best of all.'

'In point of fact, Surasa, I only outwitted you. To vanquish you I would have to kill you.' He added playfully: 'Which I have no doubt I could easily do, if I had a few more minutes to spare!'

She hissed at him. 'Silence! Insolent two-legged creature! Now go your way and unite your lady Sita with her husband. I have better things to do than stand around here bickering with vanars all day! Go, before I change my mind and swallow you again!'

He smiled and flew past her. But he kept his eyes on her until he was well out of lunging distance. She remained where she was, watching him, but she made no move to come after him. Like all ancient ones, she was true to her word.

Finally, he turned his back upon her, and flew the last few miles to Lanka.

3

In the leafy shade of the ashoka grove, Sita stood on one leg, performing a pranayam exercise to help clear her mind of fear and anxiety. It was the first free spell she had had since regaining consciousness in Lanka. The rakshasas were within sight of her, but kept their distance. They had been instructed to do so. After the chain-lashing she had given them in the sabha hall, they would gladly have torn her to pieces the instant she was back in this place. Vikata in particular seethed visibly with blood-lust, eager to do to Sita as she had done to her own companion, the unfortunate Trijata. The memory of the savagery with which Vikata, and then the other rakshasas, had fallen upon their fellow sakshi had haunted Sita. If these beasts could do that to their friend, what might they do to her?

But the Lord of Lanka's orders had been explicit, and she had a feeling that Ravana brooked no disobedience. So ever since leaving the sabha hall, they had not dared to lay a finger upon her. The endless litany of taunts and abuse, as well as the relentless prodding and scratching, had not resumed either, and that was a relief.

But they were only biding their time. The rakshasas knew their moment would come soon enough. She had no way to tell time in this unnatural place, but from the references to 'after night-fall' and 'tonight at midnight' made in the sabha hall, she had guessed it was still day at the time. Now, several hours had passed, and it was probably closer to evening. Not long now. Not long before they came for her and put an end to this farcical travesty.

If not for the unborn life within her womb, she might almost welcome it.

No. I will not think that. Death will come when it will. But I must fight it to the very last. If not for my own sake, then for the sake of my child.

Our child. Hers and Rama's.

That was her reason for living, for fighting on, for waging this unequal battle as best she could. It was her sole motivation for her defiant display in the sabha hall. She had felt a burning need to speak out against the injustice being done to her; yes, to lash out at those despicable beings for pretending to dispense justice in the name of dharma of all things. Dharma! Even Vibhisena, that brahmin brother of Ravana, had not raised his voice at the end, either because he dared not, or because he had no further argument to offer. The judgement had been made, sentence passed, and the time for execution approached.

But still she might have held her peace and allowed herself to be led from the hall in stony silence. Only the thought of her unborn child had driven her, compelled her to speak out and make an effort to appeal to any shred of decency that might exist in this godless land.

And what had she achieved by that? Nothing, it seemed. The execution was to go ahead as planned. The hours were slipping away. She did not doubt that Rama would come for her, that he would find a way to come to Lanka and fight for her release. But it did not seem likely he would reach her in time. It was too much to expect of him, that he would arrive literally at the eleventh hour, and carry her away in a golden flying chariot.

What was it one of the rakshasas had said – was it Vikata? 'She has no champions here.' It was true. And yet she was a kshatriya princess, a swordmistress of Arya. She could champion her own cause. If she could but lay her hands on a weapon, she would show them how Arya women fought – and died, if need be. She was willing to risk all to protect her honour and dignity. If nothing else, she would slay as many as she could before she fell, and she would fall praising Rama's name with her last breath.

But she had more than herself to think of now.

She had another life within her, and she must cherish that helpless unborn life. Nurture it until it was ready to join this world.

It was for the sake of that life that she had partaken of some little nourishment and water. Just enough to sustain herself.

She breathed out slowly one last time, then cleansed the crowded slate of her mind of all thoughts and worries and began her twice-daily cycle of prayer to the goddess Sri. Not knowing when sunrise and sundown came in this unnatural environ, she had taken to performing her silent prayer ritual at roughly twelve-hour intervals, judging the time as best as she could. But now she spoke aloud and prayed whole-heartedly to the goddess, pouring out her burden and raising her hopes to that ultimate court of appeal.

She was a little more than halfway through the one hundred and eighth repetition of the sacred sloka praising Sri when the familiar voice spoke.

'My lady.'

There was no mistaking Ravana's voice. Somehow, even though he spoke from different mouths each time, often changing face in the middle of a sentence, the tone of his voice always sounded the same. That flawless Sanskrit diction. That perfect pronunciation.

She continued the recitation without losing a beat. A part of her felt a twinge of surprise when he did not interrupt her again, but she sensed that he still stood waiting behind her. She paid him no heed. Nothing would interrupt her ishta, the first full pooja ritual she had performed in Lanka.

It took her a long while to finish. When she was done, she bowed and touched her head to the oblong black stone she had used as a symbolic effigy, opening her loosely held fist and showering the stone with the flowers she had picked for the purpose. She added a fruit, a portion of her own meagre meal, as prasadam. She had already washed and figuratively clothed the effigy with a strip of cloth from her own tattered garment. Crude as the arrangements might be, she made up for them with her love and devotion, leaving out no step, taking her time with the ritual, uncaring of whether the Lord of Asuras himself waited behind her. Only when she was satisfied did she rise, back away three full steps, then turn.

Ravana was standing before her. His own hands were folded as well, heads bowed. She saw the lips of more than one of his heads moving as if reciting a sloka. He unjoined his palms and looked up at her with all his glittering eyes.

Her voice, so soft and melodic during the prayer ritual, turned stony and caustic as she addressed him. 'Have you come to torment me again?'

He seemed to take no offence at her words or her tone. 'My lady, if I wished to torment you, I would have locked you in the dungeons beneath this tower, not kept you in the uppermost level under the highest degree of security.'

'Security?' She almost laughed bitterly.

'Yes, your own security. You might not know this, but the kingdom is in an uproar over the murder of the rakshasi Trijata. Many of my generals and nobles believe that I should throw you to the people and let them exact the justice they feel you deserve. Yet—'

'Why don't you do it then?'

He continued as if she had not interrupted. 'Yet I have gone to extraordinary lengths to ensure that you are given the full protection you deserve under the law.'

This time, she did laugh bitterly. 'I have seen your law at work. False accusations, rampant bias, it is a travesty of the very concept of justice.'

'Nevertheless, you have been treated as fairly as could be expected under the circumstances. Did you honestly expect a mortal in the land of Lanka to be regarded with any less hostility and derision? I would wager a year's harvest of blood-apples that a rakshasa in Ayodhya would not receive the same. You should be grateful for that small mercy.'

She folded her hands across her chest. 'I hardly call the treatment meted out by your wife and her rakshasas merciful. They spared me no pain or abuse. And before that, your own cousin sought to slay me. This, of course, was all before I was dragged in chains to a humiliating public hall, accused of a crime I did not commit, given no chance to speak in my own defence, and summarily condemned to death.' She shook her head firmly. 'Do not speak to me of mercy or fair treatment.'

'Have I treated you unfairly or unmercifully?'

She grimaced. 'You mean apart from wresting me by brute force from my husband's house and carrying me off like a slain doe?'

He sighed. 'My lady. Let us move past these old arguments. Try to see your situation in the present light. You are condemned to be executed within a few hours. People have already begun gathering in the city square to witness the spectacle.'

Which meant it was probably close to sundown. 'And yet you speak to me of mercy and fairness.'

'Yes. Because I am not one of those baying for your blood.'

'I see.' She tried not to ask the obvious question: Why is that? Why do you pretend to be so *fair* and *merciful* to me? 'And yet in the sabha, you endorsed the verdict. I did not hear you overturn it or put it aside. You showed little mercy or fairness there.'

'True. Because I am only the chosen liege of my people. Not a tyrant or a dictator. Each rakshasa in Lanka is free to feel differently and act upon their feelings. It was not always so, but it is so now in the new, resurrected Lanka.' He paused a moment, as if musing on how things had once been and how they were now. She had time enough to think that it was an odd word to use, *resurrected*. Then he continued: 'Still, I did prevail upon Mandodhari to cease this needless persecution. Even now, as I arrived, you were able to perform your evening ritual undisturbed, were you not?'

She shook her head in disbelief, genuinely amazed at his bare-faced lies. 'You dare to speak of Mandodhari? Her actions were motivated entirely by the falsehoods you told her about my husband and myself. If you had not spun that pack of lies about Rama, she would never have come to hate me with such vehemence. Nor would she have turned her rakshasas upon me. Even when they murdered their own associate and I was falsely accused of the crime, it was you who were responsible for that accusation. Do not think I am too naive to see through your strategems. Do not be fooled by my apparent passivity. I see and hear and understand everything. This is all a well-spun contrivance designed to suit your purpose. I see through it and I see your hand in everything that happens to me.'

'Then you must see that I am responsible for the good that comes to you as well,' he said mildly.

She stared at him, trying to guess which face would address her next. It was unnerving not knowing, being unable to know which one to look at when speaking. It also meant, she warned herself, that he could present a good face, and a bad, and eight shades between as well. 'Good?' She laughed bitterly. 'What good have you done me?'

'I spared you in the sabha hall when you threatened and insulted the honour of my throne. I have called off the rakshasas. I have requested my wife not to visit you again. She is very upset with me, for even though these may seem like small things to you, they are very great sacrifices for us. Would the King of Ayodhya spare a prisoner of war who behaved in his court as you did earlier today?'

She ignored his question. 'You claim to do so much for me. And yet you intend to have me executed at midnight tonight. *Death. By eating alive.*' She imitated the singsong chorus of the rakshasa nobles passably well.

'Not I. You heard it yourself. Lanka willed it. The decision to condemn and execute you was a collective one, based on the facts at our disposal.'

'But I did not murder her!' she said, struggling to keep her voice level. 'It was the other rakshasas who did it.' She turned, intending to point out Vikata. But the rakshasas were gone from the spot where they had been standing before she began her prayers. She scanned the grove.

'I asked them to leave us for a while,' he said quietly. 'What I have to discuss with you is not meant for their ears.'

She shook her head once. 'I have nothing to discuss with you. I expect no justice or redressal from one such as you. I have already spoken my heart in your court. Execute me as your sabha decreed. I have said my last prayers and am prepared to face the end of this life.'

She turned her back on him, showing that she was unafraid. Of him. And death.

But in truth, it was because she feared that he might see her face and know the truth. That she was not ready at all. That she wished to live. That she still hoped against hope that somehow a way could be found to save her unborn child and carry it to term.

'It would be a shame for you to die,' he said. 'For one so beautiful and noble and rich of heart to end her life in such a manner. Eaten alive by rakshasas in a public spectacle. Is that how you wish to die?'

She did not answer. There was no right answer to that question. But her heart pounded faster. Was he doing what she thought he was doing? Hinting to her that there might still be a way out of this? Surely she was reading too much into his words and tone.

'I do not think so,' he said, answering his own question. 'I think you wish to live. And you may do so yet.'

She resisted the temptation to turn around. But she was listening to his words with a sick fascination. What new tortuous design had he dreamed up now? Did he really believe that she would fall for his lies and deception yet again? How arrogant could he be, to think she would be duped for a third time?

In any case, she told herself firmly, there is nothing he can say that I will believe. There is no way he can undo the decision of his court without proving himself to be the very things he claims not to be: a tyrant and a dictator.

'There is one way. And one way only. I cannot repeal the decision of the court, for it is the decision of the people. And because we are a race that believes in dharma, even a king cannot overturn his people's verdict. But there is a small chance that we may be able to persuade the people to take back their decision. There is one circumstance under which they may yet agree to spare your life.'

Still she kept her back turned to him, unwilling to show him that she cared a whit for his words. But her heart pounded loudly, deafeningly. The blood roared in her head. Her stomach, long deprived of nourishment, churned its own acids. When Ravana spoke again, each of his words struck at her like a javelin point wielded by an unseen assailant, jabbed over and over into her flesh, piercing her heart.

'All you have to do is tell them that the life you bear in your womb is of my making.'

4

He decided to land on the rim of the island and spy out the lie of the land before proceeding further. The sight of a giant vanar crashing down in the heart of their city might scare the Lankans into concealing Sita somewhere where he might not find her easily. This way, he would be able to seek her out stealthily, and, when the time was right, expand himself and execute his rescue.

All his life he had thought of Lanka as an island of horrors, crawling with nightmarish demons of every hue. He had assumed the very soil and grass to be alien, perverted. But the beach he landed on seemed the very twin of the one whence he had departed the mainland. The sand crunched gritty beneath the soles of his feet, baked searing hot by the sun. The sea was gentle and calm, sloshing peacefully up to his calves, the froth tickling his soles as it drained into the porous sand. Gulls flew overhead, splattering the black rock strewn about the beach with their white splashes. Even the cliffs rising up from the beach were similar to those on the mainland. Perhaps once, in a past age, the island of Lanka had been a part of the great sub-continent his kind called Jambudwipa, and which the Aryas called Aryavarta. Perhaps Ravana himself had split it from the larger land mass through his sorcery. That would mean that these cliffs rising before him were once affixed to the cliff-face of the mountain he knew as Mahendra. He examined the line of the cliff closely. Yes, he would wager that the two were kin. In which case, it was more than likely that this cliff was also riddled with labyrinthine caves. And if those caves went far enough, they would take him nearer to the city more discreetly than an overland route.

He leapt up into the air, towards the cliffs. Hovering in mid-air, he scanned the cliff-face intently. Soon enough, he spotted what he was looking for: a place where the sunlight did not gleam off the lichen-encrusted black rock but was swallowed up entirely. He flew to that spot and saw at once that it was the mouth of a cave. He landed lightly, congratulating himself on his control over his flying ability. Two strides forward and his forehead struck a low-hanging lip of rock. The rock shattered, showering him with debris. He made a mental note not to congratulate himself too quickly. He still had a fair amount to learn about the exercise of his powers.

The cave curved and twisted, turning back upon itself. The sunlit mouth fell far behind, and soon he was in near-darkness. But he was still able to see by the light of some greenish substance that coated the irregular walls. Rubbing his finger against it, he saw that it was the same lichen that grew on the black rock outside. Apparently, in pitch darkness, it gave off some kind of luminescence. The greenish light was very faint, but his vision adjusted quickly and he was able to see his way well enough.

He stayed alert for sounds or scents. The cave smelled faintly of rakshasas, but none seemed to have passed this way recently. As he ventured deeper into the heart of the winding labyrinth, the scents grew stronger and more recent. He paused several times to choose a way between two caves, and sometimes between three or more diversions. Each time he followed the stronger-smelling way. At no time did he scent any mortal.

After travelling thus for what seemed like hours, he finally came to a place where the cave opened into a larger cavern. He moved through several successively larger caverns, until he came out through a wet passageway into which fresh water dripped constantly from some crack in the roof, and found himself in the largest subterranean chamber he had ever seen in his life.

It seemed to be a cave. But it could not be. No cave could be so vast. Or so perfectly smooth on all sides. Like the inside of an eggshell. He guessed it must be the work of sorcery again. It was the first unnatural thing he had encountered in Lanka.

There was no sign of life in here, but he sensed something. He walked out into the centre of the cavern floor, where a great heap of rubble lay. As he approached, he saw the rubble was glowing with a reddish light and stopped warily a distance away. It seemed to be the debris of a large slab of redstone. But what force had shattered it? He looked upwards and saw a mouth in the ceiling of the cavern, tapering towards the centre like a giant funnel. The hole at the very top was lost in darkness. Had something fallen from up there, shattering this slab? He shrugged. It did not matter either way. Sita was not here. He could smell the faint stench of rakshasas, though the scent was several months old. But in the rubble, the debris of the shattered slab, he smelled the unmistakable odour of one particular rakshasa, fouler and more fetid than any scent he had smelled. He suspected that it was Ravana's scent. But it was as old as the other smells.

He grew impatient and decided he must move faster. He sniffed his way to the far side of the cavern, finding a crevice where the scent of rakshasas was strongest and most recent. He sensed that the city of Lanka lay that way, to the south-west of the island. He debated flying up through the roof of the cavern and up to the surface, but decided that proceeding underground was wiser.

He moved through the crevice as far as he could go. When he came up against a rough rock wall, he hesitated only briefly, then bunched his fists and struck at the wall. The rock shattered as easily as limestone at a hammer's blow. He waited, listening for any signs that he might have alerted some rakshasa sentry somewhere in the bowels of the island. But there was nothing to be heard or smelled for miles around. All his senses told him that the rakshasas lay that way. He clasped his hands together in a wrestler's hammer and swung them again at the wall. The rock shattered again, and he passed bodily through it, like a knife through butter. Then he flew with his clasped fists before his head, driving through the bedrock. As he picked up momentum, flying through the rock, debris and dust spewed in his wake.

He drilled on, moving as rapidly as a horse galloping over open ground would have travelled. He paused every few miles to get his bearings and check the scents of rakshasa again. Finally, after some twenty yojanas, he judged that he was close to the city of Lanka and began to fly upwards, breaking through the rock just as easily. Even deep within the bowels of the earth, the unmistakable fetor of Asura blood had seeped in. He grimaced. Much blood had been spilled on the ground above. The earth was heavy with the weight of all those slaughtered souls. He smelled the residue of volcanic effluents, and recalled what Sampati the vulture had told him and Jambavan about there being a great volcano on Lanka once. He also smelled the stench of burned flesh as he rose through the tortured earth, and connected the smell with the great fires that had razed the old black fortress and city of Lanka to the ground fourteen years earlier. It took all his willpower to keep himself from being overwhelmed by the misery and pain that remained in this soil. It was true after all: this land was cursed. You only had to dig deep enough to see it.

He broke through the surface at last, and had to fight the temptation to simply soar up into the sky and leave the stench and pain below. He looked around quickly, smelling the scent of rakshasas powerfully here. Recent smells, from only hours earlier. But none was nearby at present. As he examined his surroundings, he was taken aback.

He was in some kind of garden. It was breathtakingly beautiful, the entire landscape meticulously laid out and maintained. Fountains of water sprang up, walkways wound their way through groves of beautiful flora and every variety of tree and plant imaginable. It was a cornucopia of exquisite things. He had grown up hearing vanars speak with awe and pride of the gardens of Vrindavan, where the famed honey wine of Kiskindha was made. But this garden made even Vrindavan seem a backyard plot in comparison.

He climbed a tall ash and looked in one direction then another, seeing only miles upon square miles of fountains and pathways, ponds and flower fields. After travelling through the cursed bedrock of Lanka, infused with the stench of countless slaughtered Asura, the scents of the garden were heavenly. He marvelled at the existence of such beauty and perfection on an island of monsters.

Then he turned and looked the other way, and there it was. Less than a yojana away, rising from the ground in a bouquet of pristine white spires and towers and vaulting arches, more beautiful than anything he had ever imagined. The complete antithesis of the nightmarish hell he had been raised to expect.

The city of Lanka.

Supanakha watched the vanar leap from the ash tree and land with an impact that left the imprints of his bare feet permanently embedded in the grassy knoll. He ran through the picturesque pathways of the royal botanical gardens, moving quickly and discreetly. The image turned and altered, the molecules of water spinning and changing place and colour to follow him as he made his way towards Lanka. She crept around the bowl, still keeping her distance from the holy water, snarling silently at the intruder.

The image collapsed abruptly, the water splashing back into the vessel. Supanakha leapt back to avoid a few droplets that splashed her way.

'You did that deliberately.'

Ravana grinned at her. 'There is work to be done, cousin. I have to go and speak to the prisoner. I am sure you will find something with which to occupy yourself.'

'But what of the vanar?'

Ravana's heads were already distracted, turning away. 'What of him?'

'He is in Lanka! He intends to rescue the mortal. Won't you stop him?'

Ravana laughed. 'Do you expect me, king of rakshasas, Lord of Lanka, to belittle myself by wrestling a mere messenger? A vanar at that?'

'But you saw what he can do. How he dealt with Mainika, and then Surasa. He's no ordinary messenger.' She licked her chops. 'He seems to be gifted with great powers.'

Ravana's heads examined her shrewdly. 'Why don't you deal with him?'

She feigned surprise. 'Me? Why me?'

'Sometimes guile can triumph where brute force fails. As you just pointed out, he appears to be gifted with great abilities. It would be a waste of resources pitting one of my champions against him. Oh, I'm sure they would defeat him eventually, but it might be more interesting to see how your gift fares against his.'

'My gift?'

'Seduction, cousin dear. Coupled with your ability to transform your appearance. I'm sure that you could find a form that would be attractive enough to stop even a vanar as resolute as he dead in his tracks.'

She allowed herself a catty smile. She loved praise. 'I suppose I could think of something.'

'And if my knowledge of vanars serves me well, they are a female-dominated species. It is the woman who initiates fornication, and the male invariably complies. For the sake of the perpetuation of the species, of course.'

'Of course,' she purred.

'So if you were to use your seductive skills effectively enough, you might be able to succeed where a dozen of my best fighters might not.'

'Might?' she snarled in protest. Softly.

'You certainly will succeed. Because all I need is one more night. Before sunrise tomorrow, the last die will be cast. And then Rama can send a thousand champions like that one, each capable of expanding himself to the size of the moon and the sun, and it will be of no avail. The most important battle will be won by me.'

Supanakha inclined her head, gazing curiously at the rakshasa lord. 'What battle?'

'Nothing that concerns you. You wished to toy with the vanar. You have your wish. If you play your part well, you will spend a very pleasurable night, with a partner far more enjoyable than you've had for a long while, I'll wager.'

'Surely,' she said. 'But I'm curious, too. The mortal woman has already been condemned. She is to be executed at midnight tonight, in full view of all Lanka. If the excitement I smelled in this sabha hall was any indication, then you can expect every one of your law-abiding, tax-paying, flesh-eating citizens to be present in the city square to witness her execution. I hope you don't intend to disappoint them?'

He spread his arms in mock protest. 'How could I? You heard the council's decision. Lanka has voted that she be put to death. Who am I to alter that democratic writ?'

'Only the King of Lanka,' she said. 'And a tyrant so terrible the devas named him Ra-van-a. He Who Makes The Universe Scream.'

He wagged a finger at her. 'You misjudge me sorely. That appellation is offensive. I am no longer that person. Besides, those cruel times called for cruel measures. If every one of us were to be called by the names our enemies chose for us, we would all have very ugly names indeed.'

'Ah.' She chuckled throatily. 'You have something very naughty planned, I'm sure of it. I can't guess what it might be. But I know you, cousin dearest. You will find a way to have the mortal woman for your own, won't you? I saw the light in your eyes when you came to speak with her. Never before had I seen you act so . . . *gentlemanly*. Why, you seemed almost human! But even that brilliant performance couldn't disguise your lust for her. You want her, don't you? And you want to win her over by talk and emotional bonding, the way foolish mortals do. Not the rakshasa or gandharva way, the natural way. That is why you have been treating her so kindly, so *respectfully*.'

She flicked her tail sharply, like a whip cracking.

'What do you think, cousin? If you win her over by sweet words and emotional blackmail, it will be more honourable than simply ravishing her outright? Is deceptive seduction more respectable than rape? Is that why you manoeuvred her into that moral cul-de-sac, pinning a false charge of murder upon her? So you could make her more vulnerable to your seductive wiles?' She chuckled softly, flicking her tail again, brushing the tip against his foot, tantalisingly, teasingly. 'You know, I don't think you've changed much at all. Not at heart, where it matters, anyway. You're still the same old Ravana. Except you wield a candystick instead of a chopping axe. And sweet words where you would have used poisoned arrows before.'

An impatient flicker rippled across Ravana's rack of faces. 'Enough banter, cousin. It's been entertaining listening to your theories. Do you intend to stay talking all night or do you still wish to intercept the intruder?'

She feigned a thoughtful expression. 'I suppose as long as I'm still in the king's favour, I ought to make the best use of it.'

One of the heads grimaced. 'One of these days, it might be instructive to remind you of your place. But let us not waste any more time on this foolish talk. If you still wish to dally with the vanar tonight, it would be well to seduce him before he enters the city. You will have to move quickly if you are to do that.'

He turned to go, gesturing casually to open a portal before him. Through it, she could see the foliage and shrubbery of the forest level of the tower. He moved to step through the portal then paused and turned a head back.

'Remember, all I need is for you to keep him occupied until daybreak. After that, you may do with him as you please.'

Without waiting for her answer, he stepped through and the portal winked shut behind him.

She purred in anticipation. 'I will, cousin, I will do with him exactly as I please . . .'

5

It was a city of gold. So beautiful, so perfect, he could not imagine any other existed to rival it. If a group of apsaras had appeared, greeted and garlanded him, and told him this was Vaikunta, the city-home of Lord Vishnu himself, he would not have doubted them. Or Amravarti, the capital city of the devas, eternally resplendent. Indra-loka perhaps, seat of power of Indra, lord of the devas. Or even Swarga-loka itself, the most superior level of heaven.

But instead, this was Lanka . . . Lanka! City of demons and a-dharma. Home of all ugliness and immorality. A vile and fetid place of blood and vomit and offal . . . The list of clichés rolled off so easily, the cumulative residue of a thousand treetop talks and grandma's tales. Foothold of the demon races on the mortal realm, land of death and darkness, kingdom of terror.

And yet the truth lay sprawled before him. Golden. Gleaming. Pristine.

Beautiful.

He was perched on the top of a great wall, some hundred yards high, that bordered the city limits. No doubt the wall was provided for defence, but there were no guards visible for miles in either direction. Even the enormous golden gates were locked open, secured with gleaming golden chains, as if inviting the world itself to enter and be welcome. So much for Lanka's formidable defences and hostility to strangers.

It had taken him only a single leap to bound to the top, but the wall itself had given him pause for long moments. He glanced down doubtfully now, at the broad yards-thick rampart gleaming in the dusky light of the setting sun, and reconfirmed what he had seen when he first approached it. The entire surface of the wall was plated with beaten gold, welded so perfectly that he could not discern a seam or joint; it was inlaid with an exquisite repeating pattern into which precious stones had been embedded. He raised his head and looked one way, then the other, sniffing in incredulity. For miles upon miles the wall extended in both directions, a hundred yards tall and five yards wide, stretching around the base of the great mountain upon which the city was built, circling its enormous periphery. And every square inch of it was plated with solid gold and inlaid with those gems. He had not known so much gold and treasure existed in the world, nor that rakshasa skill could craft such perfection. He had licked the gold, not believing it was real. It was. The stones were real too: pearls of many colours, and lapis lazuli, onyx, diamonds of every known hue and several unknown or unimagined. What defensive wall was covered with ornamentation enough to fill the coffers of a dozen kingdoms? What citizenry, however happy and content, could pass such a gaudy display of wealth without being tempted at least once to prise loose a diamond, or even a lapis? And yet not a gem was missing, not one gold plate out of place.

On both sides of the great wall were gardens more beautiful than the ones in the tales he had heard about the heavenly realms. He had already passed through the outer gardens to reach the wall, and they were exquisite in their immaculate perfection. The inner gardens extended for many miles, acre upon acre of undulating beauty. Meticulously landscaped walkways and lotus ponds, trees and flower fields. Several miles on, the land rose steadily upward, racing to meet its destination. The beautiful tree-lined marg that passed through the golden gates rose too, undulating in gentle chariot-friendly curves to enter an unwalled city. And that city was built in a spiralling series of layers around an impossibly tall white tower whose peak reached up so high beyond the red-tinged clouds of sunset that he could not see the top.

The rising layers of the city, built upon the mountainside, were easily accessible to his enhanced vision. As he watched in stupefied wonder, lights came on across the city to dispel the twilight duskiness. Even these were unspeakably beautiful: not the flickering, guttering jaundiced light of oil-dipped torches, but a kind of illumination he had never seen before: white luminescence tinged with rainbow hues, like drops of moonlight distilled and captured in beautifully shaped lamps, illuminating the great sprawling city and turning it into the aspect of a giant oyster, opening slowly to reveal an unimaginable treasure trove of pearls. As the lights came on across Lanka, he held his breath. It seemed something far greater than a city. A jewel box, perhaps, fit for a goddess on her wedding night.

He concentrated his senses, attuning them more finely than was possible by normal means. Granting himself the power to see, smell, hear, sense so acutely that he might as well have been there, in the heart of the city itself, walking about like an invisible surveyor among the lakhs of rakshasas that inhabited Lanka.

The moon, visible in the fading dusky light, seemed a part of the city itself, another proud ornament in this resplendent display. Somehow, he sensed, the ethereal illumination that provided light to the city was derived through some magical process from the lustre of the moon itself. As the light of the celestial orb fell upon the parts of the metropolis that sunlight had abandoned, the lamps that hung from every mansion and dwelling captured its silvery luminescence and trapped it within their bellies.

The awakening of these moonlit jewel-like sconces made everything seem even more splendid and breathtaking. It reminded Hanuman of a time when he had followed a dying great tusker for two days and a night, and after a winding, tortuous journey through the most remote reaches of the red-mist ranges, he had finally watched the great jumbo reach a

secret spot, tumble to its knees and lay itself down in a grave-
yard of dead elephants. He had gazed with awe and reverence
upon that legendary spot. The gleaming pile of ivory in that
secret place had formed an intricate pattern of its own over the
centuries, perhaps even the millennia; a pattern that resembled
a white maze that glowed from within in the sacred illumination of the moonlight, as if marking the pathway to another
realm. He had imagined that it was exactly that: a pathway for
the souls of dead elephants to travel to the next life. It was a
moment that had remained with him for ever.

But to see a place made and designed and constructed by
living hands – by rakshasas, no less! – that evoked the same
emotion within his breast was confusing and maddening.

His omniscient eyes flickered this way then that, seeing,
drinking in, barely able to accept the evidence of his senses. He
could hear music now, sweet music, wafting on the air. He could
hear laughter and conversation, lovemaking and childplay.
Carousing went on in those countless mansions and buildings.
Chariots rode the avenues, driven by richly clad rakshasas both
male and female. Palanquins bore veiled rakshasi women to
and from secret trysts and public appointments. Everywhere he
looked, he saw only beauty and luxury. Even the clothes and
jewels that draped the bodies of the denizens were scintillating.
Far from the ugly and deformed brutish aspects of most rakshasas
he had seen or heard of, almost every individual he saw was
handsomely made in form and face. Some were extraordinary,
gifted with divine looks. He found himself barely able to tear
his gaze away from a beauty who watched from an overhead
balcony, biting daintily into a blood-red apple, her body naked
for all to see, available to any who wished to come and enjoy
her embrace.

There was ugliness here too. For rakshasas were not formed
in the likeness of vanars or even mortals. They were horned
and tusked, pig-faced and wolf-snouted, carapaced and chiti-
nous, ichor-oozing and slime-seething. But somehow, here in
their natural habitat – if one could term a city natural – even

the ugliest specimens seemed to find a place in the larger scheme of things. Just as even the most hideous creeping insect seems vile when perched upon one's leg or arm, but perfectly suited to its natural environment, so now the vilest-looking rakshasas seemed to be an essential part of the great beauty of Lanka. What was more, seen thus in their home setting, even their hideous aspect, so distasteful when compared to the smooth lines and limbs of mortals or vanars, seemed almost attractive. Beautiful even. Even the most repellent rhinoceros appears perfect when seen with his mate and young ones in the secret dappled glades of the deep forest.

So it was to Hanuman's empowered gaze that even the natural ugliness of Lanka seemed wholly natural, a welcome counterpoint to the exquisite beauty that was everywhere and would have been overwhelming without some balance. And he was impressed and awed by this observation.

There were angry debates and drunken brawls. Rants and raves. Bold accusations and even bolder denials. Gruff laughter and raucous parties. He smelled the odours of rakshasi women anointing themselves with unguents and cosmetic enhancements. Despite the legends painting rakshasas as unpitying black-hearted demons, he saw now that there were many shades to the race. Just as the worth of a jewel could not be judged by any one facet alone, but by appraising all its facets, so also the rakshasa nation was a multi-faceted entity, replete with all the hues and variances that nature provided her children with. He heard mantras chanted and slokas recited by pious rakshasas, and smelled the ghee sizzling in the sacrificial fires. He focused his potent vision at various places across the city, seeking out individuals at random, and saw rakshasas strikingly handsome as well as hideously ugly, virtuous-acting and rowdy brutes. Lovemaking and carousing, fornicating and fighting. Women illuminated by their own beauty, nestled in their lovers' arms. Pairs and groups on terraces of splendid mansions, enjoying the moonlight and each other's company. Women whose feet tinkled delicately as they walked, or ran, or danced. Rakshasas with skin the colour of molten gold, others with skin like moon-light. Many alone. Many reclining in their homes and contem-plating, studying sacred texts, or uttering profane words to their spouses or companions.

None of them was Sita.

He looked high and low, seeking with the aid of his empow-ered senses. He scanned hundreds and hundreds of rakshasi women, moon-bright faces, sun-glowing countenances, eyes with lashes that curled like butterflies, neck ornaments that shim-mered like garlands of lightning, women whose eyes glowed like black pearls, who twinkled like the sun in eclipse sprinkled with motes of gold, clad in tiger furs and lion skins, naked and resplendent, beautiful and alluring, dangerous and desirable. He scoured the inner rooms and private chambers, seeking, probing, searching out. He saw sights of unimaginable couplings that would have aroused the most debauched bachelor. Scenes of heart-breaking romance and tenderness that evoked a desire to join in, become part of that family, that moment. Sights of friendship and brotherhood, the exchanging of vows and the taking of blood-oaths, the sharing of sisters' secrets, the betraying of marital bonds, the spurning of proposals and the acceptance of invitations. He saw scenes of majestic grandeur as nobility paraded its wealth and power, and scenes of unspeakable degra-dation and domination. Submission and capitulation. Brutality and remorse. Virtuosity and virtuousness. Purity and high-mindedness. Intellectual debate and foul-mouthed abuse. He heard sweet voices and smelled sweeter perfumes. Guttural accents and gutter-worthy lewdness. Tears and tenderness. Profanity and prudishness.

He sought out Sita as if she might be a barely visible flash of moonlight, a glimpse of gold hidden in the dust, an arrow-wound obscured by seeping blood, a fragment of cloud torn to shreds by the wind . . .

The evening grew later, night fell, the lights of the city blazed with their tantalising rainbow-tinted hues, and the oyster of Lanka opened fully to his potent senses, as he searched on relentlessly, resisting a thousand temptations, passing over count-less distractions, overcoming a hundred unwanted thoughts and desires and urges inspired by the things he saw and heard.

By the time the moon was fully risen, a luminous pearl floating over the oyster from which it had escaped, he had searched all of the conceivable places within the city without finding any trace of Sita. His choices were not infinite: Ravana would hardly have kept her upon an open terrace or even in any of the numerous mansions or buildings. She would almost certainly be under heavy guard, a prisoner. And not just a prisoner in a city gaol; she would be imprisoned close to where Ravana himself resided and ruled. Which left only his royal palace. But which of those magnificent mansions was the palace? He saw many important-looking structures, each vying with the rest for claim to being the city's most luxurious, most elegant showcase of wealth and prosperity and power. Yet none was significantly larger than the rest. Back in Kiskindha, the king's tree-palace was several times bigger than any other. He expected it to be much the same here. He had scoured all the palaces and mansions and estates of Lanka, which left only one likely spot.

His gaze rose to the towering white structure that dominated and dwarfed the rest of the city. The tower tapered gradually as it rose. In the cloudless night, the moonlight reflected as far up it as he could see – and he could see a hundred miles high, or farther, if he so desired. He could not estimate exactly how tall the peak was; indeed, each time he tried to follow its length with his eyes, his gaze seemed to slip. It was like counting the rings on the stump of a very ancient redwood tree. As you got closer to the centre, they were so tightly banded that if you lost your concentration for even a fraction of a moment, you had to start all over. Except that here, it was not that he was losing concentration; it was as if the tower itself were *changing height*. But how could that be? He reminded himself that this was Lanka. And that phenomenon was itself proof that the white tower was undoubtedly the personal domain of Ravana. The more he examined it and probed it and tried to look within its

milky opalescence, the more it resisted his scrutiny. He could
not sense any distinctive smell from it, nor hear a single sound
from within its moon-white walls. Most oddly, there seemed to
be no one coming or going, nor any sign of an ingress. Not so
much as a doorway or a window along its entire miles-long
length, let alone a gateway or ramp. If it was a palace, it was
the strangest he had ever heard of. Yet he had nowhere else left
to look. Unlikely as it seemed, he must explore the possibility
that Sita might be within that edifice. Since he could not scout
it out from here, he must enter the city and broach the tower.
The hour was already late.

He was about to reduce himself to the size of a gnat, after
deciding that subterfuge was the most effective disguise until
he located his goal, when the apparition appeared.

6

At first he thought it to be a mist blowing from the direction of the sea. Then, as the cloud approached closer, it coalesced to more solid form, taking the shape of a mortal woman in flowing robes. Yet she was no mortal, that was evident. She floated upon the air itself, as high as the top of the wall on which he crouched. Ethereal and angelic, she had an aura of celestial beauty that enraptured him at first sight. A devi, perhaps. At the very least, a gandharva or apsara descended from the heavenly realms.

He was on his guard at once, had in fact never lowered his guard since entering Lanka. But as he probed her with his empowered senses, he was surprised to find that she bore a scent of something quite the opposite of violence or aggression: affection, perhaps? Attraction, even? He thought that unlikely. But as he sniffed once more to confirm his doubt, he thought that the scent she exuded faintly was surely closer to desire than danger. In any case, one thing was certain – she meant him no harm.

She spoke. And he received another not unpleasant shock.

He *felt* her voice rather than heard it. It was not like the mindspeech of Jambavan. The timbre of her voice did not reach his ears at all, nor did it sound within the chamber of his thought-cage; instead it rippled across the ether separating them, like invisible waves of vibration that washed across his person and entered delicately through the pores of his skin, making even the tiniest cilia on the back of his hands and neck quiver, flowing across the entire expanse of his mostly bare body. It was a voice that found and penetrated into the most secret unguarded places within his person, soothing, reassuring . . . arousing.

~~Who is this who dares to transgress my borders uninvited? Identify yourself, intruder.~~

He had to struggle to regain a semblance of control. Her speaking had disarmed and disoriented him. Exerting his will, he joined his palms together in a respectful greeting. It felt the proper thing to do. 'My lady, I am Hanuman, servant to Lord Rama of Ayodhya, presently in exile. May I know your good name?'

~~I am Lanka,~~ she said, as if that cryptic announcement was identification enough. ~~What is it you seek here? Why do you creep across my ramparts thus under cover of darkness? And before that, why did you fly across the ocean and tunnel your way through my caverns like an iron worm? From your surreptitious actions and unfamiliar visage, I fear you mean my denizens no good.~~

'When you say you are Lanka, do you mean that you are . . .' he hesitated, 'the spirit of this land? The governing spirit of Lanka itself?'

~~What else would I mean?~~ she said with a flicker of impatience. She gestured imperiously at the island at large. ~~This is my home, my body, my flesh and blood. I take great pride in myself and in the welfare of my denizens. It is no different from the maternal care that Prithvi-maa herself lavishes upon the denizens of the mortal realm. You have violated the sanctity of my care by stealing into this land. Speak! What is your purpose in coming here?~~

'My lady, I will not lie to you. You say you are to the island of Lanka as Mother Nature is to the Earth itself. I believe and respect you. As I said before, I serve Lord Rama. His virtuous wife Sita, who is a paragon of dharma, has been kidnapped and carried here by the rakshasa lord Ravana. I have come to seek her out and rescue her.'

~~You?~~ She looked him up and down with amazement. ~~A mere vanar?~~

He did not take offence. She could hardly be expected to know him. 'I am armed with the weapons of faith, my lady. My lord Rama is no ordinary mortal. If he entrusted me with this important task, I must have some qualities that bear consideration.'

She floated a little higher above the wall on which he crouched. He turned his head to follow her. She was above and behind him, circumscribing three quarters of a circle, then she descended slowly to land on the top of the wall, as gently as a feather touching the ground on a windless day. He was enchanted by her grace and her manner. Clearly accustomed to giving orders, she bore an air of great nobility and elegance. She was commanding without being dominating or superior.

Her voice wafted more gently across him as she spoke again. It thrilled the pores of his skin, like a soft, perfumed summer breeze carried across a blossoming grove.

~~Indeed you must, ~~ she said quietly. ~~For you have come thus far already. It is a long way from the mainland to my shores. And I witnessed the ease with which you broke your way through my subterranean bedrock. No doubt you are no ordinary vanar.~~

A strange ripple of pleasure passed through him at her reluctant but honest praise. 'I apologise if I have caused injury or insult to you, my lady. Such was not my intention. I seek only to find my mistress Sita and carry her home.'

She examined him silently, her face limned by moonlight. He thought he had rarely seen such a beautiful visage in his life. Even after scanning lakhs of stunningly beautiful rakshasas this past hour, she possessed an ethereal allure that affected him strangely, deeply. ~~You believe it will be that simple? Just find her and you can take her away, back to your lord Rama? Do you expect no resistance from the king of rakshasas?~~

He hesitated.

She caught his self-doubt and smiled wistfully. ~~I see you

are uncertain of my loyalties. You assume that since I care for the land of Lanka, I must be allied with the lord of this land. That assumption would be ill founded.~~

His heart pounded suddenly. 'My lady, you said yourself that you care for the denizens of Lanka.'

~~Whomever they might be, young vanar. It is not given to the land to choose its occupants. I merely provide and care for them. As long as I am cared for as well in return, it matters little whether they are rakshasas, other Asura, mortals, devas . . . or vanars even.~~

He gestured at the gardens to his right and the city to his left, without taking his eyes off her. 'You are wise to be so open-minded. For I see that your land is very well cared for. Truth be told, my lady, I have not seen such beauty in my entire life. Never did I imagine that Lanka would be such a beauteous and spellbinding spot. Yet now that I am here, I cannot deny the evidence of my own senses.'

She beamed with pleasure. ~~It pleases me that you appreciate my beauty. Yes, Ravana and his people have cared well for me. And I have reciprocated by supporting their efforts. If they plant a garden, I see to it that it flourishes rapidly and stays in bloom a long while.~~ A shadow passed across her face. ~~Yet it was not always thus. Only a short time ago, a scant decade or so by mortal counting . . .~~ She shook her head. ~~But let us not speak of things that were and are no more. You are here for a purpose, serving your lord Rama, you say. And you wonder if I am allied with his enemy, Lord Ravana. Have I understood you correctly thus far?~~

'Perfectly.' He adored the way the moonlight fell upon her cheekbones and the nape of her neck. And her tall, graceful movements were a wonder to behold.

~~Then let me set your mind at rest. I house Lord Ravana and his legions. As long as he cares for me, I care for him. The land and her people are ever intertwined. Yet tomorrow, if Ravana abuses my love and trust, I will respond in kind as well. Just as a field when overworked becomes infertile and requires a season of rest, so also a land must be allowed time to recover. Ravana respects me because he fears me. I hold the key to the secret of his immortality.~~

'You?' His eyes opened wide at this news. 'My lady, but that means you possess power over his life and—'

She raised a hand, cutting him off in mid-sentence. ~~I say this not to offer you the means to his destruction, young vanar. For that would be dishonest and unfaithful on my part. The knowledge I possess is for me alone, it is not to be shared. I say this only to impress upon you that the Lord of Lanka and I have an understanding. He does not violate my domain, and I stay loyal to him. Anything you say to me will not reach his ears. Why else do you think I stand here alone before you? Had I been allied with Ravana, a thousand rakshasas would already have apprehended you.~~

He did not try to argue the point. 'I understand, my lady. You are independent of Ravana's influence. I see that now. You asked me if I expect no resistance from Ravana's forces. Indeed, I expect nothing *but* resistance. If there is anything I do not expect, it is mercy. If discovered and apprehended, he will surely seek nothing less than my death by the most painful means. But those are not things that concern me overmuch. I am fixed only upon my single purpose: to find out and retrieve my lost mistress. May I assume that since we are allies now, you will not hinder me in my quest?'

She arched her eyebrows. Again, like all her other gestures and actions, he found this greatly pleasing to watch. ~~You leap too far, vanar. How did we progress from a simple question to becoming allies?~~

He shrugged. 'You said you are not allied with Ravana . . .'

~~Yet it does not follow that I should therefore be allied with his enemy Rama.~~

'Mayhap. But Rama's is the just cause. He was wrongfully exiled and persecuted, in large part because of Ravana's machinations. By abducting the lady Sita and bringing her here, he has transgressed the most inviolate laws of dharma. I do not ask you to aid me in any way. I am confident I will find the lady Sita on my own. When you interrupted me moments earlier, I was about to change my form and enter the city to seek her out. I ask only that you permit me to proceed without obstruction.'

She gave him a peculiar searching look. ~~If you are willing to confront the power of Ravana himself, why do you fear the obstruction of a single island-spirit? Perhaps you think you can outwit me as you did the sea serpent Surasa, or the flying mountain Mainika?~~

He was impressed at her knowledge. And noted the tart odour that accompanied this comment – she was a little offended at his assumption that she could be so easily subdued, but she was also unsure of the full extent of his powers. 'Perhaps I could, my lady. But I do not wish to. Because you are not my enemy, nor have you done anything that gives me reason to attack or offend you,' he said seriously. 'If you seek to obstruct me, then I have no choice but to battle you. But if possible, I would rather have you as a friend and ally.'

She smiled, a slow smile that lit fires within his heart. ~~I have no cause to obstruct you, young vanar. Nor to do battle with you. If anything, I would like to accompany you secretly and see how you go about this bold and adventurous mission. Never before have I known any spy to infiltrate the heart of Ravana's kingdom and steal away something the lord of rakshasas possesses. I would see how you attempt to accomplish this ambitious task.~~

He hesitated only a fraction of a second before nodding. ~~So be it, my lady. I assume that you possess the power to change your bhes-bhav?~~

She smiled and held out her hand. It melted away to become a waterfall of mercury, flowing down into the night.

He nodded. 'I expected no less. Let us change into less obtrusive forms and enter the city then. Time is of the essence and I must not fail in my mission.'

She re-formed her hand, returning it to the semblance of a

mortal limb, perfect and smooth as the surface of newly set butter. ~~Come then. Let me see how a mere vanar unarmed and alone fares in the land of rakshasas.' She held the hand out to him to take. ~~Let us go to the city, my new friend.~~

He thrilled at the feeling of her pronunciation of those three simple words. *My new friend.* He had only just met her, and already he wished he could be more than just her friend.

7

After a brief conference, the lady Lanka suggested they would be least obtrusive if they were clad and shaped as rich rakshasa nobility. Since there were many disparate races among the rakshasa species, Hanuman chose one that was least unnerving to mortal eyes, to reduce the shock to the lady Sita when he finally found her. It was a moment's work to fly to the city's outermost limits, where the marg from the wall became a cobbled avenue. Moments later, a male rakshasa and a female rakshasi clad in rich shimmering robes strode up that same avenue. The rakshasa was a tall, well-built specimen, with stippled skin a sickly milk-white in colour, eyes as blue as the summer sky on a cloudless day, and hair as yellow as ripe corn. The rakshasi was similarly built, but with lighter eyes, almost greyish-blue, and hair so dark it bordered on reddish. Catching sight of their reflections on a polished gold pillar proclaiming the name of the avenue in some indecipherable rakshasa script, Hanuman thought they were the most beautifully repulsive creatures imaginable. But they were far less unappealing than the variety of other rakshasa forms in Lanka, and so he put aside his distaste.

If nothing else, they seemed to make a handsome couple, fitting well into their surroundings, as several pairs of eyes turned their way as they passed. More than one look was overtly inviting. This was the land of hedonistic pleasure, after all. The lady Lanka insisted on taking his arm as they walked, holding it so close to herself that he could feel her breathe.

But he did not protest, wanting to give no sign that he was not a Lankan.

She whispered continually into his ear as they walked through the city, pointing out people and places and explaining this or that. He gleaned a great deal of useful information, and as he grew absorbed in his task, he began to relax and found himself enjoying even the musky rakshasi perfume that she had assumed as part of her disguise, and the gentle tones of her voice. She used normal speech to avoid being observed, and while he knew she was speaking a rakshasi tongue – a dialect appropriate to the race they had disguised themselves as – she had enabled him to understand every word. He understood the many dialects spoken around him as well, and began to store much useful information and knowledge of the kingdom of rakshasas to report back to Rama. But after long precious moments had passed and he could still discern no clue as to where Sita might be, he began to grow restless.

The lady Lanka sensed his impatience and paused before a tavern-like place into and out of which a constant stream of rakshasas came and went, each opening of the door releasing a fresh torrent of drunken laughter, raucous rakshasa music and sounds of dancing and carousing and brawling. Not to mention the stench of soma, honey-wine, and several other kinds of inebriating drinks that he had no prior knowledge of. She informed him that it was a 'pleasure-house', a place where rakshasas frolicked in warm baths and relaxed their inhibitions. She attempted to coax him into going in with her, to partake of some of the pleasures of Lanka. He was shocked to find himself actually taking a step or two in the direction of the tavern. When he stopped still, resisting her insistent tugging, she grew briefly petulant. She attempted to cajole and coax him so desperately that a small uneasy alarum began sounding within his mind's space.

His conscience spoke quietly, sternly: *What are you doing, Maruti Anjaneya? You are not here to sample the temptations of Lanka. You are here on a service to Lord Rama. Have you*

forgotten? The lady Sita is in grave distress. You were to find
her before nightfall and already the hour is grown late . . .

He shook his head to clear it of the vapours and odours of
sin and intoxication that had surrounded him; of the alluring
perfume of the lady Lanka. For all her beauty, she was still no
friend of his, and he had a mission to complete.

Aloud he said quietly: 'My lady, I believe there is only one
place left to look. I mean to enter that tower and seek out the
lady Sita.'

He nodded over his shoulder as he spoke, for they were in
the shadow of the great tower itself now, only a few hundred
yards below it.

She looked up at him, her eyes catching the light of fireworks crackling in the sky overhead. Again he was momentarily distracted by her beauty and by the ethereal grace and
nobility that she retained even in this unpleasing rakshasi form.
Her moment of petulance had passed quickly, he noted with
relief, and she had regained the air of sombre dignity that became
her so well. 'You are wise beyond appearances, young one. That
is precisely where she is.'

He stared at her. 'Then you knew her location all this while?
And did not tell me?'

She flashed a dark smile, clearly relishing an opportunity to
pay him back for not acquiescing to her entreaties a moment
ago. 'You did not ask.'

Remember, said the voice in his head, *she may call herself*
your friend, but she is not one yet. After all, she is Lanka.

Moments later, Hanuman and the lady Lanka stood at the
base of the great white tower. He looked but could see no
guards in sight. The area around the base was empty, but only
a hundred yards away, the carousing went on. He glanced up
again at the tower. It loomed into the dark night sky. He sniffed
suspiciously.

'Can this truly be Ravana's palace?' he asked doubtfully.

'Why?' she asked in a challenging tone. 'Because it does not
have a plaque saying it is so?' When he did not respond, she

went on, 'It is more than a tower, much more than meets the eye. But have no doubt, this is the domicile of the Lord of Lanka. If it does not resemble a palace in the usual sense, then that is by choice.' She added wryly, 'Perhaps he designed it just so it would confuse intruders such as yourself.'

Paying her ironic tone no heed, he went around the base of the tower. The sounds of the city faded, and by the time he reached the far side, they had been extinguished altogether. He smelled something else, though, a strange, half-familiar odour. He crouched down, sniffing at the foot of the tower.

'I smell iron,' he said. 'And sulphur. And other scents . . . that do not seem to belong here.'

Her voice came from behind him. 'There was a volcano on this site, not too long ago. It erupted some thirteen years back, engulfing the remains of the old Lanka. This city you see laid out before you like a newly wed bride, this is the new Lanka, built over the ashes of that ancient city. And this tower stands on the very site of the old volcanic channel.'

He nodded. 'That explains much. But what madness possessed the Lord of Lanka to build his palace upon such a site? A tower no less! Surely the foundation of this edifice must rest in a bed of lava.'

'You underestimate his powers, young vanar. This edifice you call a tower, it is no construction of metal and stone, as you can attest yourself.'

Having licked the tower's surface, he could only agree. 'It is like no substance I have ever encountered before.'

'Indeed. That is because it is not a tower at all. That is why it requires no foundation or structure in the usual sense. This, my handsome vanar friend, is Pushpak, the great device of the gods.'

He stared up in newfound awe at the sky-reaching white monolith. 'Pushpak? The flying chariot of Lord Brahma?'

'Not merely a chariot, but a device that obeys the commands of its master and takes any form, any shape that he desires. It was the property of Brahma once, but Kubera, treasurer of the devas and half-brother of Ravana, won it as a gift from Brahma because of austerities he had performed. Later, Ravana wrested it away from him at the same time that he won Lanka itself in the great Yaksa war, along with all Kubera's great store of wealth. He has lost much of the wealth since then, but Pushpak remains, serving him as he pleases. At present, Ravana desires it to assume the form of a great white tower, and so that is what it is. If he chooses, he can make it resemble an entire city, or shrink itself to the size of a single chariot to carry him across the ocean with the speed of the wind – or across worlds, if he desires.'

Hanuman took a step back from the tower, marvelling at its pearl-like perfection. 'The very structure itself obeys his mind's command?'

'And none may enter or leave its environs unless he decrees it. This is why you see no guards outside the tower. He has no need of them, for Pushpak itself is the most effective protector he could ever want.'

Hanuman nodded. 'Surely then Sita-devi is inside this place. I must enter at once. Already the hour grows late.'

She chuckled softly. He turned to look at her sharply. She was laughing openly, but when he looked, she raised a hand to cover her mouth as a cultured lady would be expected to do. 'Do you think to make your way in by brute force? Even the strength of a god would not be sufficient to tear a hole in Pushpak's defences.'

He was silent.

She took his silence to indicate loss of wit. 'Oh, don't be disheartened, Hanuman. You have done a great deal already. Much more than anyone could expect of a vanar, even one with such extraordinary gifts. Even Rama cannot fault you for having tried so hard and failed. This is no ordinary place and Ravana no ordinary foe. The gods themselves have lost to him before, and been slaves in his household in times past.'

Still he was silent.

She came up to him and put a hand on his shoulder, touching

him, caressing him. 'There is nothing more you can accomplish here. Come, let us away. Stay the night with me and I will show you the true wonders of my land!'

His only response was to remove her hand from his shoulder. 'I thank you for your assistance and grace, my lady. But I request you to leave me now.'

'Leave you?' Her voice was incredulous, shocked.

'My purpose will not be thwarted by any distraction. I must proceed and fulfil my mission.'

'Distraction?' Her tone was sharper this time. 'Is that how you perceive me? As a *distraction*?'

He looked at her. Her face had contorted with a new expression, an unattractive one. It made him wonder how he had ever thought her beautiful. It made him wary of his own feelings and her true intentions in accompanying him on his quest. 'My lady, anything that delays me or draws me away from my true purpose ill serves my lord Rama's cause. I thank you for your company and your guidance until now. But I realise that I must continue my journey alone. Pray, allow me to take my leave of you now.'

She stared at him scornfully. 'And what do you expect to accomplish without me to guide you? Do you believe you can enter Ravana's palace tower alone and unarmed, seek out the prisoner and carry her away without so much as a bleat of protest?'

He shrugged. 'I will face what challenges may arise when they arise.'

He was looking directly into her eyes at that instant and saw something peculiar occur. For a moment, just a fraction of a second, they seemed to alter subtly, to become like those of a jungle predator, like the great jungle cats that his vanar race feared and detested so much. Then, before he could be certain of it, they were as before once again.

'I see that you are more resolute of purpose than I first believed,' she said.

'My lady,' he said, growing restless, 'I cannot dally here

talking all night. Sita may be in grave distress. I must find her at once.'

She was silent a moment. 'And you know that this will bring you up against the lord of rakshasas himself, will most surely earn you his wrath. Are you prepared to face Ravana and feel the blight of his anger?'

'If need be, yes. And now, I take my leave.'

He turned back to the tower, considering the best place to strike and attempt to force an entry. He joined his hands together to make a double fist, intending to hammer at the wall and see if he could not batter a hole.

Before he could raise his hands to strike, the surface of the tower shimmered like a reflection upon the surface of a sunlit lake, and a portal opened in the wall itself, large enough for him to pass through.

He turned to see the lady Lanka gesturing with a raised hand, a sardonic smile on her beautiful face. 'Let us see if you can match your actions to your intentions, bold one. I am intrigued by your foolhardy courage. Few would dare to even dream of confronting Ravana under such circumstances, and none would survive such an encounter. But I am impressed by your dedication and your zeal. I will take you to the end of your quest and watch to see how you accomplish your goal.'

She stepped forward through the portal, turning to beckon him on. 'Come. I will take you to your lady Sita.'

He hesitated, sniffing sharply. He did not trust the lady Lanka's intentions any more. In truth, he had begun to doubt that she was what she claimed to be. And this whole capitulation and the ease of her entry into the tower, it all reeked of a trap. *Beware, Anjaneya*, his mind's voice warned. *It is for good reason that you are a sworn brahmacharya. You took the vow of celibacy because you knew that desire for the opposite sex can cloud a warrior's judgement at crucial moments. From the instant she first appeared, this being, whomever she might truly be, has manipulated you with great shrewdness and skill. You cannot trust her.*

Every instinct in his body screamed that he was stepping into a trap.

But it was a trap that might just lead him closer to Sita.

With a grimace and a soft growl, he lowered his raised fists and leapt through the portal, into the tower.

8

He was plunged immediately into hell. Either hell, or a heaven designed by perverse rakshasas.

He stood still, staring incredulously. Without realising it, he had changed back into his natural form, shocked by the sights and sounds that sprawled before him. His senses were overwhelmed, his mind ignited like a lump of camphor touched to an open flame.

'What is this place?' he heard himself whisper.

The lady's voice caressed his ear, speaking in the same manner she had used before. ~~Call it what you will. Ravana terms it the palace of infinite pleasures. A place where all your desires are fulfilled. A garden of earthly delights. A cornucopia of sensual satisfaction.~~

He breathed deeply, trying to clear his mind of the thick musk that enveloped him, and only inhaled more of the intoxicating odours of the chamber. Before him, vaster than anything he had ever seen before, lay a seemingly endless space. There was little doubt that the space within was far, far greater than the external dimensions of the tower suggested. That in itself did not surprise him; he knew it was a celestial device, capable of astonishing miracles. But he had not been prepared for what lay within its deceptively pristine white walls.

The space was filled with bodies writhing and twisting in the torment of sensual pleasure. Thousands upon thousands, perhaps even lakhs, of rakshasas of every shape and colour and race. All engrossed in a frenzy of sensual pleasuring. A circus of fornication.

~~Hanuman,~~ said the beautiful one who called herself Lanka, ~~you are a handsome and virile vanar. I am impressed by your bravery and your dedication. Come. Let us dally here awhile. I would share my charms with you.~~

He fought the impulses that warred within him. With each passing moment, he saw more and more. What had seemed at first to be only one vast chamber was in fact a thousand chambers, each immeasurably vast. The entire mountain of Mahendra could have been brought into this place and it would have been as an anthill. Somehow Ravana had contrived a place that looked like a white tower only from without. Within its walls was a space as vast as imagination itself: an endless unravelling of sexual excesses, played out by more rakshasas than could easily be counted.

The more he studied it, the more it threatened to overwhelm him. Just as a man fond of drink pauses when passing the open doorway of a tavern, tempted by the reek of liquor and the sights and sounds of the revelry within, so Hanuman paused, wondering for a fraction of an instant what it might be like to participate in this feast of the senses. It was only the briefest pause, not even a considering, let alone a yielding. But it was enough to let the ocean of sights and sounds press at the dam of his self-control and threaten to burst through like a raging flood. He fought it furiously, with all his will and self-empowered strength, fought to regain his equilibrium the way a drowning man thrashes and twists his way back to the surface. The forces against him were too great.

Through his struggle, he felt the voice of the lady who called herself Lanka and whom he now knew was a rakshasi of some sort, seeking to insinuate itself through the chink in his mental armour, trying to wedge it open and let the flood come rushing through. On a more physical plane, he heard and saw and felt the rakshasas nearest to him approach, crawling and dragging themselves across the lushly carpeted floor, clutching at him, caressing his skin, calling him to join them in their depraved games, seducing him.

He thrashed and twisted, clutched by a thousand invisible hands. Tugged at by a million minds warped by an existence spent seeking only pure hedonistic pleasure.

~~Struggle is useless, my vigorous vanar. No being in all the three worlds possesses the ability to resist the allure of the palace of infinite pleasure. Even the devas hesitate to come here, for they fear they might never leave. Every fantasy you ever conceived can be fulfilled here, handsome Hanuman. It is futile to resist. Give yourself over to the call of your own libido and you will experience pleasure such as you never dreamed possible.~~

No, he shouted, *I will never—*

But no words came from his open, gasping mouth.

He flailed, tearing himself free of the clutching, reaching, caressing limbs that sought to bear him down, to crush him beneath the weight of his own subterranean desires, to awaken the reservoir of secret lust that every creature of flesh and blood must of necessity possess in order to procreate and further its species. The flailing was as much mental as physical. For every pair of hands he threw off, twisted free of, a thousand new pairs clasped him slickly. For every inflammatory, incendiary sight and sound and scent he blocked, a million more rushed in to replace it. Now it seemed the very ground beneath his feet was made of living, writhing rakshasas, engaged in the vulgar execution of primal lusts. Every mote of air he breathed was filled with the musk of sexual predation. Every way he turned, everything he did only increased the onslaught.

He cried wordlessly, caught in a bog of lust, sinking beneath the weight of a million nameless desires, his struggles only dragging him deeper into the quicksand.

He had been prepared to fight, to battle any number of opponents, wage war single-handedly if need be. He had been unalarmed by the flying mountain, by the giant sea serpent; had expected resistance, fighting, bloodshed. But this was a war for which he had no armour. A battle for which he had no weapons. A struggle for which he had no defences prepared.

Yet he fought on.

His head reeled, his senses swam. His sense of smell was over-whelmed, his mind assailed. He fought furiously, but it was as if he had been submerged in a bottomless ocean and was trying to struggle back to the surface. He swam through the ocean, racked by storm winds, teeming with great creatures and aquatic marvels and wonders, seeking only to regain the surface and breathe clean, natural air once more. But struggle as he might, he could not reach it. He was lost, lost in a world not of his understanding, succumbing to a struggle for which he had no means of retaliation.

Then a single word swam to the surface of his beleaguered mind.

Rama.

He repeated it, felt its graceful syllables upon his mind's tongue.

Rama.

It brought solace. The ocean paused in its churning turmoil, the flood abated a brief instant, the quicksand ceased its relent-less sucking.

Rama.

He recited it with adoring respect. Like a mantra against unseen evils. Like a charm to ward off his own secret temptations.

Ramaramaramaramaramaramaramaramaramaramarama . . .

'Rama!'

The sound of his own voice was like the gasp of a drowning man, regaining the surface, gulping in his first breath of air after long moments of agony.

He repeated it again, firmer and more resolute. 'Rama.'

The hands clutching at him, clasping him, caressing him began to shrink away. The hordes seeking to pull him down, to drag him into their own perverse ocean of toxic sensuality drew back fearfully.

~~No, you fool. Your master cannot save you now. Only Ravana can help you. Say his name instead. Say Ravana's name aloud, call to *him* for help. He is the only master!~~

'Rama,' he said softly, reverentially.

And flexed his body.

They fell away like shackles unchained. A space grew around him, larger, widening with every repetition.

'Ramaramaramaramarama . . .'

~~You fool. You seek your own destruction. My cousin – I mean Ravana, Ravana the Lord of Lanka, will discover you if you say that name here. It is forbidden. Outlawed.'

'RAMA!' he boomed, his voice expanding to fill the length and breadth of the mountainous space.

They were screaming now, unable to bear the sound of the Forbidden Name. He repeated it over and over, relishing his power over them, the manner in which each repetition leached the lust out of this hellish place and left it a little cleaner, less impure.

'RAMA!' The word echoed and reverberated.

~~Fool!~~ he heard her scream. ~~And I a bigger fool to bring you here in the first place. Pushpak, take us from here at once. Take us——~~

He blinked at the sudden alteration in the quality of light, at the abrupt, seamless change of surroundings. One moment he had been there, in that bottomless hell of rakshasa fornication. The next moment he was standing in a great palatial mansion, multi-levelled and richly ornamented. He took a tentative breath and was hugely relieved: the air was not pure or perfect by any means, but it was free of the nauseating reek of excess at least.

He looked around and saw a creature perched upon a golden railing that bordered the marble-floored balcony on which he stood. It was a rakshasi of some feline variety, with beautiful golden fur and glowing cat-like eyes. He recognised those eyes at once – and the sensual flow of the form, if not the actual form itself.

'Lady Lanka?' he said ironically. 'Why, what big claws and fangs you have.'

She snarled silently at him. 'Do not mock me, vanar. I am

Supanakha, cousin to Ravana himself. At a single word from me, he will tear your heart out and eat it in one gulp.'

'If you are so powerful, and your cousin so mighty, why did you need to disguise yourself and attempt to deceive me?'

She flicked her tail irritably. 'I thought you would make a good night's diversion.' She licked her chops pointedly. 'You are a handsome specimen, for a vanar.'

'And so you pretended to be Lady Lanka,' he said, shaking his head. 'The spirit of the land itself.'

She shrugged. 'There was such a being once. Except she was a rakshasi named Simhika, and she wasn't much to look at. She liked to eat anything and anyone that ventured here. It was a long time ago, back when the world was new and few creatures moved upon the land. I borrowed a little from her . . .'

'And a lot from your own imagination.'

'Actually, from yours,' she said unexpectedly. She moved closer to him, exaggerating her femininity with a sensual arching. 'Did I not please you in that form? We could have spent a night in the palace of infinite pleasures, instead of my having to eat you alive.'

He smiled at her persistence. 'And if I had succumbed to your depravity, what would you have done with me come morning?'

She cocked her head, pretending to think briefly. 'Eaten you alive.' She smiled dangerously. 'But at least we would have enjoyed the night. Now here we are.'

'And where is that?'

She gestured over her shoulder, beyond the railing. 'See for yourself.'

He kept his eyes on her as he walked to the railing, careful to keep enough distance should she try to leap. Looking down, he saw that they were on the upper level of a great palatial hall. The space below contained a dazzling display of wealth and refinement. It was created in the fashion of rich luxury that mortals usually favoured – and that vanars were also partial to if they could but afford such things. Pillars of gold and silver adorned with carvings of animals and Asuras. Stairways of gold inlaid with lapis and emerald and sapphire. Golden windows with delicate lattices. Enormous tables groaning beneath the weight of exotic foods and drinks, the heavy remnants of some sumptuous feast. Crystal floors decorated with pearls, ivory and coral. Magnificent embroidered carpets. Sweet birdsong music, divine fragrances, priceless fabrics . . . Even at a glance he was impressed by the wealth and sophistication. Yet again, Lanka had surprised him. He wondered if palaces in Ayodhya or Gandahar were as tastefully luxuriant.

But the decor was just that, decor. The real surprise lay in the centre of the chamber below. Evidently, a great feast and celebration had taken place only recently. He could still scent the odours of the food on the table, the wine drunk and spilt. The revellers had taken a respite, stealing a short rest, no doubt before resuming their revels, or going on to more advanced celebrations.

Lying upon dozens of beds, divans, couches, sofas, carpets, rugs and even across the jewelled floor were hundreds of women. Beautiful, breathtaking women wearing all kinds of clothes and jewels and garlands, and many wearing nothing at all. After the depraved excesses Hanuman had witnessed in the palace of pleasures, this sight seemed barely offensive, but he could not help but observe that every one of the women was of exquisite beauty, by any standards, rakshasa, mortal or otherwise. They possessed a perfection of limb and complexion that would have transfixed any male of any species. Singly, they were extraordinary beauties; together, they were an invaluable harem.

Every one of them lay asleep. He scanned their faces quickly but efficiently, using his superior senses to scent out whether any of them might be the one he sought. Yet even as he did so, he prayed that Sita was not among them. For her presence in this menagerie of kept females would mean only one thing, and he could not bear to allow that meaning to penetrate his mind.

There was no sign of Sita.

But lying in the midst of them, splendidly splayed out in rich robes and jewels all disarrayed from his recent revels, sleeping as peacefully as his concubines, was the King of Lanka himself.

9

Ravana lay upon his great bed in his most private of chambers, asleep after a day filled with drink and sensual pleasures. He was adorned by more jewels than Hanuman had ever seen upon a single person before. His arms, thick as flagstaffs, were ringed with beautifully filigreed bracelets that only partially concealed the rakshasa's many battle wounds. As with any great legendary personage, Ravana's scars were as famous as his ten heads. Hanuman recognised the famous rip mark said to have been inflicted by the right tusk of Airavata, battle elephant of Lord Indra, during the rakshasa king's wars against the devas. On both his shoulders were the white slashes inflicted by Indra's vajra, the celestial thunderbolt. There were any number of other scars across his body, the evidence of countless encounters and battles against celestial beings as well as mortals.

Hanuman craned his neck, peering over a curved section of the railing on which he perched, seeking a better view of Ravana's chest. At last he spied a diagonal slashing scar that was clearly of far younger vintage than the demon lord's other marks. He sucked in a breath. That scar had been inflicted by Dasaratha himself, father of Rama. Lakshman had told him the story of that fateful encounter during the Last Asura War. Dasaratha had barely escaped with his life; after his chariot was demolished by Ravana, he was carried off the battlefield wounded and unconscious by Rama's clan-mother Kaikeyi.

And now here Hanuman was, in the most private chamber

of Ravana's palace, staring down at the lord of all rakshasa-kind. His blood seethed momentarily, thinking of all the pain and suffering this being had inflicted upon so many for so long. Upon his lord Rama. His paws curled into fists, and he felt himself start to expand. It took a great effort to control himself.

A soft chuckle by his ear made him turn with a snarl. He lunged at Supanakha. The shapeshifter leapt back, startled, but recovered at once. 'So,' she showed her teeth in hostile amusement, 'the vanar has claws too.'

'She is not here,' he said, hardly caring if his voice carried. The chamber was immense, and the railing on which he was standing was a good fifteen yards above the main floor. 'Where is the lady Sita?'

She curled her tail over her rear, purring softly. 'Are you sure she isn't here? Have you looked closely enough?' She leapt up to the railing again. 'Perhaps you should take another look.'

'Rakshasi,' he said in a dangerous tone, 'I will not tolerate your games any longer.'

She swished her tail, brushing it close enough to his face for him to feel the wind, but not close enough to grab. 'Why? Do you think your mistress is too scrupulous to sleep with the Lord of Lanka?'

He snorted. 'Sleep? She will not brook him touching one hair on her head. Sita-devi is the paragon of wifely virtue.'

She chuckled. 'You'd be surprised how many paragons of wifely virtue are down there right now, lying drunk and thoroughly ravished.'

'Then you do not understand the meaning of wifely virtue,' he said, unprovoked by her taunting. 'Sita is not among those who cling to morality because their Sanskriti demands it, or because their elders impose it upon them. She does so because she is a self-fulfilled, self-empowered woman who values her own dignity. She has chosen to adhere to a code of ethics and morality, and having done so, she will not be moved a fraction of an inch from her position. Her rigidity is not demanded by her husband, her in-laws, or even her own family. It is her own desire for uprightness that makes her uphold this virtuous stance.'

Supanakha lost some of her taunting tone. Her tail flicked angrily. 'Sure, she's the queen of all virtue! But that doesn't mean she's superhuman and invulnerable. How do you know she has not succumbed to the forced embraces of my cousin? How do you know she has not been raped and ravished against her will?'

He smiled, undaunted. 'Because she is not merely a woman of strong character, she is also a warrior-princess. She would defend her virtue just as a male warrior would defend his dignity. Just as an Arya prince or king would rather have his head cut off than bow it before a being such as Ravana, or any Asura chief, so also my lady Sita would fight to the very end rather than allow herself to be used against her will.'

Supanakha scowled. 'Methinks you think too highly of your precious mistress. Perhaps you are mistaken in your fealty. Perhaps the lady is not half as honourable as you would like to believe.'

Hanuman unfolded his arms from across his chest and stared at her with narrowed eyes. 'Be careful, demoness. Your attempts to deceive me were acceptable, for you are my foe and were doing your duty in attempting to keep me from entering Lanka, and then Ravana's palace. But do not make the mistake of insulting the name of my lady. I will not tolerate any slur against her good name.'

Supanakha snarled silently, letting him see all the way down her purple throat. Spittle flew from her lips. 'Too much self-righteousness makes a person unbalanced, vanar. Be careful what you say. You may have cause to doubt the veracity of your beliefs before this night is through.'

She turned and raced the length of the balcony, away from him. He was on her heels in a trice.

The shapeshifter led him a merry dance. He followed her through chamber after chamber as richly invested and decorated as the one in which he had seen the lord of rakshasas asleep. There were apartments with courtyards paved with gold and silver and pearls. Pools of every shape and size, filled by fountains of clear sparkling water, jewelled steps leading into them, bottoms of crystal and coral and pearls. On their banks were trees such as he had never seen or heard of before: gold-hued trees which glowed luminously in the semi-darkness. Lotuses and lilies bloomed, and the cries of water birds were audible, even though he knew he was inside a great white tower, not a forest. The lines of illusion blurred further the more he pursued the demoness. He followed her through a mango grove where birdsong filled the air and the trees were made of gold and silver. Flowering trees bustled with bees drunk on nectar. Strutting peacocks pranced and preened. He saw entire townships with stone-paved streets and crossroads and buildings and fortifications. There were great numbers of rakshasas here, although none seemed to be aware of him. He recognised other subservient peoples too – vidyadharis, beautiful servants and maids who obeyed the commands of the rakshasas. Gorgeous naga women with full-moon faces. There were wonders beyond counting. He saw hillocks with streams running down them, lakes brimming with clear water with carved steps and gem-encrusted artificial banks, surrounded by landscaped gardens abounding in docile wildlife and covered with lavish pavilions.

Yet just as he was about to dismiss all these as clear signs of artifice, he came upon a samsapa tree, dense with leaves and creepers. He climbed the tree to taste the leaves and found them real. He was perplexed. Was all this really an illusion? He knew that Asura sorcery could achieve great feats, but this was a real samsapa tree, with real leaves and creepers. How could sorcery create something ostensibly *natural*? It defied everything he knew.

But this minor irritant was soon forgotten when he could not find the shapeshifter. He had seen her last at the foot of the tree, but by the time he reached her, she had vanished. He ranged up and down, in case she was hiding in the dense foliage or hanging from a creeper. But when he could neither see her nor scent her, he began to fret. It was already night, and he still had not found Sita.

He was overcome by a great thirst. The lake nearby was clear and inviting, and he went and drank from it without thinking. The water was wonderfully cool and sweet, and it refreshed him greatly. Only after his belly was full did he feel a twinge of misgiving. Perhaps he ought to have abstained from consuming anything. After all, this was the heart of Lanka. Despite all appearances, he was within the inner sanctum of Ravana, inside some artificial construct of the celestial Pushpak. Perhaps he should not have eaten those leaves and drunk that water after all . . .

His vision blurred. The lake shimmered like steaming water in a mountain spa. The entire landscape rolled, then righted itself. His ears filled with strange sounds and voices, his nostrils twitched, scenting a myriad of scents too exotic to identify. His tongue felt numb and hot where he had tasted the juice of the samsapa leaves. They were not samsapa after all, he realised, his senses reeling. Nor was that lake filled with water.

He struggled to stay upright, but a moment later found himself flat on his back. The sound of familiar laughter filled his ears. He tried to turn to see if it was the shapeshifter, but ended up falling on his face. He lay there, trying to raise his head to breathe. Moving any part of his body seemed impossible. For a moment he panicked, thinking that he would suffocate under his own weight, suffocate and die.

A train of visions floated through his delirious, drugged mind, a psychedelic line of hallucinations. He saw himself dying, succumbing to the most trivial of ruses, duped by a rakshasi shapeshifter, killed by eating a few leaves and drinking some water. He saw Rama waiting at the unfinished bridge, receiving news of his death – the hallucination did not clarify how Rama heard this news – and losing all hope and motivation. He saw Rama dying, believing Sita already lost. And then Lakshman dying too. He saw Rama's entire line extinguished – Bharat,

Shatrugan, Kausalya, Sumitra, even the rehabilitated Kaikeyi. Then Sugreeva, desolate at his failure to aid Rama in his quest, taking his own life the vanar way – by leaping from a cliff. And Sugreeva's wives, Ruma and Tara, killing themselves. Angad dying as well. And then all the vanars of Kiskindha throwing themselves to their deaths.

The vision was absurd in its exaggeration and lack of logic. Yet it carried a terrible foreboding, like a bad dream that seems utterly real and convincing at the time. He knew that it was the result of the unnatural leaves and water he had consumed, but that knowledge alone did not help him throw off the vision. He felt his body struggling with the anguish of suffocation, and although he knew that by simply moving a little to one side he could enable himself to breathe again, that little effort seemed impossible. He heard someone laugh, and recognised his own mental voice. He was laughing at himself, for being able to grow as large as a mountain and leap across an ocean, yet unable to move a few inches to stop himself from suffocating.

His mind swam with mad visions. They were worse in a sense than the earlier morass of sensual temptations in which he had been immersed. As one who had taken a vow of celibacy, he had long since mastered the art of deflecting such entice-ments. Even that epic assault in Ravana's palace of pleasures had not been sufficient to break through his wall of self-will. But these visions were his own fears and anxieties, all too real and possible, glimpses of things that could easily be. Still, he knew, they were no different from the sensual temptations. They were a form of acute battlefield depression, a sinking of the soul into the quicksand of its own anxieties, the darkness that passed through a soldier's mind when the battle was going against his side, his lines routed, his comrades slain or screaming in anguish around him, his own life-blood ebbing through his futile fingers, his general had been brought down, defeat certain.

A warm breath wafted upon his cheek, breath so redolent of rotten flesh that even the perfume of sorcery could not conceal its putridness. 'Still desire to see your lady Sita, vanar?'

She laughed, exuding an amalgam of scents that swirled like colours in his brain, dancing and leaping madly in his drugged consciousness.

Yes, he tried to say. Yes, I will find her, even if it kills me. For that is why I came here. And that is what I will accomplish.

He remembered the phrase the vanar armies had used to cheer Rama at that first gathering. What were the words? *Maryada* . . . He fought a new swirl of madness, visions of his family, his mother, his brothers and sisters, all dashing their brains out with rocks, howling and bleeding and broken. *Maryada Purshottam* . . . The women lying sprawled across Ravana's chambers, all with faces resembling that of Sita. Each one of them opened her eyes and looked up at him, and each one smiled an obscene, sensual smile. *Maryada Purshottam* . . .

'Maryada Purshottam Rama,' he gasped, his starved lungs gulping in precious breath.

Supanakha screamed and danced away as he sat up, coughing and heaving. 'Does nothing bring you down! You damned vanar! What are you made of anyway? Steel and iron?'

He retched, bringing up the contents of his stomach. It tasted vile and smelled worse, and he wondered how he could ever have been foolish enough to sample anything in this evil place of deception and desire. Then it was all out, seeping over the sandy soil that still looked and felt and smelled so real. He rose to his feet, gulping in great lungfuls of air. 'Maryada Purshottam Rama,' he said once more. 'I am the servant of Rama Who Achieves His Goals Against All Odds.'

Then he leapt, startling the birds and deer of the artificial forest, and grasped the shapeshifter as she was still in mid-air. Held her by the neck in a grip so hard that were he to tighten it but a fraction, she would be dead at once.

'Now you will take me to my lady Sita,' he said.

10

Sita started at the sight of the creature that appeared before her. It was accompanied by the shapeshifting rakshasi she knew to be Ravana's cousin. Supanakha snapped at her, as if she would dearly love to leap at Sita and tear her throat out. But the other creature, the one standing like a man on two legs, had Supanakha by the throat in a grip so tight, Sita could see tears spring to the rakshasi's eyes. She subsided, snarling softly, and turned her head up to her captor.

'Here she is,' she said in a choked voice. 'Your precious lady. Now let me go.'

Still the newcomer held on to Supanakha's neck. Sita stared cautiously, not knowing what to make of him. He looked not unlike an ape, but was less hairy, and with limbs formed to resemble a mortal more than a simian. His soft downy fur was golden in hue, and his body powerfully muscled, as if he was capable of uprooting a tree single-handedly or raising great boulders. He was taller than a mortal, and stood straighter than any ape or monkey she had ever seen. At once the word sprang unbidden to her lips: she might not have seen one before, but she had grown up hearing of the species. 'A vanar . . . ?' she asked.

To her surprise, he let go of Supankha and joined his palms together. Then he went down on his knees and bowed to her. 'Indeed, my lady,' he said in a voice as reverential as a Shaivite before his deity. 'I am Hanuman, the servant of Lord Rama, sent to seek you out.'

Her heart lifted with joy. But almost at once she drew back. Could it be true? What if it were another ruse of Ravana? Or the other rakshasas? After all, Supanakha was no friend of hers. She looked warily at the shapeshifter, twisting her neck as if to free it of a cramp. Supanakha saw her staring and narrowed her eyes, showing her teeth.

'What?' she snarled. 'Are you not happy to meet your champion? He came a great way to see you, you know. He leapt across the ocean, met the challenge of the flying mountain and the giant sea serpent, tunnelled through the rocky foundations of the island of Lanka, strolled through the boulevards of the city, overcame the temptations of the palace of sensual pleasures, crept through Ravana's private bedchamber as he slept, and he even resisted the power of Pushpak, all just to come here to find you. Aren't you going to greet him warmly at least?'

Hanuman cuffed the shapeshifter hard enough to send her flying through the grove. Supanakha squealed like a kitten, and landed with a bone-numbing thump against a treetrunk. 'Wretch!' she cried. 'Enjoy your little reunion while it lasts. When my brother finds you here, all your magic will not be enough to save you from his wrath.'

And with a snarl she vanished from the ashoka grove.

Hanuman glanced worriedly in the direction she had gone, then shook his head, dismissing her. 'She was untrustworthy. Besides, she has served her purpose by bringing me here.'

Turning to Sita, he lay down on the ground and prostrated himself before her. Touching her feet, he said, 'My lady, I beg your forgiveness for the delay in arriving. I pray I am not too late to save you from your suffering?'

She was overwhelmed. A part of her mind, already so overburdened by the strain of confinement and the tortures she had endured, felt as if she had inhaled alcoholic vapours. She felt her senses reel, and tried to take a step back. Instead, she lost her balance and had to put her hand out to grasp the nearest tree to stay on her feet.

'My lady,' said the vanar, springing up from the ground. 'Are you well?' He would have caught her but he did not wish to so much as touch the arm of his master's wife.

She forced herself to breathe. 'No.' She exhaled raggedly. 'No, I am not well. But tell me. Where is Rama? Is he here too, on Lanka?'

The vanar's large face, so much like a man's yet also so much like an ape's, lost some of its natural handsome lustre. 'I regret he is not, my lady. He awaits us on the shores of the mainland. I have come alone.'

She shook her head, unable to understand. 'But then . . . if you could come to Lanka, why not he? Why did he not come himself? Why did he send you?'

He lowered his head, understanding and empathising with her confusion and sadness. 'My lady, I was bestowed with certain abilities that enable me to leap across the ocean and overcome other obstacles. It is by the grace of my lord Rama himself that I have achieved these feats. If it were at all possible, he would certainly have come himself. Since the day you were abducted, he has done nothing but struggle to reach Lanka and bring you back. Even now, he toils to complete a great bridge across the ocean to bring him and his army here to Lanka.'

Briefly he explained to her about Rama's alliance with Sugreeva and the vanar and bear armies that were coming to Lanka. Her disappointment was still as stark as a fresh wound on her face, but as he described Rama's determination and leadership and other qualities that he had come to see during his tenure with her husband, the disappointment abated and he saw her face grow less sallow. He had been alarmed by his first sight of her. She was so different from the woman he remembered from the time he had watched Rama and his group as they battled the rakshasas of Janasthana, he would not have recognised her in a crowd. She had grown so thin and pale, the very light in her eyes dimmed to tiny candlepoints instead of the gleaming torches of lifelight they had been then. It pained him grievously to see her in this state of near-starvation and despair, her body marked and scored with a hundred minor scratches and marks. Her clothes were ragged and dirty, her hair tangled and knotted and filled with dirt and fragments of dried leaves. His heart ached at the evidence of her sufferings.

'I am glad he is well,' she said when he had finished. 'And Lakshman too. I am glad they are both well and healthy and strong yet.'

He did not want to contradict her, but there was something in her tone that disturbed him. 'He will be truly well only when you are by his side again, my lady. Recovering you has become the sole purpose of his existence now. I fear he cannot go on living without you.'

She sighed. The sound of it tore at his heart. She looked at him with great eyes filled with sadness. 'Nor I without he. I know it for a fact, good Hanuman. Neither of us can live without the other.'

'Then tarry no longer, my lady. Come, climb up on my back and hold on to my hair. I will expand myself to a size greater than this tower in which you lie imprisoned, and fly us both back to Rama. You will be free of this cursed lair of rakshasas and reunited with your husband.'

She looked at him with wide, hopeful eyes. 'You could do such a thing?' She shook her head, admonishing herself. 'Of course you could. Why else would Rama choose you? And it is true, I heard what Supanakha said. Even if she was lying or being ironic, she would not have brought you here unless she feared you more than she feared her own cousin. I'm sorry, I do not mean to doubt your abilities. I am very tired and harried.'

'Do not apologise, my lady,' he said gently. 'Even a chastisement from you would be a blessing to me. You are my master's beloved wife, and I will do anything to serve and honour you. That is why I have come, to fetch you home.'

She still remained as she was, leaning against the ashoka tree. 'Rama once had abilities too. Great powers. He could have worked wonders, accomplished anything. He was given great celestial weapons as well, enough to wage war against this entire island of rakshasas. Yet he chose to set all aside, to pursue his life as a mere mortal, vulnerable, ordinary.'

Hanuman inclined his head. 'I have heard tell of those sacrifices. Lord Rama and his brother Lord Lakshman gave up their brahmanic abilities in order to unleash the weapon of Brahma at Mithila.'

Sita nodded. 'There was no way to avoid that; he had to do it to repel Ravana's Asura army. The brahm-astra was the only force that could do it. But then later, when we were in exile, we encountered a great sage.' She recounted the tale of their meeting with the sage Anasuya, disguised as a low-caste berry-gatherer. 'Anasuya was so pleased with Rama's lack of bias against any caste or creed that she granted him powerful weapons. Yet he would not use those weapons. When we faced impending attack by a great number of rakshasas at Chitrakut and were sorely in need of aid, Lakshman and I pleaded with him to employ those weapons of Anasuya. But he refused, and later he revealed that he had given them back. That he would survive with ordinary human skills as best he could.'

'And he did survive,' Hanuman added gently. 'Indeed, he did more than survive. He defeated fourteen thousand fierce berserk rakshasas in the wilds of Janasthana, with only a handful of rebels and outlaws as his allies. He rid that entire region of demons. That is why his name is chanted first at every ritual in every hermitage in those places, for hundreds of brahmins and brahmacharyas owe their lives and the continuation of their order to Rama's championship.'

'But it took fourteen long years. And at the end of those fourteen years, look at what happened. He won the rakshasa wars of Janasthana, but this is the result. The king of rakshasas abducted me from our very home, as Rama and Lakshman watched helplessly. And here in Lanka, Rama is considered an unrighteous man who massacres species and races, and does not respect dharma. This is the reward we get for doing things the ordinary way.'

Hanuman saw and felt her anger and pain but could not

understand what to say to assuage it. 'What would you have him do, my lady? He did serve dharma, and he was and is a righteous man. He is the most righteous being I have ever known. He did what he had to, in the only way it could be done. What else should he do?'

'Use his celestial gifts,' she said. 'Call on Anasuya. Call on Brahmarishi Vishwamitra. Call on the devas. Call upon anyone and everyone who would help him. He will need their help to battle Ravana and his island of monsters. I have seen glimpses of Ravana's power. He has regained much of the ground he lost fourteen years ago at Mithila. He is ready and waiting for Rama's invasion. Indeed, he awaits him eagerly, like a bully looks forward to a smaller child's opposition so that he may smite him down and show his own power.'

Hanuman shook his head, smiling. 'If Ravana thinks that, then he is the one who will be smitten down. Rama is not a weak child. He is as powerful as any warlord in the three worlds. His fealty to dharma alone makes him the equal of all and sundry.'

'Dharma, dharma,' she cried out. 'That is all I heard from Rama's lips for fourteen years. And now you tell me the same words. Dharma is well and good, Hanumanji. But what about me? His wife, Sita? For my sake at least can he not call upon those countless boons that must be accrued on his account? With all the good he has done, surely some deva or sage will invest him with celestial weapons and powers sufficient to demolish Lanka?'

He was taken aback by her vehemence and passion. 'I do not doubt it, my lady, but—'

'Then ask him to do it! Tell him that Sita has not long to live. For I will not touch food nor drink, not so much as a drop of water, as long as I am in this hellish place. And if he wishes to recover me safe and sane, then he must act now. He must invoke his good deeds and demand a great boon of power. Then he must crush Lanka and take me home with honour and dignity.'

Hanuman struggled to find a way to appease her. 'He will

do so, my lady. He is on the verge of crossing Lanka. The bridge is almost done. Within days—'

'Days!' She laughed, the ragged laugh of one who had reached the end of her tether and teetered on the brink of sanity. 'I will not survive this night, let alone days.'

'But there is no need for you to stay here, my lady. I will ferry us both back to Rama safe and sound. Then he will invade Lanka and crush it as you desire, without fear of harm coming to you.'

She shook her head. 'What good will it do to destroy Lanka after I am rescued? Then history will only say once again that Rama conducted an excessive campaign, that he was hellbent upon the extermination of the rakshasa races, that he acted unrighteously and maliciously.'

'History will tell the truth in the end,' he said. 'No matter how the rakshasas may distort it. My mother used to say that every man believes he is the hero of his own life story and that the villain is someone else. But try as he may, Ravana will not be able to conceal the truth. He has caused so much grief to so many.'

'And so has Rama,' she said. 'For has he not massacred rakshasas by the thousands as well? Did they not have families and brethren and offspring too? Were they not missed and grieved for?'

He spread his hands. 'My lady, if you judge him thusly, then no king can ever be blameless. The only thing that matters is whether he fought to defend what he believed in or whether he instigated the conflict. And to the best of my knowledge, Rama always defended others and followed his dharma. Yes, I know you are weary of hearing that word, but there can be no other word to mean the same thing. Rama fought for dharma, while Ravana fought for his own selfish ends. History will know this as surely as they will know my lord Rama is spotless and blameless.'

She wrung her hands in despair. 'Hanuman, you do not need to convince me of Rama's integrity. I am not speaking of my own doubts or criticisms; I am speaking of the opinion of people at large, of history.'

He shrugged. 'Let history judge as it will. I have no doubt that it will judge rightly. But even if it does not, should Rama then follow the unrighteous path merely because some people foolishly believe it is the righteous one? If a nation of rakshasas judges him the villain and their lord Ravana the hero, does that make it truth?'

'In their eyes, yes.'

'But in the eyes of the supreme being, the one who is pure brahman, the essence of which we are only parts, the truth will be known.'

He paused. This debate was taking a long time, and he had no doubt that the shapeshifter Supanakha had gone to raise the alarm. At any moment, they could be surrounded by rakshasas, making their exit not impossible but possibly dangerous to Sita. 'My lady, I respect your opinions. But now is not the time to debate these matters. It is best that we depart from here at once. If you have any doubts about my abilities, please shed them. I am empowered to do great feats by the grace of my lord Rama himself. Come, climb upon my back and I shall bear you away to safety. Let us be gone before Ravana and his minions arrive with weapons of destruction.'

She sighed then. A great weary sigh as of one who had nothing else to say, no more strength to sustain her. 'I cannot.'

'My lady, I understand your weariness. My heart fills with sympathy for the suffering you have undergone. You must be harrowed, exhausted, beaten down by your treatment at the hands of these vile creatures. But I beg of you. Summon up your last reserves of strength. You need only to climb on to my back and cling on. I will do all the rest. No harm will befall you, this I swear in the name of Rama.'

She looked at him with a kindness in her tired eyes. 'Good Hanuman. You are truly a friend of Rama. You speak of him as if he was a deva. And perhaps he is. But you confuse my decision with my condition. I cannot go with you, my vanar friend.'

He stared at her. 'Why not, my lady?'

Just then, a sound came from the far end of the forest. It was the shout of a rakshasa, a snarling howl. It was answered by others, and joined by the sound of many bodies thrashing heavily through the woods. They were heading towards the ashoka grove, where Sita and Hanuman were. The alarm had been raised at last.

11

'My lady,' Hanuman said urgently. 'Please. Do not tarry any longer. Have faith in my lord Rama. If you desire vengeance against the rakshasas for what they have done to you, then have no fear. Rama will avenge this wrong done unto you a thousandfold. He will redress this crime of Ravana with just rewards. And history will record his exploits as being righteous and just. All will be well, I assure you.'

She smiled. And he saw that while her body might be at the point of collapse, her spirit was still strong. He saw her strength in her eyes. 'I am not doubting Rama's abilities, good vanar. I know my husband well. Once he sets his mind to something, he cannot be turned away from it. That is why he came to be known as Maryada Purshottam by all who knew him.'

'Indeed,' he exclaimed. 'And he will be known as Maryada Purshottam for this rescue as well. For even though I only carry out his orders, yet it is as if he himself were here in Lanka, come to take you home.' He softened his voice, kneeling before her again. 'My lady, we may not have much time; that shapeshifting demoness has already raised the alarm. I can easily deal with any number of rakshasas. But I do not wish to endanger you by fighting in such close quarters. Come, let us depart quickly.'

She shook her head sadly. 'That is impossible, Hanuman. This is what I have been trying to tell you for so long. I cannot leave Lanka with you. You must go alone back to Rama.'

He stared at her unbelievingly. 'But why? What force compels you to stay?'

'The same force that drives Rama,' she said sadly. 'Dharma.'

The thrashing and shouting grew louder and fiercer. There were a great many rakshasas, evidently, and they were all converging on this grove, beating their way through the woods like a hunting party seeking out a wounded deer.

'My lady, I do not understand,' Hanuman said. 'Why will you not let me save you?'

'Because then everyone will say, history will say, that Rama could not even come to Lanka to rescue his own wife. He sent someone else instead. You and I know that Rama fears nothing and nobody. But Ravana will use this as yet another justification to paint him in uncomely light. He will further disparage Rama's good name. And there is yet another reason. If I go with you, and am restored to Rama, then he will have to abandon his plan to invade Lanka. Indeed, knowing Rama, I do not doubt that he already hesitates to invade a kingdom and ravage its citizens only to rescue a single soul. Despite all the lies told about him in Lanka, Rama is a man who would rather subsist on herbs and leaves than slay a single deer. That is what makes him a great warrior: his love for peace.'

Hanuman was silent, struck dumb. Truly, Sita knew Rama better than anyone else.

'And I do wish Rama to invade Lanka. I wish him to storm its gates and frontiers and demolish its vain and over-proud armies. I wish him to wreak death and devastation upon this land and its people. To rid the earth of a vile corruption upon the body of Prithvi-maa, our Mother Earth. And he must destroy Ravana in fair and honest combat as well, proving once and for all that Rama is the righteous one and Ravana the enemy of dharma. For only then will the rakshasas, and the world, and history, accept beyond doubt that Rama is the champion of righteousness. And then, and only then, Hanuman, will I be restored to Rama. These are not selfish demands, for I would sorely like to go now with you to safety and not suffer a moment longer in this dread place. But it is my desire to see justice done to Rama's name and to see the earth rid of the menace of Ravana once and for all. So, go now, save yourself, and tell Rama this: that Sita remains in Lanka and awaits his righteous invasion. That her imprisonment is the warrant that grants him the unassailable dharmic right to wage war with the rakshasas. This is why I stay, and this is why he must come here and wage war on Lanka.'

'But, my lady, you said you would not last this night. How can I let you stay when I know you may not live even—'

She interrupted him sternly, as firm and as immovable as the earth itself. 'My life is no longer the only thing at stake here. Rama's honour is what matters most. Now go, loyal friend of my husband. Go, fly. And take these, my last words, to Rama.'

Hanuman stared at her. He could not find any more words with which to express himself, for she had washed every last thought out of his mind, leaving only the awareness that she was right. One last possibility occurred to him. To pick her up forcibly and carry her back to Rama. But that was unthinkable. Not only because it would violate his own sense of dharma to forcibly lay hands upon the wife of his lord and friend, and because his vows of celibacy forbade him from even touching a female of any species against her will, but also because it would be an insult to her proud and righteous spirit. She was right. His rescuing her would take away Rama's only justification for waging this war. And this war must be waged. Not just for Sita's sake, but for Rama's. And for all mortalkind. Even, as Sita had said, for Prithvi-maa herself.

The first rakshasas broke through into the clearing. 'There!' they cried. 'There is the spy! Kill him!'

Hanuman shut down all faculty of thought, acting on instinct alone. He did not care about himself, for he knew he could not be killed as easily as those rakshasas might foolishly believe. But he did care about Sita. If he fought a dozen or a hundred rakshasas here, with weapons flailing and bodies flying about, she would certainly be injured. The best thing he could do was to put as much distance as possible between himself and her. Take the fight elsewhere.

He leapt high into the air, rising up above the treetops into the peculiarly illuminated sky of this artificial world that dressed itself in the garb of a forest.

He landed a mile or more away, thumping down in the middle of a flowerbed in the heart of what looked like palace gardens. Neat rows of flowers extended in either direction, and an intricately carved wrought-iron fence ran along one side. Rakshasas patrolling the wall turned to stare at him, stunned. One of them, a larger, uglier specimen than the rest, shouted something unexpectedly sweet and melodious in a foreign tongue, and the rest lowered their spears and converged on Hanuman.

Kinkaras. He had heard of this tribe of rakshasas. They had once invaded the madhuvan gardens, where the vanars grew their healing herbs and brewed their honey-wine. In his younger days, Hanuman and a band of other mischievous young vanars had raided the madhuvan one night and got madly drunk on honey-wine, and then urinated all over the rose bushes, to make them grow yellower. When discovered, all the vanars got a sound thrashing for their prank, but Hanuman got the worst of it, for his own father was the keeper of the royal gardens. *Kinkaras*, his father had shouted over and over again. *Vanars do not behave thus. Kinkaras do such mischief.*

The kinkaras were much like other rakshasas he had seen before in Janasthana, except that their tribe favoured elaborate body and face painting and ornamentation. The kinkara rakshasa closest to him, advancing with his spear held like a javelin on his shoulder, was painted like a court dancer in some mythological re-enactment, curled lashes, heavily rouged cheeks, kohl-accented eyes and all. He, or she, Hanuman couldn't tell which it was, batted its heavily painted eyelashes at him and drew back its spear. Other kinkaras surrounded him, although, he couldn't help noticing, they seemed loath to step on the flowers.

He threw back his head, spread his arms and roared.

The kinkaras stumbled back hastily, almost impaling themselves on the spears of their comrades. The one with the spear held up screeched in dismay and threw the weapon, not the way it ought to be thrown, but straight up into the air, like a man unloosing a courier pigeon. The spear rose then fell, its weighted point causing it to bury itself in the bed of marigolds in which Hanuman stood.

He roared again, loudly. The intention was not only to confuse the kinkaras, but to draw away the rakshasas that had gone to the ashoka grove. Without waiting to see what the kinkaras did next, he leapt again, bounding to the top of the iron fence. He landed upon it nimbly, and looked to either side. Rakshasas were racing towards him from all points. The ones inside the garden were all kinkaras; the others were clad in the same purple-black uniform he had seen on his earlier passage through the myriad chambers of the tower, and which he had guessed denoted Ravana's palace guard. These latter ones seemed more aggressive than the kinkaras, shouting gruff orders and grouping in squads to advance upon him.

He raised his head and roared several times more, loud enough to be heard for miles around. When he was certain that every rakshasa within hearing distance, even those slightly deaf or feeble, was aware that the intruder was in the vicinity of the palace gardens and nowhere near the ashoka grove, he made his next move.

Reaching down, he took hold of the iron fence and wrenched hard. With an extended groan of protest, the metal yielded slowly, bent, then snapped off. He stood up, a five-yard length of iron fence in his hand, the ends jagged and curved like a mad imitation of a weapon. The rakshasas, compelled to keep a distance while he was roaring, took this as a brazen sign of aggression and came charging forward. Several threw spears, others hefted maces or wielded swords. More rushed in by the moment.

Hanuman raised the iron fence as if it was a shortsword, swinging it from side to side to deflect the spears flying through the air at him. The fence met each spear with a resounding clang, striking the missiles with force enough to throw them back. Some of them found rakshasa flesh and the unfortunate targets thrashed about screaming, or dropped dead, or did both in quick succession. He roared once more, then leapt to the ground, landing with a thump on the forest side of the gate. Behind him, he could hear kinkaras calling out in their melodious dainty dialect. No doubt they were preparing to rush him from behind through the yards-wide gap he had just made in the fence. He lifted his makeshift weapon and swung it wildly at the oncoming rakshasas on both sides. Bodies flew through the air, broken, bleeding, screaming.

'Come,' he boomed, in a voice augmented by rage. 'Come, you harrowers of Sita and enemies of Rama. Come see how a vanar fights rakshasas.'

Captains shouted orders, pressing more soldiers into the attack. Rakshasas poured in from every side, surrounding Hanuman. Behind him, the kinkaras gained courage and attacked.

He expanded himself without thinking, growing to twice, then thrice the size of the tallest rakshasas. Swinging the fence, he struck out with terrible bloody blows, each strike impacting a half-dozen rakshasas or more, smashing skulls and bodies, shattering faces and helmets, snapping swords. He roared as he fought, feeling a rage fuelled by righteous anger at all rakshasas in general for their crimes over the ages, and at these ones in particular. For they guarded Sita, his lord Rama's beloved. And that was crime enough for him. He struck again and again, growing larger with each blow, louder with each bellow. Rakshasas died every time he struck. And still more came. And still he flailed on, slaying, slaughtering.

Ravana examined the two silk body garments held up by rakshasas, comparing one with the other with the elegant ease of a man dressing to attend a royal ball.

Supanakha stalked the floor, her tail whipping back and forth like a cat-o'-nine-tails with a life of its own. 'I tell you the vanar has invaded the tower and you waste time dressing? Doesn't it worry you?'

He ignored her while he continued to decide between the two garments. Finally he chose the red one with purple piping. 'Worry?' he said distractedly. 'A mere vanar? Why should I worry about a monkey-man?'

'Because he's not any ordinary monkey-man, cousin. You saw what he could do when he crossed the ocean. And I tried my best to deceive him, seduce him, tempt him, but he still resisted everything. I even brought him here in the hope that he would be stupid enough to try to assassinate you while you took your beauty nap.'

He turned a head to her, cocking its eyebrows. 'Are you upset that you couldn't seduce him, or that he didn't try to assassinate me?' He chuckled. 'Both, no doubt.'

'He's with Sita. He could carry her off and fly back to the mainland! Doesn't that bother you? Don't you want to at least try to stop him?'

He allowed the rakshasas around him to cast off his garments, standing naked in the centre of the bedchamber. Supanakha paused in her stalking, her eyes examining his body's nether parts with a feral hunger that was both sexual and malevolent. The rakshasas began to anoint his body with oils, massaging every inch with reverential, adoring care. 'He will not.'

'How do you know?'

He chuckled softly at her naivety, and at her frustration. 'I am Ravana. I know.'

She flicked her tail angrily, sending a vase to shatter on the polished stone floor. Rakshasas shot her hateful glances, but made no sounds of protest. They began to clean up the potsherds quickly, efficiently, removing all traces within moments. Other rakshasas continued to play music and others danced or entwined themselves around each other sensuously for the amusement of the Lord of Lanka. Supanakha snarled, impatient with Ravana's refusal to take her seriously. 'He didn't come here for the sun and the climate, cousin. He means to take the woman back with him. I tell you, I have never seen any being so single-minded and determined to fulfil his will before.'

'Never?'

She paused, thinking. 'You mean Rama? Well, apart from Rama, I've never seen anyone so hellbent on accomplishing the impossible.'

He gestured to the rakshasas. They held up the robe, and she watched with fascination as he slipped all six arms into the appropriate holes with practised ease, then folded the lower pairs of arms into the slots in his own body. 'Yet you do acknowledge that his task is impossible.'

She grunted. 'I would have thought so until today. But then until today I also thought that it was impossible for any virile male to resist the temptations of the palace of sensual pleasures.'

He allowed the rakshasas to tie the sash around his waist and chest, then place plates of armour upon his arms and chest and midriff. 'Tapasvi sadhus can resist sensual temptations. My pious brother Vibhisena does so daily. Any man who devotes himself to raj-yoga can do it. Why, I myself abstained from sex and from consuming flesh or wine for a thousand years as tapasya. That was how I obtained my boons from Lord Brahma and Lord Siva.'

'But sadhus and pious penitents don't come storming into the lair of Ravana alone and unarmed,' she snarled. 'What must I say to convince you? Why will you not take this vanar seriously? I tell you, he is a threat to us all.'

'So what would you have me do?' he asked, as the rakshasas tightened the straps of his armour and strapped on his boots.

'Destroy him!' she said. 'Fight him and smash the leaping fool before he gets out of hand.'

'There are a thousand palace guards already taking care of him. And the entire kinkara tribe is at him because he violated their precious gardens. Would that be enough to soothe your anxieties?'

'I don't know,' she snapped. 'I told you. That's what worries me. I have never encountered anything like this vanar before. His zeal is fanatical. He chants . . .' She paused. She had been about to say the one name that might make Ravana lose his elegant demeanour. 'He chants his master's name as if it were one of those secret Sanskrit mantras the mortal sages use . . .'

'Astras,' he supplied, then paused to swat aside a trio of rakshasas who were trying to raise his elaborately designed ten-part armoured headpiece. His strength was such that they fell back with broken bones and serious bruises, but none of them raised so much as a whimper of protest. They removed themselves from the chamber in submissive silence. Ravana took the headpiece and put it on himself. Supanakha thought the rakshasas must be new additions to his harem, or over-eager to serve their master. Everyone who knew Ravana ought to know that he never permitted his heads to be touched by anyone, not even by his own wife Mandodhari during the most intimate moments.

'Yes,' she went on. 'Like astras. And reciting just that one word, his master's name, seems to empower him enormously, give him tremendous strength and energy. When he gets into that state, I feel like he could do anything. Face any opponent.'

'Any opponent?' he asked, turning to face her, fully dressed and armoured now. He made a formidable sight.

She gave him a smile that was also a snarl. 'Yes. That is what I feel, cousin. Of course,' she smiled sardonically, 'if you disagree, you can always prove me wrong.'

He chuckled. 'I intend to.'

12

When the rakshasas withdrew to regroup, Hanuman paused to take stock of his situation. Bodies lay piled in heaps all around him. The cries of grievously wounded rakshasas filled the air. The iron fence he had wielded so lethally was bent beyond all recognition, the wrought curves coated with a patina of rakshasa blood and fluids so that it seemed painted scarlet rather than black. On the garden side of the fence, kinkaras lay dead or howling in agony for yards around. The foppish painted rakshasas had fought bravely and intelligently, using a peculiar spear-jabbing action that he had not seen before in battle. He had noted it to pass on to the generals when he returned.

The air around him stank of rakshasa effluents and his own copious sweat. He was some five or six times his usual size, though he did not recall growing to that extent. He swiped at his forehead with the back of his hand, clearing away sweat and blood. He was stained all over with the blood of his enemies, and both his feet rested on the corpses of rakshasas. A palace guard stirred underfoot, moaning, and he jabbed the edge of the fence down, dispatching the poor fellow to a speedy end. Even rakshasas did not deserve to linger in agony.

The rakshasas were regrouping, creeping up to him steadily while he seemed distracted. They were more respectful of him now, neither shouting nor daring to launch individual attacks. They came in one close group, clustered together for courage. He spied them out of the corners of his eyes, coming from both sides. He ignored them and went on thinking.

He considered his options. What was the best thing to do next? Thanks to that devious demoness Supanakaha, Ravana undoubtedly knew already that he was here to fetch Sita. The lord of rakshasas would expect him to return to the ashoka grove and attempt to carry her away. Indeed, that was what he wished with all his heart to do. But since that option had been closed to him by Sita's own decision, he must not return there. To do so would only increase the guard around Sita and probably endanger and harry her further.

He had to show them that he was after other targets.

He inhaled, breathing in deeply enough to fill his lungs. Then, crouching to tighten his thighs like iron springs, he leapt up, away from the direction of the ashoka grove, towards the far side of the forest level.

The rakshasas, who had crept within a yard or two of him, fell back in startled horror. He saw their surprised faces reduce to dots as he flew up high, then they were lost behind him in the dense forest.

He recalled how he had followed Supanakha through the many levels and worlds of this magical tower. It was as if he had simply willed the tower to grant him access to the next level, and the next, and it had yielded without protest, letting him pass without opposition through the sorcerous membranes that divided them.

He did the same thing now, passing from the forest level on which Sita was being held to the next. This was a natural landscape too, an enormous shining lake and a township on its banks. He passed through it and to the next level, and the next. And so on. It took him a while, but finally he found what he was seeking.

The palace of sensual pleasures.

The rakshasas turned to greet him effusively, thinking mistakenly that he had returned to correct his earlier lapse, that he was ready now to succumb to the potent lure of this realm's fleshly temptations.

He roared and swung the twisted, blood-spattered iron fence

about to show them he meant war, not love. He smashed it into domes and cupolas, destroying pleasure houses and apartments, shattering marble floors and fabulous chandeliers. The rakshasas understood his intent then, and ran screaming before him. Suddenly, individual survival seemed more important than the perpetuation of the species – if that was their excuse for what they did here.

He rampaged through the palace of pleasure.

Ravana stepped through the portal directly on to the royal dais in Lanka's court hall. The agitated discussion that was raging ended at once. The assembled rakshasas turned to greet their king, bowing to pay him obeisance. He seated himself on the throne without further ceremony, and gave the rest permission to be seated. The great hall wore a deserted look, except for a dozen-odd seats near the dais that were occupied. He had called for only his war council to be present. The seated rakshasa commanders and generals looked at one another; nobody ever wanted to be the first to speak when Ravana convened a council.

He gazed down at them impassively. 'It would be helpful if someone provided an update.'

War Marshal Prahasta rose to his feet. The kumbha-rakshasa was old but still vigorous. He towered above the others with the natural size and height advantage of all kumbhas, two and a half times as tall and twice as widely girthed as most rakshasas. His uniform gleamed with gold-plated armour, set off by the rows upon rows of tiny shrunken heads dangling like medals from his lapels and chest ridges. They were the symbols of his victories, each one the leader of the force he had defeated in battle. More than two thirds of the skulls belonged to various Asura races, including rakshasas; the rest were animal species; perhaps a tenth were mortal.

Prahasta's hollow mouth horns twitched and exuded ichor before he spoke. 'My lord, the vanar has invaded the palace of pleasures and caused much destruction.' From his laconic tone, he could have been describing the completion of a municipal street-paving project. War Marshal Prahasta's inclinations were martial rather than hedonistic.

'The damned monkey has completely demolished the pleasure realm.' This voice, betraying more emotion, came from right beside Prahasta, spoken by a younger but no less impressively sized kumbha. Jambumali was Prahasta's son as well as vice-marshal, and he strongly resembled his father in physical appearance, but in every other respect the two were as unalike as could be. While Prahasta had never stepped into the pleasure realm, Jambumali spent most of his leisure hours there. It was quite natural he would be upset. His own mouth horns twitched vigorously, exuding several viscous droplets of ichor. 'My captains tell me he seemed to take particular delight in destroying property rather than taking lives.'

'But he showed no reticence in taking lives in the upper levels,' noted his father beside him. Prahasta went on: 'It seems he follows the kshatriya code of warfare. He only fights those who are armed, or who attack him first. I would not have believed until today that a vanar existed who even knew what the kshatriya code was. It seems this is a most unusual breed we are dealing with. I recommend caution.'

Ravana allowed one of his heads to show amusement at this assessment. 'Not a breed, Prahasta, merely an aberration. And one that will have no opportunity to multiply.' He paused, probing the intelligence of Pushpak with his mind. 'I see that he is currently heading through the rustic realms at a ripping pace.' He paused. 'And as Jambumali pointed out, he seems to be focusing his energy on destroying property rather than taking lives.' He followed the vanar's progress through the medium of Pushpak for several moments, then saw something that made him snort. 'Except when he is challenged or attacked, at which point he's quite willing to do violence. Indeed, Prahasta, it seems we have here a cultured vanar, if such a thing is possible.' He followed the vanar for a few minutes more, commenting on his movements to his council, then suddenly he frowned. 'He's changed direction. He sees something. What does he see?' He felt an interference in the medium and understood at once. 'The clever monkey, he's using Pushpak's powers as well as his own to seek out a destination. But what place is he seeking?' After a moment or two, 'On the move again. He's . . . ah. I see where he's going.' Scowls darkened several of his faces. 'He's heading towards the bhakti level. He's going to the worship halls.'

Several of his generals exchanged glances. 'My lord,' said General Bhasakarna, rising to his feet, 'if he wreaks havoc in the worship halls, it will be seen as a most inauspicious omen by the people. He must be stopped at once.'

Ravana grunted. 'I don't give a hang for omens, General. But we are agreed in one respect. He must be stopped. Prahasta, take your kumbhas and block his way. I am instructing Pushpak to transport them instantaneously. You go as well and ensure that the monkey-brained fool does not reach the prayer halls.'

Prahasta rose without a single word, turned, and vanished – into a portal that disappeared as soon as he had passed through.

Supanakha purred from beside Ravana's throne. He glanced at her with a half-smile on one face, knowing what she desired. 'Ah, yes, cousin. You like to watch, don't you? I think watching this will be instructive for us all.'

He clapped his hands. At once, several kinkara rakshasas kneeling below the dais fetched the large clay bowl filled with water. Ravana rose from his throne and stood before the bowl, uttering the mantras of conjuring. The contents of the bowl rose and swirled, glimmering glaucously. The image of Hanuman appeared, leaping through the air with a mangled piece of metal in his hands that seemed to be part of an iron gate or fence. The vanar landed with a resounding thump upon a grassy hillock, looked around to assess his surroundings, and began bounding uphill.

Ravana gestured again. The kinkaras moved forward at once, serving goblets of wine to the ministers of war. Their painted faces glanced occasionally at the images conjured by Ravana. He noted their stealthy looks. So. Word of the vanar's massacre of the kinkaras in the garden realm had reached down here already. He grimaced and snapped his fingers, dismissing the kinkaras. Then he raised his cup in a toast.

'Generals, tilt your cups while you watch the show,' he said. 'And make sure you drain them empty. Very shortly, we shall fill them to the brim with fresh vanar blood.'

Hanuman stopped halfway up the hill and stared at the stone edifice at the top. It looked vaguely familiar. Almost at once, he knew where he had seen it before. When flying towards Lanka. A monolithic stone temple on the top of a mountain near the southern coast of the island. It bore the unmistakable black-stone austerity of a Shiva mandir. But this temple was within the heart of the palace. He looked around, sniffing; then scratched the grass, dislodging soil, and raised a clod to his nostrils to sniff at that as well. *Waugh!* If that was real earth, then he was a monkey's uncle! He tossed the clod away disdainfully. More of Pushpak's illusion. Ravana had used the magic of Pushpak combined with his own Asura maya to create a virtual city within the city of Lanka itself. While some areas, like the pleasure realm, were wholly the product of his twisted imagination, others, like this replica of the stone temple from southern Lanka, were merely picture-perfect imitations. This was no more a real temple than this soil was real earth. He was relieved. The idea of finding the rakshasas' prayer halls had been an inspired one, but he had no desire to desecrate genuine shrines.

He reduced himself so he would be small enough to enter the temple and bounded the last few yards, roaring loudly. He was rewarded by a flurry of shouts and yells of outrage as he was seen by the long line of rakshasas waiting to go in for their daily worship – or coming out after having done their ishta. Several of them dropped their prayer thalis and drew their weapons, coming towards him. Good. He was tired of just beating down pillars and knocking over buildings. It would be nice to have some real opposition.

The rakshasas emerging from the temple didn't provide much

opposition, though. He tore his way through them in a few moments, and then he was at the temple itself. He let a crowd of screaming brahmin rakshasas, all clad in pristine white and red ochre, and with caste marks on their foreheads and black threads around their torsos, leave the premises unharmed. They ran down the hill, calling to the devas for help. He was amused to hear at least one cry out to the wind god to save them from the monkey invaders. Yes, Lord Marut would certainly save them. By demolishing this mockery of faith.

He said a silent prayer to Lord Shiva, asking his forgiveness as well as his support in demolishing this phoney edifice. To his relief, the dark god of destruction did not appear to block his path, which in his mind constituted approval. As soon as he crossed the threshold, he saw why. The temple, although a perfect replica externally, was a completely different affair on the inside. Gold pillars and jewelled walls, gem-studded polished stone floors, pearl and opal carvings, naked representations of devas and devis . . . It was an obscene mockery of what a real Shiva temple ought to be. He had no doubt that the real temple on the southern mountain was nothing like this. This was Ravana's doing, his way of subverting true faith with vulgar displays of wealth. In its own way, it was no less obscene than the palace of pleasures. A Shiva temple, of all places, was required to be as austere and simple as possible. Black stone alone was to be used, and even the effigy of the lord was to be carved as plainly as possible. Ideally, a lingam, a particularly shaped stone that resembled the forehead of the divine one, was to be installed as it was, uncut and unpolished, in the central space of the shrine.

But this place was a travesty. Hanuman expanded in size, and began roaring loudly to coax the priests and purohits into leaving. They stared at him incredulously, clutching thalis filled with precious stones, gold, and other rich offerings. Hanuman took hold of a golden pillar, wrenching it loose with a loud grating noise, and began flaying about. The priests ran, screaming, though not in too much of a hurry to remember to take their precious offerings with them. Two of them even managed to carry out a whole chest groaning with the weight of gold anklets and bangles and gems. Hanuman let them go without hurting any of them. He kept himself busy laying about with the pillar.

The temple collapsed around him in a thunderous clatter. When he emerged from the dust and debris, the pillar still clutched in one fist, an army was waiting for him.

13

If not an army, then a legion at least. He estimated several thousands of rakshasas lined up in neat formations, armoured and
armed. They were not the painted dainties he had seen before,
nor the ordinary, run-of-the-mill animal-faced ones that were
ubiquitous in Lanka. These were huge fellows (and females too,
he noted), three or four yards in height, half as much in width,
and they resembled their smaller rakshasa brethren only super-
ficially. From the burning intensity of their eyes, visible through
the slits in their headgear, they seemed to have more fighting
spirit than the smaller rakshasas too. And far more discipline.
While he had been demolishing the phoney temple, they had
cleared the area of all unarmed rakshasas and had ringed him
in completely. If he wanted, he could leap over them and be
instantly a hundred miles away, or as far as one could go within
this sorcerous illusion of a place. But why would he do that
and disappoint all these smartly lined-up, eager-to-fight demon-
faces? No. He would stay and fight.

He swept his gaze across the massed ranks and stopped at
one face. He had no doubt that that was the leader. He was an
impressive fellow, all armoured in gold – no, surely it couldn't
be solid gold, that would be as effective as tinfoil; it was probably gold-plated iron armour – and with headgear that resembled some mangled hybrid between a rhinoceros and an elephant.
But it was the rakshasa's face that caught his attention. The
fellow displayed none of the ichor-dripping hatred that seethed
in every other face in the ranks lined up before him. Only a

dispassionate curiosity. As if Hanuman were some new breed of insect the rakshasa was seeing for the first time, and it would be interesting to find out what colour his insides might be.

Hanuman looked around. A gentle wind was blowing. It felt cool and refreshing on his sweaty body. Fascinating how cleverly real this illusory world could be. Virtually as real as the Lanka outside.

Time to show the Lankans that there were other things and beings as wondrous as those in their island-kingdom. Forces greater than even the most bewitching Asura illusion.

He bared his chest and beat it once with the gold pillar. The sound it made was like a dhol-drum being thumped with a hollow stick.

'I am Hanuman,' he roared. 'Servant of the mighty Rama, King of Kosala, saviour of mortalkind, Rama the magnificent. I am the son of the wind and the chosen slayer of rakshasas. I came here to bring you the message of my lord Rama. In abducting Rama's wife Sita and bringing her here to Lanka against her will, your master Ravana has committed a mortal transgression. My lord is coming here soon, bringing an army of vanars like myself. If your lord Ravana does not repent of his crime and release the lady Sita honourably before the sun rises on this land tomorrow, then I will destroy your kingdom and kill every last rakshasa who comes in my way. And then I shall leave, and when I return, a million vanars like myself will come with me, led by our lord Rama, and we will wreak such devastation upon your homeland that no rakshasa will survive to see the dawn of another day. How say you now? Speak!'

For a long moment, there was no response from the assembled rakshasas. Unless all that twitching of the slimy hornlike appendages over their mouths qualified as a response. Those appendages quivered furiously, dripping a slick, viscous exudation the way a deer in heat exuded kasturi. Although Hanuman did not think that these exudations would smell as enticing as kasturi.

Then the leader, the one with all the gold-plated armour and the hundreds of tiny skulls dangling like decorations upon his torso, opened his own mouth horns and spoke. 'I am Prahasta, War Marshal of Lanka. We are kumbha-rakshasas, loyal to Ravana. We will not exchange words with you or trade terms. We have come to apprehend you, monkey-man. Surrender and state your demands to Lord Ravana if you dare. Resist us and you face death.'

The leader's mouth horns twitched once, then held still. But the appendages of his soldiers moved frantically. Hanuman understood that it was their way of expressing anger. So they wanted war. So be it. He would express his anger to them as well.

Hanuman beat his chest with the pillar again and yet again, roaring out the exclamation that was now his battlecry. 'Jai Shri Ram!' He shook the pillar at them, to make his response utterly clear.

The leader of the rakshasas opened his mouth appendages again and issued a loud, hoarse, bleating cry. At once the first four rows of oversized rakshasas detached themselves from the rest of the contingent and lumbered forward. The line was perhaps a hundred head wide, which meant that four hundred rakshasas were charging him in this first assault. They gathered speed as they came, trundling like a herd of rhinoceros charging at prey. The resemblance to rhinos became more obvious when they lowered their heads and pointed their long, tapering black-bone horns. The tips of those horns, Hanuman saw, were sharp enough to rip open flesh and gore through a whole body.

He expanded himself at once, stopping when he was roughly the same size as any one of the rakshasas. He could have made himself a hundred times larger – or a thousand – if he desired. But he wished to make this as fair a fight as possible. It was time to send a message to Lanka, one that would be heard and taken seriously. Monkey-man, the rakshasa leader had called him. Monkey-man indeed!

The charging rakshasa lines were almost at him when he made his move. Instead of waiting for them to come the rest of the distance, he charged at them.

Swinging the gold pillar, he struck out at the front line. The result was not quite the same as when he had struck out at the normal-sized rakshasas with the broken fence. These ones – kumbha-rakshasas, the leader had called them – were far sturdier and heavier. The pillar struck them with the impact of a mace striking an elm treetrunk. The ones who were hit directly grunted loudly in protest, their mouth appendages spewing copious amounts of that same greenish-black ichor. But they kept coming. Over their heads, he saw the leader of the kumbha-rakshasas throw his head back and issue a chugging sound that could only mean some form of laughter.

The line slammed into him. The lowered horns struck him like a bunch of pointed swords. With that much force and momentum, they probably expected to gore him through and through and toss him back over their shoulders, like a herd of bulls throwing a monkey. They barrelled into him with enough force to break down a yard-thick stone wall.

He absorbed the impact and stood his ground. With his vision control, he witnessed it as if it were taking place over several moments instead of in just a fleeting instant.

Their horns crumpled first. Some broke, snapping off and leaving ragged stumps, and one tore off at the base, leaving a gaping hole that gushed blood. Then their headgear, special armour with eyelets to allow their horns to emerge, shattered. Made of some variety of bone, they crumpled and smashed into powdery fragments. And then their heads broke, skulls cracking, breaking, shattering as well. One of them struck Hanuman's ribs with a force hard enough to press his own head back into his torso.

The entire front line crumpled, dropping dead on the spot.

Those who had not struck Hanuman directly were already into their follow-through. They swung their enormous curved blades, a cross between scimitars and battleaxes. The blades met the same fate as the horns and headgear. They shattered like glass, fragments exploding everywhere. Some were driven back into the faces and eyes and bodies of the attackers, dropping more kumbha-rakshasas.

Then Hanuman raised the pillar again and struck out. This time, he used much greater force. This time, the kumbha-rakshasas flew into the air no differently from the way the ordinary, smaller rakshasas had flown earlier. He swung the pillar again and again, felling kumbha-rakshasas like so many skittles.

A moment later, he was done. He stopped and lowered the pillar, stepping back to examine the results.

Several hundred kumbha-rakshasas lay dead, strewn in a sweeping arc that ranged from a yard before him to several dozen yards in every direction. The ranks of the remaining kumbha-rakshasas had been broken in places, disturbed by the bodies of those he had sent flying. They were repairing those breaks as quickly as possible, deeply entrenched military discipline keeping them efficient. But he could see from the face of their leader and from the change in the eyes – wider now, less angry, more shocked – that his unchallenged superiority had not been what they had expected.

'Rakshasas,' he roared. 'Once more I entreat you. Petition your master Ravana to release the lady Sita and show repentance for his transgression. Or face my wrath and see your kingdom destroyed. This is my last warning to you. I am Hanuman, servant of Lord Rama of Ayodhya.'

Again that quivering of the hornlike mouth appendages. Now that he had engaged them in close combat, he knew that the things around their mouths were horns only in shape; in substance, they were cartilaginous growths that were partly nostril-like in function and partly lip-like in the way they covered their mouths. Their appendages were quivering rapidly. He took that to mean extreme shock and outrage.

'How do you answer?' he called again.

Their leader answered for them all. 'Kumbha-rakshasas!' he

thundered in a hoarse but powerful voice. 'Kill the invader! All tribes, charge!'

With a roar of approval, the entire force obeyed.

Ravana threw the goblet of wine at the water image. The heavy gem-encrusted gold cup passed through the depiction of Hanuman slaying the last of the kumbha-rakshasas and flew on to strike the head of a bowing kinkara with a dull thud. The servant rakshasa reeled, blood streaming from his head, and fell back on the floor. His companions to either side bowed quickly, picked up their fallen comrade and removed him from the hall. Ravana failed to even notice the incident. His sunny mood had given way to a foul temper as abruptly as hot milk curdled when sour lime was squeezed into it. Supanakha kept her distance; she knew from experience that someone would end up on the receiving end of that temper, and she had no desire to be the lucky one.

Rising from his seat, Ravana gestured sorcerously and muttered a sloka in a tone that sounded as if he were cursing rather than chanting. The water image collapsed with a splash. Supanakha was far enough away that no drops would land on her, but she winced anyway.

'My lord.'

Vice-marshal Jambumali was on his feet. His face appendages quivered at the memory of the sight of his father and fellow kumbhas being slaughtered. 'My lord, permission to go confront the vanar.'

Ravana's only response was to gesture, opening a portal. Jambumali went through it and disappeared. Supanakha leapt down from the dais. One of Ravana's heads turned to track her.

'Where are you going, cousin?'

She flicked her tail. 'I want to see. I've never seen kumbhas being slaughtered like deer or rabbit. Besides,' she licked her lips, 'a lot of good meat will go to waste.'

He plucked a knife out of mid-air and flung it at her. She scampered, racing into the portal just before it blinked shut, turning sharply to the left as she went through. The knife came with her, narrowly missed her right ear and embedded itself in the earth with a snick.

The smell of blood assailed her senses. It was ripe, powerful, thick in the air. And it was all kumbha blood. She breathed it in, relishing the scent. It had been a long time since rakshasas had been forbidden to eat the flesh of other rakshasas, even when that act was part of a victory ritual in the time-honoured tradition of tribe and clan wars. And among all the tribes and clans, she particularly loved kumbha flesh. Only kinkara meat was sweeter. But Jambumali was already racing up the hillside and she wanted to see how he handled the vanar. Almost regretfully, she raced after him. He reached the top just yards before her.

'Vanar!' he cried, his voice tinged with hysteria. 'You have slain all my kinsmen, destroyed my entire tribe. These were the finest warriors that ever lived in all the three worlds.'

Supanakha scoured the hillside sharply, seeking out the vanar. For a moment, she almost didn't recognise him, splattered with blood and surrounded by kumbha corpses as he was. Then she spied the familiar proboscis shape of his mouth and the unmistakable monkey-like tail curled upwards behind him, like a bow without a string. He stood as still as a statue washed in blood, amidst the carnage of his encounter with the kumbhas.

He seemed unimpressed by Jambumali's words. 'Not the finest,' he said. Then, to Supanakha's surprise, a tinge of sorrow flickered across his features. 'But worthy opponents, all the same. I appealed to them not to fight me. They would not heed my warning. Will you?'

Jambumali responded with a bellow of outrage. 'My father lies there, murdered by your hand. There can be no armistice between us.'

Hanuman sighed, lowering the battered and bloodied gold pillar that he had wielded as a mace. 'I beg you, reconsider. As a vanar, I have no compunction about slaughtering rakshasas by the thousand. But my lord Rama abhors needless taking of lives, and as his servant, I respect his wishes. Pray, take my petition to your lord Ravana and end this violence.'

'Liar,' Jambumali said, his face appendages shaking so much that ichor flew to either side like raindrops from a trembling bough. He had strung his bow while speaking and now raised it, pointing an arrow at Hanuman. 'If you are half as treacherous as your lord Rama, then even the lowest serpent that creeps on the ground would not hold truck with your assurances. Any servant of that dastardly villain cannot be a person of honour. In killing you, I will be ridding the world of a vile spy of the worst mortal that ever lived.'

Supanakha saw Hanuman's eyes widen with surprise, then shock, then anger at Jambumali's words. 'How dare you speak of my lord Rama thus! It is your lord Ravana who is the villain. Is he not satisfied with his transgressions against my lord that he should have poisoned the minds of all rakshasas as well?'

'Silence,' Jambumali said, his quivering ceasing as he stilled himself in preparation for the loosing of his arrow. 'I will hear no more lies and deceit from your monkey lips. Defend yourself if you can.'

And he loosed the arrow so forcefully that Supanakha could feel the vibrations from the bowstring ringing in her teeth. The arrow thudded into Hanuman's left shoulder, its iron head striking bone with a sickening sound. Supanakha licked her lips. So the vanar's skin could be pierced after all. How interesting. But then why had the weapons of the other kumbhas had no effect?

Hanuman ground his teeth, clearly feeling the pain of the wound, but he neither looked at nor touched the arrow in his shoulder. 'One more time I appeal to you,' he said, 'and it is for the sake of my lord Rama that I grant you this final opportunity to redeem yourself. Will you not go to Ravana and tell him my petition?'

Jambumali had strung another arrow, this one with a crescent-shaped head. Its sharp blade gleamed like the moon in a midnight-black sky. 'Save your breath, vanar,' he said through gritted teeth. 'It is the last you will breathe.'

He loosed the second arrow. It took Hanuman in the chest, embedding itself with a sound that made even Supanakha wince. Blood flew from the wound, spattering across the vanar's body, still wet with kumbha blood and ichor.

Again Hanuman took no note of the arrow, even though she knew the wound must hurt him terribly.

'You have not given me a proper answer,' the vanar said. 'Therefore I still raise no arms against you. Tell me: will you or will you not?'

Jambumali loosed three arrows at once. These were decorated with plumes, Supanakha noted with delight. They struck the vanar on different parts of his body. One hit him in the belly, another took him in the thigh, and the third struck the flesh between his neck and his shoulder. All three went deep. Removing them would mean losing gouts of flesh, she thought excitedly. The very idea made her giddy. She wondered what vanar flesh tasted like. Even better, she wondered what *living* vanar flesh tasted like.

Hanuman raised his hand, holding out his palm in the universal gesture to halt. 'Why do you persist in assailing me, kumbharakshasa? I seek only to know your answer. Do you not honour the rules of war in Lanka? It is not meet to assault an opponent when he still wishes to speak with you.'

Jambumali looked over the top of his bow, his face noting each wound on the vanar's body with evident pleasure. 'Do not speak to me of the rules of war and the code of kshatriyas, vanar. You are the servant of Rama. And when Rama himself is without honour, why should we honour his servant?'

He loosed four more arrows in quick succession. Each one struck Hanuman in a vital part, went deep, and drew copious amounts of blood. Supanakha could barely see a limb of the vanar that had no arrows sticking in it now. Jambumali shouted as he loosed. 'Still, if you still foolishly await a response, then here is my answer. No. No. No. And yet again, no.'

Hanuman took the arrows with the same stoic grit. But the instant the kumbha-rakshasa had finished speaking, he raised the gold pillar and said, in a voice so quiet Supanakha almost could not hear the words, 'So be it, abuser of Rama's name.'

Hanuman lofted the gold pillar the way any ordinary soldier might lift a javelin for throwing, leaned back, then flung the pillar directly at the spot where Jambumali stood, some fifty yards distant.

The vice-marshal was already stringing a fresh clutch of arrows, each with different heads. The gold pillar flew through the air as smoothly and directly as any javelin. It struck the kumbha-rakshasa's chest with such force that Supanakha could hear the very veins burst. Jambumali's body was shattered so completely that his arms, his legs, his head all flew in separate directions. His chest was pierced cleanly, the pillar going through his body and passing out the other side. And still it flew on, like a javelin that had merely passed through a thin sheet of parchment. Supanakha turned her head in wonder as it sped above her, and flew on across the valley. She saw it arc downwards on the far side, where it embedded itself firmly in the soil there, some thousand yards away.

14

Ravana roared in fury. 'Sons of whores and donkeys. Can none of you face down a single vanar? Shame on the clans that bred you all!'

Portals opened and shut constantly as the sabha hall continued to fill with new arrivals. News had spread of the vanar's destruction of the palace of pleasures and the prayer level, and his shocking victory over the kumbhas, and all of Ravana's ministers had come at once. The water image had been resurrected by the king for no other reason than the need to know what was happening. The hall full of rakshasas shuddered at the demonlord's rage. He stalked the dais like a hungry lion wounded and caged. His heads babbled incoherently to one another or to themselves like a roomful of mad philosophers.

'Does none of you possess the ability to dispatch a single foe? This is but one vanar! One! What will you do when Rama's army arrives? How will you face a million like this one?'

Nobody dared venture an answer. Finally, furious and frustrated, he turned and set his ten heads to scanning the congregation. All sat up straight and silent under their lord's scrutiny, but several looked as though they wished they could shrink or turn invisible.

Ravana's eyes fell upon the clutch of seven tall-backed seats that bore the noble bottoms of the ministry of Lanka. They represented the seven chief tribes of rakshasas.

'Ministers,' he said.

The seven looked at one another with varying expressions

of disbelief and shock. The most senior among them protested in quivering tones: 'Your majesty, we are skilled in the arts of governance, not war. We cannot—'

'Save the craven apologies,' Ravana said. 'I want someone capable of killing the vanar, not boring him senseless. Each of you has an eldest son serving in my armed forces. Each a champion warrior and a leader of other warriors. Send your seven sons to battle the vanar. The one who defeats him shall replace Jambumali as vice-marshal, and his father will take Prahasta's place as marshal of the armies of Lanka.'

If there were protests on their lips, they were quickly swallowed. The rewards dangled before their greedy eyes might not have been worth risking their own lives for, but they were certainly worth risking the lives of their eldest sons. Like all the nobles of Lanka, each of them numbered their heirs in the hundreds. 'It will be our patriotic duty to do so,' said the spokesperson, bowing low enough to touch the ground with his split trunk.

He was within ten yards of her when he spoke.

'Among my people, those who feed on the flesh of their own kind are considered worthy of only the lowest levels of Narak.'

She stopped feeding, her mouth filled with a hunk of steaming kumbha innards, and looked up hatefully. He stood with his back to her, silhouetted against the bright, unearthly sky. She spat out the mouthful. There was plenty more where that had come from. 'I'm only eating the remains, vanar. You're the one who slaughtered them. Isn't killing against your karma too?'

'Not when it is for the sake of dharma.'

'Dharma!' She issued a laugh that brought out the streak of hyena in her. It echoed across the valley. 'Is that your excuse for everything? Do anything, kill anyone, take what you like, just lay the blame at dharma's feet? You know, the way you and your mortal masters bandy that term about, it sounds a very convenient excuse to cover up your own crimes.'

He turned to look at her. But there was no anger in his eyes, only the sadness she had seen earlier when he had finally deigned to defend himself against Jambumali. It startled her. She had seen that exact same look in Rama's eyes once.

'What is your role in this, shapeshifter? I do not think you serve Ravana because you need to. You pursue some other agenda, do you not? What is that? What is it you really want?'

She laughed again, this time nervously. She had not expected such a personal observation. 'I want what every rakshasa wants. Wine, sex, meat.' The answer sounded weak even to her own ears.

He watched her with narrowed eyes, a new look coming over his face. 'Power. I think it is power, is it not? Ravana is beholden to you for some reason. That is why, at your urging, he came to Panchvati and kidnapped my lady Sita. He is responsible for the crime, but you are responsible for inciting him to commit it. Why did you do that?'

She spat out a morsel of gristle. She hated gristle. 'I don't have time to teach you history, vanar. Perhaps some day, if I decide to compose my memoirs . . .' She smiled artfully. 'Though I doubt you will live long enough to hear the full story.'

He watched her with a bemused, half-distracted expression. 'It is Rama himself, is it not? In your own way, you are as besotted with my lord as I am. And your obsession has somehow infected Ravana as well. What was once a simple antagonism has turned into a personal vendetta for the Lord of Lanka. That is why, even though he possesses Sita, he will not rape or harm her bodily. Because it is not Sita he desires at all. She was only the means to an end, suggested by your devious mind. It is in fact Rama he wishes to draw here, using Sita as the lure. You have infected your cousin. Now he too is obsessed with Rama, and his obsession drives him to any lengths.'

She snarled. 'You babble too much, vanar. It shows your monkey roots. Go hop on a tree and pick your fleas. Better yet, pick up your tail and take your tall tales back where you came from. Go! Shoo! Leave me to my feast!' She dipped her head to the open belly of the kumbha she had been feeding on.

She felt the rumbling through her paws and at first thought it was the vanar, finally losing his temper with her and pounding this way to kill her. But when she looked up, she saw him gazing towards the west, at the ridge line over the hills. A dust-cloud was growing larger. She flicked her ears and caught the sound. 'Chariots. It seems I might get vanar flesh to feed on after all. Unless you decide to take my advice and leave Lanka first.'

He did not reply. She felt chagrined that he would turn his back on her so carelessly. It gave her half a mind to sneak up and leap at him. But then she recalled the way he had with-stood the temptations of the palace of pleasures, and the power of Pushpak as well as Ravana's sorcery. That had impressed her far more than his prowess as a fighter. She had seen enough renowned warriors to know that the greatest battles were fought in the mind and the spirit, not on the battlefield. Besides, he had come close to the truth when he said that she was not a servant of Ravana, even though she happened to serve him. That subtle difference had also earned her grudging respect for the vanar. Let Ravana's many minions throw themselves at him. She would watch. And maybe feed on the spoils later.

She bounded away, finding a sala tree several dozen yards away into which she climbed easily, creeping to the end of a branch and perching there, her whiskered chin on her paws.

Hanuman tried to feel some regret at this turn of events. It had not been his mission to come to Lanka and slaughter rakshasas. But he kept recalling Sita's lean, starved appearance, her pale, shocked face, those blankly staring eyes, the scores of tiny marks all over her arms. She had suffered. Not a direct assault or ravishment, it was true, nor even physical torture of the nailbeds-and-wheels variety, but that did not diminish her suffering one whit. Her mind and spirit had been battered. The Sita he recalled from Janasthana was a proud, vigorous warrior-queen. Capable of facing ten thousand rakshasas and battling them, shoulder to shoulder with her husband and brother-in-law. That Sita had been under great duress too, in exile, deprived of her rightful place of luxury and power, constantly on the run from berserk demons, constantly battling the wilderness, the rakshasas, her fate. But she had been happy. Healthy. Vigorous. Strong. He could picture her crowned with the coconut-shell tiara of a queen of Ayodhya – or whatever mortal queens wore to signify regency – seated beside Rama on the sunwood throne of that great Arya nation.

But the Sita he had found in Lanka had been a pale shadow of that woman. A half-starved, beaten-down, spirit-battered person who was sustaining herself on faith and courage alone. A woman who understood, as he did, that the battle for dharma was more important than the battle for survival. Her last words still rang in his ears. *My life is no longer the only thing at stake here. Rama's honour is what matters most. Now go, loyal friend of my husband. Go, fly. And take these, my last words, to Rama.*

They were the words of a woman who was prepared to die for her husband's and her own honour rather than take the easy way out and save her mortal body. Despite her admonition to Hanuman to leave, despite the fact that he knew Rama must be waiting in agony for his return, even though he knew that Ravana would sooner give up his ten heads than let his prize catch go, he had still lingered here in this kingdom of demons. Because he knew that those last words had not been a slip of her tongue. She was facing death shortly. And if there was even the slimmest chance that he could prevent that, then he would do anything and everything he could.

The dustcloud materialised into a clutch of chariots. Beautiful, burnished things they were, like all else he had seen in Lanka. Golden-arched, gem-studded, and designed like masterpieces of art rather than mere horse-drawn vehicles for transportation. He counted seven and almost felt disappointed. Was that all? Well, these fellows must be good warriors, or they would not have sent only seven. He inhaled deeply, cleansing his mind of all distractions, and strode forward to give the approaching enemies more accessible routes to attack him.

Supanakha recognised the seven charioteers who approached. They were all renowned fighters, masters of archery and mace-craft and . . . of all kinds of weaponry and fighting. Each of them represented one of the seven major tribes of the rakshasa race, which was to say, the seven tribes that had survived. Their chariots were adorned with satin banners decorated with the sigil and totem of their tribes. She also noted that they were the sons of Ravana's seven ministers of governance, which meant they had inherited not only their fathers' ambitions but their rivalries as well. A smile flickered on her face. Ravana must have offered a hefty reward to the one who could down the vanar. It would add an element of competitiveness that would spice up the encounter.

They had obviously been informed of the vanar's exploits already. None made any attempt to halt and parley, or to give the vanar any opportunity to do so. Instead, all seven drove their chariots straight at Hanuman, converging on him like a pack of wolves upon a bleeding carcass. As they approached, she heard shouts and caught snatches of words in several rakshasa dialects. They were egging each other on, taunting one another with boastful claims of who would be the first to draw blood, the first to chop off a limb, and so on.

Hanuman stood impassively, facing their charge without any attempt to defend himself. He had no weapon in his hands, Supanakha noted. Not for want of them; there were any number at hand. The hundreds of slain kumbhas lying about had no need of them any more. But the vanar stood bare-handed and straight-backed, staring at the oncoming chariot charge without a flicker of emotion.

His body still bore the heads of the arrows shot into him by Jambumali. He had made no attempt to remove them. Those wounds would be enough to down any warrior, mortal, deva, rakshasa – or vanar. But Hanuman seemed not to notice or care about them at all. Blood oozed from several places on his body. Against the lush green grass of the hillside, he appeared to be a statue carved out of red marble.

As the charioteers came within bowshot, they began firing. They used the tactic of most chariot-archers during battle, each shooting several arrows at once. A slew of projectiles flew towards Hanuman. At the same time, the vanar moved forward, starting to run towards the chariots.

The first hail of arrows fell to earth. Hanuman was already yards ahead of them when they landed, bristling harmlessly from the grassy soil. He picked up speed, running faster. He still had not expanded himself, she noted, and wondered why. Then she understood: fair play. These stupid dharmic principles. It was the reason why the vanar had allowed Jambumali to shoot him full of arrows before retaliating, and it was the reason why he was restraining his powers now.

The charioteers loosed again, this time aiming far lower, to anticipate the target moving towards them. The arrows flew in a line parallel with the ground. Hanuman increased his pace rather than slowing, running into the hail of arrows. Supanakha watched with great interest: the vanar would resemble a hedgehog's rear after that lot landed.

Then Hanuman increased his speed so much, he literally became a blur. It almost looked as if he was passing through the shower of missiles and they were passing through him, but Supanakha understood at once that he was in fact dodging them but at a speed so great that the naked eye could not actually see him move.

The charioteers had grown silent. They had loosed enough arrows already to slow down a legion. And the vanar was still unharmed, and still coming directly at them.

They discarded their bows quickly, taking up a variety of weapons, then spurred their horses on with their free hands, aiming to do what every charioteer did in a battle charge: run their opponent down.

Hanuman leapt into the air. He did not fly above them,

though he could have done. Nor did he fly past them, as he also could have done. He flew *at* them.

The vanar leapt directly at the closest approaching chariot, and kicked out with his bare feet. The gold-adorned cupola was torn from its stand so hard it went flying away like a discus. Hanuman landed on the rim of the chariot's front well, and balanced there as easily as a thin monkey on a fat branch. The charioteer, a young sarpa rakshasa named Anjunani whom Supanakha had once spent a pleasant hour or two with in the palace of pleasures, swung a mace edged with curved blades at the vanar's thigh.

Hanuman got inside the angle of the blow and grasped the rakshasa's arm. He snapped it off like a twig, wrenching it loose from its shocked owner's body. Then he backhanded the arm, mace and all, at its owner, smashing his face and torso like an over-ripe blood orange. A shower of blood exploded into the sunlit air.

Before the rakshasa's spraying gore had touched the ground, Hanuman had already leapt into the air again and lunged directly at the next chariot. The driver of this one was holding a long-spear tipped with a barbed point. Hanuman caught hold of the spear and drove it back into its owner, putting his entire weight behind it. The blunt wooden end of the spear pierced the rakshasa's neck and spewed out the other side. Before the rakshasa could fall back into his chariot, Hanuman had already leapt to the next one.

Supanakha watched in admiring amazement as the vanar flew and whirled through the air, crushing one rakshasa's head with his thighs – his thighs! – as he fended off the sword thrusts of another with his bare hands, then tearing the banner pole from a chariot and using it as a spear, thrust straight into the heart of the sword-wielder. Another rakshasa whirled a bladed throwing ball overhead. Before he could loose it, Hanuman lunged at his feet, grabbed his legs, picked him up bodily, then whirled *him* about, weapon and all. The last two attacked him together from front and rear simultaneously, displaying a rare moment of inter-tribe solidarity. Hanuman threw himself backwards feet first at the one behind him, caught his neck between his feet, then flew forward and grasped the throat of the other one. Then he somersaulted sideways, slamming both bodies into the ground with enough force to break them in half. Somersaulting once more, he landed on his feet on soft grass in a shower of rakshasa blood.

15

Mandodhari frowned at her brother-in-law. Vibhisena was visibly excited, something she had not seen very often before. She was wary as she came out of her bedchamber to receive him in the parlour, assuming that he was going to press the case for Sita once again. If so, she was ready to throw him out at once. She had no wish to hear the mortal woman's name uttered again, in any connection. But the first words from his mouth had nothing to do with Rama's wife.

'An emissary from Rama is here, inside the tower,' he said without preamble or formal greetings, another significant departure. 'He is on a rampage.'

She gestured at her sakshis to leave them alone. Vikata scowled. The rakshasi had been ill-tempered ever since the scene in the court. Being chain-whipped by a mortal, and an unarmed, half-starved human female at that, had not done much for the sakshi's ego. Mandodhari had no doubt that if she were not constantly supervised, Vikata would have no compunction in stealing back upstairs to the prisoner's level and tearing Sita to bloody shreds with her nails and her teeth. She would face Ravana's wrath afterwards, and would be condemned to a painful and quick death, but that would not matter. Rakshasas like Vikata were accustomed to killing first and thinking later. Mandodhari could not have given a hang if that had happened, but if she would not mind Sita being eaten alive by Vikata, she looked forward even more to seeing the mortal woman publicly paraded and then executed as a criminal of the state. So, since there was a tussle between the mistress's preferred way of seeing the mortal prisoner die, and the sakshi's, naturally the mistress had won. But only just.

Vikata left the queen's palace apartments in bad humour. If it were possible to slam the door, she would have done so. As it was, Pushpak's portal blinked shut behind her as silently and smoothly as ever.

Mandodhari looked at her brother-in-law. He was so excited, his hands were trembling. 'Sit down, Vibhisena,' she said shortly. She had not enjoyed their last conversation. If she entertained him now, it was only because she knew that she had won the battle of wills. And after all, he was still her brother-in-law. Even if he was a mortal-lover.

He sat down. His thighs twitched and he placed his hands on his lap, trying to still them. 'It is a vanar. Named Hanuman. He is empowered by some brahman shakti given to him by Rama.'

'A vanar,' she repeated tonelessly. 'That's the species of animal that looks like and lives like monkeys and apes, isn't it? And you say he has gone on a rampage? Here in Lanka?' She felt a smile come to her face. 'What kind of rampage? Smashing glass and china? Stealing sweetmeats from the kitchen?'

He did not laugh or smile. 'No, my sister-in-law. He has destroyed the palace of pleasures, and the prayer world, and several other levels and realms that even I had not known existed. It seems he has ranged freely through the realms of the tower, demolishing everything in sight. He has caused a great deal of destruction.'

She raised her eyebrows. It sounded like the subject of a street performance, one of those things where feeble-minded rakshasas tumbled and danced and smashed open their skulls or cut off fingers to get a few laughs from their equally feeble audiences. 'Are you sure your information is correct, Vibhisena?'

He nodded vigorously, wiping sweat from his neck with the end of his ang-vastra. It was practically drenched with perspiration, she noted, as were the rest of his garments. 'Aye, milady. It is the talk of Lanka. Did your sakshis not tell you about it? But then, they deliberately keep you ill informed and spy on you for Ravana.' He shook his head as she opened her mouth to protest. 'No, let us not argue now. I only came to tell you these things because I wish you to come with me to your husband.'

'Why?' she asked suspiciously.

'Because he is out of control. He does not understand the vanar's powers and he will not listen to anyone who tries to tell him. I have already tried thrice to gain access to the throne room, but he has kept me out.'

'I am not surprised,' she said. 'This sounds to me like a matter for the royal guard.'

He clucked his tongue impatiently. 'The royal guard is almost completely destroyed. So are the kinkaras.'

She blinked. 'What? Destroyed? By whom?'

'By the vanar, my lady. Did you not hear what I said earlier? He is on a rampage! Blood and destruction. He will destroy all of Lanka if he is not stopped. But Ravana thinks he can be halted by brute force, and that is completely absurd. He does not understand the extent of this creature's powers.'

She leaned forward, stunned. 'Are you telling me that this vanar intruder, an emissary from Rama, has single-handedly killed the royal guard and the kinkaras?'

'And Marshal Prahasta. His son Jambumali. One entire kumbha-rakshasa legion. The seven champions of our seven ministers. And now Ravana has ordered five more legions, led by five generals, to join the attack. And they are being slaughtered as well.'

She rose to her feet, her hands flying to her mouth in disbelief. 'But this is impossible. A single enemy? A vanar? How?'

'He is the son of the wind god, Vayu. But his powers were realised and activated only because of his devotion to Rama. He fights for dharma. He came here to ask that Sita be released and permitted to go back with him. But Ravana will not even listen to his petition. He thinks that by throwing armies and warriors at him, he can destroy the vanar. He does not understand that this is no mere warrior.'

She looked around, unable to process this flood of shocking news. 'Why was I not told about this—' She stopped herself. Perhaps there was some truth in Vibhisena's accusations after all. All this while, she had thought she was the one keeping an eye on Vikata. What if it had been the other way around? 'But even if I agree with you, Vibhisena, what do you expect me to do? Ravana is handling the situation, isn't he? Even I don't presume to match his knowledge of military matters. This is beyond me, or even you.'

He sighed, wringing his hands. 'My lady, he knows now that he cannot deal with the vanar by force alone. That is why, even after sending in the five generals and their legions, he has still summoned two more warriors.'

'So?'

He looked at her with large, unhappy eyes. 'He has called for your sons, Indrajit and Akshay Kumar. He intends to send them in to battle the vanar. And if they do so, they will be killed just like the others. Only you can stop him. Not as a wife, or as a queen. But as a mother.'

Supanakha howled with glee at the sight of the five generals of Lanka lying on the battlefield. The entire level, once nothing more than an idyllic rustic landscape, a perfect replica of the southern part of Lanka, had been turned into one vast charnel house. She scanned the hundreds upon hundreds of corpses of foot-soldiers of various rakshasa tribes, shattered chariots, slain broken-surs and horses. It looked like the aftermath of a clash between two sizeable armies. Hard to believe that one vanar had wreaked so much death and destruction.

Hanuman was standing in the midst of the carnage, looking at the bodies of the fallen generals. He turned his head as she approached cautiously, pausing now and then to take a nip of one, a lick of another. 'I tried to tell them. But they would not listen. Why will nobody hear my plea? Do they wish me to destroy the whole of Lanka?'

Supanakha chuckled.

He looked at her. 'Why do you laugh? Do you find the death of your fellow rakshasas amusing?'

'Rakshasas, mortals, devas, Asuras . . . they all die sometime or other,' she said matter-of-factly. 'I don't let myself get upset over it. I was laughing at your hubris.'

'Hubris?'

'Do you really think this is all of Lanka?' She gestured with a nod of her head and a grin. 'This is all illusion, a non-place created by Pushpak. Nothing you do here will destroy the real Lanka.'

He pointed at the field strewn with corpses. 'Are all these illusions too? Non-rakshasas?'

She lost her smile. 'They're real. And yes, they were some of Ravana's best warriors. But mark my words, I said "some of". He has many more champions to replace these. You haven't faced the best yet. He's underestimated you, that's all.'

Hanuman regarded her thoughtfully. 'Who are the best then?'

She chortled. 'Think I would tell you that? Not in a million years! I enjoy watching you slay his incompetent goons. I'm sure sooner or later he'll send a couple of slightly less incompetent ones your way. You'll find out for yourself.'

He shook his head. 'I will kill them all. No rakshasa will stop me.'

She arched her eyebrows. 'Vain for a vanar, aren't you? You don't know what Ravana is really capable of, my simian friend. And you haven't even seen his real champions. Why, take just one for instance. Kumbha—' She broke off. 'You almost tricked me there.' She grinned. 'Anyway. Once Ravana's oversized ego accepts that you're more than a run-of-the-mill warrior, you'll have your chance to test that assumption to the limit.'

She cocked her ears. The sound of a conch shell blowing was audible. It was coming from just over the next rise. 'I think you may get your chance sooner than you think.'

She backed away, then stopped and looked back. He was standing in the same place, as if rooted to the ground. 'In case I don't get an opportunity to exchange pleasantries with you again, let me take this chance to say that you aren't half bad at all. The last opponent I saw who could harry Ravana's forces so skilfully was . . . Rama.'

He looked pleased at that. She chuckled and scampered away to find a safe perch from which to observe the next round in this conflict.

Ravana was pacing the throne dais when Mandodhari burst in. She came in the old-fashioned way, through the door. The surprised sentries on duty had to dance aside to avoid being struck. She strode up the carpeted aisle, her white robes billowing, face as dark with fury as a stormcloud over a black ocean. Vibhisena followed behind her, wringing his hands and muttering mantras.

The assembled ministers and generals turned to look at her with only slight curiosity. Everyone's attention was riveted on the water image. Few were seated. Most stood about, anxious looks on their faces. Several wore fixed snarls, others expressions of shocked disbelief.

Mandodhari stopped before the water image. It showed the vanar Hanuman standing alone in a field of corpses. The devastation was considerable. Off to one side, a feline figure scampered to the silhouette of a tree and leapt up, climbing to the top, where she perched on a branch. Despite the sorcerous clarity of the image, it was not possible to make out the identity of each and every corpse, but Mandodhari didn't have to recognise them all to understand the scope and significance implied by the image.

'A single vanar,' she said. 'Unarmed.'

Ravana flung down the goblet he was drinking from. It bounced hard on the stone floor, the metal rim crumpling with the force of the throw, and settled with a ringing echo on its side.

'What does he want?' she asked her husband.

Every pair of eyes turned to Ravana.

'What do you think he wants?' he growled.

'And is she worth all this?' she asked, indicating the field full of corpses.

He waved dismissively. 'This is not about her any more. It is a question of dealing with an intrusion.'

'An intrusion?' she repeated. 'Is that what you call it? It looks more like an invasion to me.'

Ravana glowered down at her with three of his heads. The others seemed to be muttering arcane things to each other or to invisible persons. 'It will be dealt with. Within the hour, I will have the vanar bound in chains and paraded through the city streets. Then he will be executed.'

'Along with the mortal woman?' she asked.

He turned away, avoiding her gaze. 'Let us deal with this impudence first. The mortal woman is no immediate threat.'

She stared at him until she felt that her gaze must bore through his back and pierce his flesh. But then she recalled the real reason she had come here. In that sense, he was right. The mortal woman could wait a while. There were other things more pressing to deal with first.

'I am told you have sent for my sons.' She kept her voice calm.

He turned to face her again. 'What of it?'

'And that you intend to order them to go into battle against this invader . . . intruder . . . whatever you wish to call him.'

'Lanka is as much under their protection as mine. They have a right to defend their kingdom against this intrusion. They are, after all, princes of Lanka.'

'And you are, after all, King of Lanka,' she responded, more than a little curtly.

He stared down at her, ignoring the mild buzzing that had started in the rear of the hall. 'Your point being?'

'That you are the chief defender of this kingdom. If you can justify sending Akshay and Indrajit, then you can send yourself as well.'

A long moment of stunned silence passed. The buzzing in the rear was replaced by a sense that most of the occupants of the hall were holding their breath.

'You expect me, Ravana, Lord of Lanka, to go and personally deal with a single intruder?' he asked with deceptive mildness. She could see the rage dancing in his eyes, leaping from face to face too quickly to be noticed easily unless you knew where to look. And she knew exactly where to look, oh, she knew all too well. 'What next? When a dog comes to the city gates and urinates, will you expect me to go flick a stick at him too?'

She walked up the steps of the dais. Even when she stood at the top, on the same level as Ravana, he was still a good two heads taller. Well, for that matter, he was a good ten heads taller! But she felt better, if only for having asserted her queenly prerogative. 'I expect you not to put my sons into any situation into which you would not put yourself.'

He stared at her so long and so silently that she was certain that this time she had overstepped the invisible line that had always encircled her in their relationship. She expected a mantra to issue from one of his pairs of lips at any moment, blasting her into a charred skeleton, or a fist to swing out, smashing her dead with a single blow. Things had always been that fragile between them, only one utterance or a single blow away from the end. Yet she knew that if she did not assert herself, constantly test the limits, she would be diminished daily, ground down into the earth, until finally one day she would wake up to find that she had no more power than a joy slave in a perverse rakshasa's cellar.

But his anger dissipated suddenly. His eyes, smouldering until now, turned opaque and moved away from her, looking over her shoulder at something in the sabha hall.

'Of course,' he said. 'Any risk I would bid them undertake, I would be willing to undertake myself. They are my sons too, after all.'

She almost sighed with relief. She had won another battle, however minuscule. 'Then we are agreed. You will not send Akshay Kumar and Indrajit to face this vanar.'

He laughed. 'Perhaps you misheard me,' he said, then glanced to the left of the dais where she knew Vibhisena was standing. 'Or perhaps your sources of information are too slow. Our sons have already gone to face the vanar.'

'What!' she cried out despite herself. 'But you just promised me—'

'I promised you that I would not send them to do this if I was not willing to do it myself. And I stand by that. If they should fail, which I doubt very strongly, then you have my word. The next opponent I will send to face this vanar will be I myself.' He strode past her. 'Now let us see how our sons fare in this unequal battle.'

She turned to see the thing he had been staring at over her shoulder. The water image. It depicted Hanuman facing a single chariot. Even in this diminished depiction, she could not fail to recognise the sigil and banner of her younger son, Akshay Kumar.

16

Hanuman knew that the opponent who faced him now was someone of greater significance than all the others who had come before. He knew this because even before the distant rumble of the chariot came to his ears, the ground beneath his feet began to groan. Until now, the sun had traversed a course similar to the real sun in a real sky. It had been sometime in the late morning when he had entered this level of the tower, and by now it had moved perhaps an hour or so westwards. But now, even as the earth groaned underfoot, the sun began to visibly dim, its solar light dulled to a matt glow, like a lantern before which a mesh screen had been positioned. The wind, which had been wafting gently until now, suddenly died down, leaving a stillness that was accentuated by the utter absence of insect or bird sound. From somewhere in the distant west came the sound of an ocean swelling and crashing against a rocky shore. And the silhouetted mountain range along the northern horizon trembled and boomed, as if with great avalanches. Finally, the sky itself thrummed and clashed though no storm-clouds were visible, nor any other visible cause.

He thought of asking the shapeshifter who his latest opponent was, then thought better of it. Would knowing change anything? He would still have to fight and slay, no matter who it was. Better then that he faced the challenger as just a warrior, and ignored the light-and-sound show as yet another boastful flaunting of rakshasa maya.

He flexed his muscles and without consciously debating the

choice, began to expand himself. It seemed warranted. He swelled
with strength and power, growing to only a few times his size.
When he was perhaps the height of a mature oak tree, he stopped,
spread his legs to anchor himself, and slapped the insides of his
thighs to get the blood circulating, an old wrestling habit from
his young days in the akhada. Something made him think of
Sakra, and a small smile tweaked his mouth.

He was standing that way when the chariot came into view.
It brought no dustcloud, which was yet another indication of
the driver's importance. It was an impressive machine. Six-
wheeled, drawn by a team of seven horses, and ornamented in
gold and platinum with massive fist-sized diamonds studded
throughout its length. Even the spokes on the hubs of the
wheels, designed to slice off limbs as the chariot passed through
close-ranked legions, were made of gold alloy spokes tipped
with razor-pointed diamonds.

The rider himself was virtually concealed in the fortress-like
well of the chariot. A suit of armour could hardly have protected
him better, so artfully was the chariot designed. All Hanuman
could see of his opponent was a small section of his face and
a strip of his chest at a little below shoulder height – the space
through which the charioteer would fire his arrows.

The chariot stopped when it was about a mile away. Hanuman
waited. The stillness of the air made the artificiality of this
world more obvious than ever; a peculiar odour, like camphor
mingled with rusted iron, tingled his nostrils, cutting through
the charnel stenches of the battlefield.

After a pause during which the sky continued to boom and
echo, and the earth beneath his feet groaned like an unoiled
hinge to the netherworld, the challenger made his first move.

Three arrows emerged in quick succession from the well of
the chariot, arcing towards Hanuman's position. He was too
far away for them to reach him, as the archer must surely know,
but he soon saw that it was not the warrior's intent to inflict
damage upon his body, but to attack his fear.

The first arrow plummeted sharply downwards, to strike the

earth. The second flew up toward the sky, in a trajectory that should have been impossible. And the third sped straight on, as if aimed precisely at some unseen object midway between Hanuman and the charioteer.

As soon as the first arrow struck the ground, a great gnashing sound erupted from the earth, followed by a spume of dark fluid that rose a hundred yards high before falling back upon itself. At the same instant, the arrow that flew upward disappeared, and a clashing sound reverberated, followed by a release of the same dark fluid from a puncture in the fabric of the blue sky. The liquid spewing down from the hole in the sky met the top of the plume rising from the earth to form an uninterrupted line.

The third arrow, arcing directly towards Hanuman, stopped perhaps five hundred yards short, as if it had struck something in mid-air. A scream of anguish, like the wail of a cyclone in a seaside storm, issued forth, and a great wind sprang up, blowing in every direction at once.

Hanuman pressed his feet down firmly and hunkered lower to keep his balance.

He was impressed by the demonstration of the charioteer's powers. The archer had displayed the extent of his prowess by firing arrows straight at the earth, the sky and the wind. All three had struck home, injuring their targets. It was no mean feat to be able to wound three of the elemental devas, Prithvi, Akasa and Vayu. Only someone gifted with divine astras could accomplish such a feat.

But he would have been more impressed had the demonstration not been conducted within Ravana's sorcerous tower. In this magical place, part tower, part palace and part multiple worlds, anything was possible. For everything was controlled by Pushpak. And Pushpak obeyed Ravana's will. Despite the impressiveness of this display, neither Prithvi, Akasa nor Vayu had been involved. The archer's arrows had only struck Pushpak's illusions. That was the essence of maya, the web of illusions that passed for reality in this world of rakshasas.

In a typical battle situation, where one famed opponent had displayed his own powers and challenged his adversary, the other warrior would usually respond with a display of his own strength and skill. This exchange of demonstrations and displays could continue for hours, with each party seeking to upstage the other through increasingly impossible feats. Finally, when they joined arms through mutual agreement, the fight itself was only a culmination of that long stand-off.

But this was not the real world, nor was it a typical battle situation. Hanuman had no intention of acknowledging his opponent's strength and skill. Indeed, he abhorred and despised such a vulgar display conducted gratuitously within the auspices of one's own controlled environment.

He roared like thunder and leapt forward. In two great bounds he reached the spot where the third arrow had ostensibly struck the wind god, his own father. He wrenched the arrow out of mid-air and snapped it in two. The wailing wind died down immediately. Then he crouched down and leapt up high, miles high, to the spot where the second arrow seemed to have embedded itself in the navel of the sky god. He wrenched that arrow out too, crushing it like a toothpick into fragments. And as he fell to earth, he pounded the spot where the first arrow had struck the back of Prithvi-maa, Mother Earth.

Both the upward spume and the falling shower of dark fluid, ostensibly blood from the wounds of sky and earth, slowed to a trickle and died out.

Silence and stillness reigned again.

He turned and faced the chariot, now less than half a mile away. He could see the whites of the charioteer's eyes, watching through the slot in the well. There was respect in that gaze, and amazement too. He thought that perhaps the rakshasa ensconced in that diamantine chariot had never seen nor heard of a vanar of such capabilities before. The battlefield strewn with corpses was no doubt an added consideration. Well, he was about to give him another reason to goggle.

*

Supanakha munched on a haunch of rakshasa as she watched the one-on-one fight. Hanuman probably didn't know, or care, whom he faced, but that chariot belonged to Ravana's younger son, Akshay Kumar. Now there was a rakshasa who defined the word handsome. She mulled on the encounters she had enjoyed with him. Akshay Kumar ranked high on her personal chart of sexual prowess.

She hoped his prowess on the battlefield matched his excellence in the boudoir.

The vanar was standing about half a mile from Akshay Kumar's chariot, staring at it. He seemed to be narrowing his eyes, concentrating his gaze. Was he trying to see through the slots in the chariot well, to lock eyes with his opponent?

She continued watching, unable to see anything of any note happening.

Then it began. At first there was only a snicker from the lead horse, a magnificent stallion a whole head taller than the rest of the team. His snicker turned into a whinny as he turned his head this way, then that, as if trying to avoid a pesky gnat. That horse was much too well trained for battle to act that way. There must be something far more serious than a gnat bothering him, but for the life of her she couldn't tell what it was.

Then she saw a spot brighten on the front of the chariot well, bang in the centre where the prince of Lanka's sigil was embossed. The sigil seemed to be glowing. She thought at first it was only a reflection of the sun, which had begun to shine brightly again now, but the position of the chariot was wrong for it to catch the sun's rays. Still the sigil glowed, brighter and brighter, until it turned red-hot, then white-hot. The lead horse whinnied in a tone that suggested real alarm, rather than irritation, and now the alarm spread to its mates as well, who began to toss and turn their heads and stamp their hoofs. One horse turned its head inwards, and for a moment she saw the loose hair on its mane suddenly ignite, as if lit by a sun's ray passed through a dense glass. It cried out in panic, wanting to bolt, but the discipline drilled into it and the stoic stubbornness of the lead horse stayed the team.

The sigil burst into flames.

Supanakha caught her breath. For once, even she was amazed. What level of heat did it take to set solid metal on fire? She had no idea, but thought it must be volcanic. How could such heat be striking Akshay Kumar's chariot? Where was it coming from?

Fool, she told herself, turning her eyes to the vanar. Where do you think?

As she watched, Hanuman tilted his head very slightly, as if tracking something with his eyes. The fire on the chariot moved in a straight line, like a slash drawn by a magical sword, cutting across the front of the well. Inside, Akshay Kumar cried out in a startled tone, and through the slot she saw him backing away hurriedly.

The vanar turned his head to one side, then slowly downwards, then the other way. She kept glancing from him to the chariot and back again, trying to make out what he was doing. Then she understood. He was using some kind of heat power from his eyes to cut out the chariot well.

In moments, the entire front of the armoured well fell to the ground in a heap of steaming, overheated metal. The terrified horses went wild as pieces of half-molten metal clattered by their flanks and lay sizzling on the grassy field.

From an elaborately fortified riding machine, the chariot had been reduced to a ludicrous-looking open horse cart. Its owner, Akshay Kumar, stood exposed on the platform, reins clutched in his fists as he sought to regain control of his team. He was armoured lightly, as was his style, and she could clearly see his handsome face. He was staring white-eyed at the vanar, unable to believe what had just happened.

Then he rallied. With a yell to his horses, a rakshasa sloka popular for its efficacy in calming mounts, he regrouped their heads, then yanked on the rein to the leader. With a snort of relief, the horse whinnied a command to its fellows and the entire team moved forward, hoofs pounding. The chariot rolled smoothly enough, undamaged in any other way, driving directly at the vanar.

Supanakha expected the vanar to simply use his heat gaze to blast Akshay Kumar. If he could burn through metal like a welding flame, he could surely scorch the rakshasa to ashes easily. But Hanuman did no such thing. Instead, he simply stood and waited for Akshay Kumar to come to him.

Akshay Kumar had recovered his wits. The team set on their course, he took up his bow and began his onslaught without further ceremony or preamble, loosing a hail of arrows that might have been shot by an entire legion of archers. Hundreds of missiles of varied types, sickle-headed, barb-headed, snake-headed, flew towards Hanuman.

They fell upon the vanar as hail upon a mountain.

None pierced the vanar's skin, just as no other weapon had pierced it apart from the dozen-odd arrows shot by Jambumali during the parley. But even so, Supanakha winced. Even if the vanar could harden his skin to resist penetration, those arrows must still hurt. From the impassive look on Hanuman's face, you could hardly tell.

Akshay Kumar loosed a second onslaught at the vanar. Twisting, turning, writhing, the arrows sped straight towards Hanuman's nostrils, his ears, his eyes, seeking to enter through the natural channels. That was brilliant, Supanakha thought.

Hanuman only shook his head once, vigorously. The arrows struck his face and head and neck and fell off harmlessly, like a shower of pine needles.

There was no time for a third loosing. The chariot had reached the vanar's feet.

Bending down, Hanuman opened his fist, the size of an elephant's flank, and slapped the chariot's horse team.

The chariot, horses and all, was suddenly diverted from its headlong charge. It flew sideways, tumbling over and over, until it came to a rest a hundred yards away. Akshay Kumar, ever nimble and quick on his feet, leapt from it the moment the vanar struck, and rolled, rising to his feet even before the chariot stopped tumbling. Every last one of the horses was dead, rendered lifeless by the vanar's single blow. Akshay looked at them and turned his attention back to his opponent.

He drew his sword and charged towards Hanuman like a wild boar in the deep Southwoods. He didn't waste his breath on any war cry.

Hanuman didn't waste his breath either. Not bothering to roar or perform any of the preliminary shows of strength that he had used against larger groups of foes, he raced forward to meet Akshay Kumar.

The difference in their sizes was so immense that to Supanakha they resembled a boar charging an elephant. Still, even a boar as skilful as Akshay Kumar with his sword could rip out the elephant's intestines with one well-aimed slash.

Akshay Kumar sprang through the air, leaping up to aim himself at the vanar's groin. Supanakha saw what he intended: he would launch himself at the vanar and feint, twisting in one direction while slashing in the other. And then they would know whether the vanar's groin and lower belly were as resistant to pointed blades as the rest of his body.

But Hanuman's hand flashed out, quicker than the rakshasa, quicker than his sword as well, and the next thing Supanakha saw was Akshay Kumar's feet clutched in Hanuman's fists. The vanar swung the rakshasa around in a circle, leaping to turn himself round. He swung and spun, leaped and turned, increasing speed until both he and his victim were but a blur, like a gigantic top spinning madly around on the field. Supanakha tried to count how many times he whirled around, but soon lost track. The vanar turned and turned until she thought Akshay Kumar's brain must be addled and turned to mush from the speed and the motion alone. A hundred times? No, much more. Five hundred? Six? Closer to a thousand, she thought. And there was something significant about the number one thousand and eight, wasn't there? She had no way to know for certain, but that was as good a number as any to guess at.

One thousand and eight times Hanuman swung Akshay Kumar around.

Supanakha expected him to release the rakshasa. She was looking forward to seeing how far Akshay Kumar flew. She guessed a yojana, but any distance was possible.

Instead, Hanuman twisted the rakshasa's body over his shoulder and smashed it into the ground.

She felt the impact all the way up in the tree. The branch on which she sat shuddered, and lost a few dried leaves. Pushpak had been imitating late autumn in this level.

The place where Akshay Kumar had been smashed down looked like the chopping block of an abattoir. The ground was flattened in a roughly rakshasa-shaped pattern. But there the resemblance to any form or structure ended. So forcefully had the rakshasa been flung that his sinews, muscles, entrails, eyes, bones, head, limbs and blood were all commingled into one formless heap.

17

No sooner had Hanuman killed Akshay Kumar than he heard a sound from nearby. It came from the place where the bodies of the kumbha-rakshasas lay. He frowned but could not see anything clearly, so crowded with bodies and debris was that part of the field. He leapt up and over Akshay Kumar's fallen chariot, landing with a thump in the midst of the slaughtered kumbha bodies. Unlike in the real world, no flies or other insects had begun swarming over the corpses yet, nor were there any scavengers circling in the sky above. They lay much as they had when slain. He looked around, seeking the source of the sound.

He saw an arm move. A forearm, with the six fingers of a rakshasa hand at its end, wriggling fitfully.

It was buried beneath a pile of kumbha corpses and the torso of one of the misshapen-headed creatures that seemed as ubiquitous in Lanka as camels in the desert. He picked up the bodies and tossed them aside. Beneath the third one he found the source of the sound. It was a kumbha-rakshasa, still alive. From the looks of him, and the still-bleeding gash on his head, he had been knocked unconscious and then buried beneath a pile of his fellows. Hanuman looked closer, then saw that it was the kumbha who had spoken to him first, the leader who had called himself War Marshal Prahasta.

The kumbha retched, coughed violently, then opened his eyes, wiping them clear of blood with the back of his horned hand. He stared up unseeingly at first, then focused on Hanuman, and blanched.

Hanuman bunched his hand into a fist. A little tap on the head and the kumbha would be oatmeal like the rest of them. The kumbha, too weak and shaken to defend himself, closed his eyes, breathing fitfully.

After a moment, Hanuman lowered the fist and allowed it to relax. The kumbha sensed something and opened his eyes.

Hanuman stretched out his hand, offering it to the kumbha. The rakshasa stared at it dumbly for a moment, then wheezed and turned over on his side, struggling to rise of his own accord. The effort was futile. His legs were trapped beneath the torso of his fallen mount, thrice his own weight. Hanuman waited, letting him thrash and twist helplessly for a moment. Finally, the marshal turned back to look at him, purple eyes blazing with humiliation and fury, and reached up to take the vanar's hand. Hanuman closed his own oversized fingers around the kumbha's like a father holding his child's hand, and yanked him bodily out of the pile.

The marshal groaned loudly, then sighed with surprise as he found himself upon his feet again. He seemed unharmed except for the gash on the head, which was not fatal. He glared at Hanuman.

Before either of them could say a word, the rumbling of a chariot came to their ears.

Hanuman strode away from the kumbha, turning his back upon the rakshasa uncaringly. Behind him, he heard the marshal gasp and exclaim in horror as he saw the carnage and slaughter that had occurred after he had fallen unconscious. The kumbha cried out as he recognised each fallen compatriot by their brahman emanations, the soul-signatures that only a few enlightened creatures could read. 'Jambumali, my son! The five generals! And Akshay Kumar too!'

Hanuman ignored him and watched the approaching chariot. It was the complete antithesis of the one ridden by Akshay Kumar. No gaudy golden plates or fancy carvings. This chariot was jet black with a simple silver-embossed sigil on the front of its barely waist-high well. It was large enough to accommodate only a single rider, built for speed and manoeuvrability rather than to pound foot-soldiers into the ground. It was drawn by a team of four splendid white horses who moved with a gait that was poetry to behold. A warrior's chariot, not a poseur's.

The charioteer proved himself as undesiring of artifice as his vehicle. He wasted no time on demonstrations or protocol. He was armed with a bow, Hanuman saw, and the moment he came within range, he slowed his chariot. As he put an arrow to the bow, he whispered a mantra to the tip, then took careful aim. The air shimmered, the world shook, and a great rumbling erupted from deep within the ground. Hanuman frowned. He was inured to rakshasa sorcery by now, but something about the very simplicity and directness of this rakshasa's method rang true.

'Vanar,' the charioteer called in a clear but grating rakshasa voice. 'I will fire but one missile at you. But one is sufficient to accomplish that which a thousand have failed to do before it. This arrow I have strung to my bow is empowered with a mantra you must surely have heard tell of. It is the famed dev-astra of Lord Brahma. The same which your master Rama unleashed upon my father's armies at Mithila fourteen years ago. If you believe yourself capable of withstanding its celestial power, then face it by all means. But if you do not, I have orders from my father to take you as my captive and bring you before him. Tell me, what is your will?'

Hanuman sensed that this warrior spoke the truth. Of all the rakshasas who had faced him thus far, he felt that this one was the mightiest. If he was indeed wielding the famed brahm-astra, then there was only one response to his query. But he still had one doubt. 'The brahm-astra, once spoken and unleashed, cannot be recalled. If you have uttered the sacred mantra already, then why do you tarry? Unleash it and let what will be be.'

The rakshasa answered in a steady voice, without anger or

impatience. 'I have spoken only one part of the mantra. The rest remains to be uttered. So tell me quickly, shall I unleash Brahma's weapon, or will you yield gracefully?'

Hanuman did not have to think very long. With a great sigh of relief, he let his hands fall by his sides, and allowed his specially enhanced strength to leave his body. At once his size diminished and he became his normal vanar size once more. He held out his hands in the attitude of a supplicant, offering them to be bound.

'I will not resist the weapon of Brahma. It has been ordained that I should be overcome by His celestial power, and His alone. Therefore I am prepared to endure submission to your superior might. Take me as your captive. But first tell me one thing, rakshasa. What is your name and calling? For no ordinary kshatriya is usually given the right to wield the greatest weapon of all. Who are you, and what is your claim to fame?'

The rakshasa leapt from his chariot, putting his bow and the arrow back in his rig. He approached Hanuman with a grim expression on his face. 'I am known as Indrajit,' he said shortly. 'He Who Defeated Lord Indra In Combat. That is one of my claims to fame. I have overcome many devas by my prowess on the battlefield and in single combat, both unarmed as well as armed with a variety of weapons. Several of those devas have then been compelled to serve in my household as servants to me and my father and brother, for the victories belonged to all three of us jointly.' He paused, then added as an afterthought, 'I am also sometimes known as the eldest son of Ravana.'

Hanuman nodded. 'I had no doubt that you were someone highly placed. The crown prince of Lanka no less. It is not dishonourable for a warrior to place himself in the custody of another warrior who has a superior reputation and wields a weapon so great.'

Indrajit looked at him with a lowered brow, his lashes almost concealing his dark eyes. The rakshasa was not handsome like his younger brother, but there was a powerful menace in his aspect that recalled his father's terrifying visage. 'You are arrogant, vanar. That will be your downfall. Just because you are empowered with your father's gifts does not make you a great warrior. You have a long way to go and much, much more experience to gather before you become worthy of facing a kshatriya of my stature. Although under the present circumstances, I doubt you will have the opportunity to gain that experience.'

Hanuman shrugged. 'I could take offence at your words, but I shall not. You speak mostly the truth. I am not arrogant, Prince Indrajit. Yes, I am complacent in my powers, but it is my faith in my lord Rama that gives me this complacency and supreme confidence. I have possessed my father's gifts for all my life, but they were worthless to me until Rama put his faith and trust in me and awakened my hidden shakti. As for experience, no doubt I will gain much, much more, just as you say. And I look forward to facing kshatriyas not only of your stature, but even greater than yourself! For what good is experience without ambition?'

Indrajit's heavy brow lowered further, until his eyes were visible only as slits through which two smouldering black-red coals glowed out. 'My orders were to take you captive, vanar, not kill you. And I always follow the orders of my superior. But you would be wise not to test my resolve. Especially when the body of my brother lies only yards away.'

Hanuman stared back at him levelly, making it clear that he was submitting himself of his own accord, not out of fear or compromise.

Indrajit stared back, the coals of his eyes glowering more fiery the longer he stared.

War Marshal Prahasta coughed loudly, breaking the stand-off. 'My lord prince, it would be best if we move quickly.' He did not need to add anything more; the implication was obvious: *Before one of you loses control.*

Indrajit stepped back, keeping his eyes still on the vanar. He did not waste time asking Prahasta how he had survived. He was a soldier, accustomed only to taking and giving orders. 'Tie his hands,' he said curtly.

Prahasta started to protest, then stopped. Without another word, he found a bloodied sash that had belonged to a kumbha and used it to bind Hanuman's hands. The vanar gave him no trouble, but Prahasta finished the job without once looking at his face, and when he was done, he moved backwards stiffly but not slowly.

Indrajit stepped forward, raised his chainmailed fist and smashed it backwards against Hanuman's face. 'Now we shall show you how we treat intruders in our kingdom.'

Hanuman felt a trickle of blood escape the cut on his lip inflicted by the rakshasa's horned sixth finger, but remained standing as he was. He said calmly to Indrajit, 'Will you take me to Ravana now?'

Indrajit turned to look at him with smouldering eyes. 'Aye, that I will. Those are my orders.'

He looked around and saw a mace lying beside the body of a slain general. He picked it up, hefting it easily. He was magnificently muscled, with evident power and familiarity with warfare. He raised the mace and swung it hard, striking Hanuman across the abdomen. This time Hanuman could not help but bend over from the pain and impact of the blow. His stomach felt as if it had been pressed against his spine.

'But first,' Indrajit said, raising the mace again, 'I have a few lessons to teach you about pain and endurance.'

He brought the mace down again on Hanuman's body. And again. And again.

Supanakha sighed with disappointment as Indrajit continued to batter and pound Hanuman with the studied efficiency of one who had done the same thing hundreds of times before in his life and knew just how to infict the maximum pain. Not because she cared about the vanar, but because she had enjoyed the battles. She always felt let down when the fighting ended. Despite all the victory marches of history and the grandiloquent claims of supremacy, the truth was that nobody ever really won a war or conflict. It was only the bloody brutality itself that mattered in the end; the song of blood and pain. And that was what she loved most.

She watched for a while longer. Indrajit was thorough in the beating he adminstered, as he was in everything he did, be it drinking, eating, statecraft, warmongering, or fornication. He was not as inventive or innovative a lover as Akshay Kumar had been; which reminded her, she would miss Akshay. Oh well, once this was over, and the palace of pleasures had been rebuilt, she would surely find some new lover to help her get over her loss. More likely, she would find several hundred new lovers!

She slipped down the tree and called up a portal. This part of the show was over. It was time to go backstage and see what the dramatist had in store for the next act.

Mandodhari was beside herself. Yet she knew better than to unleash her grief before a hall full of Lanka's top military and ministerial rakshasas. If she gave in to the black darkness that threatened to overwhelm her now, she would be branded a weakling and a civilian, the worst epithets any rakshasa could be given. For the rakshasa race, war was the natural way of life. Peace was abhorrent, undesirable. Even the pacifists, of whom there were a small but steadily growing number these days, tempered their talk with phrases like 'preventive action' and 'positive force'. But the truth was her son was dead, and nothing would bring him back.

She uncovered her face and forced herself to sit up straighter. She had slumped back into her seat the instant Akshay was killed, and after witnessing his gruesome end, she didn't have the heart to raise her eyes to that water image again. Her mind must have blanked out for several moments, because when she roused herself from her inward-looking reverie, the image showed the vanar bound and lying on the floor of a chariot at the feet of the charioteer. Indrajit, her eldest son, was driving his team fast but not too fast, with his customary efficiency. War Marshal Prahasta was standing on the running board of the chariot, clinging on with a fierceness that suggested it had been a very long time since Lanka's chief warlord had travelled in such discomfort. She cared not a whit for the marshal's comfort. He had survived while her son had perished. Damn him. Damn all these warmongers. What did they ever achieve except death and destruction? What use were all their marble monuments and statues and speeches and medals in the face of the grieving mothers of the slain, or the orphaned children, or the desolate wives?

She fought back tears as Indrajit passed through a portal and rode towards two enormous wooden doors lined with gold. She recognised them belatedly as the doors to this very sabha hall, just as they crashed open across the chamber and the chariot entered, the horses neighing and shying as Indrajit rode them without a pause through the crowded room. Several of Lanka's seniormost military commanders and chief dignitaries were forced to make undignified leaps and jumps to escape being run over by the chariot, but Indrajit drove all the way to the foot of the royal dais without any mishap. Marshal Prahasta stepped off the running board with a great sigh, all but collapsing on the spot.

Indrajit picked up the vanar, now bound hand and foot with a variety of sashes, belts and even the partly severed chain of a mace, and carried the being who had been the cause of so much devastation – and the death of her younger son – up the steps of the dais, depositing him roughly at the feet of the black-wood throne.

'As ordered, my lord, I bring you the vanar, bound and tied and incapable of further violence.'

Ravana remained seated on his throne. The King of Lanka seemed to be in a reverie of his own, Mandodhari saw. For once, his heads were neither babbling nor arguing. In fact, every last one of them seemed present in their consciousness, focused on the here and now. The water image had been dismissed a moment earlier, before Indrajit's chariot reached the dais, and the bowl removed. Now Ravana sat stone still, gazing at the vanar at his feet with ten expressionless faces.

18

Vibhisena felt outraged at the sight of Hanuman. The vanar had been badly beaten by Indrajit. He had watched with chagrin on the water image as the beating was administered, and even the reduced size and distance had not diminished the brutality of it. Even now, Indrajit yanked the chain with his fist, tightening the noose-like coils around the poor fellow's throat as if he would hang the beast here and now. And still the vanar managed to make not a sound of protest, but stood ramrod straight, in the same stoic silence he had maintained throughout the beating. His face, already coated thickly with the blood and ichor of the many opponents he had slain, was now wet with his own freely running blood as well. The many arrows he had taken during the parley with Jambumali – which, Vibhisena felt strongly, had been rudely violated by the vice-marshal – still protruded from various parts of his body. Indrajit, in his typical meticulous way, had pointedly aimed the mace at those places, snapping off the heads of some of the arrows, and driving some further into the vanar's flesh and organs. Vibhisena longed to protest and lament such abominable behaviour; even an enemy deserved to be treated with dignity once he surrendered with grace. But he knew the futility of attempting such a protest. After the massacre the vanar had perpetrated, every rakshasa in Lanka lusted for only one thing: his execution. If I were king, Vibhisena thought with cold rage, then stopped himself. He was not king. And likely would never be.

He watched as Hanuman gazed up at the rakshasa who *was*

king with a curious expression on his vanar features. There seemed to be no rancour or malice in that gaze. Indeed, the vanar seemed almost to be . . . admiring, or something close to admiring, Ravana.

Vibhisena wondered what thoughts were passing through that simian head right now. With the power he had seen displayed in the battles, the vanar could undoubtedly give even Ravana a good fight. Yet he had submitted so meekly, so graciously. Why? Because he wished to be brought here before Ravana? That was what he had said, over and over again, but of course nobody had paid him any heed, until the body count was sufficiently high to earn him grudging attention. And now that he was here? Would he only talk and entreat Ravana? Or . . .

Vibhisena leaned forward, holding his silence until he could learn what the vanar intended to do next.

Hanuman gazed up at the King of Lanka in adoration. He was not ashamed of what he felt. The lord of rakshasas was worthy of such an emotion. Ravana sat upon his great throne like a king of kings. His jewels were dazzling, his armour unmatched, his body had been anointed with rare red sandalpaste, his golden pearl-studded crown sat upon his central head like a ring of solar fire. His rack of ten heads upon his immense neck was awe-inspiring. Any one of them could have been the face of a great king; together, they presented an aspect that was unmatched by any ten kings. He blazed with splendour, serene and certain in his own power. The shakti in his spirit was palpable, illuminating him like a great shroud that pulsated with different hues of throbbing light.

How magnificent he is, Hanuman thought. What beauty, what grace and dignity. To his eyes, Ravana seemed to have all the qualities of a great king. It was possible to understand now, sitting before the rakshasa in person, how this single being had acquired the stature of such a great legend, a mythology unto himself. For the first time it occurred to Hanuman that had Ravana not been unrighteous and violated dharma so relentlessly, he might well have been made protector of the three worlds by the devas themselves. Lord Indra would surely respect such a warrior, and gladly grant him all the wealth and power he desired, for no other ruler could command as much respect and adoration as Ravana.

His beauty is beyond reckoning, Hanuman thought. He is the most beauteous being created since the beginning of time. Even the terrible things he has done, the heinous crimes he is capable of, only add to his beauty. Is not the tiger that slays without forethought or hesitation beautiful in the dark dappled mangrove forests? Is not the great bull elephant, trampler of serpents and ravisher of any cow elephant that catches his fancy, undeniably beautiful in his lustful rage? Is not the serpent himself beautiful, with his diamond-patterned scales and wedge-shaped head, and terrible, hypnotic eyes, those fangs dripping deadly venom, capable of bringing death with a single strike? Is not the pale floating predator beautiful that glides through the valleys of the undersea world, his jaws opening and closing endlessly, killing and consuming without measure like a primordial killing machine, perfect in his elegant simplicity?

He is beautiful. If only he was righteous. If only he was a faithful adherent of dharma. If only he was respectful of the sanctity of all life and a seeker of peace and knowledge. If only he was not an abductor of other men's wives and slayer of innocent souls.

But then, Hanuman thought, if he was not all these things, if he had not done what he had done, had not the nature that he possessed, then he would not be Ravana at all. Then he would be . . . Rama. Or something close to Rama. A virtuous warrior beyond compare.

And in that moment of insight, he came upon a realisation that was beyond thought or knowledge. It was wisdom itself. The ultimate goal of all study and worship. A fragment of pure brahman. If he could but verbalise it, he would know truly what Ravana was, and why a being so beautiful was capable of such ugly acts. And knowing that, he would know the deepest secret of the rakshasa king, the one thing that nobody else had ever found out about Ravana. The secret of his true strength.

And the secret of his true weakness.

The hall was growing impatient and agitated. Prahasta could not understand why Ravana was not speaking or doing anything. The king just sat there, staring blankly at the vanar. And the vanar stood there and gazed back at the Lord of Lanka with a look of, well, he did not know what that look meant. But it was not hatred. That much he was sure of.

It was almost as if both Ravana and Hanuman were locked in some mental bond, examining each other like two great sages who had progressed past the point of words and spoken language and communicated through pure thought alone.

He stepped forward, clearing his throat and speaking in a cautious voice.

'My lord, with your permission, may we question the vanar about his actions?'

'Yes,' a voice shouted from behind Prahasta. 'He has much to answer for.'

'He deserves to be tortured and broken into pieces,' shouted another voice.

'He should be executed at once, right here and now.'

'No. He should be eaten alive, a piece at a time, every day, so he suffers for the longest time possible.'

'He should be—'

'We must—'

'Let us—'

'Make him—'

The chorus of angry shouts grew louder, clamouring for inventive and progressively more horrible punishments to be inflicted upon the vanar, all eventually ending in his death. Prahasta turned to face the hall and tried to restore order by calling out in a commanding voice. But everyone was seeking to be heard by Ravana, using the opportunity to show their fealty and initiative. Many of them, the marshal thought bitterly, felt guilty that they had not had the opportunity to fight the vanar and die as so many others had. As his son had.

'Enough.' Ravana's single word sliced through the cacophony like a volcanic-glass blade through coarse cloth. Silence fell on the hall. Prahasta saw his king raise a head or three to scan the assembly. One pair of eyes found him, bored into him, then was joined by two more pairs. Ravana pointed a single finger at him. 'War Marshal, proceed.'

Prahasta thought that was an abrupt command even by Ravana's curt standards. But he wasn't about to argue. Every warlord and minister in the chamber was looking for an opportunity to turn this situation to his own advantage, or at the very least to show solidarity and competence. There were at least half a dozen high ranks to be filled, and if Ravana's previous attitude to failure was any basis to judge by, then more heads could roll before the night turned. He bowed and spoke swiftly. 'Your majesty, it would be my privilege. As a first-hand witness to the damage caused by this intruder, and as one who faced him and lived to tell the tale, I am entitled to interrogate him personally.'

He paused, aware that every rakshasa eye in the room was glaring jealously at him now. 'However, in view of the fact that the situation is one that concerns the entire nation, I shall conduct my enquiry right here and now, before the entire body of governance. With your leave, of course,' he added quickly.

Ravana gestured impatiently. The king was still staring at the vanar, whose own gaze seemed riveted to Ravana. Prahasta went up to Indrajit and held out his hand for the end of the chain by which the prince held the prisoner. Indrajit looked at him darkly but handed it over, then went and took his seat on the dais, watched by his mother, whose eyes shone wetly.

Prahasta rattled the chain to attract the vanar's attention. Hanuman seemed barely aware of him, and only by yanking the chain hard enough to choke off breath could the war marshal get the prisoner to even glance at him.

'Speak. Identify yourself. Who are you and why did you come to our land?'

Hanuman looked at him unseeingly. Slowly, in stages, the vanar seemed to return to his senses like a person surfacing from a deep trance. He sighed, releasing a long-held breath, then spoke. Utter silence prevailed as every rakshasa in the hall hung on to his words.

'If you would know the answers to these questions, then you must grant me leave to tell the whole tale. I have heard some things spoken about my lord Rama that are patently untrue. It saddened my heart to listen to such lies and slander about a man so pure of heart and deed. If you will hear the truth about Rama, I will speak gladly. If not, then do with me as you will.'

Prahasta regarded the vanar. 'First answer the questions I have put to you.'

'I am Hanuman, a vanar. Son of the wind god Marut, and Anjana, who was once an apsara in Indra's court before she was cursed to spend a lifetime as a vanar. I leapt a distance of a hundred yojanas or more to fly across the ocean here to Lanka.'

Prahasta held up his hand to still the commotion that erupted in the wake of this extraordinary revelation. 'Are you an emissary of the mortal named Rama?'

'I am his servant.'

'So you represent his will here?'

'It was at Rama's behest that I came here to Lanka.'

'Very well. What is it you wish to tell us about your master?'

'The truth.'

Prahasta read the rumbling of discontent in the hall and interpreted it carefully. He injected the appropriate amount of scorn into his voice as he said, 'Why should we listen to you? You have slain a great many of our warriors and wreaked great destruction in our land. You are now an enemy of the kingdom. Why should we sit here listening to you rather than put an end to your life at once?'

Hanuman considered the question for a moment. 'Every warrior is prepared to die. But to die for a purpose is far more honourable than simply to die unknowingly. If you would understand the reason why I slew your rakshasas, then listen to my words. If you do not desire to know, then do with me as you will. I have already surrendered my life to you.'

Prahasta glanced quickly around the chamber. There was grudging silence now, and even the glowering stares held a tinge of curiosity. 'Very well, vanar. As you are an emissary of the arch-enemy of Lanka, and since we rakshasas honour the rules of war, we will hear your words. Make them brief and quick, though. And bear in mind that no insult to any Lankan will be brooked here. Speak one ill word against any of us, and you will speak no more.'

Hanuman nodded once. 'It is gracious of you to hear me out. I begin then, taking the name of my lord Rama.'

And he began to tell, in as brief a manner as he could, the story of Rama, sketching out the bare facts of his life. Prahasta was surprised to find himself listening with greater interest than he could have expected. From the relative silence in the hall, the same applied to the rest.

When Hanuman spoke of Ravana, every rakshasa in the hall listened intently. Even Prahasta was ready to respond should the vanar speak a single syllable of abuse. He knew that his own reputation, and likely his life, might rest on any such utterance. But he had permitted the vanar to speak and he must allow the prisoner a fair opportunity now.

To his amazement, Hanuman began praising Ravana. He lavished compliment after compliment upon the Lord of Lanka, extolling him in such elaborate detail that Prahasta had to remind himself that this was the same being who had killed Ravana's son only a little while earlier. And what was even more amazing, Hanuman seemed to mean every word he spoke. The vanar genuinely felt strongly that the king of rakshasas was an honourable and noble being at heart, that except for a wilful choice to pursue certain courses of action – 'paths of karma', Hanuman termed them – for as yet inscrutable reasons that he alone knew, the Lord of Lanka was a great personage deserving to be recorded as one of history's finest monarchs. This unexpected extolling provoked drawn breaths and startled grunts and stares from around the hall. Even Mandodhari and Indrajit seemed to be puzzled and confused by it. Only Ravana remained as he was, staring impassively and silently with all his ten faces at the vanar, his expressions inscrutable.

Finally Hanuman drew a long breath and added: 'All that you need to know, you know. All that remains now is for your king to release the lady Sita and allow her to return home to her husband Rama. You may view this as a warning if you will, or as a gentle offering of friendly advice. Release Sita, and you may yet be spared the coming devastation. Ignore this message, and not a single one of you will live to see the end of this long night of death.'

There was a long-drawn-out pause, largely because of the vanar's shocking praise of Ravana. Prahasta himself had to take several moments to consider how best to proceed. On one hand, the vanar had committed unspeakable outrages against the kingdom – for pity's sake, he had killed his own son, Jambumali, in the prime of his life. A veteran soldier who lived by the code of warfare, Prahasta could not possibly see the creature as anything other than an enemy, and as an enemy he deserved the harshest penalty available. But on the other hand, so effusive had been his outpouring of praise for Ravana, so well balanced his tale of Rama and the conflicts between the two over the years, so reasonable and empathetic his narration, that doubts had been raised that Prahasta never thought he could feel. The vanar had professed to speak the truth. And if that was the truth, then Rama was not the villainous, unrighteous dastard that they had all taken him to be, nor was their own lord Ravana the villain of the piece either. In fact, to hear Hanuman tell the tale, there was no clear black and white here. Only greys, with both Rama and Ravana painted in alluring and admirable shades ranging from pristine ivory to soft shadowy damask. Prahasta was finally facing the one thing no soldier should ever have to face: a genuine moral dilemma. And like all trained soldiers, he was incapable of solving it. For a soldier's only purpose is to follow orders. And in dharma, in morality, in the realm of spiritual truth, there are no orders or directions. Only guidelines and multiple choices, each one right in its own way, none wholly incorrect or wrong.

At a loss, he turned finally to the throne. 'My lord, you have heard the testimony of the emissary. What is your will now?'

Ravana spoke without hesitation or any flicker of doubt. 'Put him to death at once.'

19

After a moment of confused silence, during which everyone looked at each other to see how the other was responding, a ragged chorus of ayes broke out, followed soon after by a rousing roar of approval. Execution was always popular in Lanka.

Vibhisena sprang to his feet. 'My lord Ravana, on what grounds do you demand the execution of the vanar? It is neither moral nor sanctioned by the rules of war. The moral aspect is open to all of us to judge. And Marshal Prahasta will testify to the veracity of the kshatriya code that would never permit such a thing.'

But Marshal Prahasta was listening to the roars of the assembly and the silence of his king rather than the voice of his own conscience, and he kept silent, his eyes averted. Vibhisena strode up to the marshal, forcing him to meet his eyes. 'Prahasta, you are an honourable warrior. Speak! Is it right that we execute an emissary sent to us by another king? Is it not a violation of the rules of warfare?'

Prahasta glanced around nervously, but found the gumption to speak. 'That is so, Minister, but there are extenuating circumstances here . . .'

'If you mean the destruction and violence wreaked by the vanar, then yes, I accept that,' Vibhisena said. 'Punish him for those acts. Disfigure him. Scourge him. Shave his head and brand him and parade him through the streets. But you cannot take his life!'

Someone shouted angrily, 'What if we had killed him on the

field, as he killed our rakshasas? Would that have been acceptable under the rules of warfare, brother Vibhisena?'

'Yes,' Vibhisena agreed. 'That would have been acceptable. But that is not what we are discussing here. The vanar surrendered gracefully, and put himself in our hands, so he could deliver his missive from Rama. In fact, he made it clear from the very outset that he had no wish to fight, but none would heed his entreaties and bring him here to be heard. So he fought on as any warrior would.'

'Then he must be treated as a warrior, not an emissary,' said another objector.

'Aye,' echoed several others.

Vibhisena turned to Ravana. 'My lord, you have heard the vanar praise your character and your true nature. You yourself know that you are famed throughout the Asura races for your wisdom and kingship. Do not let this travesty of justice be implemented. Do what is just and fair.'

Indrajit sprang to his feet. 'My father is doing just that,' he said. 'He is implementing a wise and just decision. If you respect his kingship, then do not presume to question his verdict. Let the vanar be put to death.'

A chorus of resounding approval seconded his words.

Vibhisena continued to appeal to Ravana directly, ignoring everyone else. 'My lord, my king . . . my brother,' he added forcefully. 'I feel the pain of Akshay Kumar's death too. He was my nephew. I watched him grow and play and learn. I share your grief at his loss. But he was a warrior, and he died a warrior's death. He will be honoured and commemorated for ever. His name will come to be taken by any hero who seeks to prove that he is the epitome of beauty, grace and martial skill. But you are not only a father. You are a king first and foremost, and as a king, it is your moral duty to put righteousness before your personal ends. If you desire revenge, then go seek the person who sent this emissary here. Fight Rama! Kill Rama if you will. Or better yet, send out emissaries of your own, tell them to go to Rama's camp and wage a battle with

his forces. But if you do this, if you kill this emissary after he
has surrended peaceably and trusted your fairness and morality,
then you will be casting a slur on your own name that will
never be erased. You have heard how highly this vanar thinks
of you, how effusive his praises. He considers you a paragon
of dharma, as virtuous a personage as his own master, whom
he compares to a deva. That is akin to calling you a deva too!
How can you repay such veneration with vengeance? I pray to
you, reconsider your judgement. Inflict any pain or penalty
upon this vanar for the violence he has done, but do not put
him to death and spoil your own good name.'

The court exploded in a flurry of outrage, some rakshasas
spewing ichor and venom and others yelling at a hundred different
pitches until the din was deafening.

Ravana raised a finger.

Silence fell as suddenly as a dropped stone.

'I have listened to your arguments, Vibhisena. And for once,
I agree with you. The vanar's actions are deserving of punishment. But because he is an emissary and because he willingly
submitted himself and allowed himself to be bound and brought
here, it would be morally reprehensible to execute him. He will
not be killed. Instead, we will punish him in another way,
appropriate to his actions.'

The silence continued, but its quality altered to one of stunned
shock. Nobody could believe what they were hearing, least of
all Vibhisena himself.

He found his voice at last. 'You are great and merciful, my
lord Ravana. You will be eternally praised for your wisdom
shown at this juncture of history. Your name will be recorded
and remembered for all posterity as a king who upheld dharma
and the laws of warcraft.'

He turned to Hanuman, beaming happily at the vanar.
'Messenger of Rama, remember this day well. For it is the day
your life was spared by a righteous king.'

Hanuman dipped his head. 'I did not doubt it.' He looked
up at Ravana.

Indrajit stared from the vanar to Vibhisena, then at his father. The look of disbelief on his features was priceless. The prince was a fighting man, better suited to the battlefield than the parlour – or the sabha hall. He seemed not to know how to deal with this turnaround. He turned to look at his mother. Vibhisena saw his lip tremble.

Mandodhari rose and came to her son's aid. 'My king,' she said in a tone that could have passed for either arctic coldness or volcanic rage, 'if this is your judgement, then permit me to enquire, what is the punishment you desire to be implemented on the vanar, *appropriate to his actions*?'

She did not have to spell out the reason why she had emphasised that last phrase. Vibhisena could see the hurt in her heart, the pain of a mother who had seen her younger, and in many ways her best, son slaughtered like any common foot-soldier. He felt a moment's guilt at his arguments, the more so because he had won so unexpectedly, but he stayed his course, firmly resolved that he had done the right thing. This reversal of Ravana's verdict, however painful it might be to his sister-in-law personally, was one small reparation for all the wrongs that had been done to Rama and his family by the Lord of Lanka and his minions.

Ravana turned his rack of heads to Mandodhari. He still remained aloof, detached from the fury of the arguments that had raged. Vibhisena did not understand it, especially since Ravana was usually the most passionate of personalities. But a part of him felt glad of it. Perhaps the vanar was right after all. He had perceived a side to his brother that even he, Vibhisena, the eternal optimist, had all but forgotten existed. Perhaps Ravana was balancing his karma after all.

'Vibhisena said earlier that the code of warfare dictates that an emissary who commits bodily harm or violence upon the people to whom he brings his missive can be treated harshly. He can be beaten, whipped, injured, interrogated, shaved and branded, and humiliated. The vanar has already been soundly beaten by Indrajit. And as any of you who has ever faced my son in combat must know, a beating at Indrajit's hands is less preferable than death at the hands of most other warriors.' One of his heads smiled a very small smile as it looked at Indrajit. 'He does not know when to stop.'

'Is that all?' Mandodhari asked incredulously. 'He has been beaten and that is punishment enough?'

The smiling head lost its smile. Ravana looked at Hanuman. 'Vanar. What is the part of your body that is most precious to you?'

Hanuman bowed his head, thinking. Vibhisena was flooded with a rush of warmth at the vanar's sincerity. He will answer truthfully, he thought, even though the information he provides may lead to a terrible result.

'A vanar's tail is the most prized part of his body,' Hanuman replied. 'Some vanars even believe it is the repository of all their strength and virility. At the very least, a tail is a symbol of pride and beauty, and a means of gauging stature among my kind.'

Ravana received this information without any change in expression. 'And what is the weapon that you fear the most?'

Hanuman sighed. 'We vanars do not like to admit to our links to the monkey races, but the truth is that we are more closely linked to them than to any other species. And like all monkeykind, we mortally dread fire. Even today, we prefer to eat our food uncooked than go near a flame. I have overcome that innate fear to a large extent, thanks to my self-mastery. But deep within me, it resides still. I have an abiding fear of it and I believe that whenever I die, my destruction will be brought about by the weapon of Agni, lord of flame.'

Ravana seemed pleased with the answer.

'In that case,' he said, 'we shall set your tail on fire and burn it off. And when it is scorched to a stub, you will be sent back to your master. Let your friends and family and comrades see you with your burned stub of a tail, pathetic and miserable. It will also mark you out on the field of battle so that one of us may seek you out easily and take revenge for the slaying of our fallen mates.'

Vibhisena stared up at Ravana. For the second time in as many moments, his brother had done a remarkable thing. He had given a perfect judgement. Not only was his chosen penalty truly fitting and sanctioned by the terms of the warrior's code, it was shrewd as well. Among the rakshasa races, maiming or crippling was considered more humiliating than death. There were virtually no crippled rakshasas in Lanka, because none who suffered such injuries in war or accident could bear to go on living afterwards. And even those few who dared to outrage the mores of their culture by continuing to live – a right which Vibhisena and his brahmin comrades defended vigorously against all odds – often met sudden ends, mostly at the hands of their own family members. By ordering that the vanar's most prized limb should be destroyed, Ravana would not only fulfil the demands of dharma and just kingship, he would earn the respect of all rakshasas.

The cheers of acceptance and approval that greeted the decision confirmed Vibhisena's assessment.

But there was one thing that tainted the beauty of Ravana's judgement.

Fire rarely restricted itself to one place. Even though the royal edict called for only the vanar's tail to be set on flame, how would they ensure that the vanar himself was not wholly consumed by the fire, or, at the very least, injured in other parts of his body as well? Vibhisena looked at the vanar, covered with a liberal coating of furry hair all over, right to the tip of his long bushy tail, and thought that Ravana might well have outsmarted them all.

Sita was ready when they came for her. She had said her final prayers and prepared her mind and spirit for the end. She had not doubted that it would come soon. After the fracas at the ashoka grove and the escape of the vanar, she had been escorted quickly but non-violently to a new prison. It was a cold, stark place, made of marble and lined with great white pillars, and the ceiling was so endlessly high that she could actually see clouds – real clouds – drifting above. There was no relief, no greenery around her or soil beneath her feet, even though she knew everything here was only artificial, and even the pillars held nothing up. It was a museum without any displays, a prison that entrapped because it was as vast and empty as a desert, with nowhere to run to.

Even the guards who had ordered her to accompany them through the magic portal that led here kept their distance, standing in a great circle several hundred yards away, their backs turned to her, spears and swords held ready, as if they expected an army of vanars to attempt to rescue her at any minute. She walked the cold marble floor endlessly, then sat and prayed to calm her soul. She did not know what had happened to Hanuman. Had he left Lanka? Had he been captured, killed, wounded, imprisoned? A variety of alternatives passed through her mind as the hours passed. She received no information, nobody spoke to her. Even the guards who brought her food and drink at regular intervals, neither of which she touched, simply put the vessels down on the marble floor and went back through the portal, which winked shut at once.

The portal opened now, letting in light of a different hue from the colourless, mindless illumination of this hellish place. But instead of the guards she had been expecting to lead her to her promised execution, Ravana himself stepped through. He was alone.

The portal shut behind him and he came forward, stopping several yards away.

'Have you considered my offer?'

She rose to her feet. She wished to look up to him as little as possible. Even so, she still had to raise her gaze by over a yard above her normal line of sight. 'It was not an offer worthy of consideration.'

He was silent a moment. 'I expected you to be wiser than this.'

'I am as you find me, neither more nor less. Perhaps you expected me to be something that I am not.'

'I expected you to be considerate of the life of your unborn child.'

She clenched her jaw to keep from shouting. It galled her that he even knew of the life she bore in her womb. How dare he speak of it with such feigned *gentleness*. As if he cared what happened to her or her offspring? 'Our child,' she said levelly, 'is Rama's and my responsibility, not your concern.'

'But it *is* my concern. For you are condemned to be executed. And if you are executed, then your unborn child will die as well. But that need not come to pass.'

She permitted herself a bitter smile. 'I was not the one who condemned us to death. If I recall correctly, it was you who had a hand in that verdict.'

'It was my people's choice. They were baying for the blood of the vanar too. After the havoc he wreaked in my palace, they wished him to be executed summarily as well. But my better judgement prevailed over the mob mentality. I said that it would be wrong to slay an emissary. He was permitted to deliver his message, and now he is being allowed to return to your husband.'

Her heart increased pace so suddenly, her head began to swim. Could it be true? 'Return?'

'Yes,' he said. 'Despite your misconceptions and your prejudice against rakshasas, we are an honourable race. In fact, if you like, you can view the vanar's punishment and his departure with your own eyes. I can arrange it.'

'Punishment?'

'The rules of war call for an emissary who has instigated violence to be punished. He himself was allowed to choose the method of his punishment. It is nothing very severe.'

She did not ask the obvious question, merely waited in silence till one of his faces smiled slyly and said, 'His tail is to be set on fire.'

She was surprised. That really did not sound very severe. After all, she was condemned to be eaten alive. A tail-burning paled in comparison.

'Will you watch it?' he asked. 'It is time.'

Without waiting for her answer, he gestured sorcerously, and the marbled floor several yards before her split with a resounding crack, as if struck by invisible lightning. The crack travelled to the left and the right, until the entire realm in which they stood was riven by a great crevasse. A deep rumbling came from far beneath her feet, and then the crevasse expanded itself with a methodical grinding motion, the two halves of the realm separating as neatly as a stone door being drawn open by unseen winches and gears, hauled by invisible horses. But even a million horses could hardly move such a great weight, for, she realised suddenly, the entire tower was cracking open, split vertically into two perfect halves. A railing emerged from the edge of the crevasse before her, rising to sufficient height that someone as tall as she could lean upon it and look over the edge without fear of falling.

Ravana walked with her to this balustrade, and she peered over, hardly knowing whether to be afraid or excited at what she might see.

20

Hanuman experienced a moment of pure terror as the flame was brought towards him. His hands were still bound before him, and his legs were shackled loosely. They had wrapped his tail in coarsecloth rags and dipped the whole in oil. He felt more constricted by the binding on his tail than by those on his wrists or ankles. But when they lit the torch and carried it towards him, he forgot about everything else. For one heart-stopping moment, the flame was all he saw, flickering like the hungry tongue of a primordial beast, licking the air, feeding on it greedily, seeking to consume. He reverted to the state he had been in when he first began spying on Rama in the wilds of Janasthana, a scraggly vanar only one step removed from a monkey, terrified of his own shadow at sunset and sun-up.

They had brought him to the lowermost level of the tower; he recognised some signs from the time he had walked around its base with the shapeshifter, sniffing and examining its substance. Then the tower itself had cracked apart and the two halves separated. Looking up, he could see the whole length of it, all the levels visible, hundreds upon hundreds, rising up to the very clouds. It was a kingdom unto itself.

But he was about to be taken through the old city. The real Lanka. The wide boulevard before him was filled to bursting with rakshasas, citizens and soldiers alike – in Lanka, there was little difference between the two, because when war came, all fought side by side, even younguns. The windows and galleries and balconies of the mansions and houses lining the street were filled with watchers too, eager to witness the slayer of Akshay Kumar being punished. Although 'punished' was not the word he heard repeated often, over and over again. The word he heard was 'executed'. His suspicions had grown when they bound his tail in cloth, and when they dipped it in oil, they were confirmed. Once they set his tail on fire, there was no way he could prevent the fire from spreading to the rest of his fur. He had thought Ravana's change of verdict a sign of the rakshasa's fairness and wisdom. He now thought otherwise.

But he had permitted this. It was a fair verdict in theory, if not in implementation. Even the brahmin rakshasa who had argued his case so heatedly had said that an emissary who committed violence must be punished. He had known as much; it was why he had submitted to Indrajit's brutal battering. All that mattered then was delivering his missive to Ravana personally, and he had done so.

The rakshasa holding him tight and the one carrying the torch were kumbha-rakshasas. Myriad reflections of the torchlight danced in their serpentine eyes. 'This is to repay you for the slaying of Jambumali, best-born of all kumbhas,' said one. 'And the slaughter of our comrades.'

His companion snarled. The reek of his breath filled the vanar's nostrils. 'If you ask me, even this is too good for you. If it were up to us kumbhas, we would ask that our lord be awakened.'

'Aye,' said a third. 'Then we could see how boldly he faces Kumbhakarna himself!'

The first kumbha made a lewd comment about vanars wetting their nether fur at the very sight of Kumbhakarna, then from somewhere on a level above, the watching War Marshal Prahasta called them to attention. They shut up.

Prahasta read out a short proclamation, announcing the names of the commanding rakshasas slain by Hanuman and the legions he had wiped out. He ended with the name of Akshay Kumar, at which the crowd roared angrily. They were echoed by roaring for yojanas around. It sounded like every single living rakshasa in the city-state of Lanka was out to watch him being cremated alive.

Then a chant began, slowly at first, and halting, rising gradually, then building into a crescendo that filled the sky and seemed to reach up to the clouds themselves. It was a repetition of two simple words, over and over:

'Burn him! Burn him! Burn him! Burn him!'

So intense was the wave of hatred that emanated from their screaming throats that the very flame of the torch tilted away.

Some order or gesture from up on the tower silenced them. They fell quiet, eyes gleaming and glistening eagerly.

The voice of Prahasta ordered the kumbhas to light the vanar's tail.

Hanuman saw the kumbha holding the flickering torch leer one last time at him as he walked around behind him. When he went out of sight, he felt his heart sink, and for one brief instant he felt utterly alone, misunderstood, incompetent, useless, pathetic. He was only a vanar after all. His father and mother were dead. He had finally found a being who believed in him enough to entrust him with a great responsibility, who had given him this one mission to fulfil, and he had failed in that. Failed utterly. Sita was still Ravana's prisoner, so bereft of hope that she herself did not expect to survive until Rama arrived. And Lanka's forces were far, far greater than any of them had ever imagined. Through his visionary powers, he had seen entire levels where great armies of rakshasas drilled and trained endlessly, lakhs upon lakhs of them, millions all told. His fellow vanars would be sadly outmatched. The bears might fare better, but on the whole, Rama's army was little more than a great gathering of . . . animals. There was no other word for it. Unarmed animals, untrained in warfare. These were rakshasas, the fiercest fighting race in the three worlds. Led by Ravana, the being who had invaded even the heavenly realm and destroyed Indra-lok. His son was named Indrajit because he had defeated Lord Indra himself, the god of warfare! Even if Nala's bridge was completed quickly and the armies of Rama crossed to

Lanka soon enough to save the lady Sita, it would be a slaughter rather than a battle.

Unless.

He felt the heat of the torch at the tip of his tail. He smelled the crisp, pungent reek of his own fur burning, the smells of his sweat and bodily odour mingled with the oil and the unmistakable stinging stench of the fire itself, for as every vanar knew, each fire had its own smell. His smelled like charred corpse.

Unless he could return to Rama, and tell him what he had learned about Ravana, about his forces, about his magic. About his secret.

The tip of the tail caught, then the edge of the cloth, and then the oil itself ignited, and the whole went up in a roar. The crowd echoed the roar and the din was deafening. The kumbhas laughed in his ears, their foul spittle falling on to his face, his snout.

Unless he could even the odds a little. Tip the balance just so. And in the process, show them that even a single vanar armed with weapons of faith and dharma could stand up to their combined might. That way, when Rama arrived, the armies of Lanka might hesitate a fraction before starting the slaughter, and in such a war, even that tiny fraction of doubt could be leveraged into an advantage.

And there was a chance he could do a bit more than that as well.

He felt the fire scorch his entire tail now, the whole length of it burning quite thoroughly. The kumbhas had turned him around so the watching hordes could see. He was forced to show his back to the boulevard, which made him face the tower. It lay yawning like a length of bread split open and put to stand on its end. He could see tiny antlike shadows of rakshasas on every one of the hundreds of levels, waving and cheering and applauding and chanting. 'Burn, vanar, burn!' they were shouting. The guards continued hustling him till he had completed the full turn and was facing the boulevard again. Now he was truly a dancing monkey act put on display for the viewing pleasure of millions.

'Burn, vanar, burn!' they sang.

And he felt the excruciating agony of his tail, his flesh and blood and skin and fur, that part of himself that was to a vanar no less than a hand or a leg, even more valuable than those limbs, for it was the mark of a vanar, his badge of race.

'BURN, VANAR, BURN!'

And now the fire was creeping up to the top of its length, to the place where the tail met his lower spine. In another instant, his nether fur would ignite and then he would be lost.

He closed his eyes, shut out the deafening roar, and focused. Willing his tail to do as he desired. A simple enough thing for a vanar who had mastered his inner powers. Who had overcome his self-doubt and realised his true self-worth. A vanar who served . . .

'Rama.'

The kumbhas were the first to see it. One of them said something to the others, who bent and peered and stared disbelievingly. All three of them squatted down and tried to get a better look at what was happening. Then, as one, they looked up at his face, and the look on their features was not disbelief, but fear.

He was the slayer of Akshay Kumar. And Jambumali. And the seven champions and the five generals. And legions of fierce rakshasa warriors.

The kumbhas backed away. A shout from above made them glance up briefly. It was Prahasta, enquiring what was going on. They shouted an incomprehensible reply, then pointed to Hanuman, to his tail. They continued to back away, almost falling over in their eagerness to put as much distance as possible between themselves and the vanar. Prahasta yelled at them furiously, ordering them to stop.

Hanuman had crushed Mount Mahendra beneath his feet, leapt a hundred yojanas across the ocean, confronted the flying mountain, and outwitted the great sea serpent. He had endured the temptations of the palace of pleasures and the realm of intoxication and had triumphed over both.

The crowd saw it now. The chanting died out and they began to shout to one another, pointing, gesticulating, staring. Hanuman took one step forward, then another, then yet another. The fire was no longer lapping at his back, it was well away from him.

He took several more steps, then stopped and looked back.

The burning end of his tail, still wrapped in oiled cloth, lay back there, several yards behind him. The rest of its length, extending to his back, trailed along the street. As he watched, the flames spread further, like a fire finding its way along the length of a fuse.

It needed to be longer. Much longer.

He willed it once again. It took a great effort to expand just the tail, not all of himself. But he did it. The tail grew ten yards, then twenty, then forty . . . And kept on growing.

He began to walk towards the crowd. Directly at the hordes of watching rakshasas.

They parted quickly, to make a pathway for him to pass through. All of them were in awe of him, staring at the slayer of their great champions. Some at the back of the crowd peeled away and ran. Those at the fore and centre had no choice, and in any case, they were too eager now to see what he did next.

He walked down the street, his tail growing longer and longer behind him, the fire growing at almost the same pace. Then he began to run, to leap, and bound. Now he allowed himself to grow. To expand himself. Twice his size. Four times. His chains and bindings fell to pieces like confetti. A dozen times. A hundred times . . .

The crowds broke at last. They began to run screaming from the giant vanar with the leagues-long burning tail.

He laughed and laughed at their fear. At their panic. They stampeded. Not a single one dared stop and confront him. The whole scenario was too bizarre for them to comprehend. A giant vanar, growing larger every eyewink, with a burning tail now a mile in length, now two miles, now ten . . . What were they supposed to do? How were they supposed to fight him?

He flew up into the air, the size of a mountain now. But still he continued growing, his tail elongating at as fast a rate. It snaked through the whole of Lanka now, like an endless serpentine coil, burning. He twitched it this way, and a street full of marbled mansions went up in flames. He flicked it that way, and an avenue of stables blazed. Houses, palaces, camps, parks, he set them all on fire. In mere moments, the whole of Lanka was burning. The fire lit up the night sky for yojanas around, illuminating even the night-darkened ocean's white swells beyond.

He stood in the midst of the burning city and continued to expand himself. His head rose so high, he could barely hear the screams of the frightened, stampeding Lankans any longer. They were far below, minuscule pawns in a great game of fire and death.

He faced the tower. He was still only half its height.

He grew faster, shooting up through the clouds to the stars.

Finally, when the clouds were around his waist, and the city below was barely visible, when the back of his feet rested on the gritty sand of Lanka's southern shore, he was head to head with the tower.

On the uppermost level, in a realm of pristine whiteness, the lady Sita was standing, leaning upon a balustrade of white marble.

Hanuman bowed to her, folding his palms together. 'My lady, I am relieved that you are safe from the fire. I would not wish you to be harmed by it.'

She smiled and returned his greeting. 'The lord Ravana is good enough to keep me safe. At least so long as he desires me kept safe.' She glanced around, as if making sure the subject of her words was not standing behind her. 'He was here until but a moment ago. I think he has gone to attempt to undo the havoc you have caused.' She smiled, and his heart leapt to see it, so wondrous a thing was it to behold. 'Again,' she added.

'It is my parting gift to you, my lady,' he said. 'Now I will go back to Rama and tell him that I have seen you here safe and sound and much else besides.'

'Go, my brave Hanuman. And tell him to come quickly. And

then let him wreak havoc too. You have lit the funeral pyre of Lanka. Rama must inter the corpse and turn it to ashes.'

He bowed one last time, then said to her, 'My lady, hold on tightly to the railing before you.'

She did as he asked, without questioning. He reached out and grasped a great section of the marbled level on which Sita stood, and wrenched it apart from the rest of the tower. It came free with a peculiar screaming sound, not like marble cracking, but like metal being torn apart by a great force. Then he turned and sought out a place near the outer wall of Lanka which he recognised even from so high up by the shining gold and many gems, all of which reflected the flames of the burning city. There he put down the section of marbled floor, so gently that the lady Sita was not discomfited one bit. She smiled up at him.

Then he turned back to face the tower, crouched down, and leapt.

He landed on top of the tower itself. He teetered there a moment, getting his balance. When he was sure of his equilibrium, he crouched down, then hopped. He rose up a few leagues, then landed on the tower. It groaned and protested loudly. He leapt again, then came thumping down on it. It screamed now. He continued jumping up and down, just as he had done before departing the mainland, building up momentum for his great flight across the ocean. Each time he leapt up higher, and each time he came down, he crushed the tower further. It began to shudder, then to collapse on to itself, whole levels demolished, pushed one into the other. The entire island thundered and echoed with the reveberations of his jumps, and the screaming rakshasas fleeing the flames below were further startled by the amazing sight of the giant Hanuman jumping up and down, pounding on the great tower.

Finally, he launched himself into the air. 'Jai Shri Ram,' he bellowed.

Looking back over his shoulder, he saw that he had pounded the tower into the ground on which it had stood. All that remained of it was debris and shattered refuse. Soon even that was obscured by the gouting smoke from a thousand fires. He let his long trailing tail fall into the ocean, dousing the fire. He relished the cool relief for a moment, then drew his tail into himself, to a length proportionate to his size, and sighed. The night wind was cool and refreshing on his face and limbs. The sky was clear and cloudless. And the ocean stretched before him, vast and dark and empty, a desert of brine demanding to be crossed.

He flew back to Rama.

GLOSSARY

This 21st-century retelling of The Ramayana *freely uses words and phrases from Sanskrit as well as other ethnic Indian languages. Many of these have widely varying meanings depending on the context in which they're used – and even depending on whether they were used in times ancient, medieval or present-day. This glossary explains their meanings according to their contextual usage in this book rather than their strict dictionary definitions. AKB.*

aagya: permission.
aangan: entrance; courtyard.
aaram: rest.
aarti: prayer ceremony.
aatma: spirit; soul.
aatma-hatya: suicide.
acamana: ritual offering of water to Surya the sun-god at sunrise and sunset.
a-dharma: the opposite of dharma; unrighteous; an action or belief that is against the natural laws.
agar: black gummy stuff of which joss sticks are made.
agarbatti: incense prayer sticks made of agar; joss sticks.
agni: fire; fire-god.
agnihotra: fire-sacrifice; offering to the fire-god agni. Originally, in Vedic times, this meant an animal-sacrifice. Later, as the Vedic faith evolved into vegetarian-favouring Hinduism, it became any ritual fire-offering. The origin of the current-day Hindu practice of anointing a fire with ghee (clarified butter) and other ritual offerings.
ahimsa: the opposite of violence; pacifism.
Aja-putra: literally, son of Aja, in which Aja was the previous Suryavansha king of Ayodhya; it was common to refer to Aryas as 'son of (father's name)'; e.g. Rama would be addressed as 'Dasarathaputra'.
akasa-chamber: from the word 'akasa' meaning sky. A room with

the ceiling open to the sky, used for relaxation.

akhada: wrestling square.

akshohini: a division of the army with representation from the four main forces – battle elephants, chariots with archers, armoured cavalry, and infantry.

amar: eternal.

amrit: nectar of the devas; the elixir of eternal life, one of many divine wonders produced by the churning of the oceans in ancient pre-Vedic times. The central cause of the original hostility between the devas and the Asuras, in which the Asuras sought the amrit in order to gain immortality like the devas but the devas refused them the amrit.

an-anga: bodiless.

anarth ashram: orphanage.

anashya: indestructible.

angadiya: a messenger of Prince Angad; loosely, a courier.

an-atmaa: soulless.

angoor: grape.

ang-vastra: length of cloth covering upper body – similar to the upper folds of a Roman toga; any bodily garment.

anjan: kohl; kajal.

apsara: any of countless beautiful danseuses in the celestial court of lord Indra, king of the devas.

aranya: wilderness.

arghya: the traditional washing of the feet, used to ceremonially welcome a visitor, literally by washing the dust of the road off his feet.

artha: meaning, purpose, motive.

Taken together, artha, karma and dharma form the trifold foundation of Vedic philosophy.

Arya: literally, noble or pure. Commonly mispelled and mispronounced as 'Aryan'. A group of ancient Indian warrior tribes believed to have flourished for several millennia in the period before Christ. Controversially thought by some historians to have been descended from Teutonics who migrated to the Indian sub-continent and later returned – although current Indian historical scholars reject this view and maintain that the Aryas were completely indigenous to the region. Recent archaeological evidence seems to confirm that the Aryas migrated *from* India to Europe, rather than the other way around. Both views have their staunch supporters.

asana: a yogic posture, or series of postures similar to the kathas of martial arts – which are historically believed to have originated from South-Central India and have the same progenesis as yoga.

ashirwaad: blessings.

Ashok: a boy's given name.

ashubh: inauspicious.

ashwamedha: the horse ceremony. A declaration of supremacy issued by a king, tantamount to challenging one's neighbouring kingdoms to submit to one's superior strength.

astra: weapon.

Asura: anti-god: literally, a-Sura or anti-Sura, where Sura meant the clan of the gods and anyone who stood against them was referred to as an a-Sura. Loosely used to describe any demonic creature or evil being.

atee-sundar: very beautiful. Well done or well said.

atma-brahman: soul force; one's given or acquired spiritual energy.

atman: soul; spirit.

avatar: incarnation.

Awadhi: Ayodhyan commonspeak; the local language, a dialect of Hindi.

awamas: the moon's least visible phase.

awamas ki raat: moonless night.

Ayodhya: the capital city of Kosala.

Ayodhya-naresh: master of Ayodhya. King.

ayushmaanbhav: long life; generally used as a greeting from an elder to a younger, as in 'live long'.

baalu: bear (see also rksa).

badmash: rascal, scoundrel, mischievous one.

bagh: big cat, interchangeably used for lion, tiger and most other related species of large, predatory cat.

bagheera: panther or leopard.

baithak-sthan: rest-area; lounge.

balak: boy.

balidaan: sacrifice.

balu: colloquial term for bear.

bandara: monkey; any simian species.

barkha: rainstorm.

ber: a variety of wild Indian berry, yellowish-reddish outside, white inside, very juicy and sweetish.

bete: child.

beti: daughter.

bhaang: an intoxicating concoction made by mixing the leaf of the poppy plant with hand-churned buttermilk. Typically consumed at Holi celebrations by adult Hindus. Also smoked in hookahs or traditional bongs as pot.

bhaangra: robust and vigorous north Indian (punjabi) folk dance.

bhabhi: brother's wife or close friend's wife.

bhade bhaiya: older brother.

bhagyavan: blessed one; fortunate woman.

bhai: brother.

bhajan: a devotional chant.

bhakti: devotion.

bharat-varsha: the original name for India; literally, *land of bharata* after the ancient Arya king Bharata.

bhashan: lecture.

bhayanak: frightening, terrifying.

bhes-bhav: physical appearance.

bhindi: ladyfinger, okra.

bhojanshalya: dining hall.

bhor: extreme; as in *bhor suvah*: extreme (early) morning.

bhung: useless; negated.

bindi: a blood-red circular dot worn by Hindu women on their foreheads to indicate their married status. Now worn in a variety of colours and shapes as a fashion accessory.

brahmachari: see brahmacharya.

brahmacharya: a boy or man who devotes the first 25 years of his life to prayer, celibacy, and the study of the Vedic sciences under the tutelage of a brahmin guru.

brahman: the substance of which all matter is created. Literally, the stuff of existence.

brahmarishi: an enlightened holy man who has attained the highest level of grace; literally, a rishi or holy man, whom Brahma, creator of all things, has blessed.

brahmin: the priestly caste. Highest in order.

broken-sur: broken-head, where 'sur' is coll. for head.

buddhi: intellect; mind; intelligence.

chacha: uncle; father's younger brother.

chaddar: sheet.

Chaitra: the month of spring; roughly corresponds to the latter half of March and first half of April.

charas: opium.

chaturta: cleverness.

chaukat: a square. Most Indian houses were designed as a square, with an entrance on one wall and the house occupying the other three walls. In the centre was an open chaukat where visitors (or intruders) could be seen from any room in the house.

chaupat: an ancient Indian war strategy dice game, universally acknowledged to be the original inspiration for chess, played on a flat piece of cloth or board by rolling bone-dice to decide moves, involving pieces representing the four akshohini of the Arya army – elephants, chariot, foot-soldiers, knights.

chillum: toke; a smoking-pipe used to inhale charas (opium).

chini kulang: a variety of bird.

chital: a variety of spotted deer found in the forests of the Himalayan foothills, considered the most beautiful of all deer.

choli: breast-cloth; a garment used to cover a woman's upper body.

chotti: pigtail.

chowkidari: the act of guarding a person or place like a sentry or chowkidar.

chudail: banshee; female ghost; witch.

chunna: lime-powder or a mixture of lime-powder and water; used to whitewash outer or inner walls; also eaten in edible form in paan or mixed directly with tobacco.

chunnri: a strip of cloth used by a woman to cover her breasts and cleavage, also used to cover the head before elders or during prayer.

chupp-a-chuppi: hide and seek.

crore: one hundred hundred thousand; one hundred lakhs; ten million.

daiimaa: brood-mother, clanmother, wet nurse, governess. A woman serving first as midwife to the expecting mother, then later as wet-nurse, governess and au pair.

dakshina/guru-dakshina: ritual payment by a kshatriya to a brahmin on demand.

daku: dacoit; highway bandit; jungle thief.

danav: a species of Asura.

darbha: a variety of thick grass.

darshan: the Hindu act of gazing reverentially upon the face of a divine idol, an essential part of worship; literally, *viewing*.

dasya: slave; servant.

Deepavali: the predominant Indian Hindu festival, the festival of lights. Also known as Diwali.

desh: land; country; nation.

deva: god. Several Indian devas have their equivalents in Greek and Norse mythology.

dev-astra: weapon of the devas; divine weapon.

dev-daasi/devdasi: prostitute.

devi: goddess.

dhanush-baan: bow and arrows.

dharma: sacred duty. A morally binding code of behaviour. The cornerstone of the Vedic faith.

dharam-patni: wife; literally, 'partner in dharma'.

dharamshala: a traditional resthouse on Indian roads in times past, where travellers could partake of free shelter and simple nourishment. Literally, 'shelter of dharma'.

dhobi: washerman (of clothes).

dhol: drum.

dollee: palanquin; travelling chair.

dosa: a flat crisp rice-pancake, a staple of South Indian cuisine.

dhoti: a white cotton lower garment, worn usually by Indian men.

diya: clay oil lamp.

drishti: vision; view; sight.

dumroo: a small x-shaped drum with sounding tassels. Dumroo-wallah, or He who Plays The Dumroo, refers to Lord Shiva the Destroyer, who plays the dumroo to make all us monkeys (mortals) dance to his rhythm.

gaddha: donkey.

gaddhi: seat; literally, a cushion.

gaja-gamini: elephant-footed.

gandharva: forest nymph; when malevolent, also a species of Asura.

ganga-jal: sacred Ganges water.

ganja: charas; opium.

garuda: eagle, after the mythic giant magical eagle Garuda, the first-of-his-name, a major demi-god believed to be the creator and patron deity of all birdkind.

gauthan: village; any rural settlement.

gayaka: singer.

Gayatri: a woman's given name; also the most potent mantra of Hindus, recited before beginning any venture, or even at the start of one's day to ensure strength and success.

gharial: a sub-species of reptilian predator unique to the Indian sub-continent, similar to crocodiles and alligators in body but with a sword-shaped mouth.

ghat: literally, low-lying hill. Burning ghat usually refers to the places in which Hindu bodies are traditionally cremated.

gobi: common term for cauliflower as well as cabbage.

gotra: sub-caste.

govinda: goatherd.

gulmohur: a species of Asian tree that produces beautiful red flowers in winter.

guru/guruji: a teacher, generally associated with a sage. The 'ji' is a sign of respect; it literally means 'sir', and can be added after any male name or title: eg, Ramaji.

guru-dakshina: see dakshina.

guru-dev: guru who is as a god, or deva; divine teacher.

gurukul: a guru's hermitage for scholars; a forest ashram school where students resided, maintaining the ashram and its grounds while being taught through lectures in the open air.

gurung: a variety of bird.

hai: ave; hail; woe. An exclamation.

halwai: maker of sweets.

hatya: murder.

havan: sacrificial offering.

hawaldar: constable.

himsa: violence, bodily harm.

Holi: a major Indian festival and feast day, celebrated to mark the end of winter and the first day of spring, the last rest day before the start of the harvest season; celebrated with the throwing of coloured powders and coloured waters symbolising the colours of spring, and the eating of sweetmeats (mithai) and the drinking of bhaang.

Ikshwaku: the original kshatriya ancestral clan from which the Suryavansha line sprang. After the founder, Ikshwaaku.

imli ka butta: tamarind.

Indra: god of thunder and war. Equivalent to the Norse god Thor or the Greek god Ares.

indra-dhanush: literally, Indra's bow; a rainbow.

ishta: religious offering.

jadugar: magician.

jagganath: relentless and unstoppable Hindu god of war; another name for Ganesha; juggernaut.

Jai: boy's given name; hail.

Jai Mata Ki: Praise be to the Mother-Goddess.

Jai Shree: Praise be to Sri (or Shree), Divine Creator.

jaise aagya: as you wish; your wish is my command.

jal murghi: a variety of Indian bird; literally, water-fowl.

jal-bartan: vessel for drinking water.

jaldi: quickly; in haste.

jalebi: Indian sweet, made by pouring dough into a tureen of boiling oil in spiralling shapes, removed, then drenched in sugar-syrup.

jamun: a common variety of Indian berry-like fruit, purplish-black, deliciously sour.

janayu: ceremony marking the coming of age, usually of a brahmin male. Also known as thread ceremony.

japmala: a beaded prayer chain used for rote (jap) recitations.

Jat: a proud, violently inclined, North Indian clan.

jatayu: vulture, after Jatayu, the first-of-its-name, the giant hybrid man-vulture, second only to Garuda in its leadership of birdkind.

jhadi-buti: literally, herbs and roots; herbal medicines.

jhadoo: Indian broom.

jhilli: a variety of Indian bird.

ji: yes (respectfully).

johar ka roti: a flat roasted pancake made from barley-flour.

johari: jeweller.

kaand: a section of a story; literally, a natural joint on a long stick of sugarcane or bamboo, used to mark off a count.

kabbadi: a game played by children and adults alike. India's official national sport.

kachua: tortoise.

kaho: speak.

kai-kai: harsh cawing sound.

kairee: a raw green mango, used to make pickle.

kajal: kohl.

kala: black.

kala jaadu: black magic.

kala kendra: art council.

kalakaar: artist.

kalarappa: ancient South Indian art of man-to-man combat, universally acknowledged to be the progenitor of Far Eastern martial arts – learned by visiting Chinese delegates and later adapted and evolved into the modern martial arts.

kalash: a brass or golden pot of a specific design, filled with rice and anointed ritually, tipped over by a new bride to bring prosperity into the house during her homecoming ceremony. A symbol of the good fortune brought by a new wife to her husband's home.

Kali: the goddess of vengeance. An avatar of the universal devi.

Kali-Yuga: the Age of Kali, prophesied to be the last and worst age of human civilisation.

Kama: god of love. The equivalent of the Greek Eros or sometimes Cupid.

kamasutra: the science of love.

karmic: pertaining to one's karma.

karya: deeds.

kasturi: deer-musk.

katha: story.

kathputhli: puppet.

kavee: poet.

kavya: poem.

kesar: saffron, extremely valuable then and now as an essential spice used in Indian cooking; traditionally given as a gift by kings to one another; worth several times more than its weight in gold.

khaas: special; unique.

khatiya: cot; bed.

khazana: treasure-trove; treasury.

kheer payasam: a sweet rice-milk preparation.

khottey-sikkey: counterfeit coin/s.

khukhri: a kind of North Indian machete, favoured by the hilly gurkha tribes.

kintu: but; however.

kinkara: a tribe of rakshasas and celestial beings.

kiran: ray (usually of light); a girl or boy's given name.

koel/koyal: Indian song-bird.

Kosala: a North-Central Indian kingdom believed to have flourished for several millennia before the start of the Christian era.

koyal: Indian song-bird.

krita: the first age.

krodh: wrath.

kshatriya: warrior caste. The highest of four castes in ancient India, the armed defenders of the tribe, skilled in martial combat and governance. Kings were always chosen from this caste. Later, with the Hindu shift towards pacifism and non-violence, the brahmin or priestly caste became predominant, with kshatriyas shifting into the second-highest position in contemporary India.

kul-nari: schoolgirl; *kul* being Sanskrit for school, *nari* meaning girl/woman.

kumbha-rakshasa: dominant species of demons, lording over their fellow rakshasas as well as other Asura species because of their considerable size and strength; named after Kumbhakarna, the mammoth giant brother of Ravana, who grew to mountainous proportions owing to an ancient curse that condemned him to absorb the physical mass of any living thing he killed or ate. Unlike Kumbhakarna, the kumbhas (for short) do not grow larger with each kill or meal.

kumkum: red powder.

kundalee: horoscope.

kurta: an upper garment with a round neck, full sleeves. Like a shirt but slipped over the head like a t-shirt.

kusa or kusalavya: a lush variety of grass found in Northern and North-Central India, long-bladed and thick.

lakh: a hundred thousand.

langot: loin-cloth.

lingam: a simple unadorned representation of Lord Shiva, usually made of roughly carved black stone, shaped like an upward moulded pillar of stone with a blunt head that is traditionally anointed. Typically regarded by some Western scholars as a phallic object; a controversial view which has been repeatedly disproven by Indian scholars and study of ancient Vedic texts.

lohit: iron.

lota: a small metal pot with a handle, used to carry water.

lungi: a common lower-body garment; a sheet of cloth wrapped around the waist once or more times and tucked in or knotted, extending to the ankles; unisexual but more often worn by men.

maa: mother.

maang: the centre point of the hairline on a person's forehead.

madhuvan: literally, honey-garden; a garden where honey was culled for the purpose of making honey-wine.

magarmach: Indian river crocodile.

maha: great. As in maha-mantra, maha-raja, maha-bharata, maha-guru, maha-dev, etc.

mahadev: great one.

mahal: palace; mansion; manse.

maharuk: a variety of Indian tree.

maha-mantra: supreme mantra or verse, such as the maha-mantra Gayatri. A potent catechism to ward off evil and ensure the success of one's efforts.

mahout: elephant-handler.

mahseer: a variety of Indian fish.

mahua: a variety of Indian tree.

malai: cream

manai: a variety of Indian tree with heavy creepers.

manch: literally, platform or dais; also, a gathering of elders or leaders of a community.

mandala: a purified proscribed circle.

mandap: a ceremonial dais on which prayer rituals and other ceremonies are conducted.

mandir: temple.

mangalsutra: a black thread necklace worn by a married woman as proof of her marital status.

mann: mind.

mantra: an invocation to the devas.

mantri: minister.

marg: road.

marg-darshak: guide, mentor, guru.

marg-saathi: fellow-traveller; companion on the road.

martya: human; all things pertaining to humankind.

mashaal: torch.

masthi: mischief.

matka: earthen pot.

maya: illusion.

mayini: witch, demoness.

melas: country fairs, carnivals.

mithai: traditional Indian sweetmeats.

mithaigalli: sweetmeat lane; a part of the market where the halwais (mithai-makers) line up their stalls.

mithun: Indian bison; a species of local buffalo.

mochee: cobbler.

mogra: a strongly scented white flower that blooms very briefly; worn by Indian women in their hair.

moksh: salvation.

mudra: gesture, especially during a dance performance; a symbolic action.

muhurat: an auspicious date to initiate an important undertaking. Even today in India, all important activities – marriages, coronations, the start of a new venture – are always scheduled on a day and time found suitable according to the panchang (Hindu almanac) or muhurat calendar.

mujra: a sensual dance.

naachwaali: dancing-girl or courtesan.

naashta: breakfast; also, an early evening refreshment (equivalent of the British 'tea').

naga: any species of snake; a species of Asura.

nagin: female cobra.

namak: salt.

namaskar/namaskaram: greetings. Usually said while joining one's palms together and bowing the head forward slightly. A mark of respect.

namaskara: see namaskar.

nanga: naked.

Narak: Hell.

naresh: lord, master. A royal title used to address a maharaja, the equivalent of 'your highness'.

natya: dance.

nautanki: song-and-dance melodrama, a cheap street play.

navami: an infant's naming day.

neem: an Indian tree whose leaves and bark are noted for their proven, highly efficacious medicinal properties.

nidra: an exalted, transcendental meditative state, a kind of yogic sleep.

odhini: woman's garment used specifically to cover the head, similar to pallo.

Om: the trisyllabic universal invocation believed to purify the soul and attune it to the infinite brahman.

Om Hari Swaha: Praise be to the Creator, Amen.

Om Namay: Praise be the Name of . . .

paan: the leaf of the betelnut plant, in which could be wrapped a variety of edible savouries, especially pieces of supari and chewing tobacco.

pagdee: turban; headpiece; headdress.

pahadi: a hill dweller or mountain man. Often used colloquially to connote a rude, ill-educated and ill-mannered person.

paisa: in the singular, a penny, the smallest individual unit of coinage, then and now. In the generic, money.

palai: sandy ground. Also pilai, or pillai.

palas: a variety of Indian flowering tree.

palkhi: see *dollee.*

pallo: the top fold of a woman's sari, used to conceal the breasts and cleavage of the wearer.

panchayat: a village committee usually of five (panch) persons.

parantu: but; however.

pari: angel; fairy.

parikrama: a ritual demonstrating one's devotion to a given deity, often consisting of walking several (hundred) times around a temple as well as the performance of related rituals and prayers.

Patal: the lowermost level of Narak, the lowest plane attainable in existence.

patang: kite.

payal: a delicately carved chain of tiny bells, usually of silver, worn as an anklet by women.

peda: a common, highly popular Indian sweet made of milk and sugar.

peepal: a species of tree with hanging roots and vines.

phanas: jackfruit.

phera: ritual circling of a sacred fire.

phool mala: flower-garland.

pisaca: a species of Asura.

pitashree: revered father.

pitchkarees: water-spouts; portable hand-pumps used by children in play.

pooja: prayer.

pradhan-mantri: prime minister.

Prajapati: Creator; The One Who Made All Living Things; also used as a term for butterflies, which are believed to represent the spirit of the Creator.

pranaam: a high form of namaste or greeting.

pranayam: a yogic method of breathing that enables biofeedback and control of the senses.

prarthana: intense, devout prayer.

prasadam: food blessed by the devas in the course of prayer; a sacramental offering.

prashna-uttar: question-answer.

pravachan: monologue or lecture, usually by a guru or mentor; to be imbibed in rapt silence.

prayaschitt: penance.

Prithvi: Earth.

pundit: priest; master of religious ceremonies.

purana: an ancient treatise or narrative; literally, old, ancient.

purnima: full moon; full moon night.

purohit: see pundit.

pushpak: a flying vehicle described in ancient Indian texts, anti-gravitational devices whose technological basis was said to be once known but is now forgotten; also 'chariots of the gods'.

putra: son.

raag: a scale in Indian classical music, consisting of a certain blend of notes in a related confluence, designed to produce a specific effect on the environment. E.g. Raag Bhairav was said to be capable of inducing rain, Raag Deepak to cause oil lamps to light.

raat ki rani: colloquial name for a common Indian flower that blooms only at night; literally, 'queen of the night'.

rabadi: a popular Indian dessert of thickened sweetened milk, over-boiled until the water drains and only thick layers of cream remain.

raja: king; liege; clan-chieftain.

raje: a more affectionate form of 'raja'. The 'e' suffix to a name ending in a vowel indicates intimacy and warmth.

raj-gaddhi: throne; seat of the king.

rajkumar: prince.

rajkumari: princess.

raj-marg: king's way; royally protected highway or road.

rajya sabha: king's council of ministers, a meeting of the same.

raj-yoga: an advanced form of yoga, the ancient art of meditative self-actualisation.

rakshak: protector.

rakshasa: a variety of Asura; roughly equivalent to the Western devil or demon. Singular/male: rakshas or rakshasa. Singular/feminine: rakshasi. Plural/both: rakshasas.

rang: colour; usually, coloured powder.

rang-birangi: colourful.

rangoli: the traditional Indian art of creating elaborate patterns on floors, usually at the entrances of domiciles, by carefully sprinkling coloured powder.

ras: juice.

rasbhurries: a very sweet, sticky and juicy wild berry; literally, 'juice-filled'.

rath/s: chariot/s.

rawa: a type of flour.

rishi: sadhu.

rishimuni: holy man.

rksa: black mountain bear.

rudraksh: red beads, considered sacred by Hindus.

radraksh maala: a Hindu rosary or prayer-bead necklace strung with rudraksh beads.

rupaiya: rupee. The main unit of currency in India even today.

sabha: committee; parliament.

sadhu: literally, 'most holy' or 'most auspicious'; also used to denote a penitent hermit; holy man.

sadhuni: a female sadhu or woman whose life is dedicated to prayer and worship.

saivite: worshipper of Lord Shiva.

sakshi: a woman's close female friend.

sala: a variety of Indian tree.

samabhavimudra: celestial meditative stance.

samadhi: memorial.

samasya: problem, situation.

samay chakra: the chariot wheel of Time, turning relentlessly as god rides across the universe. A cornerstone of Hindu belief.

samjhe: 'understood?'

sammelan: a friendly gathering; a meeting.

sandesh: message.

sandhyavandana: evening oblation; ritual offering of water and prayer to the sun at sunset; see also acamana.

Sanskriti: Arya culture and tradition.

sanyas: renunciation from the world; the process by which one gives up all one's worldly possessions, attachments and relationships, taking sanyas, and becoming a 'sanyasi'.

saprem: supreme.

Satya-Yuga: Age of Truth.

sautan: husband's second wife; one's rival for a husband's affections.

savdhaan: caution.

seema: borderline; boundary.

sena: army.

senapati: commander of armed forces, a general.

sesa: rabbit.

shaasan: a type of low-lying couch with a backrest or armrest.

shagun: a variety of Indian tree; an auspicious event or occurrence.

Shaivite: a worshipper of Lord Shiva.

shakti: strength, power, force. Used to describe divine power of a god, as in Kali-shakti or Goddess Kali's power.

shama: forgiveness. Colloquially, 'excuse me'.

Shani: god of weapons and destruction. Equivalent to the Roman god Saturn.

Shanivar: Day of Shani; now marked as Saturday because Shani is believed to correspond to Saturn; but probably a quite different day in the ancient Vedic calendar.

shantam: quiet, calm, serene; litterally, 'be at peace'.

shanti: colloquialisation of shantam.

shastra: a science; an area of study.

shatru: enemy.

shikhaar: the hunt.

shikhsa: education; learning.

shishya/s: student/s of a guru.

shraap: curse; terrible invocation.

Shravan: a month in the Hindu calendar; usually the month of the rains; also, a boy's given name.

siddh: successful; blessed.

silbutta: grinding stone and board; pestle and mortar.

sindhoor: a blood-red powder used in marital rituals. Traditionally applied by a husband on his wife's hairline (maang) to indicate her status as a married woman. Hence, unmarried women and widows are not permitted to wear sindhoor. Although a bindi (dot) is now used as a modern equivalent and worn universally as a fashion accessory.

siphai: soldier; guard.

sitaphal: a variety of Indian fruit with sweet milky pods.

sloka: sacred verse.

smriti: hidden; secret.

soma: wine made from the soma plant; a popular wine in ancient India.

som-daru: a kind of wine.

sona: gold.

spasa: spy, informant.

stree-hatya: murder of a woman.

sudra: the lowest caste, usually relegated to cleaning, hunting, tanning and other undesirable activities. The lowest in order.

suhaag raat: wedding night.

supari: betelnut.

Suryavansha: the Solar Dynasty, a line of kings that ruled over Kosala; literally, the clan of the sun-god, Surya.

su-swagatam: welcome; the traditional ritual greeting offered to a visitor.

sutaar: carpenter.

swagatam: greetings, welcome.

swaha: a term used to denote the auspicious and successful completion of a sloka or recitation; corresponds to 'Amen'.

swami: master; lord; naresh.

Swarga-lok/a: Heaven.

swayamvara: a ceremonial rite during which a woman of marriageable age was permitted to select a suitable husband. Eligible men wishing to apply would line up to be inspected by the bride-to-be. On finding a suitable mate, she would indicate her choice by placing the garland around his neck.

taal: rhythm; beat.

tabla: an Indian percussion instrument, a kind of drum sounded by striking the heel of the palm and the tips of the fingers.

tamasha: a show; performance; common street play.

tandav: the frenzied sexually charged celestial dance of Shiva the Destroyer by which he generates enough shakti to destroy the entire universe that Brahma the Creator may recreate it once again.

tanpura: an Indian stringed musical instrument.

tandoor: an Indian barbecue.

tann: body.

tantrik: a worshipper of physical energy and sensual arts.

tapasvi: one who endures penance, usually with an aim to acquiring spiritual prowess.

tapasya: penance.

teko: prostrate one's head, touching the forehead to the ground as a demonstration of devotion and obeisance.

thakur: lord; landowner.

thali: a round metal platter used for eating meals or for storing prayer items. The Indian equivalent of the Western 'dinner plate'.

thrashbroom: a broom with harsh bristles, used for beating rugs and mattresses.

three worlds: Swarga-lok, Prithvi, Narak. Literally, Heaven, Earth, Hell.

tikka: ritual marking on forehead.

tilak: ash or colour anointment on one's forehead, indicating that one has performed one's ritual prayers and sacrifices and is blessed with divine grace to perform one's duties.

tirth yatra: pilgrimage.

Treta-Yuga: Age of Reason.

trimurti: the holy Hindu trinity of Brahma, Vishnu and Shiva, respectively the Creator, Preserver and Destroyer.

trishul: trident.

tulsi: a variety of Indian plant known for its efficacious medicinal properties and regarded as a symbol of a happy and secure household; always grown in the courtyard of a house and prayed to daily by the woman of the house; also, a woman's given name.

upanisad: an ancient sacred Indian text.

uraga: a species of Asura.

vaahan: vehicle

vaid: physician trained in the art of Ayur-vaidya, the ancient Indian study of herbal medicine and healing.

vaisya: the trading or commercial caste. Third in order.

vajra: lightning bolt.

valakam: welcome.

valmik: termite, white ant.

van: forest, jungle. Pronounced to rhyme with 'one'.

vanar: bandara; simian; any monkey species, but most commonly used to denote apes, especially the intelligent anthropomorphic talking apes of this saga.

vanash: a variety of Indian tree.

varna: caste; literally, occupational level or group.

varsha: rain; a woman's given name.

Veda: the sacred writings of the ancient Arya sages, comprising meditations, prayers, observations and scientific treatises on every conceivable human area of interest; the basis of Indian culture.

vetaal: a species of Asura; somewhat similar to the Western concept of 'vampire' but not usually synonymous.

vidya: knowledge.

vidyadhari: a scholar or student.

vinaashe: destruction; death.

yagna: religious fire-ritual.

yaksi: a female yaksa; a species of Asura capable of shape-shifting; closely corresponding to (but not identical to) the Western concept of Elves.

Yama: Yama-raj, lord of death and king of the underworld; literally Death personified as a large powerfully built dark-skinned man with woolly hair, who rides a black buffalo and carries a bag of souls.

yash: fame; adoration; admiration.

yodha: great warrior, champion.

yoganidra: the supreme state of transcendence while meditating, usually indicated by the eyes being partly open yet seeing only the apparent nothingness of brahman; a divine near-sleep-like state.

yojana: a measurement of distance in ancient India, believed to have been equivalent to around nine miles.

yoni: female sexual organ; the 'yang' of 'yin and yang'.

yuga: age; historical period.

Look out for . . .

KING OF AYODHYA

Book Six of the Ramayana

By
Ashok K. Banker

orbit

www.orbitbooks.co.uk

MEDALON

The Demon Child Trilogy: Book One

Jennifer Fallon

A breathtaking fantasy adventure is about to unfold. Enter the extraordinary world of Medalon . . .

According to legend, the last king of the ancient Harshini race sired a half-human child. Now the demon child must be found – and it must be killed.

It is a time of upheaval among the ruling elite of Medalon. Intrigue is rife and treachery is the only means of political advancement. It is a time when lies conceal more lies and the truth has been long abandoned. It is a time when only the most ruthless survive.

It is into this world that a forgotten magic is about to be unleashed. And it is two siblings, R'shiel amd Tarja, whose story will become one with the legends of the land.

The first volume in a stunning epic fantasy trilogy, *Medalon* is Jennifer Fallon's debut novel.

orbit

www.orbitbooks.co.uk

SOUTHERN FIRE

The Aldabreshin Compass: Book One

Juliet E. McKenna

A major new epic of empire and intrigue from an author whose storytelling has set fantasy fiction alight.

Their coming has not been written in the stars, and no augury had foretold the terror they would bring. The first sign was the golden lights from the beacons, a clear message from every southern isle that a calamity had befallen them. But it was still too late for many.

Daish Kheda, son of Daish Reik, reader of portents, giver of laws, healer and protector of all his domain encompasses, must act quickly and decisively. His people will be looking to him to guide them, as they looked to his father.

But there is only one defence against the dark magic that threatens to overrun every island of the Aldabreshin Archipelago — and to wield it means certain death.

www.orbitbooks.co.uk